D1557756

PRIESTESS OF
POMPEII

Ariadne—the Light in the Darkness

PRIESTESS OF
POMPEII

THE INITIATE'S JOURNEY
BOOK I

SANDRA C. HURT

THYRSUS PUBLICATIONS

Priestess of Pompeii is a work of fiction. All incidents and dialogue and all characters, except for well-known historical figures, are products of the author's imagination.

Published by:
Thyrsus Publications
1967 Chelmsford Street, Carmel, IN 46032
www.thyrsus-publications.com

Printed in the United States of America
First Edition Printing 2020

Map of Pompeii used with permission of: John Joseph Dobbins, and Pedar William Foss. Based on map in the book, *The World of Pompeii. 2007* London: Routledge.

Design: Erika F. Espinoza
Illustrations and book cover art: created by Carol Spicuzza, owned by the author.

Frontispiece: Roman marble copy of a Greek original. Classical Period. Museum: Musei Capitolini, Rome.
Statue of Artemis: Roman marble copy, 1st or 2nd century CE, of lost Greek bronze attributed to Leochares, c. 325 BCE Museum: Musee du Louvre, Paris

Project of Hawthorne Publishing, Carmel, Indiana

ISBN 978-1-7923-3488-7
ISBN 978-1-7923-3711-6

Library of Congress Control Number: 2020906307

1. Pompeii—Villa of the Mysteries 2. Ancient Women—Religious life 3. Rites and ceremonies 4. Jungian Psychology 5. Roman Republic—Greece 100-44BCE 6. History 7. Sandra C. Hurt

To my first and final storytellers
My parents
Rufilla Istacidia

The task is to give birth to the ancient in a new time.

—Carl Gustav Jung, *The Red Book*

CONTENTS

CONTENTS

MAIN CHARACTERS

ITALY

Istacidii Family:
Numerius Istacidii, **Rufus** husband, father, vintner and landowner of numerous farms outside Pompeii
Aridela, his wife
Cil, (pronounced Kyle) their son
Rufilla, their adopted daughter (a.k.a. Arianna)

Lucius Marcius Philippus, Aridela's brother, Roman Senator
Cassia, his wife
Zosimus, their son

Key Servants of Istacidii Household:
Melissa, Rufilla's nursemaid
Theo, Roman freedman, head of household servants, tutor to Istacidii children
Junia and Selene, their servants

Friends of the Istacidii Family:
Victor Bucci, a vintner, landowner
Clodia, his wife
Titus, their son
Aula, their daughter, married to Aper Melissaei

Marcus Arrius Polites, import/export business, landowner
Aricia, his wife and Aridela's best friend

Gnaeus Melissaei, ship builder, importer and exporter
Aper, his son and commander of his family's merchantman ships.
Hostia, Rufilla's best friend

GREECE

Epidaurus
Camilla, a girl from Praeneste that Rufilla befriends
Kharis, Greek priestess at Epidaurus Sanctuary

Athens
Kallistê, friend of Aridela, Arianna's aunt
Stephanos, her husband
Dionne, Kallistê's maid
Timo, head servant

Delphi
Nikolaos, friend of Aridela and Stephanos
The Pythia, Priestess to the Oracle of Apollo

HISTORICAL Characters

G. Julius Caesar, Roman military general, statesman, Roman Consul
Julia, his sister
Atia, Julia's daughter
G. Octavius, Atia's son and grand-nephew of Julius Caesar

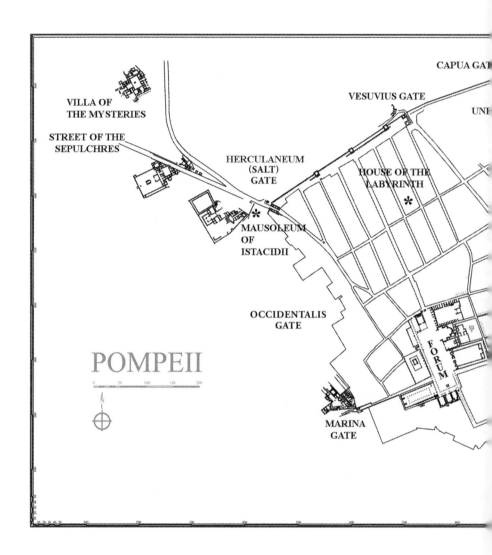

CAPUA GAT

VESUVIUS GATE

UNI

VILLA OF
THE MYSTERIES

STREET OF THE
SEPULCHRES

HERCULANEUM
(SALT)
GATE

HOUSE OF THE
LABYRINTH

MAUSOLEUM
OF
ISTACIDII

OCCIDENTALIS
GATE

FORUM

POMPEII

0   50   100   150   200

MARINA
GATE

**Plan of Pompeii: Gates, Public Buildings,
Structures related to the book**

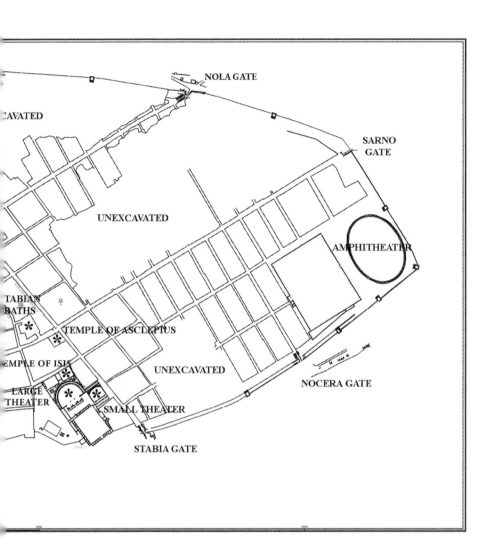

NOLA GATE

SARNO GATE

CAVATED

UNEXCAVATED

AMPHITHEATER

TABIAN BATHS

TEMPLE OF ASCLEPIUS

TEMPLE OF ISIS

UNEXCAVATED

NOCERA GATE

LARGE THEATER

SMALL THEATER

STABIA GATE

PROLOGUE

1991

I am listening to a lecture about women and art when an image flashes on the giant screen behind the speaker's head—it is a fresco of a woman who lived in Pompeii first century BCE. She resides in the Villa of the Mysteries. It is an image that my mind says I have never seen before, and yet I recognize. I am suddenly no longer in the room. In my mind's eye, I am in a dark place, can feel cold stone beneath me, and when I look up, she is looking right at me, chin in her hand as if she has all the time in the world. I leave the lecture shaken. Days, weeks, years go by. I can't get her image out of my mind.

1994

My trip to Greece and Italy.

Pompeii was a destination for me. I'd read up on the art and architecture of the town, including the Villa of the Mysteries. The Villa housed the room where megalographic frescoes filled the walls. The fresco of the woman I had seen in the lecture three years ago was there. I had to see her.

I arranged for a tour guide and took friends with me. The guide finished his well-rehearsed tour and thanked us for our attention.

"But we haven't seen the Villa of the Mysteries," I said.

"Signora, we have seen all the important things. And, anyway, it is not open."

I was irritated that he did not think the Villa was important.

"But I came thousands of miles to see the woman in the frescoes," I said. "I will not be turned away."

My outspoken Italian companion says something to him in dialect, and suddenly, we are off.

Of course, the Villa is open. She is waiting for me, has been for millennia.

PROLOGUE

I take my place once again on the cool stone of the ancient floor. Painted crimson walls are the backdrop for the frescoes of life-size women who envelop the room. The entombed silence allows for memories to surface, images to arise for which I have no words.

2004

A new millennium is underway.

I have spent years doing research, cultivating the classics, finding my way into her story, the story I know I am meant to write. It is a long and sometimes difficult journey.

A book I am reading falls open onto this passage:

"The way.....is a blind waiting, a doubtful listening and groping. One is convinced that one will burst. But the resolution is born from precisely this tension and it almost always appears where one did not expect it.

"But what is the resolution? It is always something ancient and precisely because of this something new, for when something long since passed away comes back again in a changed world, it is new. The task is to give birth to the ancient in a new time." —Carl Jung, *The Red Book*

2020

Her journey is mine. Her journey is yours.
Initiation. Ritual. Wisdom.
I am a daughter of the Priestess of Pompeii.
There are things worth knowing.

Corona Borealis

CHAPTER I

BIRTH AND DEATH

OUTSKIRTS OF ROME, 60 BCE

According to ancient myth, Ariadne, a princess of Crete, wore the diadem given to her by the Greek god Dionysus during their wedding ceremony. Afterward, he threw the crown into the night sky, where it formed a semicircle of stars, the Corona Borealis. From that time forward, those who gazed skyward witnessed it as a tribute to their love.

On a frigid night in the era of Julius Caesar, the crown of stars glowed in the nighttime sky. Cosmus, a stocky Roman freedman, paced the barnyard, the crown of his balding head reflecting the moonlit sky. Despite the winter chill he was sweating. His wife Lucilla had started labor, and the cries of her pain had driven him into the slap of winter air. As he made his way from the kitchen fire to the barn lot, he peeked into their bedroom. She looked at him with a torment in her eyes that he hadn't seen in the other two births. He kissed her brow, just as another pain gripped her stomach.

Outside, the hushed countryside seemed oblivious to his wife's suffering. Cosmus appealed to Zeus to grant Lucilla safe passage, but he saw nothing. No stars streaked across the sky in response to his plea.

At the barn, he lit a lantern and busied himself with farm equipment. The racket he made succeeded in drowning out his wife's cries of pain, but when he paused, out of breath, the cold air brought her suffering to his ears once again.

Hours earlier, as soon as the midwife arrived, he had taken his two sons to his master's villa. His mistress had made it clear that when Lucilla's time came, she would take care of the boys.

The trusted midwife was the same woman who had delivered his younger son eight years before. She had assessed his wife's condition and declared that tonight would be the night for the birth. Of his third son, he thought.

Three sons! He would be a rich man, indeed.

The crisp night air cleared his mind as he surveyed the vineyards of the aristocrat who had hired him. He tried to divert his attention by plotting his dream of owning his own vineyard one day, imagining that it would not be long before all three of his sons were old enough to help him work the land he would soon purchase.

Lucilla had worked for her mistress for several years when Cosmus and his father came to work for her master. When his father died, Cosmus took over as foreman. Lucilla had never wanted to marry but was attracted to the brawny man with his witty ways. Encouraged by their patrons, the two married after a brief courtship. She ran both the household and her family with a keen eye for what was required. She loved her boys dearly, but secretly longed for a girl who she could love and teach womanly life lessons.

For hours, Lucilla sat in a birthing chair in excruciating labor. Then her water broke, and instead of helping the labor, it seemed to stop it. After more than an hour and many supplications to Lucina, the goddess of childbirth, her labor resumed with even more fervor. She sighed as the pain of a contraction subsided. The midwife wiped Lucilla's brow with a damp sponge. "You have a generous mistress," said the midwife. "She not only made sure I was here for you, but also instructed me to bring the birthing chair."

"Yes, yes, I only wish she could have been here," she whispered. "I must think of a gift for her—Ack!" Lucilla screamed. "It is coming!"

The midwife bent over, her nimble fingers feeling the baby's head start to emerge. Her face paled for a moment at what she felt next. Gently, she said to Lucilla, "I must make an adjustment here, and then you must push very hard."

Unable to speak, Lucilla nodded and her eyes closed.

The midwife placed one hand on Lucilla's belly and felt the uterus relax. She knew she did not have much time. She spoke softly to her apprentice, a hesitant girl standing nearby, but her fierce look revealed the urgency of the situation. "Help me get her to bed."

The two women put Lucilla's arms around their shoulders. They paused, raised her from the chair, and with all their strength, moved her dead weight back to the bed.

This time, with Lucilla on her back, the midwife could now clearly see what she had felt—the head with the cord wrapped around it.

As Lucilla screamed and pushed, she heard the midwife's raised voice command: "Lucilla, listen to me. It is very important now that you breathe and do not push."

By the next contraction, the midwife had oiled her hands and placed them on either side of the baby's bloody head, urging its release from the entanglement of the cord.

Lucilla made an effort to sit up again, her body swaying on the edge of her bed. "Support her," the midwife cried to her apprentice as she slid her feet under the bed and sat on the floor beneath her.

The midwife moved with expert hands to facilitate the birth. The shoulders popped out. The arms and the back slid through, and then the buttocks, legs, and feet followed in quick succession. The baby's body glistened in the light of the oil lamp as the midwife held her upside down, quickly removing the cord from around her neck.

Lucilla raised her head. "It is a girl," she cried, raising her arms, giving thanks to the goddess for granting her covert wish.

"It is a miracle," the apprentice proclaimed.

The midwife gently lowered the baby into her lap and turned her on her side, firmly stroking the length of her spine. The baby choked a cough and took her first breath. With the second breath came a cry.

The midwife measured the cord from the baby's belly—four finger widths. She reached into her basket of medical tools to find the piece of glass fashioned into a sharp knife, and with one swift movement, severed the cord, separating the baby from placenta and mother, tying the cord with a strand of wool twine. She used her apron as a blanket and gently laid the baby on the floor beside her, awaiting the father, who would pick up the newborn as a gesture of acceptance.

Cosmus had already entered the room. He started toward the bed and the infant lying on the floor, but was stopped short by the sight of the placenta emerging from Lucilla. With it came a gush of blood. As Cosmus watched in disbelief, the gush turned into a torrent.

"Help me," the midwife shouted to the apprentice. "Take these sponges and apply pressure between her legs. Hurry!"

Cosmus staggered and fell back against the wall as he watched the midwife and her assistant work feverishly to contain the bleeding.

As quickly as it had started, the bleeding ceased. The bed was soaked. The smell of fresh blood filled the small room. It was silent, save for Lucilla's shallow breathing and the baby's whimpering. Cosmus moved to Lucilla's side, nudging the baby out of the way with his foot, and kneeling next to her bed, taking his wife in his arms he cried, "Lucilla, my love, by all the gods above, you cannot leave me!"

She slowly opened her eyes and a faint smile crossed her lips. Then her eyes closed, and her breathing ceased.

"Take the baby away," Cosmus howled. "Because of her, my wife is dead. Expose it!" He shoved the bundled baby across the room, collapsing over his dead wife's body.

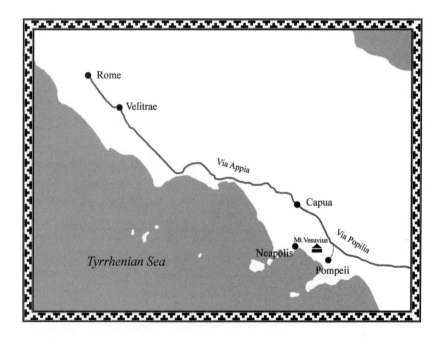

Pompeii to Rome

CHAPTER II

A GIFT FROM THE GODDESS

Travel time from Pompeii to Rome depended on how one traveled, where one caught up with the *Via Appia*, and how many friends and relatives one stopped to visit along the way. Numerius Istacidii, otherwise known as Rufus and his wife Aridela, had made the journey several times. When they arrived in Rome, they would stay with Aridela's brother Lucius, his wife Cassia, and their son Zosimus.

Rufus and Lucius met while serving in the Roman army under the consul, Lucullus, where they fought in the battle of Tigranocerta. Lucius was an officer who had been wounded early in the battle and hospitalized. As he healed, he had offered to help the *medici* with their patients, and these doctors, in turn, encouraged him to stay on as he seemed to have a real gift for helping with patients and surgery. Rufus, an *Equite* or cavalryman, came in as a patient with a severe leg wound. He could no longer return to the battlefield, so Lucius found him a position in the fort hospital doing administrative tasks.

Acting as a matchmaker, Lucius brought Rufus home after they were reassigned to duty in Rome. Aridela and Rufus had an immediate attraction to one another. When he completed his tour of duty in the military, they married. As was common in many Roman marriages of the upper class, the age difference was significant; Rufus was thirty-eight, and Aridela was twenty.

Once settled into his family home in Pompeii, they wanted to start a family as soon as possible. Their first-born, Numerius Istacidii, was nicknamed Cil.

And so it was that Cil and his nursemaid, Selene, accompanied his parents on this trip to Rome, along with Junia, Aridela's maidservant.

Pompeii was a walled city with many gates. As they left early in the morning, Rufus led the way on horseback, the carriage for the women followed, and behind them were the mule-drawn carts that held the luggage, food and necessities for the trip, gifts for relatives and friends, and even emergency equipment for any breakdowns, including a ladder and ropes. They passed through the Salt Gate built of brick and block, with three imposing arches. An arched path on either side afforded a walkway for pedestrians while the middle arch, taller and wider, accommodated carriages and carts, making it a monumental passageway. According to Roman law, no one was allowed to be buried within the city limits, so as they made their way beyond the gate, they passed the tombs and monuments of the town's elite families that lined either side of the street.

Turning onto *Via Pomeriale*, the caravan paused first at the street shrine that marked the religious boundary of the city, Rufus and Aridela reciting prayers to ensure a safe journey. Moving on, they bowed their heads as they slowly passed the resting place of Rufus' parents, an elegant mausoleum built for the Istacidii *gens*.

They made their way down the hill to the bay, where the salt flats seemed to stretch out forever. Some men were raking the slowly forming crystals in the salt beds, while others were piling them up, building blinding white hills of salt that glistened in the morning sun. The road skirted the flats, making its way up the coast to Herculaneum, then inland to connect to the *Via Appia*, the Queen of the Long Roads.

The journey required that when meeting someone on one of the lesser, more narrow roads, one had to give way to the other. The bigger one's carriage, like the Istacidii's, the more leeway one was granted. The high travel season was yet to come, so they encountered only small, mule-driven carts, transporting goods like amphorae of wine, olive oil, and fresh produce, ready for sale in the forum markets located in the center of small towns.

South of Capua, they merged onto the *Via Popilia*, a smoother road. They arrived in the late afternoon, in time to meet their hosts, family friends of Greek descent, who offered them *Xenia*, a Greek gesture of hospitality that included a refreshing bath and a sumptuous evening meal.

The next morning brought a flurry of activity. The main street of Capua was a famous market for women to buy cosmetics, perfumes, jewelry, and exotic cloth. Aridela was looking for cushions and blankets to replace the ones in their carriage. She and her hostess pored over the colorful wares in the different booths, servants standing behind them, ready to carry the purchases back to the house.

Rufus held meetings with local wine merchants who bought and sold amphorae of his wines and olive oil. Instead of sending an emissary, he enjoyed making deals in person.

The following morning they left Capua, traveling now on the broader, paved road of the *Via Appia* heading north. Even with the better roads, they had three days of travel in front of them before reaching their friends in Vellitrae. Horses and mules were exchanged at rest stops along the way.

By the second day, young Cil was getting restless. "When do we get to Vellitrae?" He had practiced saying the name of the town. "Will Octavius be there?"

"By the end of the day tomorrow, we will be there," Aridela said. "Yes, Octavius will be there. I think he and his mother will be delighted to see us, but we will be staying with friends of your pater's. We will visit Octavius the next day."

As planned, they reached Vellitrae by the end of the third day, staying with a merchant friend. The next day Aridela and Cil went to visit Atia and her son, Gaius Octavius. They were living with Atia's mother. Julia was the sister of Julius Caesar and the grandmother of Octavius. Aridela and Atia visited while the boys played. The two women had met through a mutual friend the year they both had given birth to their sons. That same year, their friend died from a fever, and the grief Aridela and Atia shared brought them closer together.

Octavius had few friends to play with in this small town, so he looked forward to Cil's visit. He took Cil to his room. "Shh, this is a game that my servant showed me how to play, but we cannot tell our maters." He removed a pouch from under his pillow. In it were two ivory dice. "Let me teach you how to roll the *tesserae*—it is easy."

Octavius was a good teacher but made up his own rules as he went. "Let us throw the two tesserae and whoever gets the highest number wins!" Even when Octavius won, which was most of the time, he shared the prize, his hidden stash of figs, with Cil.

"Octavius is my best friend," Cil told his mother as they returned to the home of their hosts at the end of the day.

In the predawn darkness, Aridela and Selene, the nursemaid were awakened by Cil, who had a stomach ache. Selene gave him a tonic of caraway followed by some sweet mint, and this potion started to bring Cil some relief. Rufus was awake and decided to get an earlier start, so he roused his servants and slaves to make ready.

Back on the road, they left the hilltop town of Vellitrae, turning north onto the *Via Appia*. This road, having been built by the Roman military, continued in a straight line toward Rome. As usual, Rufus rode at the head of the procession on horseback, accompanied by his manservant. Within the carriage, the women and little Cil were nestled on the new cushions and wrapped in blankets to keep out the brisk morning chill. This carriage had a suspension mechanism that rocked the cabin, and soon everyone within was lulled back to sleep.

Aridela woke after an hour and felt the need to stretch her legs and use the chamber pot. As if he had read her mind, Rufus dropped back and leaned in toward the carriage. "Is it time?" he asked.

"Oh, you know me too well," Aridela said.

"That I do." A knowing smile passed between the two.

Rufus directed the porter driving the carriage to stop, and the three women got out with the chamber pot carried by Selene. The men went in the opposite direction.

"Pater, take me with you," Cil shouted to his father. Rufus turned and motioned for the boy to break from his mother and join the men to relieve themselves.

After a brief respite, they forged ahead, Rufus wanting to arrive at his in-laws' villa in time to use their private baths, have a good meal, drink some aged Falernian wine, and take his luscious wife to bed.

In the carriage, Aridela watched Cil as he slept. At the age of three, he was smart and curious, and Aridela could see already what a compassionate heart he had. He will be a doctor of substance, she thought. Like Hippocrates. She had had two miscarriages but was able to carry Cil to term, and Rufus was thrilled when it was a boy, someone to carry on the family name as well as taking over his business.

Why then, with her life so full of blessings, had Aridela been feeling a sense of emptiness? Even though she had been warned by the physician not to attempt another pregnancy, there was a yearning within her—she wanted a girl. Why was she having recurrent dreams of holding a smiling baby?

By late afternoon, Aridela started to recognize familiar sites. Monuments and burial tombs lined either side of the road, indicating that they were just outside the gates of Rome. She signaled the coachman to stop.

As the porter helped her from the carriage, Cil jumped to the ground beside her. "I am going to walk for a while," Aridela said. "If you want to walk with me, hold my hand."

By then, Rufus had circled behind the two. He asked his son, "Do you remember the last time we stopped at the Sacred Tree, Cil?"

The child shot a questioning look at his mother. "Why do we have to stop at a tree?"

"Because it is a Sacred Tree and the altar of the goddess Fortuna is beside the tree. We need to give thanks to her for our safe journey."

"But I got sick this time."

"Yes, you did. But Selene and I were with you, so you were safe. You were sick because you ate too many figs. Do you understand the difference between safe and sick?"

"Yes, I think I do," he said. "And now I am better."

"Yes, you are."

"Can I help you give thanks?"

"I would like that," Aridela said. As Cil and Aridela climbed the hill, she handed Cil some acorns that she had brought. "Place them on her altar and give her thanks."

At the Sacred Oak Tree, Aridela and her son made their way a little farther up the hill to the shrine honoring the goddess Fortuna. It brought good luck to put an oak leaf in your shoe when traveling, so Aridela had saved some leaves from the preceding fall and put one in her shoe.

Cil stood quietly until his mother patted his shoulder, and then bounded happily down toward the Sacred Tree while Aridela arranged the acorns with a few oak leaves as she recited her prayers to the goddess. A low, eerie whine caught her ears.

"Cil?"

Wild animals often scouted these hills. Perhaps a wolf was sniffing around.

"Cil! Answer me!"

Cil emerged from the tree area below and ran into her arms. "Mamma, it is after me!"

"What is after you, Cil? Rufus!" she called.

"The tree. The tree is after me."

Aridela pulled him close with a laugh. "The tree is rooted to the ground, Cil. It cannot chase you."

"But the tree is crying, Mamma. Listen."

He turned toward it and pointed. They both fell silent.

"Hear it? The tree is crying."

Her husband ran up the hill to join them. Now she felt safe. Together they went to inspect the Sacred Tree.

The sound they heard from within the tree was low and weak.

"It is just some harmless little animal," her husband said. "Come."

"It is not an animal," Aridela said. "Bring the ladder," she called down to the porter.

"Aridela," her husband scolded lightly. Before he could object, she had climbed onto the ladder. He gently pulled her off and as he ascended Aridela steadied the bottom. "What do you see?" she said.

"There is something here," Rufus said as he reached between a large branch and the tree trunk.

"Oh, Aridela," he said.

"What, what?" she asked.

As he came back down the ladder, carefully, one rung at a time, he had cradled in one arm, a tiny bundle. Back on terra firma, he unfolded the cloth. They both looked down at a newborn with lots of red hair.

Aridela gasped. "Oh yes," she said, taking the baby from Rufus, unwrapping the blanket.

Tears streamed down her face. "Rufus," she said. "This was my dream."

"Mamma, mamma, do not cry."

"These are tears of joy Cil," Aridela said, kneeling so that Cil could see the baby. "Would you like a baby sister?"

He was hesitant. "I think so, but will she do a lot of crying?"

"No more than you, my son. It will be fun to be a big brother—you will see," she said. She turned to her husband. "What do you think, Rufus? You heard what the doctor said. And she has *your* red hair!"

The late afternoon sun broke through the clouds and lit up the shock of hair like a flame. Rufus remembered his mother telling him that he was so named Rufus because Rufus meant red-haired. People often called him

Numerius, but to Aridela, he was Rufus, that red-headed man with whom she had fallen in love.

Rufus gathered his wife and the baby in his arms. "Your dream has come true. You have received your long-awaited baby girl—from the goddess!" He was already smitten. "She is beautiful."

They slowly made their way down the hill with the baby, and as their caravan pulled away, two figures, the midwife and her apprentice, emerged from behind a nearby tree.

The midwife smiled with relief. "I was hoping a wealthy family would find the baby," she whispered. "They will surely give her a good home."

CHAPTER III

SACRED SEIZURE

ROME

Lucius was standing at the front door of the villa when they arrived. "Welcome!" he said. "Good timing. I just told the porter that you might be coming early—and here you are—Officer Numerius!"

"Yes, Officer Lucius. We are all present and accounted for, *Sir!*"

The two men broke into laughter as they grabbed each other's shoulders.

"What do we have here—my dear sister with a bundle in swaddling clothes! Please come in out of the chill." Lucius greeted Aridela as he and Rufus helped her from the carriage.

"My dear brother, you will not believe what happened." Aridela stood with the baby in her arms, her eyes welling up. Cassia appeared as they entered the villa.

Rufus smiled. "We have been given a gift from the goddess at the Sacred Tree."

Aridela opened the blanket so they could see the baby. Cassia's dark eyes opened wide.

"Dear Aridela," Cassia said. "We know how much you wanted a girl baby. Praise the goddess Fortuna for her gift!"

That evening, as the wine was being poured, Lucius said to Rufus and Aridela. "I took the opportunity to send for Cassia's midwife to come to the house and examine the baby to make sure everything is in order with her health."

"You are such a thoughtful brother," Aridela said.

The midwife came declaring the baby physically sound, "and beautiful." Rufus and Lucius walked her to the door.

"We want to know the parentage of this baby," Rufus said. "No need to worry our wives. Just let us know."

"I have heard about this baby," she replied. "We midwives are a very close community. I should warn you. It was a difficult delivery, and the child may have problems as she grows."

"Problems?" Rufus interrupted. "What kind of problems?"

"I will talk to the midwife who delivered the child and find out more," the midwife said. "With your permission, I will arrange for you to meet with the owner of the estate where Cosmus, the baby's father, works."

The following afternoon, Lucius and Rufus went to the communal baths, where they were introduced to the landowner. He had a kind, tired face with dark eyes and heavy eyelids. Rufus listened as he talked about the couple who had worked for him so loyally. "They have a long history," he began. "Their family lived in servitude in Neapolis. When Cosmus' father was able to buy his freedom, he took his family and moved to Rome. Because of his experience working in the vineyards, he came to me highly recommended. He instilled his strong work ethic in his son, Cosmus, who took over as foreman when his father died. He is a good man, but devastated by his wife's death, as are we. She was a valued personal servant to my wife."

"What happened to the mother?"

"It was a difficult birth according to the midwife. Shortly after the baby was born, Lucilla died," he said, wiping away his tears.

Rufus sat with the men in the communal hot bath, his head in his hands. Not a good sign, he thought to himself.

"Cosmus needed another son to help him with the land," the man said. "A girl is of no use to him, and since she would be a daily reminder of his wife's death, he told the midwife to take her away."

"Have you spoken to this midwife?" Lucius asked.

"I have," the landowner said. "A better midwife you could never find. She did all she could. She told me that Lucilla was thrilled that she had birthed a girl."

"The baby is our daughter now, and the gods have granted my wife's wish of a girl-child. She will have the best of care," Rufus said. He stretched out in the tub of hot water, the *caldarium,* and closed his eyes.

Later that day, Cassia's midwife returned with a wet nurse for the baby. Again, Rufus and Lucius spoke to her as she was leaving, out of earshot of the women.

"The cord was around the child's neck at birth—always a potential problem," the midwife said. "Epilepsy is a definite possibility."

"Epilepsy—seizures? Rufus said.

The midwife continued. "Yes, I think you and your wife should be prepared that she could eventually develop seizures. I can talk with both of you before you leave for Pompeii," she said. "The women are talking right now about getting a permanent nursemaid. She should know too."

"I will ask you to return later, but I do not want to burden my wife, so we will keep this among the three of us for now," Rufus said. "Thank you for finding a wet nurse." He drew some coins from his leather pouch and gave them to her.

"*Gratias tibi valde, dominus,*" she said, bowing and taking her leave.

On the baby's fourth day of life, the wet nurse noticed her spitting up a milky pink substance. She reported it to Aridela, who examined the inside of her mouth. At that moment, the men entered the house laughing and joking about something that had happened at the baths that afternoon. Rufus saw the look on Aridela's face.

"What is it?"

"The baby has bitten her tongue, but she has no teeth. I do not understand," Aridela said.

Rufus let out a deep sigh. "Dearest wife, I was hoping not to have to give you the whole story quite so soon."

Lucius sent the porter for the midwife, who explained that the baby had probably suffered a seizure in her sleep. "That is good in that she was lying down and supported by the crib," she said. "Often the body tenses with this affliction, and if one is standing, one can fall and be injured. Depending on the severity of the seizure, the jaw may clamp down, and if the tongue is in the way, even though she has no teeth, this bleeding may happen." She examined the baby's mouth and tongue. "Her tongue is a little swollen, but pray to Mother Gaia that it will heal in a few days."

Lucius, who was interested in medicine, asked, "Will these seizures lessen as she grows?"

"They may," the midwife said, "but it is unlikely that they will go away."

She was familiar with the healing god, Asclepius, and suggested that when they return to Pompeii, they establish a relationship with the priests at the Asclepian Temple. "Over the years they will prove a valuable bond between you and your child."

Rufus would have preferred to dedicate the child upon returning to Pompeii. Instead, he chose the eighth day of life, which under Roman law was the usual dedication day for girls. So he performed the naming ceremony on the prescribed day while still in Rome. The custom of the time was that the maternal uncle, in this case, Lucius, would give the child her name. And so it was that Lucius, Cassia, and Zosimus attended the ceremony along with a few close friends. The entourage returned to the Sacred Tree, and Aridela and Cassia placed fresh garlands of flowers at the base of the Tree and the nearby altar. With that, the *lustratio*, the purification ritual, began. Rufus placed the baby on the ground beneath the Sacred Tree and proceeded to walk around the baby and the tree in a full circle. Cil was allowed to walk behind him. This circle of footprints defined a magical boundary around the child to rid her of any harmful spirits that may have been present at her birth. Rufus lifted the newborn from the ground as a sign of his acceptance. Water, from a sacred spring nearby, had been collected and now Rufus dipped his hand into the basin and bathed her head in the Sacred Waters. Holding the baby in his arms, he began, "Thus in the past, we have buried two children, sending them to a peaceful afterlife. Hence today, we walk the fields of this earth, glorifying, honoring, and praying that all the gods and goddesses of nature will be with this child, Rufilla, today and all her days. She has already been blessed by the spirit world, in that she was placed in the arms of this Sacred Tree. I declare that henceforth, before all those present, seen and unseen, that I will protect her, love her and see that her spiritual life is fully realized, in whatever form that the gods choose. I humbly invoke also, all the nature spirits to give us their divine approval on this day of celebration for the girl child we now adopt." Lucius stepped forward. "The name Istacidia Rufilla will be the name that will honor our family," Lucius said. "May she be nourished by all the fruits and bounties of this land."

A feast at the home of Lucius and Cassia followed the ceremony, starting with plates of raw vegetables, fish, and egg dishes. A second course followed with meat dishes, including a pig that had been sacrificed for the occasion. Numidian chicken, rabbit with fruit sauce, liver sausages with white grits, cooked vegetables, and freshly baked bread rounded out the meal. There was plenty of wine, which was always cut with water as Romans thought it barbaric to drink it undiluted. For dessert, dried fruits and nuts, including Neapolitan chestnuts roasted slowly until tender, were served.

Rufus made one of many toasts that day. "May I become so near and dear a relative that one day your cook will share with my cook the secret ingredients for the Numidian sauce. I have tasted this dish in many households, near and far, but never as sweet as here."

Lucius smiled. "Although I hasten to say our wonderful cook has some secrets that she may or may not want to share, maybe it is the sweetness of the day that has influenced the sweetness of the sauce."

Days turned into weeks. The day before Rufus would return alone to Pompeii, he and Lucius went to the Temple of Saturn in the Roman Forum, recording an official declaration of Rufilla's birth. He then accompanied Lucius to the assembly of senators, of which Lucius was a member.

That night at dinner, Cassia asked, "What was the gossip in the Senate today?"

"Today was all about the talk of a secret pact that Caesar, Pompey, and Crassus have formed," Lucius said. "It is only a rumor, but it is said that Caesar has arranged to help consolidate his power with these two influential men in the hope of winning the election to the next consulship."

"And well he may succeed," Rufus said. "From the conversation, I heard he is quite the political manipulator. But be careful what you say." Rufus winked at Lucius. "Aridela will give our names to Caesar's niece, Atia, who is a friend of hers, and he will have you and me on his proscription enemy list when he wins the consulship."

"What do you mean?" Cassia asked.

"May I?" Aridela looked at her husband.

Rufus nodded his consent.

"First of all, Caesar is quite aware of the danger of proscriptions," Aridela said, looking directly at her husband. "Having been proscribed by Sulla, Caesar was condemned to be killed at a mere 19! Besides, from what Atia tells me, I do not think he is of the disposition to kill his Roman enemies once in power. He saw enough of that with Sulla. And truly, you and Lucius are not his enemies," she said.

Cassia tilted her head as her eyebrows lifted.

"Atia is a good friend," Aridela said. "We met through a mutual friend in Vellitrae, and it felt like we had known each other all our lives. I love her sense of humor. We consider each other sisters—almost twins, born the same year! Cil and Atia's son Octavius have become good friends. They were born in the same year as well."

Anticipating Cassia's next question, Aridela continued. "When we stay with our friends in Vellitrae, we often see Atia. Her husband, Gaius Octavius, is serving a term as Roman governor in Macedonia at the moment, so she is living with her parents. It is thought that when he returns, he will run for the consulship. We will see how that works since Julius Caesar is her uncle, and he wants the consulship too. She and I always have the best conversations. She is quite bright and since her uncle has taken an interest in young Octavius, she has become politically ambitious for her son."

Aridela continued. "Atia revealed to me that Octavius was born just before dawn, so his father, a Senator, was late to the Senate. When he told another senator, one who had studied astrology, that senator asked him the time of the birth, and when he disclosed it, the senator proclaimed that a new ruler had been born that day! Atia has never forgotten that."

"I am duly impressed, sister-in-law," Cassia replied.

"As are we," Rufus said, gesturing to Lucius.

Then looking at the two men, Aridela said, "I know you were joking, but you should know that I would never betray my brother or you, my husband,"—an impish smile crossed her lips—"especially since you have given me my beautiful baby girl."

"Well, if I do not return to Pompeii soon, someone may take over my land and then where will our baby girl live?" Rufus said.

"There are vineyards and olive groves to purchase near Rome," Cassia said, "You could always move here."

"Ah, yes, but then it would not be Pompeian wine. It may not be the best wine in the region, but it sells well abroad and has a strong bite. And it does get better with every passing year, just as our marriage thrives and grows." Rufus kissed Aridela on the cheek. "Time for bed, dear wife," he said, extending his hand, "I must leave early tomorrow, and I need the warmth of my wife tonight."

After Rufus left for Pompeii, Aridela interviewed several women to become the permanent nursemaid to Rufilla. No one seemed quite right.

Then a neighbor of Cassia came to visit. As they talked, the neighbor relayed the story of a young girl, Melissa, who had come to her with such a sad tale. Melissa and her husband were in an unfortunate accident. The husband was killed, run over by a carriage. She was injured and shortly after that lost the baby she was carrying. The neighbor had been looking for help in the kitchen, but when she found out that Melissa had just miscarried, and more importantly that her milk was in, she decided to recommend her to Aridela.

Cassia arranged the interview. Melissa, a dark-haired girl, entered the room where Aridela and Cassia were waiting. Her hands were coupled as if in prayer, eyes lowered.

"Did I hear you speaking Greek to the neighbor?" Aridela asked Melissa.

"Yes, Domina," Melissa said, looking up. "I always do that when I get anxious. It will not happen again, I promise."

"Είμαι πάρα πολύ ελληνικής καταγωγής," Aridela said.

The young girl collapsed into Aridela's arms and started speaking rapidly in Greek.

"Slow down, slow down," Aridela said, answering her in Greek.

Cassia interrupted. "Latin, please speak in Latin for those of us not well versed in Greek."

"Sorry, dear sister-in-law, this young girl—Melissa, is it?" The girl nodded her head. "She is from a Greek section of Neapolis, so she is naturally excited to be able to speak her first language. You know that Melissa is an ancient name?"

"Yes, I do, Domina. It was my mother's name and her mother's too."

"It is even more ancient than that," Aridela said, smiling. "I am sure you know it means honey-sap, but did you know that legend has it that Melissa was the name of the nymph who cared for Zeus in his infancy?"

"No, I did not," Melissa said.

After listening to the neighbor's story, Aridela had Rufilla brought to her.

As Melissa held her for the first time, she exclaimed, "Oh, she is so beautiful!" Rufilla opened her eyes, made the sweet smacking sound of lips wanting to nurse.

"My milk is in—would you like me to try?"

"Of course, please sit in the wicker chair," Aridela said.

Melissa bared her breast, took her nipple between her two fingers and gently rubbed the baby's cheek. Rufilla responded, taking the nipple between her lips.

"The goddess Artemis has certainly brought us together." Aridela was exuberant. "Or should we call her by her Roman name, Diana?"

"Whatever you wish, Domina. I am grateful to serve you and the goddess."

"Then so be it—if Melissa is good enough for Zeus, then she is good enough to care for our sweet baby daughter."

With a nursemaid secured, Aridela was now anxious to return to Pompeii. She spoke to servants, Melissa and Selene, and also to Junia, her maidservant. "I intend to keep a contented household, especially now with this baby girl and her delicate nature. If problems arise, please take them to Junia." Looking at Melissa, she continued. "Junia is my maidservant, but she also helps keep the peace among the women servants. If she thinks that I should intervene, she will talk to me. That does not mean that *you* cannot talk to me. I am ultimately in charge of running our household, and I want above all, *Pax*." She drew out the word slowly. "Understood?"

"Yes, Domina," they answered.

"Good. I am excited for you to see Pompeii, Melissa. It is a lovely little town, and I hope that you will like it." Aridela clapped her hands. "Let us prepare to leave!"

CHAPTER IV

LESSONS AND RITUALS

POMPEII

The household settled into its routine. As *paterfamilias*, Rufus was responsible for the *familia's* health and well-being, and for bringing up his children, through blood or adoption, to be moral Roman citizens. The extended family included servants—freedman and slaves. He had learned from his father's example that servants well treated gave a good day's labor. The Istacidii's primary residence was in Pompeii, but they also owned a farmhouse just outside the walls of the city. Rufus's father owned many acres of the fertile farmland that surrounded not only Pompeii but lands that reached all the way north to the foothills of Mount Vesuvius. The Roman general Sulla had incorporated the town perforce into a Roman colony twenty years earlier. Because of his father's loyal service to Sulla, he received more land and had planted much of it as vineyards. When his father died, Rufus added to the family wealth by purchasing even more land as it became available. He hired tenant farmers to help manage the vast estate and share in the harvests. He eliminated some of the olive groves, which weren't producing well, turning them into vineyards, but kept some of the orchards so that he could produce olive oil for his family and local buyers. Arable farmland adjacent to the farmhouse was used to produce acres of grain, as bread was the essential food for all Romans. Groves of fruit trees and vegetable gardens provided food for his ever-expanding family of servants and slaves. A forest of beech trees in the valley had been planted by his father and nourished by Rufus, in memory of his father. On hot summer evenings, he rode his horse into the forest to feel close to his father and the land they both loved.

Rufus loved being in the out-of-doors, and as Cil got older, Rufus sometimes took the boy to the farm in the morning, a special treat for father and son. He taught Cil to ride a horse, and slowly introduced him to Rufus' duties as a gentleman farmer. They could sometimes be seen riding in the early morning at the edge of the fields and winding their way, single file, through tidy rows of grapevines in the terraced, emerald vineyards. Most mornings were spent at the farmhouse, meeting with clients. Rufus was a man of wealth and influence. In his capacity of the *patron*, he saw to it that his clients—freedmen—were given protection, representation in court, or even loans of money. They, in turn, offered their services to him as needed. In the afternoon, Rufus joined his comrades in the public baths, to talk politics, be entertained, and make business deals.

Roman matrons went to their bathhouse in the morning, so often, Aridela would address the house staff first thing with whatever needed attention for that day. She had seen the civility that her mother had shown her servants and ran her household the same way. Junia helped her oversee the running of the residence in town and the farmhouse. Selene was in charge of Cil, seeing to it that he received a daily bath. Roman children learned early in life that bathing was part of their spiritual upbringing, as water was sacred and not to be wasted because it was given to humans by the gods. Melissa often joined Selene in the bathing of both children and supervised their playtime. After household tasks were assigned, and if nothing urgent called her attention, Aridela would be off to her favorite bathhouse to meet with her friends and hear the latest news from Rome. She loved politics, and there were always juicy rumors going around. She and Atia frequently exchanged letters, so Aridela supplied other women at the bathhouse with news about Atia's famous uncle, Julius Caesar, and her son, Octavius. The women often knew the latest happenings before the men. Their lines of communication were well known.

Into this world of Pompeii, a town perched on the ledge of a prehistoric lava flow, Rufilla began her life again, thriving in her new home with the help of her loving parents and nursemaid. Her delicate and unstable condition reflected the uncertain landscape around her. Mount Vesuvius, located just a few miles north of town, loomed large, as did her affliction. Those living in this era were unaware of how often the mountain had erupted, or how the shaking of the earth was related to the fiery volcano. Likewise, no one could anticipate how violent the nature or frequency of her seizures, her body's shaking movements being the only outer manifestation of the intense explosions going on inside her head. They were hardly noticeable at first, but as time went on, Aridela and Melissa could read the signs and tried to protect her as best they could. Since they often occurred in her sleep, Melissa spent every night bedding down next to her cradle. One morning, as Melissa wiped the baby's mouth, she noticed a pink-tinged froth coming from between Rufilla's lips. Another seizure had occurred. Melissa found Aridela. "She must have had a seizure in the night," she said. "Even though I sleep next to her bed every night—"

"It is all right, Melissa," Aridela said. "Remember the midwife in Rome warned us that this could happen. We cannot catch them all. Heaven knows you need your sleep!" Aridela stayed close by until Rufilla finished nursing and then said, "I am ready for my morning prayers. Follow me and bring Rufilla."

The *lararium* in their home was in a small room off the kitchen, where family members offered their daily prayers. The room contained a shrine dedicated to the *Lares*, the deities who protected the household. The frescoes on the walls of the room emulated a garden filled with plants and garland decorations. On the back wall, small clay statuettes symbolizing each Lar stood on a sacred bench. The center was left open to receive daily offerings. Earlier that day, Rufus had burnt fragrant dried herbs as his oblation, and the scent still permeated the room. A stunning feature on the wall above the table was a fresco of the goddess Fortuna. She wore a crown and a white tunic and mantle. The red background on the walls made her look almost three-dimensional. In her left arm, she held a cornucopia with fruits flowing forth. On her right, a ship's rudder rested on a globe, indicating that she steered the lives and fates of those who sought her blessings. Around her feet, a serpent coiled and looked up at her as if to assure her of its protection. Melissa lit an oil lamp and then added to the sacrificial herbs, a small spark catching the new alms, the scent of rosemary refreshing the air. Aridela held the baby and began her morning invocation. "Today, in our morning prayers, we beseech you, dear goddess Fortuna, to give our family abundant life and make whole this child, whom you have chosen to give to us. Also, we call upon the goddess Hygeia to send healing powers to her and ask for help from the *genii*, her guardian angels Cunina and Cuba, to protect Rufilla as she sleeps in her cradle."

The following week, Aridela remembered the midwife's advice and decided to take Rufilla to the Temple of Asclepius in Pompeii. "Her malady is called the Sacred Disease," the older priest said. Then he whispered in Aridela's ear, "It is thought that Julius Caesar has this affliction too. It is a curse and a blessing." The priest continued, "Often those afflicted have special gifts because of their sensitive nature." The priests offered animal sacrifices and uttered incantations to Asclepius, the god of healing. That was all they could do, except they did suggest seeing the astrologer who served the temple. She told Aridela, "Your baby suffered a horrific birthing with this incarnation. Because of this, these seizures will be with her all her life, although they might lessen with time. Rufilla is a strong-willed, intuitive child, an old soul who has the potential to accomplish great things during her lifetime."

As Rufilla grew older, the family spent many summer days at the farmhouse. Often, Rufus and Theo, Rufus' right-hand man, joined Aridela in the *exedra*, a roofed, open-air room that revealed their elevated garden terrace beyond. Below was the undulating sea, and beyond, the setting sun. Melissa and Selene brought the two children to enjoy the nightly ritual of watching the sunset and listening to stories. Rufus and Theo loved telling stories including the one about the founding of Rome, Romulus and Remus, the adventures of Theseus, and the travels of Ulysses. The women added tales of Penelope's bad-mannered suitors and her plight in the story of Ulysses.

One evening, Aridela had started with the story of Ariadne of Crete, and Melissa chimed in with a different version that her family told. That was the first time that Melissa and Theo realized that they had similar Greek backgrounds. Cil was restless that evening and kept pulling on his mother's gown and whispering in her ear. "Cil, your turn will come," Aridela said. After a few more tugs, Rufus spoke. "What is so important that you cannot wait your turn, young man?"

Cil was quick to respond. "It is about Asclepius, Pater. You and mater talked about maybe going to Epidaurus and visiting the Temple of Asclepius with Rufilla. Is the god there? What happens when someone visits that place? And what is a sanctuary? Could they help Rufilla?"

Days earlier, he had been present when Rufilla had a particularly severe grand mal seizure. It had visibly shaken him, and he couldn't forget the conversation concerning Asclepius.

"Dearest, Cil," Aridela said, "It is sweet of you to want to know how to help your little sister, but the Sanctuary I spoke of is not the one we have visited in Pompeii but the one in Epidaurus, Greece, far, far away."

"Yes, I know about Greece. You talked about Theseus and Ulysses living there. When can we go?" he said. "I want to go with her."

"One day, when Rufilla is much older, we will see, Cil, we will see."

For the first six years of a child's life, the Roman mother managed the education of her children. And so, Aridela was in charge of teaching Cil the necessary alphabets in all three languages that were popular at the time in Pompeii; Latin, Oscan, and Greek. The next phase of learning took place from six to seven years of age. Cil's began at home with Theo as the tutor. He was of Greek ancestry and had been educated to teach basic reading, writing, and math, and was also versed in Latin and Greek literature. Cil, who was joined by his friend Titus, started a daily school regime of reading and writing, which began by incising with a stylus on a wax tablet. When they became proficient, they were allowed to write on paper with ink pens and paper scrolls made from papyrus. An abacus was used to teach basic math. Memorization was crucial, as there were no books for Cil and Titus to read. Theo was able to obtain some writings transcribed on scrolls, pertaining to literary texts. The boys were quick learners and easily bored, so it was Theo's challenge every day to keep his students engaged.

Lessons for Cil and Titus took place in Theo's apartment next to the main house in Pompeii. Rufus had given Theo his own apartment because he had shown himself a talented and competent servant. Word had spread that Theo was an unusual teacher. Unlike most teachers, whippings and beatings were not part of his curricula. Several of Rufus' friends asked if their children might be tutored by him as well. So a private school of sorts started in his apartment but soon moved to the peristyle garden in the Istacidii home. If students could not follow his rules, their parents threatened them with having to go to an alternative teacher, one whose name struck fear in them. All remained with the help of their parents' persuasion.

One sunny afternoon, just before the classes were due to end for a well-deserved break, it was test time in the garden. Theo had introduced the boys to some advanced courses that they would be taking in the fall when they entered their secondary schooling in Neapolis. The boys, now between 10 and 12, sat on chairs with their backs against the walls of the shaded colonnade that surrounded the peristyle garden. Curtains had been placed on both sides, so the boys would not be distracted by the movements of house servants. That day they were given a list of questions to answer. The students had graduated from making their letters with a *stylus*, which was used to incise the wax on the tablet, tiring to young hands, to using the *calamus*, a writing tool that merely drew the letters on top of the wax. The boys listened intently. These questions covered subjects concerning local cultures as well as those of faraway lands, including the legend of Ulysses. Their penmanship counted too, breaking any ties so that there could be a clear winner. Theo, who usually let his assistant administer the tests, was in attendance that day.

Unbeknownst to them, there was one other student present, Rufilla, sitting on the other side of the curtain. She had been secretly listening to the lessons, and so she wanted to take the test, too. Aridela, who had been teaching her privately, told her she was too young to join the boys. Just then Celer, Cil's dog, came up to her, nuzzling her to pet him. He had taken a liking to Rufilla. "Shh, you must not make any noise," she whispered. She sat with stylus and wax tablet in her lap, drawing a rosebud that she saw on the rose bush in front of her in the peristyle garden.

The first question was to differentiate between Etruscan and Greek cities and give an example of each. Rufilla had remembered Theo giving this lecture. He had said that Greek cities like Athens had an acropolis, or an area of high ground that was usually fortified, with the city where the people lived below. Etruscan cities, like Pompeii, were built on high ground and were often walled cities to protect the people. She preferred the latter plan.

The last question concerned the story of Ulysses. Rufilla was restless, twisting and turning as she sat on the tiny cushion. The boys seemed to take forever to write the answers to the questions she quickly recalled.

Then it happened. The dog caught sight of a mouse moving between two rose bushes in the garden.

"Celer, come back," Rufilla shouted, deserting her hiding place to chase after the dog.

The boys and teachers looked up at Rufilla, whose words spilled out behind her.

"You boys are so slow," she said. "The answers are easy. U-l-y-s-s-e-s went on the voyage; C-y-c-l-o-p-s was the one-eyed monster. And for your information, P-e-n-e-l-o-p-e was the patient wife who waited ten years for her husband to return home."

At that moment, Melissa rounded the corner. "So sorry she interrupted your—" She stopped mid-sentence as Theo's laughing eyes met hers. "I," she said, pleasantly surprised, "I did not know you were here, too."

"It is fine, Melissa. But it sounds like we might think about including her in the lessons next year."

Cassia and Lucius had planned their annual spring visit to Pompeii to coincide with the return of the boys from their schooling. Rufilla, who had turned eight, had written a play, with the help of her mother, Melissa, and Theo. Cil, Titus, Aper, and her best friend, Hostia, would participate in her production, and she had added a small part for her cousin Zo.

Aridela and Cassia sat on the porch of the farmhouse in the late afternoon, sipping *mulsum,* honey wine, and talking. They could see Mount Vesuvius, topped with clouds a few miles to the north, and a colorful sunset to the west.

"I have missed you since your visit last fall," Aridela said. "As I recall, you arrived before the rainy season and after the Eleusinian Mysteries. I remember that because I had just received a letter from my friend Kallistê in Athens, telling me of her involvement in the rituals."

"Yes, the leaves were starting to turn, and we had to leave so that Lucius could oversee the grape harvest back in Rome. Spring is a much better time of year to come, as the floods in Rome are so difficult to endure," Cassia said.

Zo had been sitting patiently near his mother. "Junia, would you take Zo and find Cil so that they might play together," Aridela said.

"Thank you, auntie," Zo said.

After the boy had left, Aridela turned to face Cassia. "I have wanted to talk to you about Rufilla. I am concerned about her. She is so thin, and she has had many seizures recently."

Cassia took Aridela's hand. "She is so striking with her red hair and brown eyes and that beautiful milky white complexion. I cannot believe there is anything wrong with her. She looks more like you every day."

"Yes," said Aridela. "I think it must be my Etruscan heritage. My mother used to tell me I reminded her of her grandmother. She would say, 'You have the tiniest mouth, and those large, dark eyes can read my thoughts before I say them!'" Yet, she often wondered if Rufilla looked like her birth mother. Was she of Etruscan heritage too? Rufus had assured her that he would find out about the family and the circumstances of Rufilla's birth, but Aridela made him promise not to tell her. For reasons she couldn't quite understand, she did not want to know. She only wanted to love and nurture this 'dream' child that the goddess Fortuna had given her.

In the atrium, Rufilla and Hostia were playing with their dolls.

"When I grow up, I am going to marry Julius Caesar and live in his villa," said Hostia. She put a small veil over the doll's head and walked her across the couch, singing the wedding march.

"Oh, he is far too old for me," said Rufilla. "I will marry Titus. He is older but not as old as Caesar."

"I do not care," Hostia said as she pounded her doll's feet on the sofa. "Papa says that he thinks Caesar wants to be king and I want to be his queen."

Rufilla gave Hostia a blank stare.

"I am sorry," Hostia said. "I did not mean to make you angry."

Rufilla's eyes rolled back in her head, her chin snapped upward, and her back arched. She dropped the doll and fell backward onto the sofa, her arms and legs thrashing in unison. A gurgling noise came from deep in her throat, and her jaw became rigid as if she were biting something.

"Melissa, come quick," Hostia said, running to the door. "It is Rufilla—hurry!"

Melissa yelled for Aridela and Cassia to follow her as she ran to the atrium.

"Now, now, my sweet, it will be all right," Aridela said, cradling her child.

Rufilla's body was still shaking.

"I did not do anything, honest," Hostia said. We were playing with our dolls and—"

"It is all right, dear. I know you did not do anything wrong."

Melissa came back from the kitchen carrying a damp cloth with smelling salts. "I have sent for the doctor," she said.

Aridela looked up at Cassia. "This is what I was worried about—the seizures seem to be getting worse." When Aridela passed the smelling salts under Rufilla's nose, the child reacted immediately. She turned her head from side to side, and as she opened her mouth, her mother saw blood around her lips.

"Oh, the poor dear, she bit her tongue again," Aridela said, investigating Rufilla's mouth. "Melissa, please fetch some cold water and bring another clean cloth."

"Let me do it," said Cil. He and Zo had heard the commotion and come to see what was happening. He ran from the room and returned from the kitchen with a cold cloth and a sprig of dried lavender. He placed it under Rufilla's nose. She opened her eyes, looking dazed.

"You are all right, baby sister," he said. "We are all here for you. Come here, Hostia. See that she is awake now. It is a frightening thing to see, but know that you did not cause it."

His words seemed to comfort Hostia as he put his arm around her.

Melissa and Aridela exchanged glances. Cil was such a loving brother.

Cassia went to her sister-in-law's side and hugged her. "I am so sorry."

"I am sorry for Rufilla," Aridela said as she rocked her child in her arms.

When the doctor arrived, Rufilla was still groggy. He took Aridela and Cassia aside after the examination. Looking at Aridela, he said, "When was the last time you took her to the Asclepian temple?"

"Not since she was a baby," Aridela said. "They shared with us the remedies they thought might help."

"I think it is time to go again. You must appease the god."

"I agree." Aridela looked at Cassia. "We will go to the temple in a few days after she has recovered. Rufus will want to make a sacrifice to the god. Following that, Rufilla will be able to present her special surprise to you and Lucius. She will want to be in her best form."

CHAPTER V

THE PERFECT PIG AND PROPHECIES

A week later, Melissa directed Theo to go to the family farm to select a pig that Rufus and his friends would offer as a sacrifice at the temple later in the morning. "Make sure the pig is male and perfectly formed," Melissa began, "with no blemishes on his skin. He must be perfect. Here are the ribbons to put around his neck," and as she handed them to him she whispered, "Make sure that the musician plays his flute loudly so that—"

"So that he will drown out any ill-omened noises." Theo chuckled as he finished her sentence. She blushed at their familiarity, and then switched to Greek with some final instructions. As worried as she was about Rufilla, Aridela had recently noticed the natural intimacy between the tutor and the nursemaid as well as the way Melissa spoke to him in an intimate Greek dialect. Aridela felt she had the right to listen in on the conversations of her servants. Keeping the peace was her responsibility. The other servants and slaves looked to Theo and Melissa for guidance. Aridela had talked with Rufus, and he agreed that marriage was in the future for these two loving and generous people.

Theo picked the "perfect" pig from the family's farmyard. He tied a rope around its neck, washed it down, and led it to their home in town. Melissa was there to greet him. "Here, give me the rope," she said, walking around the pig and checking it carefully. "I want to make sure it has no blemishes." After closely scrutinizing it, she handed the rope back to Theo, his hand over hers for just a second, long enough to cause Melissa to blush once again.

The group was starting to assemble. The men would take the pig to the Asclepian Temple as a sacrifice to appease the god. Theo pulled on the rope. The pig did not budge, which brought howls of laughter from Zo, Cil, and Titus. After a series of snorts and squeals, imitated by the boys, the pig went along peacefully. The three boys followed behind the pig, cooking up some mischief, Theo was certain. He warned the boys to behave.

And so at the given time, the *pompa*, the procession, commenced. Rufus and Lucius took the lead, followed by the other men who would partake of the upcoming meal: Victor Bucci and Marcus Arrius Polites. Gnaeus Melissaei was away on business, but his son Aper was there with Theo, Cil, Titus, Zo, and the sacrificial pig bringing up the rear. It was a formidable group.

To pass the time during their walk, Theo quizzed Cil and Titus on their most recent lessons about Asclepius. "I want to be a physician just like him," Cil said.

Once in a while, the pig balked, and Theo had to give it an extra hard yank. That made the trip fun for the children, and in no time the "house of sacrifice" loomed before them.

The Temple of Asclepius was narrow yet imposing. The procession paused on the sidewalk at the entrance. Rufus rang the chimes, and the priest appeared, allowing all to enter.

The priest motioned the group to move to the altar, where he began the ceremony with the washing of his hands, followed by a formal cry for silence. Rufus covered his head with his toga and the rest followed. The priest recited the opening prayers of the petition. Rufus sprinkled the *mola salsa*, the salted flour, onto the head of the animal and also onto the sacred knife that would be used. The priest called for all the boys, Cil, Zo, Titus, and Aper, to stand before him. Rufus instructed Cil to pour an offering of wine over the head of the pig, which gave a loud squeal, but Theo was in control and held the pig as still as possible. The boys could barely control a snicker. A stern look from Theo squelched that. They had been warned that this was a solemn occasion. If anything out of the ordinary happened, they would have to cancel the ceremony and return at another time with another sacrifice. None of the boys wanted to be responsible for that.

Two men who had been hired to carry out the sacrifice took control of the pig. One man called out, "Am I to strike?" then stunned the animal with the blow of a hammer. The other man took the knife, turned the pig's head upward toward the god, then slit its throat with the consecrated knife. The men drained the blood and cut the belly open, examining the entrails for omens. The omens were favorable. There were no abnormalities in the organs. The fire had been started on the altar, and so the pig was placed upon it. The priest offered the internal organs to Asclepius as a burnt offering, and the rest of the pig would be roasted and shared among the priests and the guests at the dinner that evening.

As fate would have it, just then Aridela and Cassia, along with Clodia Bucci and Aricia Arrius were coming from the baths, having attended the opening part of Rufilla's purification ritual, they were heading toward the home of the Asclepian priests. Aridela had decided to take them past the Asclepian Temple first, wanting Rufilla to experience the sacrificial ritual even if women couldn't participate. When they turned the corner, they caught the scent of incense burning in the temple and heard the lyric sound of the flute and the rhythmic tempo of the tambourine. It mesmerized the women, drawing them to the open gates of the Temple. The priest had gathered the group of men in the courtyard in front of the altar. They had their backs to the street with togas over their heads, singing a ritual song, so they did not see the women. Aridela stopped the women's procession and pulled Rufilla close to her. "This is the sacrifice in progress. Look at the spectacle—men and boys with their heads covered in religious obeisance gathering around, watching the flames of the sacrifice upon the altar. See the wide flight of stairs in front of them?" She pointed her finger upward. "Let your eyes follow the stairs and behold—in the *cella*, the sacred inner room, the statues of Asclepius and his daughter, Hygeia. His left hand holds his staff, a knotty tree limb with a single serpent encircling it. Remember this image always, seeing these men and boys who love you, wishing for you the best of health." Rufilla felt honored, her heart open to the love.

After a few moments of silence, the priest started the song to Hestia, the goddess of altars and the hearth.

"Hestia—come now into this house—and bestow grace upon my song."

The women took their leave and continued to the priests' home. The entrance to the house had an unusually elevated walk above the regular sidewalk, which spanned almost the entire width of the property. Aridela remarked that this short set of stairs on either end made it easier for the infirm to gain entrance.

They were standing at the small front door waiting to be admitted when down the street came the group of men. Having been dismissed by the priest, they were now headed to the baths. Theo approached Aridela and Cassia with Zo and Cil in tow. Zo was still imitating the pig and being a bit unruly.

"I will take the boys home, with your permission," Theo offered.

"I would like to go inside," Cil said.

Aridela gave him a tentative look.

"But I want to learn," Cil said. "I want to be like Asclepius, like Hippocrates."

Aridela remembered being a young girl and hearing her brother say those exact words. "All right, Cil, come with me," she said. "But remember to be quiet and respectful."

The group turned its attention to Zo. He started to say something, but Cassia spoke to him sternly. "You may come in, with my permission, but if you show any irreverence—"

"No, no, I will be good, I promise, Mater, I promise."

At that moment, a porter opened the outer door and directed them inside. "Welcome to the Sanctuary of Asclepius." The vestibule was narrow and dark and, Aridela had to admit, a bit intimidating. But she could tell by the way Rufilla held her hand, ever so lightly, that she was entirely at ease, confident and unafraid. "It feels like I have been here before, Mater."

"You were only a baby," Aridela said, recognizing the intuitive nature of her daughter.

The porter opened the main door within so that now they were able to see well. One Ionic column on either side of the vestibule held ornately decorated capitals. As they walked past, Aridela whispered to Rufilla, "Look behind you at the capitals on the columns—are those women etched in stone maenads or goddesses?" They grinned at each other. Rufilla didn't answer her mother's question.

Beyond, they stood looking at the most remarkable atrium Rufilla had ever seen. It was enormous. An open skylight in the center of the room allowed rainwater to flow into the large *impluvium*, a shallow basin set in the floor, which drained into the cistern below. "Count each column, Rufilla," Aridela said.

"Sixteen?" Rufilla had already been counting.

"Yes, sixteen Doric columns, four on each side of the *impluvium*. And notice how tall they are!" They were at least two stories.

"May I touch one?" Rufilla asked.

"Yes, you may," Aridela said. "They are made of local rock and are very strong. See, they are holding up the roof."

From behind them, they heard footsteps. The steps did not belong to Theo, who tended to lift his sandals high with each step. This sound was more of a scrape. Aridela turned and saw the older priest from the temple. He moved forward, around the *impluvium*, stopping amidst the back four columns where a water fount stood. He motioned for all to join him.

"You must be the celebrant, Rufilla?" the priest said, and Rufilla nodded. "I saw you and your mother standing outside the temple a short while ago. I am so glad you have come." When everyone had gathered around him, the priest said, "Let us begin *our* ceremony."

Rufilla showed no signs of nervousness as the older priest cupped his hands into the water and performed the purification ceremony over her wavy red hair. He gave Rufilla a penetrating gaze before leaning down to say something to her that Aridela couldn't hear.

Another priest approached them from behind and led them to the back of the Sanctuary, where two more small fountains stood at the start of a luxurious garden. The sight of the beautiful foliage and flowers eased Aridela's heart. "This is my daughter who is ill with seizures," she said to the second priest.

"You are the girl that we made the sacrifice for this morning."

Rufilla nodded.

"Come with me," the second priest said as he led Rufilla into the garden, where they picked spring flowers together. He explained to Rufilla what the flowers represented. Roses symbolized love. Rosemary was for remembrance. "We will present them to the gods along with the offerings you brought, Rufilla."

Aridela was alone when the older priest approached her. He lowered his voice for a private conversation. The words he spoke made her face turn ashen.

"She is that sick?" she replied in alarm.

"Yes, but take heart, your daughter also has unusual powers."

"When she was an infant, I brought her to you and you said she had the sacred disease."

"As well as the gift of prophecy," the priest continued.

Aridela's eyes narrowed as she considered this startling news.

"You have not seen instances of this?"

Aridela shook her head.

Rufilla came towards them, excited about her handful of flowers. Aridela held her finger to her lips so that her daughter would show the proper respect and not speak until someone spoke to her. Rufilla saw her brother and walked toward him, leaving the two alone again.

"I remember when you visited us and your grief at losing your first two pregnancies," he said. "You weren't sure that you had done the right thing by marrying."

"I love the man I married, but my earlier experience as a youth, my time in Athens with my Greek sister, those were formative moments in my life."

"Those were precious times for you, especially the Dionysian ritual you experienced." He looked deeply into her eyes. "I remember everything you told me. Aridela, you have gifts to share with your daughter."

She gasped, close to tears. Attempting to maintain her composure, she said, "You seem to understand even beyond my comprehension."

"Your innate sensibilities give you the wisdom that will benefit both your children," the priest said as Cil joined them. "Your son is a healer, and your daughter, when she approaches puberty in a few years, should be able to learn more from our brothers at Epidaurus. The same gift that you have chosen not to develop fully must be encouraged in your daughter."

The two priests gathered everyone together in front of the alcove next to the atrium. It was set off by two columns with exquisite carvings of Ionic capitals. Within was an altar made of marble and upon it was a small, lidded basket.

The two priests asked Rufilla and Aridela to join them inside the alcove. Rufilla, as instructed, put the flowers she had picked in front of the basket. Then she placed her gifts, a small jar of goat's milk and a honeycomb, on either side of the flowers.

The first priest reached behind the altar, retrieving a tree limb shaped like the club of Asclepius, complete with a snake entwined around it. He moved to the basket and set the lid ajar. Then he began to pray. He finished with the words, "Just as you accepted the earlier gift of the sacrificial pig, generous Asclepius, please accept these well-meaning gifts, placed before you by the celebrant within this sacred *lararium*." The priest put his finger to his lips. "Wait in silence."

Anticipating something, Theo placed a hand on the shoulder of each boy.

The basket lid started to move. Aridela put her arm around Rufilla. Slowly the cover opened more as a tiny snake emerged and wrapped itself around the bouquet. "The symbol of Asclepius is moved to accept your gift, dear girl," the priest said. "Rejoice at this wondrous act!"

Ariadne Play by Rufilla Istacidia

CHAPTER VI

ARIADNE'S STORY

The morning of the sacrifice, Junia and Melissa had accompanied Marcia, the cook, to the *macellum*, which was the large market area located in the *Roman Forum*, the public center. Vendors set up shop early in the morning, selling everything from flowers to fish, poultry to seasonal fruits and vegetables. Marcia had learned from Aridela to drive a hard bargain with the merchants, getting what she thought was a reasonable price for the freshest fare. She and her kitchen staff took the purchases to the farmhouse, as that is where all the festivities would take place later in the day.

The dinner parties of Pompeii were celebrations of a boisterous society at its best. Men used this time to further their friendships and establish business bonds. Often it was only the men who dined in the *triclinium*, the main dining room, reclining on long couches covered with cushions and pillows. But this dinner, hosted by Rufus and Aridela, would be attended by a group of men and their wives who dined together regularly, this time celebrating the coming together of their children performing in Rufilla's play. She had requested that they hold the performance in the farmhouse's spacious atrium, which could entertain the entire audience of parents and friends. Later, adults and children would move into their separate dining rooms.

Guests arrived and mingled in the atrium. The men were eager to sample the previous year's wine. Excellent weather conditions had produced a vintage crop, and Rufus watched with pride as the men raised the silver *scyphus*, ornate drinking cups his father had willed to him, and smacked their lips as they sipped the delicious wine. The women migrated to the garden to admire the flowers and the newest addition, a figure of a young Dionysus with a cluster of grapes in his hand.

Among the guests were Victor and Clodia Bucci. They brought their daughter, Bucia, and son Titus. Victor's gregarious, fun-loving nature always made him the center of attention. Already he was laughing and joking and holding out his *scyphus* for the second pouring of wine. He was stocky with a big chest and broad shoulders, but as a young man, he had had exceptionally narrow hips, and his build had turned many heads. Wine and good food had, throughout the years, thickened his belly, and age had thinned his hair to the point where he now wore a wig, expensively threaded with gray. Still, he remained an attractive man. He could have had his pick of any woman but deferred to his family's wishes that he marry Clodia.

His wife, Clodia, however, was the sour partner in their arranged union. Even the presence of her daughter did not relax the prunish scrunch of her face. She seldom laughed or smiled except, Aridela had noticed, when her adored son Titus was in the room. Aridela tried to be understanding. Perhaps it was Clodia's sickly nature. She was too thin, and her coloring was that of a faded narcissus. It was commonly known that she suffered some ailment of the kidneys. Almost as soon as the women were alone in the garden, Clodia motioned to a servant, who led her to a private room with a chamber pot. The other women had the good manners not to notice. Instead, Aricia loudly exclaimed how well the new garden design had turned out, and the women gratefully had an excuse to turn their attention elsewhere.

Aricia had been Aridela's friend for a long time. Although she was as thin as Clodia, she looked healthy and beautiful. Her large, almond-shaped eyes and broad, sensuous smile made one think of a Greek goddess. No one would ever have guessed her barren. Her inability to bear children was the biggest disappointment in her life, but instead of making her bitter, she decided to find consolation and enjoyment in her friend's children. Aricia loved Rufilla and Cil as if they were her own. Aridela knew how much Aricia cared for them, even though Aricia was not a demonstrative type. She hid her deep capacity for love under a reserved exterior. Aridela believed it was because Aricia's arranged marriage to Arrius Polites had sapped something vital within her. Aricia had tried to be a dutiful wife. At first, she had gone along with the patriarchal hierarchy, obeying her strict Roman husband who put rules before the relationship, dictating, among other things, how she should run her household. He saw how beautiful she was and grew more demanding and jealous when other men were present. Even to his fellow business colleagues, Arrius Polites was imperious and adamant, always setting down moral codes for others to follow. He had had the rules of conduct for his dinner guests painted on the dining room wall. Aricia had put up with his attitude for a long time, but her powerful feminine identity began to emerge as she became a follower of Artemis. As her priestess, Aricia would be the one to guide Rufilla through the Artemis rituals in two years, when Rufilla turned ten.

The last couple coming to the play and party was the Tintirii, whose family had moved to Pompeii from Nuceria after Spartacus had plundered the town. They were asked to join the dinner group when the two families decided that the Tintirii's daughter, Tintiria, would marry Cil when she came of age. They had purchased a house just around the corner from the Melissaei.

Aper Melissaei, son of Gnaeus and Sulpicia, would represent his parents at this gathering. His family had a fleet of ships that traveled from port to port, transporting wine and olive oil, trading products that were produced in the regions near the harbor towns. The imports, from exotic cloth to expensive herbs and spices, were from areas far from the Bay of Naples. The sailing season had started, keeping Gnaeus away for long periods, including now. Sulpicia refused to attend the party alone, but she had insisted that their son Aper make an appearance before Victor and Clodia, his future parents-in-law. After a brief stint in the military, Aper would marry Buccii's daughter, Bucia, and carry on in his father's shipbuilding and an import-export business.

With the sound of a gong, the women joined the men in the atrium for the pre-dinner performance. Everyone was looking forward to it since the entertainment revolved around their children. Aridela knew that good or bad, the adults would love it, but she hoped for her daughter's sake that it went smoothly. Rufilla was directing a production of what she called *Ariadne's Story*. Aridela, Melissa, and Theo had helped her put together the scenes and write the narration. She took it seriously, throwing heart and soul into it. Having heard the story since she was a baby, Rufilla felt that it was part of her being. Now, as an eight-year-old, she knew what she wanted. Her mother had taken her for a visit to the theater in Pompeii, so she adapted what she had seen there to her family's atrium. There were doors on either side of the atrium, leading to the peristyle garden. She closed those off and asked Junia to arrange for two transparent curtains to hang front and center in the archway between the two rooms. These drapes would be the entrance and exit for the actors. The stage was a slightly elevated wooden platform made to fit in front of the curtains. Around the stage, chairs were placed in a semi-circle to simulate the theater seating.

To Rufilla, the play touched something deep inside her, something she did not understand but which called to her as her destiny. She cast herself as narrator and also as Ariadne, to whom she felt such a close affinity. Titus, of course, would be Theseus, the man who fell in love with Ariadne and saved her. That was how it should be since Titus was her betrothed. At age eleven, an awkward period for most boys, Titus was slim, muscled, and taller than other boys his age. His hair was dark and curly, and with his unusual blue eyes, it was easy to see that the cutest boy in the room would grow to become the most handsome man.

Cil had agreed to play the monstrous step-brother with a human body and a bull's head, the Minotaur, who lived in the labyrinth. She cast Aper as Dionysus. At sixteen, Aper was almost too old for this child's play, but he enjoyed playing big brother to Cil and Titus, as well as protecting Rufilla when necessary. He had warned Cil not to wave the bull's head around clownishly.

Hostia, Rufilla's best friend, had been instrumental in helping Rufilla complete the preparations for the performance and would play Ariadne's mother, Pasiphaë. Her parents had been called away due to the illness of Hostia's grandfather, and she was staying with the Istacidiis.

Melissa and Theo were behind the scenes in the peristyle area, busy trying to get the children organized. Even though the boys were older than Rufilla, and far more interested in getting the play over with so they could go outside and roughhouse among themselves, they were good sports. But they were having fun too.

Theo, Melissa, and the children had positioned themselves behind the translucent curtains.

"All right!" Theo called out to the children clapping his hands together. "Is everyone ready?"

The adults had taken their seats in front of the curtains and were anticipating the show.

The natural light streaming from the open peristyle behind the curtain was bright enough to backlight the actors in silhouette. The audience saw, through the curtains, a tall boy on the left holding a double flute; to the right, a figure of the Minotaur; and in the center was a petite girl holding a scroll, dressed in a diaphanous gown that made her look like a goddess. The flute player stepped from between the curtains and began playing a haunting melody reminiscent of music heard in Greece. It was Aper. The women in the audience sighed. Joining Aper in front of the curtain was Rufilla as the narrator. As she unrolled the scroll, all the nervousness that she usually felt in front of a group fell away. The music had soothed her soul. This was her myth.

"On the island of Crete, Ariadne stood on the windswept hill overlooking the bay," Rufilla started. "She had heard that the ship was coming from Athens with the yearly tribute—seven men and seven maidens. She always felt sorry for these young people her age, going to their deaths because of her father, King Minos. She watched the procession of the tribute coming up the hill and noticed something different this year. Among the men was one who was taller, more muscular than the rest. His black hair and bronze body caught her eye. He seemed almost mysterious.

"She hurried back to the palace to be present when they stood before her father as he condemned them to the Labyrinth and their fate with the Minotaur. The whole court was buzzing about the handsome Athenian among the booty. Ariadne was determined to meet this man who had touched her so deeply at first sight."

Titus joined Rufilla on the makeshift stage and read his opening monologue.

"I, Theseus, son of King Aegeus of Athens, conceived a plot. I told my father that my plan was simple. I would volunteer to be one of the tributes who would take the long journey to Crete to be sacrificed to King Minos. I had already heard of the beautiful Ariadne, daughter of the king. I would enlist her as my accomplice to kill the Minotaur and free my people once and for all from this tyranny. My father agreed, and I set sail for the island of Crete.

"After arriving on the island, we were taken to the king's court, where I saw this young woman standing next to her father. I looked into her eyes, and it was as if Zeus had let loose one of his thunderbolts. Sparks flew between us, and I knew from that moment on that I would accomplish my mission."

As the play proceeded, Hostia played a sympathetic version of Ariadne's mother, Pasiphae. She seemed to be enjoying herself despite the absence of her mother and father. Cil relished the role of an ogre. He spoke his lines behind the curtain, with his body hunched over and his Minotaur's bullhead poking from behind the curtain to roar at Theseus and duly frighten his step-sister, Ariadne. The battle between Theseus and the Minotaur also took place behind the translucent curtain. Cil made all the right noises for an animal being killed. Finally, Aper as Dionysus rescued Ariadne after Theseus abandoned her on the island of Naxos. Rufilla had made a crown that Aper placed on her head for the marriage ceremony. Afterward, he tossed it into the air to replicate Dionysus throwing the crown into the night sky to form the Corona Borealis. This earthly crown looped around a rod that had been set up next to the curtains, which were dotted with stars imitating the evening sky.

"Good toss," Theo whispered behind the scenes.

Aper grinned. "With this gesture, I signify my love for this mortal woman by returning the crown to the nighttime sky where it once again becomes the Corona Borealis, a symbol of our love, visible to the world for all eternity."

The adults clapped loud and long. Theo and Melissa handed Rufilla and Hostia congratulatory bouquets. One could hear Titus' father, Victor, with his booming voice, cheering more loudly than the rest. Aridela was proud of Rufilla, for she knew the play had been all hers. As the children took their bows, Melissa brought Hygeia to Rufilla so that they could, together, take a bow. Her cat had been a real crowd-pleaser in its role as the common bull sacrificed instead of the rare white bull played by Cil's white dog, Celer. Rufilla had never felt so proud and happy. Instinctively, she plucked two roses from her bouquet and handed them to her mother and father. The guests murmured appreciatively at this gesture, and at the love the roses signified between Aridela and Rufus.

Rufilla plucked two more roses, handed one to Aricia and said, "To my mentor," and one to Victor and for a second was lost for words. "To my future father-in-law," she finally said.

Immediately Rufilla realized her mistake. She should have given one to Clodia also, but it was too late.

In the embarrassed silence, Hygeia saved the day. She jumped out of Rufilla's arms and onto the lap of Arrius. When Aricia grabbed at the cat, Hygeia leaped long and high right onto the head of Victor. The gray wig slipped down Victor's face, and the cat flipped to the floor and scampered away, dropping the wig partway across the atrium.

Everyone laughed as they headed toward the dining room. Victor went to retrieve his wig and passed Aricia, giving her a devilish smile. She looked up at him, then at the heavens, and made an audible prayer: "Artemis, be with me at this moment." Anyone else might have seen the way she looked at Victor as dismissing him. He saw it as a sign that she would be guided by Artemis—into his arms.

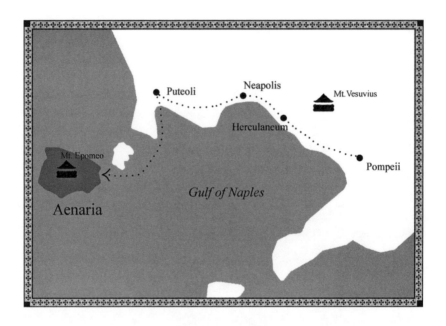

Island of Aenaria

CHAPTER VII

JUNE 52 BCE

Later that evening, Melissa and Theo went to check on Rufilla. She and the cat were asleep in her bed. As they stood at the foot of Rufilla's bed in silence, Theo put his arm around Melissa's shoulder. "How lucky we are," he said, looking down at the sleeping child.

Melissa put her hand on his and looked into his eyes. "Yes," she said.

He leaned down and touched his lips to hers, their sweet first kiss, so long-awaited.

"My love," Theo said, uttering a feeling that he had never spoken to her before. "Will you marry me and be with me as long as we both shall live?"

"I will."

The moment had been a long time coming, and with those words, they sealed their bond of engagement. The only witnesses were a sleeping child and her cat. But that was enough. In this Roman era, these two Roman citizens chose to become husband and wife. There would be no dowry as they were servants, not aristocrats. No written contract was necessary, only showing *consensus*, or consenting to live together.

That night they decided to find Rufus and Aridela and tell them. "We would like permission from you, Dominus, to announce our engagement and marry thereafter as soon as possible."

"It is time," Rufus said.

"It is past time," Aridela said, "Rufus and I have been talking about this for months. We will start planning the wedding tomorrow!"

The month of June was named in honor of the Roman goddess Juno, the wife of the god, Jupiter. She was the goddess of marriage. The day after the Ides of the month was the first day acceptable for weddings in June, and so that was the day Rufus and Aridela planned this celebration for the two most important servants in their family. Melissa did not want anything extravagant. Some of the discussion included Rufilla. "Hostia's mater says that you must at least wear a veil as that will show your consent to be married," Rufilla said.

"Hostia's mother, you say," Aridela said. "You have been talking to other people about this?"

"Hostia can come," Melissa said, "but none of your other friends, and certainly not their parents. Theo and I want it to be a family gathering."

And so the plans came together. The household servants and slaves could barely contain their excitement. They had noticed the attraction between the two for some time and wanted to participate in the event in any way they could. Both house and farm servants would join in the ritual meal after the wedding.

"I will cook all my special dishes for the celebration dinner," Marcia, the cook, said. "With your permission, Domina."

"Of course," Aridela said. "Theo and Melissa would like the dinner held at the clearing near the farmhouse. Marcia, call upon the services of the foreman to roast two pigs and a lamb, and order fresh fish so that there will be enough for all of our family."

Aridela bought the material for the bridal veil from her favorite seamstress. The accomplished weavers of the Istacidii household helped Melissa spin a simple woolen *tunica recta,* wedding dress. Other servants used saffron to dye the veil and matching shoes a traditional deep gold for the bride-to-be.

Since Melissa had been married before, she decided to forego the hair-do that resembled the traditional hairstyle of the Vestal Virgins. She did go to the temple of Venus to honor the goddess with flowers and ask for her blessing.

The day of the wedding feast, Aridela and the women Melissa had chosen, including Rufilla, accompanied her to the pre-wedding bathing ritual at the public baths. After that, they all walked to the farmhouse. On the way, Rufilla told Melissa of a dream she had dreamed the night before. "I dreamed that I saw you and Theo standing arm in arm, next to the railing of a ship," Rufilla said. "Are you going on a trip?"

"Not that I know of," Melissa said.

At the entrance to the farmhouse, Rufilla blindfolded Melissa so that she could lead her nursemaid into the room where Melissa would be dressed for the wedding, surprising her with all the accouterments of her wedding day.

"Do not peek," Rufilla said. "I will not lead you astray," she said, giggling.

Melissa walked into the farmhouse acting apprehensive, as though someone had set a trap for her, a little someone who held Melissa's hand, their roles of child and nursemaid briefly reversed. Rufilla led her into the dressing room.

"Bend over," Rufilla said, "so that I can remove your blindfold."

That was the cue for the musicians in attendance to start playing.

Melissa drew in a deep breath as she raised her head, looking past Rufilla to her friends, holding her wedding dress, veil, shoes, and bouquet. Looking around the room, she said, "What are all these other clothes?"

Aridela entered the room, saying, "My gift to you. I thought you deserved some new clothes. You have been a loyal and faithful servant and I wanted to show my appreciation."

"I am indeed blessed by the goddesses. Thank you, Domina!"

The women all helped Melissa put on the full-length dress followed by the colorful shoes. Aridela gave her three coins for the ceremony that followed the wedding. Melissa put one of the coins in her shoe, dancing a few steps, turning round and round to the music. Aridela continued her duties, performing the task of the mother by putting a sash around Melissa's waist and tying it into a "knot of Hercules"—Hercules being the guardian of married life. "You are now officially ready for your wedding night," Aridela said, with a glimmer in her eyes. The tradition was that only the groom could untie the knot after the bride and groom had entered the privacy of their bedroom.

Finally, Aridela secured the veil on Melissa's head with a fragrant crown of flowers. After sharing a prayer with all these important women in her life, Melissa emerged, holding her bouquet.

Theo and Rufus were waiting for her in the atrium. The other women servants that had helped Melissa dress now stood around the couple.

"You look stunning," Rufus said. "Melissa, do you consent to marry this man, Theo?"

"Yes, I do," Melissa replied.

"Then let us begin this ceremony," said Rufus. "As paterfamilias, I hereby order any evil spirits who might be present to leave this house and ask the spirits and ancestors of the household for their blessing. I invoke the god and goddess of marriage, Jupiter and Juno, and also the god of new beginnings, Janus, to bless these two people, once separate, now united in marriage."

Next, Aridela stepped between the two, performing the final sacred act of placing their right hands together, wrapping them with a ribbon, and saying only, "With this act, I join this couple in marriage. May the respect, honor, and love you feel for each other at this moment last the lifetime of your marriage."

Melissa spoke the words, *"Ubi tu Gaius, ibi ego Gaia."* This meant that wherever life took them, they would go as husband and wife.

The couple leaned their heads together, chanting their vowels to one another. In the end, Theo took Melissa's left hand in his, saying, "Love of my life. I see you are wearing the ring I gave to you at our engagement."

"I wear it with love and commitment," Melissa said, beaming with joy.

Finally, Theo raised Melissa's veil and they sealed their bond of marriage with a kiss.

The married couple now sat down together, making an offering of oatcakes to Jupiter, then shared a piece of cake.

The guests who had attended the ceremony offered congratulations to the couple. "Let us proceed with this celebration!" Rufus said.

Theo and Melissa walked hand in hand around the garden peristyle, into the tall, vaulted hallway, and out through the massive front doors of the farmhouse. Outside, in the bright sunshine, cheering friends lined either side of the roadway as Rufilla ran in front of the bride and groom, her headdress bouncing up and down as she tossed rose petals in front of the couple. Accompanied by musicians, she sang a wedding song that Melissa had taught her.

After a short walk, the couple stopped at the picnic area by the side of the road. Decorated couches, one for the bridal couple and one for the pater and materfamilias, were set up so that they could recline and enjoy the wedding meal. The women servants who worked the farm had decorated the clearing with flowers and garlands adorning the couches, ribbons tied to the chairs and tables where the large family of servants would sit. Rufus' father had planted cork oak trees around the clearing many years before, their height giving shade to the area. Close by, the farm servants had planted a cultivated garden of vegetables and herbs, and the fragrance of lavender filled the air. Up the hill, terraced rows of grapevines were intermingled with the last of the poppies, their red blossoms dotting the surrounding fields. At the top of the hill, umbrella pines stood towering against the cerulean sky.

As a special treat, Rufus provided the new wine that many of them had harvested last fall from the vineyards that surrounded them. At dinner, after a cup or two of wine, some of the guests gave boisterous toasts to the new couple. Musicians played songs while servants sang and danced with castanets, cymbals, and tambourines.

Rufus finally calmed the group and pointed to the tympanum player who gave a drum roll. "Theo has been a godsend to me for many years now," Rufus said to the group. "Melissa was sent by the goddesses to help raise our sweet girl. I propose a special trip." The gathered guests applauded with whistles and cheers.

Rufilla shouted to Melissa, "Remember my dream from last night!"

"Is anyone familiar with the Roman name *Aenaria,* or the Greek name *Pithekoūsai?*" Rufus asked.

"I believe I remember both names," Theo said, squeezing Melissa's hand. "It is an alluring little island not too far from here, with a mountain in the center and plenty of shoreline with sandy beaches."

"An ideal setting for these two people to start their married life together, do you think?" More cheering ensued. "I propose," Rufus said, "that this Istacidii family gather together and help out for a few days while we send these two off for some well-deserved time to themselves."

CHAPTER VIII

THE MAENADS

Another year had passed, and it was the harvest season. On this warm fall day, Rufus had ridden his horse, visiting most of his vineyards to check on the grape pickers. He was hot and tired as he entered the cool wine press room called the *tocularium*, attached to the farmhouse, adjacent to the servants' quarters. Several slaves had unloaded a wagon full of grapes, pressed them, and left to refill their carts. The *must*, grape juice, was still flowing across the sloped, waterproof concrete floor. It was captured at the end of the room by a row of concave tiles that funneled the flow of the liquid down to a lower fermentation room. There the must was collected into the *dolia*, large terracotta jars buried in the ground for climate control.

Rufilla, age nine, would sometimes enter the room, squatting to retrieve a sip of the grape juice from the concave tiles as they turned a corner at the far end of the room. She had first seen Cil and Titus do this, but Cil had warned her not to do it because their father had forbidden her. That was enough to ensure that she would steal into the room when no one was watching her. This day, she had taken a cupful of the sweet juice to quench her thirst. When she heard her father come into the room, she tried to avoid him by hiding behind a large dolium in the corner. He saw her and shouted, "You are a bad girl. Boys are allowed to drink the must. Girls are not."

Her father had never spoken to her so harshly, so she threw down her cup and went running to her mother in tears, with her father following close behind.

"I will not have my daughter grow up to be one of those Roman maenads," he shouted as he entered the portico.

Aridela had been sitting under the roofed porch, spinning with her spindle and distaff when Rufilla ran into her arms, crying.

"Rufus, what on Mother Gaia's earth is going on," Aridela said as she held the whimpering child.

"She is to be brought up a proper Roman girl. She is not allowed to have the run of the house, especially the wine press room. It is dangerous enough without a young child underfoot. Where is Melissa? Does she not watch this child?"

Melissa appeared, breathless. "Dominus, I am sorry. I just stopped off for a moment to talk to the cook. Rufilla was only out of my sight for a moment."

"If she gets a taste for the grape then who knows—next we will find her in the fermentation room drinking from the dolia. I do not want her to go into that room ever again. Is that understood?"

"Of course, dear husband. I will take care of it," Aridela said, noticing his limp from his war wound. "Make sure you have your leg massaged when you go to the baths."

Rufus gave his wife, daughter, and nursemaid a stern look, then turned and left, muttering to himself as he passed over the threshold.

"Oh, mother," Rufilla said, "I do not understand why I am so different from the boys." Her mother smiled. "Well, I know I am different, but—"

"Yes dear, I understand that it was only grape juice. But you must understand your father. Years ago, when he and your uncle Lucius were in the military, they were assigned to duty in Greece. He would never tell me the exact details, but he heard a story about some Greek women in a wood one night. He said that if it was true, he could understand why the Roman Senate put restrictions on the behavior of Roman women at Dionysian rituals. Maybe we should talk further about the maenads. There is more for you to learn about that realm."

"Realm?"

"Yes, it is time now that you are growing older."

Aridela put down her spindle and took Rufilla's hand.

"Come with us, Melissa."

The three walked down the hill, past the terraced vineyards and through the stand of beech trees, till they came upon Rufilla's favorite shade tree, a large plane tree with full branches that offered shelter from the sun.

"Come sit beside me as we talk about some Greek customs," Aridela said. Rufilla sat and nestled her head in her mother's lap.

"Maenads were Greek women who were followers of Dionysus." She had to be very careful not to give her nine-year-old daughter more information than she could handle. "These women had been unfairly controlled in their day-to-day life by their husbands. At some point, women mentors secretly introduced them to a realm where they could be taken over by the god Dionysus. The wine they drank caused them to be carried to a primitive place, where they got in touch with—their untamed nature."

Aridela looked down and saw her daughter's eyes looking up with dread and confusion.

"I am sorry. I did not mean to frighten you. But this is why your father is so concerned. Roman women do not do the wild things that ancient Greek women were accused of."

"Do they do those things now?" Rufilla said. "Did you see them when you went to Athens when you were a girl? Will I see them if I ever go?"

"No, I did not see any of this. By the time I was there, the Dionysian ritual was a rite of passage that took place under specific conditions. There was a supervised time in nature, and there were spiritual lessons learned thereafter. These women lived a very long time ago. Who knows what cruelties they endured? We are lucky to be living here, where Roman husbands value their wives. It was a sad time for women in Greek history. Greek men, even today, impose more restraints on Greek women than we Romans. It is not that Melissa and I do not revere the Greek heritage that has brought Greek art, architecture, and literature to our country," Aridela said, "but their treatment of women is a different situation. It is complicated."

The sun was setting in the western sky. After a moment of silence among the three women, Aridela spoke again. "One more thing I will mention about Dionysus. He is also the god of the theater—tragedy and comedy. You, as a young Roman girl, have honored Dionysus by writing and performing your play, and telling the love story of Ariadne and Dionysus. You have taken their story into your heart and mind and will carry them with you always."

"Yes, I will, Mamma—always."

"I think that is enough for now," Aridela said.

Melissa nodded.

"But I have a question, Mamma. What is a rite of passage?"

"Next year, your aunt Aricia will be taking you through a series of steps that will introduce you to the goddess Artemis and her rituals, helping you grow and develop from a little girl to a young woman. Those steps are called a rite of passage."

Aridela took a deep breath, hugged her daughter and said, "Time to go back, that is enough conversation for one day."

Rufilla called out as she left the two women behind. "Mamma, watch how fast I can run."

"I will watch," she shouted to her daughter. "Do not fall."

Aridela continued the conversation with Melissa as Rufilla ran up the hill. "So, first the maenads, next, the Artemis bear clan—the arktoi! The Artemis ritual is what Rufilla needs to experience now. There is a fine line she must travel to be strong yet compliant with Roman views and values—Roman male rules, that is," she said, giving Melissa a knowing woman-to-woman look. "She has already shown that she has an open heart, and this ritual will help her learn her place of strength and compassion within the family."

CHAPTER IX

ARIADNE'S RED THREAD

Rufilla wove in and around her mother as she sat spinning thread. The child picked up a long, loose thread from the floor and danced with it, swirling it around her own lithe little body, humming a tune she had learned from the flute player. It was late afternoon the following spring and eight months had passed since Rufilla had learned about the maenads. The breeze coming in from the portico filled her tunica as she twisted and turned, her curly red hair flashing in the brightness of the sunset.

"What a happy child she has become," Aridela said to Melissa as they spun the wool into thread.

As Rufilla swirled the natural string above her head, she said, "Color, it needs color."

Aridela smiled and glanced at Melissa. Melissa stopped her weaving and took Rufilla and her thread to the kitchen. She found a saucer, added water to it from the bucket of water kept at the ready, and went to the garden. "Surely we can find some clay earth somewhere in this flower patch," Melissa said. She knew the garden intimately and loved to work there when she had time. But with Rufilla growing and so active, her time was limited. "Now we will immerse the thread in this mixture and let it sit overnight. In the morning, you will have your red thread."

"How did you know I wanted it to be red?" Rufilla asked.

"What is the color of Ariadne's thread?"

Rufilla lowered her head and grinned. "You know Ariadne well."

"I know *you* well," Melissa said as she drew Rufilla into her arms.

The next morning Rufilla awoke to see the copper-red thread hanging from her bedpost. She quickly tied the string around her neck and went to find Melissa, who was in the kitchen, talking to the cook.

"Look at my lovely necklace," Rufilla said, twirling around in the morning sun. "Let's go for a walk and see who can see me." The women laughed.

"Come with me." Melissa held out her hand, and Rufilla gently slapped it and ran out the door.

"You are It," Rufilla shouted over her shoulder. "Chase me!"

"I am getting too old for this," Melissa shouted back to the cook as she followed Rufilla out the door. Down the hill they ran and soon met up with Cil and Titus.

"Look at me. Look at my new necklace. Am I not beautiful?" Rufilla shouted to the boys.

Cil came over to her as if to admire it, then quickly jerked on the necklace, pulling his sister toward him and dislodging the thread from her neck.

"Give it back," Rufilla screamed as the boys ran down the hill, rolling the string into a small ball and throwing it back and forth to each other as they went.

Cil stumbled then tumbled down the hill with Titus soon rolling behind him. Rufilla was in hot pursuit. "Give me back my thread!"

At the bottom of the hill, the three tussled for possession, until Melissa caught up with them. Rufilla ran to Melissa, crying, "Make them give it back."

"She is your little sister, Cil," Melissa said, "and not as strong or as big as you. Now give it back."

"Whiner, whiner," Cil taunted as he threw the thread into the air, batted it to her with his hand, both boys running away into the olive grove at the bottom of the hill. "Little piece of thread" were Cil's parting words. "Who wants it anyway?"

Melissa gathered Rufilla in her arms, turned her face upward. "We both know the power of Ariadne's red thread. But for now, we will keep that mystery to ourselves. Boys cannot appreciate such things."

Later, as Rufilla related the story to her mother, Aridela said, "Melissa, remember last fall—the incident at the tocularium—we talked about the Artemis ritual? We were exactly right to think she was ready. With warmer weather coming on, it is time for us to introduce the teachings of Artemis and all the outdoor activities related to it. Cil will be going through the *Liberalia* festival in a year or two. But first, Rufilla will become an *arktoi* of Artemis. My children are getting older, and so am I."

Rufilla's face turned from a frown to a smile when she heard the name Artemis. "Oh, yes, whatever that means, I want it. Ar-te-mis, I love the goddess Ar-te-mis," she chanted, twirling round and round. She stopped and looked at her mother. "What is a *Liberalia* festival?"

"It is a coming of age for your brother. He will remove the protective amulet, the *bulla* that he has worn around his neck since he was a baby, and also replace his childhood toga with the all-white toga *virilis* of a citizen of Rome."

"But I will become an *arktoi* first? And Hostia too?"

"Yes, you both will. Hostia's Aunt Aricia and I are meeting tomorrow at the baths to discuss it."

CHAPTER X

AN ARTEMIS FOREST

50 BCE

At the women's entrance to the Stabian Baths, four muscular slaves carefully lowered the *lectica*, a long, wooden, canopied litter, to the ground. Gently, the slaves pulled aside the curtains that protected their mistress from the light mist of the early morning. Aridela and her maid, Junia, alighted and noticed another litter near theirs. "Aricia is here," Aridela said.

The slaves positioned the empty litter beside one of the long stone benches outside the door to the women's bath complex and took their seats. Aridela entered the baths followed by Junia. "Good morning," the bath supervisor said as the door closed behind them.

"Yes, it is a good morning, crisp and a little chilly for this late in spring," Aridela said, "but it certainly feels warm in here."

"We stoked the fires early this morning to take the chill out of the air. I remembered that you like to bathe early."

Aridela smiled and nodded her approval, leaving the coins on the table for payment.

"Your friend just arrived," the supervisor said. "She may still be changing."

The fragrance from the fresh-cut lilies sitting on the supervisor's desk filled the air, and the flickering candelabra that lit their way gave the long, arched corridor a warm glow. She thought of how Rufus liked to tease her by saying that the women's bath area was smaller than the men's. "And how would you know that, my dear husband?"

A woman's lyrical voice could be heard coming from the dressing room. As Aridela and Junia stepped through the doorway, they saw Aricia seated on one of the benches, her maid removing her shoes. The two Dominae exchanged greetings as the maids helped them disrobe and put their clothes into the niches overhead.

"Find the *capsarius* to watch the clothes and then join us in the *tepidarium*. Give her both coins as she keeps a good eye on our clothes," Aricia called back over her shoulder.

The two dominae and their servants relaxed for a while in the *tepidarium*, the room that housed a large tub of warm water. Then they all moved to a sauna-like room, the *caldarium*. There they slipped slowly into the hot water basin. This tub held the most heated water: the hypocaust system originated under this room, warming the floors as well as the water. Their maids wrapped them in towels, and they moved to the massage room, where masseuses awaited them. The maids carried their domina's favorite perfumed oils of attar of roses and sweet rush. The massage beds were side by side, and so the conversation continued.

"Remember the dancing in the streets oh, so long ago," said Aridela.

"And the singing, do not forget that." Aricia sang a few bars of a song from the Artemis bear clan ritual.

"Aricia! I had forgotten what a melodic voice you have. You must surely teach Rufilla and the other initiates the songs."

When the massage was finished, the *strigil* was next. The masseuse applied more oil to their bodies, and then the strigil, a curved, metal tool, was used to scrape off the oil and dead skin cells.

"Thank you. That is the best part of the bath," Aridela said as she raised herself from the bed. Both women walked back to the tepidarium. The heated room felt good after the massage. The bath ritual ended in the *frigidarium*, a brief dip in the cold water basin to close the pores and stimulate their minds and bodies for the rest of the day.

Returning to the dressing room, they dressed and made their way to Aricia's home for lunch.

Aricia's husband, Marcus Arrius Polites, and his father and brothers owned a large estate outside Pompeii. The parents had since died, and two of the brothers and their families lived across town in a spacious elaborate complex. Marcus and Aricia preferred the quiet home that belonged to his father, and since he was the oldest, he had first rights to the property. They had combined the house next to it with theirs and created a generous living space with gardens. Marcus, along with his brothers, owned several farms that produced vegetables for much of the area. However, the primary family business was the import and export of wine.

"As you know, we have two entrances because we've combined two houses. Let us go in this door as this is the one I will use for the initiates' entrance," Aricia said as they entered the house on the left, pausing in the atrium. "When we combined the two houses," Aricia continued, "a relative of Marcus', an architect, suggested that Marcus use this side of the house to entertain his clients. The other side is for family and entertaining friends."

"Like our wine group," Aridela said. "Thank you. I do not think I ever heard this explanation."

"Marcus will be staying at the farm the night of the initiation," Aricia said, "so the girls can gather here first. We can take them back to the winter dining room, for a short orientation, returning them to the atrium for the beginning purification ceremony. This is the moment when I usually have them remove their tunicas and put on the saffron-colored tunica of Artemis." Aricia was glowing as she spoke.

"You enjoy doing this ceremony."

"Since I have never been able to bear a child of my own, I enjoy doing this for the children of the community. It is my way of giving back for all I have been given." There were tears in her eyes.

Aridela embraced her. Aricia stiffened. "I do not talk about my feelings much, as sometimes, no, oftentimes, the emotions are too strong. Marcus does not like to see my tears—even joyful tears."

"You know I am always here if you want to talk," Aridela said.

"I have been going to the Temple of Isis," Aricia said. "I have been disturbed about my mood lately, and since I have known the priestess and priest for some time and value their opinions, I have been able to discuss my feelings as well as Marcus' feelings with them."

"Yes, men have feelings too," Aridela said.

"Come, walk with me," Aricia said, taking Aridela's arm and walking past the small inner garden. "This is where we connected the two houses. It certainly isn't in the traditional Vitruvian style, but it is functional for our needs."

"Vitruvius?"

"Yes, he is an architect whom Marcus' relative knows. He talks of a conventional design for Roman homes—yours would be a good example where the entrance flows into the atrium, then the peristyle garden and beyond that maybe even another garden."

They walked over the threshold and entered the hallway that took them to the summer triclinium of the second house. Aridela saw a door that stood open at the far end of the garden. "It feels like I am seeing your house for the first time. The door?"

"We rarely have it open for dinner parties. But you saw what is beyond, once, several years ago. We will explore it again—after we eat. I am starving!"

As Aridela reclined on one of the couches in the dining room, she remembered the upcoming festival. "Speaking of dinner parties, will you and Marcus be hosting our group for the Vinalia this year?"

"Yes, we will," Aricia said. "And after that, it will be time to start the meetings with the mothers and daughters and classes for the girls' Artemis ritual. Then the ritual itself. A busy spring."

"That is a great deal of preparation," Aridela said. "Are you sure you want to host the dinner?"

"Oh, I will enjoy the preparations for both. Do not worry about me."

It had been four years since she had gathered a new group of girls for the ritual. Rufilla and Hostia participated their first time as the sacred basket carriers, and this year they would be fully initiated into the Artemis arktoi "bear" clan.

Aridela leaned back on the couch pillows and noticed the white lettering on the walls of the triclinium. "Would you please explain how these writings came to be on your dining room wall? I know Marcus told Rufus about this at one of our gatherings, but I have forgotten."

"Let me see—where do I start? This is a family house going back to Sabellian Pompeii," Aricia said. "Somewhere in the generations of wine merchants past, my father-in-law, or maybe his father, used to quote his rules of etiquette for his clients and some of his friends, I am sure. That is how several of the family earned the nickname Polites. When we re-decorated, Marcus decided to write them on the walls. Their manners have preceded them on many occasions." She muttered to herself, "Though sometimes rules are meant to be broken."

Aridela read aloud the sentence on one of the walls: "*Let the slave wash your feet with water and wipe them dry; let him cover the dining couch with a napkin. Take care with our linens.*"

"Yes, we insist that the servants wash the feet of everyone who enters—as every Roman does," Aricia said. "Then, as the guests recline, the servant puts a linen cloth under each one's bare feet to protect the cushions. But you do this, too. I think that rule was written for foreigners or 'barbarians' as Polites calls them." She had switched to the nickname of her husband without even thinking.

"*Remove lustful expressions and flirtatious tender eyes from another man's wife; may there be modesty in your expression.*"

"Someone might remind Victor about this." Aridela smiled.

Aricia looked puzzled and then shrugged. "Oh, he does that to all the wives. Clodia acts like she does not see it, but she has to. It is so obvious."

"Does she care?" Aridela said. "More comes to my mind, but I will refrain from gossip."

"Oh, why—tell me more!" Aricia pleaded.

"Have you not heard that he has probably taken a lover? He is very discreet, so no one knows who it is."

"Well, I will keep my eye out for her," Aricia said, her heart racing. She hoped she hadn't blushed.

Aridela continued. "*Let decency abide in your speech. Speak pleasant words and avoid troublesome quarrels if you can; if not, take steps to your own house.*"

"I think that says it all. Clodia and Victor could also be reminded of that," Aridela said. She changed the subject. "Oh, Aricia, I love your garden." She stood and peered out the dining room window. "It looks like a sacred grove of Artemis."

At that moment the servant appeared with lunch. They ate a modest salad of fresh vegetables garnished with quail eggs, followed by fruit and cheese. Then they lay back on the couches and rested for a short while. A wood thrush singing in the garden ended their nap.

"What a lovely sound to awaken to," Aridela said.

"Let us go into the garden," Aricia said.

As they entered the formal garden, Aridela saw the statue of a goddess. In front of it stood a pedestal, which held a bronze and iron brazier for burnt offerings. She looked at Aricia, who anticipated her question. "Marcus bought it and put her there. I think he attempted to please me after an argument we had. But lately, as I said earlier, she appeals to me as well."

On either side of her statue were two huge rose bushes that were ready to bloom. They walked through the tree-shaded garden filled with shrubs and plants honoring Isis. She took Aridela's arm. "We will walk the girls through this small, sacred garden, and out the back door." Beyond the walled garden, and encompassing the backyards of both houses bloomed an orchard of fruit trees, flowering plants, and bushes, a veritable Artemis wilderness.

"I remember seeing this now. How tall the trees are. It must be three years since I have seen this area. It is gone from a garden to a forest!"

"An Artemis forest," Aricia replied as she stood smiling, her arms crossed, proud of all the fruits of her labor. "We will have fruit ripening on the trees by the time we initiate the girls. The roses and lilies will be in bloom so that they may be made into garlands. The florist down the street does beautiful work."

"Are those—yes, they are—wild berry bushes," Aridela said as she looked even deeper into the wooded area, seeing two tall Cyprus trees in the distance, forest green against the blue sky. As they walked on, they came to a small clearing where she recognized a statue of Artemis, the goddess reaching into her quiver for an arrow, by her side was one of her hunting dogs. A palm tree grew behind the sculpture. "this will remind the girls that Artemis was born beneath a palm tree," Aridela said. The tall Cyprus trees stood on either side of the statue as guardians, protecting the goddess within.

CHAPTER XI

WINE AND FIRE

Spring in Pompeii officially started in April with the Roman festival of wine and fire, the *Vinalia Urbana*. It lasted for two days. Early on the first day, the sacrifice of many lambs had been made by the official head priest to assuage the patron of the festival, Jupiter. The group would partake of that roasted meat at their dinner. Pompeii also honored Venus on that day, as she was the protectress of the *hetairae*, or dancing girls, who performed several functions at many of the celebrations. Marcus, whose turn it was to host their private wine group, found no need to pay for that kind of entertainment. Wives would be present.

Aricia hurried into the triclinium, two of her slaves following on her heels. "Make sure the pillows and mattresses are clean," she said. "Air them in the garden and watch the skies for rain. We must not have wet coverings for our guests to recline on at the dinner tonight!"

She recited her list of things to be done. The older servant had prepared for dinner parties before. She knew how to please the mistress of the house. "Yes, Domina," she said. "You and the Dominus will be pleased with my work."

Aricia caught her husband as he was leaving for the vineyards. "Marcus, be sure to return in time to select the new wines for dinner tonight," she said.

"They are already in the atrium—I am ready for tonight. Are you?" Marcus said in a demeaning tone as he headed out the front door.

"Please bring back some grapevines with the new growth on them—you know the ritual," she shouted after him.

Aricia bubbled with excitement. Included in the group were two other vintners, landowners with vineyards as well as olive groves, a local merchant who sold wines and olive oil, and a shipowner who exported and imported not only wines but exotic items from ports of call, near and far. And their wives were always included.

At the designated hour, the invited couples arrived at Marcus Arrius

Polites' home carried on litters by their slaves, who would remain with the litters near the front door, playing games of chance and getting hot food from the nearby *thermopolium*. The Arrius home was located on the main east-west street of Pompeii where there were many large mansions, as well as inns and restaurants. A lively street, it was always filled with the locals making their way on foot or by litter.

"*Salve!*" "*Bonum vesper!*" the friends said as they greeted each other with a kiss. When Aricia and Victor exchanged kisses on their cheeks, Victor whispered in her ear.

It gave Aricia a start, and she gave him a disapproving, "Victor!" Everyone knew he liked to flirt. Marcus did not much care for it.

After the foot-washing amenities, they all reclined on the couches in the triclinium. Marcus initiated the ceremony of the festival of Vinalia by opening a wineskin from his fall harvest. He had chosen a wine from an area of his vineyard where he knew the wine matured more quickly and would thus afford an excellent example of his vineyards.

When all the gleaming silver cups had been filled with wine mixed with water, Marcus raised his cup. "On this festival of Vinalia Urbana, we are thankful to Venus for last year's generous harvest and ask the goddess for continued good weather this year, with another abundant harvest in the fall." Cups clinked and the evening began.

In between sumptuous courses of food, the friends sang verses of their favorite songs to the lively accompaniment of flute players. A few guests ventured out into Aricia's garden, where an early spring had produced the succulent buds of flowering fruit trees, plus a brilliant display of narcissus, wild crocuses, and hyacinths.

"Here," Aridela said, handing Aricia a potted plant that had sprouted spiky green leaves with tiny flowers still in bud. "This is to plant in your garden. Remember, we talked about this unusual miniature hyacinth last fall, and I promised to give you some starts."

"What a lovely gift," Aricia said, "and I have something for you." She led her to a shed in the back corner of the garden. There within a terra-cotta pot were crocuses already in bloom.

"What surprising color combinations," Aridela said. "I have never seen one like this." She leaned over to inspect the pot of deep purple crocuses with a white stripe down the middle of the petals.

"Leave it to Aricia to find an unusual plant for her garden," Victor said as he joined the two women. "I love my garden. Maybe you will find something special for me too."

Rufus suddenly appeared and interrupted. "Dearest," he said to Aridela, "you must come back to the table and enlighten our friends about your journey to Athens those many years ago. They did not realize I had such an adventurous wife."

After Aridela left with Rufus, Victor came close to Aricia and said, "Meet me tomorrow to discover our mutual gardens."

"How bold you are!" Aricia blushed and turned her back to the house, feeling eyes prying at them, giving them away. "We are breaking rule number two of Marcus Arrius' *distichs*."

"Which one is that?" Victor asked. "Is it the one about taking care not to dirty the linens that cover the dining couches?" he said. "Or maybe the other one about postponing one's quarrels and taking them home with them." Victor's rambunctious laughter was heard all the way into the open-air dining room.

"Remove lustful expressions and flirtatious tender eyes for another man's wife," she said, her broad, sensuous lips turning up at the edges, hardly able to restrain a giggle as their eyes locked.

Victor sighed. "Then let us stroll among your plants and trees as you pause and enlighten me," he said, lowering his voice. "They all know that I have cultivated a beautiful garden at my home and that I am always interested in finding new and interesting plants."

They strolled along the path that meandered through the garden, stopping from time to time to dote on a plant here, a bush there. Dusk had fallen, and the servants lit the candelabra that Aricia had placed at strategic points to grace the garden as well as the dining room. A warm glow shone on the faces of all the guests—but especially the hostess.

"You look stunning," Victor whispered.

"Stop it," she whispered back. "It is time to return to the party."

Aricia and Victor made one last stop in front of a marble statuette of a goddess figure standing on a tall pedestal. On the ground below was a bronze incense burner in the shape of a wooly lamb. Incense was burning in the receptacle below it, the sweet scent of frankincense and myrrh filling the air.

"I do not remember seeing this the last time I was here," Victor said.

"I suspect that Marcus Arrius gave it to me to temper his guilt—

another sweet tart in his vineyard, I presume," Aricia said. "He could not decide if it was a statue of Diana or Isis, but he thought either might please me. He has no idea that I have turned to the temple of Isis lately—because of you."

"Me?"

"Yes. Although my husband has his trysts now and then, I have remained faithful."

Victor bowed his head. "I am sorry but I cannot help my feelings for you."

Marcus Arrius' disapproving voice called from the house, "Aricia, you have other guests to tend."

"Coming, Marcus."

Behind her, she heard Victor say in a low voice, "*Cras.*" On the morrow.

The next morning, Aricia sat on the ground in her garden before what she chose to see as the statue of the Egyptian goddess Isis. The week before, she had gone to the Temple of Isis and gone through a purification ceremony. Today, she would take the next step. She had covered her head with her cloak in the spirit of humility. She lowered her eyes, watching the smoke spiraling from the incense of rosemary burning in the brazier in front of the statue. She collapsed, rocking back and forth, imploring the goddess, "Please hear my prayers. I am torn in two, loving a man I should not, not loving a man I should. Is it my fate to suffer and never be understood? I need your guidance, your understanding, and if possible, your forgiveness."

An hour later, she appeared in front of her house, her head still covered and face shielded from the bright sun. She let her slaves carry her in the litter and then dismissed them when they reached the Temple of Isis. The priestess was waiting for her in the sanctuary. Together they walked to the altar of Isis and offered a small sacrifice, burning some dried rosemary Aricia had brought with her. The priestess prayed for Aricia. "The rosemary represents our gift to you, Sacred Isis, for its healing properties and for remembrance, a recollection of who we are in this life and how that carries us forward." She looked at Aricia. "The Great Mother understands that there may be a need for change that feels like a destruction of the old ways, but always a new and redeeming path opens up. She is both stone sculpture and living woman, working through you to determine your fate."

The priestess left her side and walked up the stairs of the temple into the *cella*, the sacred room, the holy of holies, and returned with a large basket.

"Come, follow me," the priestess said. They made their way around the small sanctuary to the back of the temple. There, a niche held a statue of Dionysus. The priestess paused, raising the basket in dedication to the god. They returned to the front of the temple, near the altar where they had started.

"If you are ready to meet your fate, touch your forehead to the ground," the priestess said. Her destiny was in the hands of the goddess.

As she knelt and lowered her head, the earth had a sweet, pungent odor. "I am ready."

Slowly the priestess lifted the lid of the basket. "Rise, woman, and meet your fate."

She brought her body to an erect position, still kneeling. Next, she removed the veil from her face and slowly opened her eyes. Aricia looked into the eyes of a serpent, and it returned her gaze.

"When you are ready," the priestess said, holding the large snake upright in her hands.

Aricia, trembling, took a deep breath, closed her eyes, and pressed her lips, kissing the serpent. She could feel the cool scales against her mouth, could feel the pulse of venom throbbing in its fangs. The seconds seemed to her an eternity. She quietly exhaled and withdrew her face, unbitten.

"Goddess of relationship, birth, death, and love," the priestess said, "please accept your humble servant's kiss as an acceptance of her fate, Your Divine Will. You are the giver of understanding and wisdom. In the years to come, we ask that you watch over this woman, giving her guidance on the difficult path she has chosen."

Aricia sat back on her heels, watching the priestess return the serpent to the basket and then to the cella.

The priestess and Aricia sat in silence. Finally, the priestess spoke. "As we feel the earth beneath us, so keep us grounded in our humility and duty to you, dear goddess. Praise forever to you, Isis, and the wisdom that you choose to share."

With that, she took Aricia's hands and helped her to her feet. "Return to me soon, and we will speak again about what it means to keep your path."

Back outside, Aricia clutched another bouquet of dried lavender in her pocket, still aromatic from being stored in her root cellar over the winter.

She walked briskly down the elevated sidewalk. At the street corner, her stride lengthened as she crossed, using the large stepping stones that were elevated above the street to reach the other sidewalk. She made her way to the back entrance of a local inn. She gently knocked on the door of one of the rooms.

"Enter."

For a moment, she hesitated, but then slowly opened the door, and grateful for the dimness of the room, quietly closed it. When she turned around, Victor stood directly in front of her. "We must be very careful, someone—" He put his finger to her mouth, pulled her close, and replaced his finger with his lips for a deep, slow kiss that made her body go limp in his arms.

"Hello to you, too." He smiled. "Come in. The lavender smells delightful." He took a deep whiff. "It will take the musty smell out of this room." He laid the bouquet down on the end table next to a vase of two red roses. He always brought two.

She stared at the roses. "I will always wonder why Rufilla gave the roses to you and me."

"She is very intuitive. My son says that sometimes she knows things before they happen."

"I must talk to you," she implored. "I heard from someone reliable that you have taken a lover. I am very concerned that people are talking."

"And who is this mysterious woman. Or is it a man?" His eyes sparkled.

"Please be serious, Victor. She did not know who the woman was, only that someone thought they saw you with a woman. I do not think she was fishing. Oh, I am not sure about all of this. What a risk we are taking."

He sat her down on a chair next to a desk and pulled the other chair beside her. "My sweet one, I am not sure who saw me. Where did they see me—on the street? I think your friend was trying to see if you knew something or would admit to something.

"Yes, but—what if they—she—saw *me* entering the inn?"

"But we never come in together, Aricia," he said, taking her hands in his. The sound of his voice speaking her name usually calmed her. "I know you feel vulnerable. But let me assure you that you are safe. No officers are checking the identity of veiled women in the streets."

"Do not make light of my concerns," she said. He knelt beside the chair and comforted her.

"I am torn in two. My love for you defies even the gods," she said. "But what would happen to me if someone discovered us? The Roman matron in me wonders if I have gone completely mad."

Victor lowered his head into her lap, his arms enveloping her hips. She embraced his shoulders.

"I am so sorry. I know this is mad, but I have loved you for so long," he said.

"And what is this flirting you are doing with all the women in our dining group? And who else?"

"I have always been a flirt, but this is different. How long have we known each other?" He lifted her chin. "You are even beautiful when you cry. Come to the bed and let me hold you."

"No."

He stayed sitting on the floor, holding her hand, stroking and caressing it. He got on his knees and started to speak. Aricia pressed his head against her breasts, the heat of his breath and lips, intoxicating.

She finally took a deep breath and moved him to arm's length. "How could I be so naïve as to believe there could be more to life for me than being married to a rule-driven money monger whose greatest joy in life is in making a deal? Money is his mistress."

Victor got up and moved his chair across the room and sat, hands folded, looking at her. There was no logic to this moment.

"I love the intensity in your eyes," he said.

He chuckled.

"What is so funny?" she said.

"Do you know that when there is a lull in the conversation, it means Hermes has just walked through the room?"

"So which one of us is he taking to Hades?" she asked.

"I would imagine we would go together."

She closed her eyes. He walked over, took her hands in his, and lifted her up. She opened her eyes, and like the gaze of the serpent just an hour before, she looked deeply into the eyes of her fate and surrendered to it.

Diana-Artemis

CHAPTER XII

ARTEMIS ARKTOI RITUAL

Less than a week after the Vinalia festival, Aridela and Aricia were busy planning the initiation. Within a few days, they had composed a list of eligible girls. The two women talked at length, developing the ritual that Aricia would lead. It was time to share their plans with the group. They contacted the parents, and within a week, the first meeting of mothers and daughters took place at Aricia's home. "I have brought you all here because Aridela and I feel it is time we talked about preparing our girls for the Artemis initiation," Aricia said to the mothers. "I understand that Artemis included boys in her arktoi activities, but there are things that girls need to experience without boys. The activities we have developed will help them realize their worth so that they will not be intimidated by young men as they are finding their way to adulthood."

The girls nodded to each other in rapt attention.

"I have been thinking about that myself," Hostia's mother said. "My boys are in the rough and tumble stage, and my daughter needs to learn how to take care of herself."

"Exactly," Aridela said. "My daughter is experiencing the same problem."

Aricia began her instruction. "In the beginning there was Chaos. Out of Chaos came Gaia, also called Mother Earth, and Uranus, Father of the Sky and Heavens. They gave birth to many children, including Kronos, who took Rhea as his wife, and they had a son Zeus. Zeus mated with Leto, a daughter of the Titans. She gave birth to twins. Artemis was first born and saw her mother having difficulty giving birth to her brother, Apollo. So Artemis helped her mother with the delivery. That is how she became known as one of the goddesses of childbirth.

"As a favored daughter of Zeus, she asked for and received permission to live her life as she desired without being married. She chose the wilderness as her domain. As a nature deity, she and her nymphs lived in the forests, guided by their self-confidence and independent spirit. She became the revered guardian of girls and women—a mother she-bear.

"And so she gave of her wisdom to young girls, instructing them to respect their independent thoughts and feelings within, even while living in the outer world. This wisdom was passed down from mother and aunt to daughter and niece, preparing the next generation for the tasks to come."

"Are there any questions?" Aridela asked, taking over.

Hostia asked, "Does that mean that if we ask our fathers if we can remain unmarried, they will grant us this wish?"

Aricia smiled. "Good question, Hostia. First, you must realize that Artemis is a goddess, and we are only humans. She is there to help us develop our minds so that *when we marry,* we might become women who can love our families, support our husbands and children, *and* live a fuller life ourselves. But at this point in your life, it is essential that you learn these early lessons of thinking and making decisions.

One of the girls raised her hand, gesturing to be heard. "Yes," Aricia said.

"When my mother and I disagree," the young girl said, "she makes me sit and write down my side *and* her side of the argument, and then talk it out. Sometimes I wish she would just say no and use the switch!" Both mothers and daughters laughed out loud.

"Well," Aricia said, "maybe now is a good time to mention that you will be learning firsthand some of Artemis' ways by spending two days and one night in the woods? Without your mothers!"

There was a general shout from the girls. "Hooray!"

"That is what is important to you right now—enjoying each other. These next few years are precious times of learning what it means to have other girls in your life with whom you share a bond—a sisterhood that can last all your lives."

"So that takes us to the next step—the ritual," Aridela said. "Honoring Artemis is our focus, and she is always delighted to see happy young girls enjoying her ritual. The oldest girls will be going through the entire initiation. That means those of you who are at least ten or eleven."

"I am ten," Rufilla said.

"I am eleven," Hostia said.

"You younger ones, ages six through nine," Aricia said, "are here to help with the ritual and thus prepare yourselves for when, in a few years, it will be your turn. There will be music and dancing." The girls all shouted their approval. "Then the older girls will be taking part and becoming the *arktoi*, or young she-bears who will learn what it means to be fierce and protective of their family, friends, and loved ones. Then some surprises as well."

"That is all for now," Aricia said. "You girls are free to go out into the garden and play while we talk with your mothers."

"Ark-toi, ark-toi," the girls chanted as they walked to the garden, imitating the walk of the bear.

Aricia and Aridela smiled at each other. "These girls are a blessing to us all," Aricia said.

Aricia distributed the saffron-dyed material to each mother so that the *tunicae*, dress, could be started promptly. They asked questions. Some were concerned about the overnight in the woods. Aricia assured them that the outing would happen *after* the initiation and that the girls would be watched over and protected, but from a little distance to let them feel their aloneness and interdependence. Each girl would be paired with another, so no one strayed too far. In the end, all were delighted to take part and even offered their relatives—aunts, grandmothers, and nurse-maids to help.

She then walked the mothers out into the extended garden where the girls had gathered, standing silently around the statue of Artemis. Aricia raised her hands, palms open, and spoke to the mothers of her arktoi. "In exchange for the advance of culture, these girls will explore a period of ritual wildness. We are their mortal forms of Artemis, watching over them while giving them the freedom to enjoy this brief interlude between childhood and puberty."

CHAPTER XIII

THE GODDESS OF WILD THINGS

Pompeii is a town built on top of a lava spur perched strategically on the edge of a lava flow. In ancient times, it overlooked the Sarnus River to the south. The river flowed west into the Tyrrhenian Sea, making it the perfect seaside port for small merchant ships, commerce, and travel. Farmers, vintners, and olive growers populated the fertile valleys that extended east of the town, toward the foothills of the Apennine Mountains, northwest toward Mount Vesuvius, and south toward Mount Lattari. Many of the wealthy landowners and sea merchants lived in homes within Pompeii and also owned villas in the countryside. These were the parents and relatives of the young initiates.

"Do you remember that I gave you an assignment before you left the last meeting?" Aricia said. "I requested that you ask your parents where your ancestors originated. I will start with mine. My ancestors came from Greece and helped settle the area that we call Magna Graecia. My immediate family came from Neapoli."

"Mine, too," one girl said. "Pater said that the Greeks had to fight for their land."

Another spoke with an air of authority, "My pater said our ancestors were fierce warriors from the mountains in the center of Italy. They were called Sabine and were among the earliest settlers who spoke the Oscan language."

"My mater's ancestors were both Greek and Etruscan," Rufilla said, "and Pater says his family was Etruscan, Sammnite warriors and Romans—and the Romans won. And did you know that the Etruscans were the first settlers? And all names with a double I, like ours, are Etruscan. I learned all that from my tutor, Theo. My parents speak that language to each other when they do not want my brother and me to understand them." The girls giggled and nodded, recognizing that the

Oscan language was the secret lexicon of many parents.

"Mine were Samnite," said another girl.

"So were mine," said two others.

After everyone had shared, Aricia spoke. "Now, we have explored our heritage. We see that over hundreds of years of conflict, mostly over land and citizenship, we are now all Latin-speaking Romans—at least our fathers and husbands are—having adopted the ways of many cultures."

One of the younger girls raised her hand. "You said that our patres were Romans. Are we not Romans?"

"Women are Roman citizens," Aricia said, "but we cannot vote or hold political office. We must not, however, lose sight of the fact that these lands remain, first and always, the realm of the sacred goddess. Who?" She motioned to her young audience.

"Artemis!" was the resounding answer.

"Some of her woodlands are now our cultivated farms and gardens, giving us beauty and sustenance. Whether we call her Artemis or Diana, she watches over us all."

"I like the way it sounds—Artemis arktoi," one of the girls said.

"Yes, that is her Greek name, but understand that there will be a time when, during the ritual, you will use the Roman name Diana," Aricia said. "That is all you need to know for now. Let us talk about her as Diana, goddess of the hunt, the moon, and wild animals. Our ancestors, ancient hunters and gatherers, believed that any living thing, including animals, were intelligent beings, deserving of respect. So it is important for us today to be aware of this and show reverence to nature and wildlife."

Another girl spoke up. "My mother still believes this. She talks to her plants."

"As do I," Aricia said as she motioned for the group to follow her into the garden. "You will notice as I take you through my garden that I will speak to certain plants and bushes, and especially the flowers." She paused to caress a rosebud starting to open. "Bloom dearest, let us see you in all your glory." Turning back to the girls, she said, "Diana is also a protector of wildlife, with areas or sanctuaries in the wilderness where no killing of animals is allowed. Also, no hunter should ever kill more than he needs for food. That is one of her strongest mandates. She has been known to punish those who disobey her rules."

Aridela now spoke. "She is also known as the protector of young girls, a mother bear goddess. In ancient times, initiates wore the actual bearskins, but now they have been replaced by a short saffron-yellow *chiton tunicae* meant to symbolize the bearskins. Your mothers have probably started making your dress." The girls nodded in agreement. "Everyone receives a dress, but only the oldest girls go through the complete initiation. You younger girls will be eligible next time. This time you will have the opportunity to participate as wreath and sacred basket carriers." The younger girls' sighs turned to smiles.

The women took the girls through the rest of Aricia's garden, introducing them to the statue of Isis and then out into the area of trees and vegetable garden beyond to see her statue of Diana with her bow and arrows and trusted hound.

"These bushes full of rosebuds will all be in bloom when you go through the ritual. We will make garlands from the roses and lilies that will be blooming."

"What is that tree?" Rufilla asked.

"That, my dear, is a cherry tree. Are not the blossoms beautiful? And do not miss the rosemary that is starting to open, and see the purple clematis that climbs the trellis." Aricia's enthusiasm spread to the girls as they asked her to describe the flowers, bushes, and trees that were favorites of the goddess.

Later that day Rufilla spoke to her mother. "Tell me about rosemary, Mamma. Of all the flowers we saw today in Aunt Aricia's garden that is the one I remember."

"It is about exactly that—remembrance. It is often used at weddings because it represents fidelity and love."

"Humm, there was something more—something in Aunt Aricia's eyes when she said the word. She looked right at me."

"Maybe she was thinking about Titus. She knows you and he are betrothed to each other," Aridela said. "Why, I have known young girls to slip rosemary into their pillowcases, so that they might dream about their true love."

"No, this was different." The past weeks of lessons meant she was not around Cil and Titus. She was beginning to hear her own 'wild' mind as Aricia had called it. Part of it was separating from mothers, too. Rufilla was more ambivalent about that thought.

Could it be the remembrance was of the future? Rufilla held that question in her mind. She laughed. That was it—her mother had talked about Mnemosyne, the Titan goddess of memory, in one of the lectures she gave. She spoke of two kinds. There was the memory used in learning—like memorizing the nine muses on her knuckles. Calliope, Clio, Erato, Euterpe, Melpomene, Polyhymnia, Terpsichore, Thalia, and Urania, she recited, fingering each knuckle as she went. Mnemosyne was the tenth. Mother of them all.

There was yet another kind of memory—a remembrance or innate ability to intuit other people's thoughts and feelings, and sometimes a premonition of events that were about to occur. "It is a unique 'memory,'" Rufilla could remember hearing her mother say, "That only a few can claim as their truth." Aridela had been describing to Rufilla's friends who Rufilla was without speaking her name.

Rufilla was grateful for her mother's compassion.

The evening they chose for the ritual turned out to be warm and clear with a bright moon rising. Aridela gathered the girls at her home, and then they made their way to Aricia's home, single file, in silence. A purification ceremony began with water poured over the hands and feet of each initiate. Next, the girls received the new dresses, which were the physical representation of their initiation into the bear clan. The girls whispered to each other as they changed their clothes. Melissa's task was to help each girl secure a diadem of rosebuds that crowned her head.

She kissed Rufilla on each cheek. "You look beautiful." Rufilla beamed.

The double flute players appeared, and by the music they played, set the tone for what was to come. The older, already initiated girls brought garlands, and the younger girls carrying wreaths were waiting for the initiates in the garden. The initiates followed the youngest girls through the gardens, stopping to pay homage at Aricia's statue of Diana, and then out the gate, where their female relatives were waiting for them. Each woman held a torch that lit the way for the initiates. Aridela caught Rufilla's eye. "I love you, Mamma," Rufilla mouthed as she passed by.

The older girls started their bear dance, the *arkteia*. They motioned for the initiates to imitate what they had all been taught—to move their arms and legs with broad "bear" gestures to the rhythm of the flute music as they made their way down the *decumanus maximus*, the longest east-west street of the town. There was even an occasional growl. Lining the street were curious people who had emerged from their homes and inns when they heard the flute players and then saw the young girls. They understood that these were the girls selected to represent the community in their tribute to Artemis.

The initiates were instructed to follow the pace of the music, which increased, so they ran a short distance to the next group of mothers waiting for them. They alternated dancing and weaving their way down the long street, keeping time with the music. They passed the forum and reached the enormous marina gate heading down toward the river. There, the girls were separated by age. The women stopped the younger girls at the gate.

The culmination of the ritual was at hand: the moment when they left the safety of the town and entered the wilderness. The initiates walked through the long, double-arched brick gateway, entering the narrow pedestrian side. Inside was a darkness they had never experienced. Just as they were starting to feel anxious, they saw the light of torches below, near the water's edge.

"Make your way through the trees." Aricia sang the words loudly, from her post down the hill. "Diana will protect you!"

As they emerged from the darkness, they ran down the paved cobblestone street toward the light of the torches and the sound of Aricia's voice as she stood by the edge of the stream. The calm waters rippled at the shoreline. Upon instruction, each girl removed her dress. Guided by the garland carriers, they reached the edge of the stream and were asked to take a few steps into the slow-moving current, supported by two women who stood on either side of each girl. Letting their bodies sink into the water for a few seconds, the women uttered these words, whispering into each initiate's ears: "Let the cool, running waters flow over your animal body and awaken your soul. Diana blesses your devotion to her. This is your moment. She gives you the grace and courage to live your life fully. She will watch over you all the days of your life."

Back on land, other women were waiting with towels to dry and warm them and returned the dresses to the girls. With the initiation completed, everyone made their way back up through the gate to the Temple of Apollo at the edge of the forum. There stood the statue of Apollo on one side of the sanctuary, and Diana, in all her glory, on the other side. Torches lit the night as the women and girls encircled the statue of Diana, and one by one, the initiated girls made their offerings to the goddess of Wild Things and the Moon. In turn, the older girls helped the younger girls, who had been waiting in the sanctuary, place handmade fig necklaces around the necks of the initiates as a gift from the generous goddess.

Aricia spoke. "Remember that Diana is your guardian, the keeper of animal wisdom. She teaches you how to be independent and, more importantly, how to be true to yourselves. You will be able to join your initiated friends in the Sanctuary, appreciate the sisterhood of older girls, mentor younger ones, and learn to honor your emerging feminine ways, enjoying the dance of animal life, your life."

The older women encircled all the girls, giving them a moment of silence to feel the closeness of their "sisters" and the omnipresent goddess. A chant started—*arktoi, arktoi, arktoi*— growing louder and louder, filling the sanctuary and forum with resolute feminine voices.

"Congratulations, Rufilla," Aridela and Melissa chimed together as the group dispersed.

"Thank you for helping with this ritual, Melissa. And thank you, Mater. I am truly grateful."

"Oh, so it is mater now? No more mamma—you're all grown up?" Aridela said. The three laughed, hugged, and walked home arm and arm through the moonlit streets. The night was clear as Aridela looked toward the star-filled sky. She stopped and pointed to the north. "I see The Bear," she said, gazing at a group of stars shaped like a ladle. "Look to the left," she said.

"I see the head of the serpent, and above it, the Northern Crown— Ariadne's crown!" Rufilla shouted, jumping up and down. "She saw us tonight, I know it. She saw us!" She ran ahead of Melissa and Aridela, doing her bear dance from earlier in the evening.

"I am dancing for you, both of you, goddess Artemis and goddess Ariadne."

CHAPTER XIV

THE GIFT

A few weeks after the initiation, the girls met for the trek into the woods, the one they would go on without their mothers. The villa where they would stay was in a beautiful valley, the Sarnus valley. Woods surrounded it so that they could enjoy their nighttime forays yet return to a place secured by the women who watched over them. There were Artemis Rules. No girl ever went outside without another girl. That was true even when they were home. But at home, it was an older woman, a mother or nursemaid, who accompanied them. Free time, which included a walk in the woods, was part of each day so they could be with one another. There were times when the older girls decided on a more structured day. One day, they decided to test the younger girls' skills of storytelling. They chose Rufilla, giving her the word Quartus, meaning *fourth born*, and told her to develop a brief story from that word.

After concentrating for a minute or so, eyes closed, she started. "This is a story about a young girl who seemed very happy on the outside but was often very sad on the inside. One day the girl was talking to her doll, and she heard someone in the room talking back to her. She turned but saw no one. 'Where have you been, my friend,' she asked again, and the answer came back, 'Right here, all along.' Now she was frightened. But for some reason, she did not run for her nursemaid or her mother. She sat very quietly with her eyes closed and said, 'Where are you going?'

"'With you, of course.' With that, her eyes flew open. There, sitting in the other chair, was a bald little boy, his head shaped like an egg. 'Will you be my friend?' he said.

"'Yes?' she said, not sure about this. 'What is your name?'

"The answer came. 'Quartus. I am fourth born. I make your family complete.'

"She did not understand, but number four was her favorite number. After that, when she was alone and needed a friend, she could call out, 'Quartus!' And he would come. Sometimes he came on his own.

"One day, her mother passed by the door of her bedroom, came in and sat down in the chair. 'Who are you talking to?' her mother asked.

"The girl started crying. 'You just sat on my friend Quartus.'

"Her mother gave her a worried look. 'There will be no more of this,' she said. 'You can no longer have your imaginary friend. Go next door and play with the neighbor girl. But do not tell anyone about Quartus!'

"And that was that. Quartus never came back. She called his name over and over when she knew no one else could hear, but he never came back."

No one spoke. One of the older girls broke the silence. "Thank you, Rufilla. That was a good story. I think we should go into the woods now and do our bear dance and sing songs."

Another girl said, "Then we can hunt for wild berries."

As the girls filed out of the room, Hostia stayed behind with Rufilla.

"No one liked my story," Rufilla said, bowing her head.

"I did," Hostia responded. "It is my story, but how did you know? I have never told anyone!"

"I have told you about how things come to me—like that story I just told," Rufilla said. "How do I know these things? Maybe I am mad! I do not know how I know. I just do."

CHAPTER XV

TRANSITIONS 46 BCE

As the years passed, Rufilla grew. She was not very tall but started to "fill out," as her mother called it. She had received the lecture from her mother about how dogs and cats procreate, and then she had broadened it to include humans. Rufilla found it disgusting. The thought of having a man do that to her. She would never allow it. Artemis would help her. She made a pact with Hostia, never to let it happen to them, but in case it did, then one must tell the other. And most important—they would remain best friends. No one would come between them.

When Rufilla turned 14, Hostia went to visit her relatives in southern Italy. Cil, 17, left for Rome, staying with Lucius, Cassia, and Zo. Cil was passionate about military medicine. Uncle Lucius was well connected to that branch of the military, and so Cil spent the summer being educated by Lucius and his doctor friends. He learned the basic duties of a medical officer on and off the field of battle.

Rufus and Aridela went on a vacation with Victor and Clodia. Rufilla and Titus would join them, and Theo and Melissa were delighted when Rufus invited them as well. They had had little time off since their wedding. They traveled by ferry to the island of Aenaria in the sparkling waters of the Bay of Napoli west of Misenum. This island was where Theo and Melissa had gone for time alone after their marriage. It was a wonderful time of year, due in part to a constant westerly breeze. Rufilla and Titus were allowed to take long walks together around the small island. Without Cil or Hostia around to distract them, they started to enjoy each other's company. Just what the parents had in mind.

One day on their way back to the villa where they were staying, the two stopped at a small secluded cove. They climbed a rock formation and found a massive spike of rock that jutted skyward with a flat rock in front that faced the sea, and formed a natural seat, giving them privacy from those passing by on the road. They sat in silence, watching and listening to the waves crash onto the rocks below. Titus put his arm around Rufilla and they kissed each other for the first time.

"Hello. Is anyone there?" said a familiar voice.

Both jumped up and peeked around the rocks behind them. Melissa and Theo stood there, arm in arm, looking for all the world like the happy, loving couple they had become.

Melissa said innocently, "This is where Theo kissed me the first time we were on this island. It is quite a romantic spot, do not you think?"

Theo winked.

CHAPTER XVI

A DREAM OF FOREBODING

Rufilla awoke, screaming. Melissa, asleep in the alcove outside her door, rushed to Rufilla's side. "Are you all right, dear?"

Rufilla sat up in bed, sobbing. "Oh, Melissa, I had a terrible nightmare." Melissa held her in her arms as she had done so many times over the years when nightmares invaded Rufilla's dream life.

Rufilla calmed herself and said, "I want to write down this dream. I think it is important." Melissa lit the oil lamp. Rufilla retrieved her pen, ink, and papyrus from beneath her bed. "I am fine now, Melissa, thank you. Get some sleep."

I feel myself descending into the murky waters of a turbulent sea. It is shallow water and the seaweed hinders my vision. I am underwater, but I can breathe. I see a large wooden ship close by. It has run aground and its bow is embedded in the sand between huge rocks. I can see the waves moving overhead on the surface, jostling the ship as if it were a toy. From above, I watch a man as he plunges into the water. He is dressed in a white nightshirt and falls headfirst, hitting his head on a large rock. A strong wave forces the stern of the ship to rise, and the man's lifeless body is pinned between a boulder and the underside of the ship! His body and the ship move in tandem, swaying side to side, at the mercy of the tides and the storm above.

I awake screaming.

The next morning, she told her mother who had helped her interpret her dreams in the past. "I know it is a sign. I am going to tell Titus and Cil. We need to warn them. Do you think they will listen?"

Her mother stroked Rufilla's face. "Knowing them, I doubt it."

She fell into her mother's arms and sobbed. "But they must, Mater, they must."

"You know," Aridela said, "this is their chance to establish themselves as soldiers in Caesar's army. Octavius can help them advance their careers."

"But Mater, you of all people should understand how important dreams are."

"Yes, but I also understand how men think and what they are driven to do."

Spring had arrived early, and the olive trees were already in full bloom. An unusually warm evening with its gentle breeze filled the open-air dining room of the Istacidii home. Aridela and Rufus had asked Titus and his parents to dine with them. As each person entered, a servant removed their shoes and washed their feet. Three couches were arranged in a U-shape around the tables of food. Aridela and Rufus reclined on one, Victor and Clodia sat opposite them, and in between, on the third couch were the three children, Cil, Rufilla, and Titus.

Tables of food filled the center of the room. Marcia had prepared her special soufflé of small fish garnished with eggs and rue leaves. The first lettuce salad of the season announced spring. Fresh bread was served with wine from their vineyards mixed with honey. Everyone had his or her spoon and napkin, but they ate most of their food with their fingers. They scooped up a portion of the fish soufflé with the rue leaf, remarking on its light and fluffy texture.

During the first course, the adults and Cil had a lively discussion about the upcoming adventure of the two sons, while the two lovers huddled together, deep in their banter.

"Rufilla, do not worry about the dream," Titus said, taking her hands in his. "Octavius says that the voyage will be an adventure most soldiers do not get to experience. Anyway, the trip from Neapoli to *Hispania* is not such a long way."

"But Titus, you know I have been right about my dreams before," Rufilla said. "Do not you understand this might be one of those prophetic dreams? And I know how long the journey is. You forget that I studied geography too. Anyway, it is a long way from me. I miss you already."

Titus pulled her toward him in an embrace. He gently wiped her tears away. She looked up at him, and they smiled what felt like their secret smile. "Why not start planning the engagement party, my love?" Titus said, stroking her forehead.

"You know he is right, Rufilla," her mother said, who had been eaves-dropping. "While Titus is gone, we will be able to spend some precious time together. Preparing for the engagement will make the time that the two of you are apart pass quickly. You will also be learning the duties involved when you become the domina of your household."

The servants appeared, clearing the first course. They wiped the hands of everyone at the dining table, and then placed the second course before them.

"Tonight," Rufus announced, "we have fresh chicken from our barnyard and asparagus, the first of the season, from our vegetable garden."

Aridela continued. "This is Marcia's version of Numidian chicken. The fig sauce is flavored with salty liquamen, dill, coriander, cumin, and pepper for tartness, and defrutum from the grape."

"A toast," Victor said, raising his wine cup. "To our two families, soon to be joined in matrimony, and to our two sons and their venture into manhood."

"Long live Rome and long live Caesar!" Rufus added.

"I thought you had reservations about Caesar and his motives," Aridela said.

"I have changed my mind since I found out that Caesar has chosen a sage, Apollodorus, to be Octavius' teacher," Rufus said. "When our sons go to Rome, they will also learn much from this scholarly man."

The servants refilled their cups from a *krater*, a large vessel of wine mixed with water.

Rufus turned toward Titus. "I have heard from my son, but will you tell me more about this adventure? I know that your friend Octavius is often in poor health. How do you think he will fare? And where does Caesar fit into all this?"

"Octavius can hold his own," Titus said. "Do not you remember when we were younger, how that bully was going to beat up Octavius, and he not only talked him out of it but persuaded him to join our group to help us with other bullies? What he might lack in physical strength he makes up for with his wits. He has also been in physical training for quite a while, preparing for this chance to be in combat with his great uncle. Caesar has seen Octavius' potential on several occasions and wants to prepare him for the military first and then for the Senate. After that, who knows?"

"That is what your father and I want for both of you," Rufus said. "A military career so that you might enter the equestrian ranks. Caesar will be a great help, I am sure."

"Yes, I know," Titus said, smiling at his father. "That is why Octavius asked us to join him. He wants to have some friends with him when he enters the Senate."

"That is good thinking, Titus. We enjoy giving the new senators a challenge or two." Victor winked at Rufus and then turned serious. "To have one another to rely on will be very helpful, both in the physical combat of war and the political conflict of the Senate."

"We look forward to it," Cil said in his newly found grown-up voice, smiling at Titus. "I hear initiations are sometimes rigorous but also necessary for the long term."

Rufus looked at Aridela, and then to Victor and Clodia. "We raised them well. Their time has come."

The servants reappeared at the end of the second course, removing the table and bringing back a new one set with a sweet date dessert, cheese, olives, and yes, more wine.

CHAPTER XVII

OCTAVIUS AND JULIUS CAESAR

Gaius Octavius, the future Roman Emperor, who would be known as Caesar Augustus, was born in Rome on the morning of September 23, 63 BCE. Gaius Octavius and Atia Balba Caesonia were his parents, Atia, the niece of Julius Caesar. He had two older siblings, Octavia Major, a half-sister, and Octavia Minor, a full sister. In his memoirs, Gaius Octavius claimed that he was born into "a rich old equestrian family." The men of the Octavii family were wealthy bankers who lived in a hill town south of Rome called Velitrae. They had acquired enough wealth to qualify them to join the equestrian class, second in rank below the senatorial level. His father decided on a career in politics, hoping to become a senator. By 70 BCE, he had amassed enough wealth from his banking business and land holdings to qualify for the Senate. He was elected *Quaestor* around that time, which automatically made him the first man in his family to become a senator, a *Novus Homo*. He was elected *Praetor* in 61 BCE. After serving his Praetorship, he was sent overseas, as was usual, to serve as *Propraetor*, a magistrate who governed a province—in this case—of Macedonia. He proved to be an accomplished official, and some thought that although he came from the provinces, he was qualified to seek the consulship, the highest office in Rome. On his return trip to Rome, he unfortunately and unexpectedly died of unknown causes at the family's country villa near the foot of Mount Vesuvius. Octavius was four years old.

Because his parents saw Rome as an unhealthy environment in which to raise a child, Octavius had been sent in his infancy to live with his maternal grandmother, Julia, the sister of Julius Caesar, at her country home near Velitrae.

In 59 BCE, after her husband's death, his mother, Atia, joined her son to live with her mother. Atia, as a member of the Julian family, had excellent qualifications for remarriage, and Caesar would take an interest in finding her an appropriate husband. He was in Rome during that time, having been elected consul in 59, and having taken his third wife, Calpurnia Pisonis, in that year. He visited his sister, Julia, introduced his new wife, and met his grandnephew for the first time. The four-year-old Octavius was a precocious child and reminded Caesar of himself—intelligent, self-confident, and with only adults around him, mature beyond his years. Octavius was in awe of Caesar, as he rarely had a fatherly role model in his life.

Two years later, Atia married a member of a Roman senatorial family, Lucius Marcius Philippus, and moved to Rome with him when he was elected consul in 56 BCE.

The young Octavius remained in Velitrae and was brought up by his grandmother. Atia took charge of his early education, if only from a distance. A father or male relative usually took over the tutelage of his son at age seven. But in this case, Octavius relied on only one male—a slave called Sphaerus, who served the boy well in those formative years. As he grew older, he was sent to a private elementary school, accompanied by Sphaerus. Octavius must have loved his slave because when he was an adult, he freed the slave, and when Sphaerus died, he gave him a public funeral.

Atia and Julia told Octavius many stories of his great-uncle, Julius Caesar, beginning with the fact that *his* father died when he was sixteen, and he had to take over the family. A few years later, Caesar joined the military and distinguished himself by winning the Civic Crown for bravery while fighting in the siege of Mytilene. Caesar returned to Rome and became a lawyer at age twenty-three. Along the way, he raised an army and fought in the Third Mithridatic War. He started climbing up the political ladder of offices first as a military tribune. Then in 69 BCE, he was elected to the quaestorship, serving in Hispania. Both his sister, Julia, and his wife Cornelia died in that year and were given public funerals. Around 67 BCE, he married Pompeia. In 62, he divorced her due to a political scandal.

By 59 BCE, he had won the consulship, Rome's highest office. After serving his year in office, Caesar became governor of Roman Gaul in 58 BCE, setting into motion a plan to secure the borders of the Roman province of Transalpine Gaul. In short order, Caesar saw that the situation was untenable and that he needed to conquer all the native tribes of Gaul. The Gallic wars lasted for eight years, with Caesar finally subduing both Cisalpine and Transalpine Gaul and turning the defeated tribes into allies. During that time, Caesar wrote his book, *Commentarii de Bello Gallico*, describing each successful battle and sending them to Rome. His popularity with the people of Rome was unsettling to the Senate. Each communique to the people strengthened his cause. Octavius undoubtedly read every one.

The political situation back in Rome became so dire that in mid-course of the war, Caesar met in secret with Crassus and then Pompey, his two political allies. Historians consider this the First Triumvirate, bringing Crassus and Pompey together with Caesar as a mediator. But it was tenuous at best. To bolster his situation, he convinced them that if they could delay the elections of new consuls, he would bring his soldiers back home long enough to elect Crassus and Pompey as the consuls for the following year. In return, he asked for ten more senior officers and the funds to hire four more legions, close to twenty-four thousand men. In the end, they found an ally in the Senate, Cicero, who helped arrange the funding. After they were elected, Pompey and Crassus passed a bill that allowed Caesar to stay on as governor of Gaul for five more years to win the Gallic Wars.

All this is to say that Julius Caesar, a shrewd politician, began as a soldier with little military experience, and ended up as one of the most powerful men in the Roman Republic, and, some say, the most exceptional military leader of all time.

Octavius' grandmother, Julia Caesaris, died in 51 BCE when he was around twelve. By then, he had become so close to her and was so well-spoken that he was given the privilege to perform the eulogy at her funeral, thus making his first public appearance. Funerals were not just about the deceased person, but also about family and their accomplishments. It was a pious occasion but also a political one. Atia would have told Octavius that his great-uncle, Julius Caesar, had given the eulogy for *his* aunt, Julia, the widow of Marius. The eulogy usually started by recalling all the famous deeds of their ancestors, followed by those who were alive, and finally, the recently deceased person. He would have mentioned his great-uncle, Julius Caesar, as a vital politician and an outstanding leader of the Roman army. After the funeral, he went to live with his mother and step-father in Rome, continuing his secondary education in a private school.

Octavius showed great promise as a future politician, displaying *pietas,* piety, that is, performing his duty to family and country. The second virtue he learned was *fortitudo,* meaning strength, courage, and bravery. Both virtues were necessary, for he was a sickly child. Octavius was not tall, but it was said that he was well built, handsome, and blond-haired. He had a presence about him that drew people to him, including girls, who were kept in check by Atia. At an early age, he already had a following of male friends who respected him.

One of the friends, Marcus Vipsanius Agrippa, he met at school. The two became very close and would remain lifelong colleagues. Agrippa, about the same age, was also a son of a provincial family, but of obscure and humble origin. Both boys were trained in the humanities, the sciences, and literature.

However, there was a clear difference between them. Agrippa enjoyed the physical challenges and tactics of military life, while Octavius had the mental capacity to lead, but seemed physically unable to join in combat. In their later years together, Agrippa would indeed prove to be a competent general, statesman, and architect for Octavius as Emperor. They would conspire to build and improve the city of Rome, as well as the entire Roman Empire.

During Octavius' early teenage years, Atia had kept her uncle informed about his grand-nephew's politically savvy nature. When Julius Caesar, who had been fighting in Gaul for eight years, returned to Rome, he took an active role in Octavius' education. Over the next few years, when he was available, Caesar passed on a great deal of wisdom to his eager student, specifically about his two favorite subjects— politics and war.

At around fifteen, Octavius and his family observed a rites-of-passage ceremony held for every Roman boy of the upper classes. He had worn a *bulla*, or amulet, around his neck to protect him and symbolize his boyhood. Now he performed a ritual in his home, where he offered the bulla to his ancestors, the household gods, or *Lares,* leaving behind his childhood amulet and putting on the white *toga virilis*, indicating his transition into manhood. Soon after, Caesar presumably appointed

Octavius to the priesthood in the college of pontiffs, of which Caesar was the chief priest or *pontifex maximus*. It was a prestigious moment for Octavius. He took off his newly donned *toga virilis*, and put on the garments of the priestly office and, for the first time, conducted a public sacrifice—his first public act as a priest. According to the historian Cassius Dio, Octavius' toga unraveled and fell to the floor. Maintaining his composure, he said, 'I shall have all the senatorial dignity at my feet.' Octavius possessed an agile mind and the political ambition to go with it.

Around that time, the triumvirate had collapsed, and the power struggle between Caesar and Pompey raged on in what is called the Great Roman Civil War. The politics of Rome were complicated. Although there were two parties, the *optimates,* and the *populares,* the Senate's control of the city teetered back and forth with whoever was the most influential senator and military leader at that particular moment. When he returned to Rome, Caesar would not leave his legions behind as Pompey had demanded, so in a bold move, he crossed the Rubicon and entered Rome with his troops, thereby committing a treasonable act. The Civil War began. As consul, Pompey had taken over control of Rome, but his troops were in Africa and Hispania, so he was forced to flee to Greece and then Egypt. In the end, after defeating some of Pompey's troops, Julius Caesar pursued Pompey to Greece, defeating Pompey's army at the Battle of Pharsalus. Pompey escaped with his family and headed to Egypt, thinking he would find asylum there. Instead, King Ptolemy sought Caesar's favor, and so had Pompey beheaded. Instead, Caesar was appalled. His relationship with Pompey was a complex web of politics and power plays that were used by both men. They were longtime rivals, sometimes allies. Respect for each other could only be surmised. They were also family as Pompey had been allowed to marry Caesar's daughter, Julia. With the murder of Pompey, Caesar was robbed of the opportunity to pardon his rival magnanimously, and with that would have gained political favor in Rome.

After winning the Battle of the Nile, he secured Cleopatra and her brother Ptolemy XIV's place as joint rulers and continued an affair with Cleopatra.

Octavius was almost seventeen when Caesar returned to Rome. The Senate granted him a total of forty days of public thanksgiving, which included celebrations and games, and four triumphal processions celebrating his victories over Gaul, Egypt, the Pharnaces, King Zuba, and Africa. He had been absent from Rome for many years, but his list of accomplishments had a strong influence on Octavius. Nothing went unnoticed with this young man.

Dictators were political leaders who were given absolute power for short periods. Caesar was appointed dictator in 49 BCE and again in 48 BCE for a one-year term. Caesar set about establishing a new constitution to strengthen the central government, unifying the provinces, and appointing many senators who were then sympathetic to him. He also set into motion many improvements, including the revision of the calendar, setting up a police force and fire brigade, and initiating land reforms.

But he still had to deal with Pompey's sons and their armies. In 46, he was appointed dictator of Rome for ten years. He chose to go to Africa first to confront the troops and wanted Octavius to go with him to gain some military experience. Atia refused to let him go, stating that his participation might permanently "injure his health." Octavius remained at home, probably not happy, but understanding his physical limitations, he worked to strengthen his physique.

Upon his return, Caesar was given many honors. There seemed to be a movement toward giving him all the powers of a divine monarch, the title of king, which the Romans had detested in earlier times, overthrowing the system of kingship hundreds of years before. Was history repeating itself? This was not a good omen.

In October, 46 BCE he resigned as sole consul, and in November traveled to Hispania to do battle with the remaining opponents—the Pompeian army that included Pompey's two sons. This time Octavius would join him.

CHAPTER XVIII

JANUARY

45 BCE

Octavius summoned Cil and Titus to Rome. All the young men who would accompany him were there. Octavius' physician was also there, as was the captain of the ship that they would sail on to Hispania. Lucius had encouraged Cil to introduce himself to the physician and tell him about his interest in medicine, which he did. They had a lively exchange, and both looked forward to their time together.

"My great uncle, Julius Caesar, is already in Hispania battling Pompey's sons," Octavius said. "I am now ready to leave and am so glad that all of you can join me. It should be quite an adventure and a good start for all of us in our military careers. I brought you together so that we can make plans and set a sailing date. Letters from Caesar since he left late last year have confirmed that this is a decisive battle and that the skirmishes with the enemy have been formidable. Hopefully, we will make it in time to participate in the final battle."

Titus and Cil returned from Rome with such excitement. Rufilla had the recurring nightmare, but this time chose to tell no one. She did not want to spoil their last days at home.

The night before they left, Titus and his parents hosted Rufilla, Cil and their parents for dinner. Family and friends of both boys joined the festive occasion, offering many toasts and good-natured jokes. The two lovers insisted on some time alone after dinner. Theo, as usual, followed at a discreet distance. Titus and Rufilla strolled down the hill, stopping in a public garden overlooking the river. They sat for a while, silent in each other's embrace, watching the water flow past them. Titus sensed that Rufilla still felt anxious about his leaving, and he broke the silence. "Look at the water, how it flows endlessly by, waiting for someone to join it in its journey." He searched her eyes for understanding. "This is my moment, Rufilla. This is the time to look destiny full in the face. I know it sounds dramatic, but the sense of duty I feel is powerful. I cannot deny it."

"I understand, and I am happy that you are driven and passionate about this opportunity. You know that I want the best for you. It is just that I have known you all my life. You are not only my betrothed, but you and my brother are two of my best friends. If anything happened—"

"Shh." He touched her lips gently with his finger. "Let us not spoil this last night together. Keep in mind what I taught you about the Stoics. Fortitude is the state of one's soul unmoved by fear. Your heart must be fearless."

He tipped her chin upward to meet his face, his mouth on her mouth. "Oh, I will come back to you. We will sit here again in the moonlight and remember this night."

"And laugh about how silly I was to worry."

"No, I want you to worry and stew and fret so that on my return, you leap into my arms and never let me go."

"You will write to me, will you not?"

"More often than you will write to me."

"I will write to you every day."

"I will write to you twice a day and three times on my day off." Titus laughed. He turned to gather her into his arms, looked over her shoulder, and noticed Theo standing at a distance. "Come, I had better get you back before they send the hounds after us."

They rose to leave, walking arm in arm. From a distance, one could hear their laughter, winding its way up the hill toward home.

As the families parted for the evening, Titus took Rufilla aside and whispered in her ear, "Just so you know, it cannot be me in your dream because I do not wear a nightshirt—or anything else for that matter. Dream about that if you dare."

He picked her up and twirled her around until they were both giddy.

"Sounds like the laughter of youngsters in love," Rufus said.

"Yes," Aridela said. "We had better have everything prepared for the engagement party by the time he returns."

Everyone laughed, hugging and kissing their goodbyes.

As they left, Aridela and Rufilla rode on a litter, while the two men, father and son, walked beside them. Rufilla waved goodbye to Titus and his parents until they were out of sight and she could no longer hear their voices. Then she collapsed in tears.

CHAPTER XIX

LETTERS

Every day Rufilla watched for a letter. Almost a month went by, and then three letters came, two from Titus to Rufilla and one from Cil to the family. The letters told of their rough voyage, the seasickness, and how they had been driven into other ports more than once by intense spring storms. They had both learned a lot about sailing. At the time of their writings, they were getting ready to sail southwest from the island of Majorca to Cartagena, Hispania, and then march inland to meet Caesar and his troops. A troop of soldiers would meet them at an appointed place. They would be fighting against the army of Pompey's sons, Gnaeus and Sextus.

My Dearest Rue,

You would not recognize me. I am as brown as one of those honey cakes you love so much. I have decided to grow my beard and it is rough, dark, and curly. You would not let me kiss you, I know. But for now, it is fine. We do not bathe every day as we do at home. I miss the feel of that waterfall near your farm. We are now in port on the island of Sardinia. There are beaches here where we can swim. It feels luxurious. But it makes me remember our times by the sea in Pompeii, and my body grows sick with longing.

It is ironic that aboard ship, we are surrounded by water that we cannot drink. The small amount of drinking water that we carry is such a precious passenger. It seems that I am always thirsty. Or am I just thirsty for your kiss? We have too much time to think out here. I will not be the same man, or what I want to say is that I will be a man for the first time when I return to you.

Your brother and I are closer now than we ever were on land. The close confinement of the ship, the camaraderie of the men, I am not sure what it is. I only know that I—we are changed. He is a good man, Rue. I love him like a brother. We are both lucky to have him.

*The sun is scorching hot, and I am running out of precious
papyrus, so I close for now.*
I give you all my love, now and for eternity.
Titus

The following morning she re-read his letter. Then she turned to
Sappho. After a few minutes, she threw her treasured collection of poems
against the wall. Why do I read this? It just makes me miss him more. I
must write to him. That will make me feel better.

Dearest Titus,
*I am writing because I am missing you so much. I did not find
solace in reading Sappho this morning, which usually helps. Here is
what she said:*
*"Some an army of horsemen, some an army on foot and some say
a fleet of ships is the loveliest sight on this dark earth; but I say it is
whatever you desire—"*
*I would settle for seeing your ship come into port, but not before
your "adventure," as your pater called it, is complete.*
*I am making progress in learning my duties of running the
household. Lots of things to remember, but I think I am doing very
well. Mater thinks so too.*
Give my love to my brother, but save most of it for yourself.
Remember our first sweet kiss on the island.
I remain faithful to you forever.
Kisses, Rue

COMING OF AGE

The dawn gave Rufilla enough light to read, but the household wasn't
stirring yet. Her mother and Melissa had decided that, since Rufilla was
older now and having fewer seizures, Melissa could spend most nights
sleeping with Theo in their apartment next door.

Rufilla usually heard Theo when he started to wake up all the other
servants, but it was too early for that. She loved this time of day, the few
minutes when she could feel the stillness of the household and read her

poetry books, with no one to interrupt the quietude. At that moment, she heard a messenger pigeon land on its perch just above the kitchen. It cooed as if to signal its landing. She knew that someone had sent a message from the farmhouse and that the bird would soon be retrieved. So much for quiet time.

Out of nowhere, Melissa appeared in the doorway. "Good morning, angel." Melissa recited her usual greeting to her charge. "It is time to ready yourself for the baths," she said. "Your mater will be ready shortly."

"But I just started telling Ariadne's story to Hygeia," Rufilla said.

Seeing then that Rufilla had been crying, Melissa said gently, "I am so sorry."

"I am missing Titus and feeling sorry for myself," she said, throwing her bed covers off. "Tell mater that I am ready too. I need a walk to change my mood.

"You know your mother does not like you to walk. The roads are strewn with all sorts of foul things."

"Then I will walk on the side of the road," she replied.

"With all the rain, there will be so many *insectae!*"

Rufilla rolled her eyes and with a deep sigh, acquiesced. "Bring out the *lectica*. I will ride."

Mother and daughter made their way down the hill, sitting high atop the litter shouldered by four slaves. A long, rectangular linen cloth supported by four stakes stretched above their heads and furnished the women with cover from the sun overhead. Their maids followed behind, carrying fresh clothes, oils, and strigils for the pair. Aridela chose to take her daughter to the baths only when and where women bathed. At fifteen, Rufilla was well developed with shapely hips that drew the attention of too many men in her mother's mind. The time would come soon enough when Rufilla would share the baths with her husband.

The bathhouse had been built and donated to the city by a friend of Aridela. Since it was small, she had set appointed times for women and then men to bathe. Later in the day, it was coed; men and women could share the baths and meet their friends in preparation for dinner. It was a social place, and in this particular establishment, most everyone knew one another.

"Welcome back," the hostess said. She handed them clean, white towels, and they made their way down a short hall and into the dressing room. It had a vaulted, tiled ceiling with frescoes of women and cubicles built along the walls. Because the hostess knew her clientele, it was safe to leave one's clothes unguarded, unlike at the Stabian baths.

All four women, now naked, moved down the tiled corridor to the next room, the tepidarium. Beautiful frescoes lined the walls with scenes of bathers, and the floor was warm with the heat of the boiler located under the floor in the adjacent room. Friends of Aridela were already in the pool. They greeted the others and slipped into the warm water of the rectangular pool at one end of the room. They could faintly hear the droning of the hot water boilers, as the animated conversation nearly drowned out the noise.

"Well, have you two heard from the boys at sea?" one of Aridela's friends asked.

"Yes," answered Aridela. "I am delighted to say that the letter delivery system is working. We both received letters from Sardinia. Their ship had been moored in the harbor for a few days due to storms."

Hostia was there and asked Rufilla about Titus.

"He misses me," she offered and then was silent.

"Looks like you miss him, too."

Rufilla wiped her eyes.

Rufilla stood up in the shallow pool. "Mater, I want to take the hot bath and have a massage today, so I will not linger here any longer." Rufilla stepped out of the pool, wrapped the towel around her, and bid everyone a pleasant good day. Melissa rose to go with her, but Rufilla waved her back. "I can take care of myself, Melissa. Stay and enjoy the water."

Melissa looked at Aridela, and she nodded. "Let her have some time alone."

Rufilla left the room quickly.

"She seems to need more time alone lately," Aridela said to her friends. "We are both worried about the spring storms."

Rufilla's wet feet slapped the tile floor as she strode down the hallway toward the next room. She was grateful that she saw no one as she entered. "Thank the gods for small favors," she said as she entered the caldarium.

She sat on the edge of the small pool, letting her feet dangle in the steaming hot water. It took several minutes before she could immerse her whole body. Then she relaxed and tried to think of nothing. She must have dozed off because the next thing she heard was the sound of a woman's voice. "Excuse me," the woman said, "would you like a massage?"

"Yes, I would. Did my mother send you?"

The masseuse nodded. "Would you be more comfortable in one of the rooms at the end of the hall?"

Rufilla heard voices coming from the other direction.

"Definitely," she said.

The woman showed her into a room with a stone table in the center. It was padded with cushions and covered with two sheets.

"Just climb between the sheets, and I will fetch some warmed oil and be with you shortly."

Rufilla dropped her towel and hoisted herself up, pulling the top sheet over her. This ceiling was vaulted as well. She looked up and saw the familiar frescoes of men and women in various phases of getting a massage. She thought of Titus. The woman came back, carrying the heated oil and fragrant unguents, and asked if she would like a flute player to provide some music.

"Yes, outside the door, please, not in here," Rufilla said.

The masseuse started at her head, gently rubbing the soft skin of her face with olive oil. The flute player started with a familiar tune. At once, with her eyes closed, she saw Titus' face before her. She gasped, and her eyes flew open.

"Are you all right?" the woman asked.

"Yes, go on," she said.

After a few moments, the masseuse moved to Rufilla's side and touched her shoulder. Instantly, Rufilla broke into tears. She curled up onto her side and lay there sobbing.

The woman moved behind her and started to rub her back. Again the tears began. Rufilla grabbed the woman's hand. "Hold me, hold me," she pleaded.

The woman bent over her and embraced her, rocking her, stroking her brow. When Rufilla felt calm, the woman asked her to turn over onto her stomach. She began at her shoulders, massaging Rufilla's back, her buttocks, and the back of her legs and feet. Then she took the strigil and, with sweeping motions, scraped the oil from the young woman's body. Rufilla loved the feel of the strigil. It sent shivers down her spine. She imagined Titus with her, experiencing the same sensations, and then, they would take their "pleasure," as her mother called it, together. She looked forward to that time. "Soon," she whispered, "please make it soon."

Next, she turned over and felt the fresh air on the front of her body. The massage felt even more sensual as she enjoyed the stroking of her breasts and belly. She closed her eyes and imagined Titus touching her. She spread her legs so that she could feel the strigil on her thighs. As it slid down the inside of one thigh and then the other, she exploded. With one hand, she touched her most tender place and felt her warmth, moisture, and pleasure. Enjoying the moment, she grabbed the arm of the masseuse. Then, opening her eyes, she smiled and self-consciously laughed. The woman laughed with her, a warm laugh, full of womanly wisdom.

"Thank you," Rufilla said.

"You are very welcome." The woman said. She pulled the sheet over Rufilla, saying, "Rest for just a little while."

Rufilla did not need coaxing. She fell asleep immediately and woke relaxed and refreshed.

The pool, she thought. Yes. She grabbed her towel and made her way up the hall and jumped into the pool, surprising several women, including her mother.

"Well, look who is here." Her mother beamed at the sight of her beautiful daughter. "You look refreshed."

"Rested and hungry," Rufilla said. "Let us eat!"

CHAPTER XX

TWO LETTERS

Ten days passed, and then one letter arrived—from Cil. Aridela opened it immediately. She broke the seal, unrolled the longer than usual scroll, and saw that inside there were two letters.

"Here is one for you from Titus!"

Rufilla grabbed it and ran to her bedroom to read in private.

> *Dear Rue,*
>
> *As we sat watching the sunset this evening, Cil and I talked about many things. We are both looking forward to being in battle with Octavius and Caesar. But there were also thoughts of you, my sweet. Cil has often said that we were lucky we were betrothed so many years ago, and then he gets a gleam in his eye and proclaims that he is far from ready to feel those bonds of matrimony around his neck. Even though Cil is betrothed, he does not want to commit yet. But when you are as in love as we are, there will only be bonds to make, not break.*
>
> *I have decided to sleep on deck tonight because it is the first warm day we have had since we sailed. We reached sight of terra firma today, and tomorrow we will be landing on the shores of Hispania. Already, we are close enough to see the coastline. I volunteered to help with the setting of the sails tomorrow morning. By now, the stench of spoiled food and the men's filthy bodies makes it almost impossible to sleep below deck. Several others have decided to sleep on deck, too. The air grows chilly even as I write this, and one of the men has just offered his other nightshirt. I may take it, but do not fret about your dream—the night is calm.*
>
> *Good night, my love, sweet dreams.*
> *Titus*

LETTER FROM CIL

Aridela was grateful to see her son's familiar writing addressed to her, Rufus and Rufilla. She took the letter to the porch and sank into her chair. She held the scroll next to her breast, unwilling to open it just yet. So many years passed quickly through her mind, memories of her son's playfulness and pranks, but also his tenderness toward her. He enjoyed teasing his sister, but loved her dearly and showed it more with every passing year.

Just one more moment to enjoy the anticipation of reading his letter, she thought. He hadn't written as often as he said he would, but she could forgive him for that. As she waited, Rufus came home from the baths. She held up the missive and smiled. He sat beside her.

"Open the letter, woman! Read me the latest from our sea-bound soldier." She began:

> *Dear Pater, Mater, and Fila,*
> *I find it difficult to start this letter. I do not know how to tell you this terrible story.*

She gasped and, unable to go on, handed the letter to Rufus. He read it aloud.

> *We were sailing down the east coast of Hispania. The night was the warmest so far, and several of us, including Titus, were sleeping topside. This much he told Fila in the letter of his that I have enclosed. I awoke in the middle of the night. I thought I heard a noise and, after several minutes, realized it was thunder. The boards of the ship were creaking, but there was no wind. The sea was so calm that I could hear the men snoring below decks. Then the ship started moving, ever so gently, side to side. We had anchored the vessel off the coastline, but I realized there was a breeze now, and we were going in a circle around the anchor. The sky filled with heavy thunderclouds overhead, and the breeze turned into a strong wind. Within a few minutes, the storm was upon us. Lightning lit up the sky, the wind velocity increased, and then the wind carried the waves over the sides of the ship.*

Aridela interrupted, shouting, "The turbulent sea!"

"What?"

"Rufilla's dream! Go no further!"

Rufus collapsed into the chair beside his wife, reading the rest of the letter to himself.

> *The ship was taking on water. I saw Titus in the bow, and then he turned to see a wave, no, a wall of water taller than the mast, heading toward us. It broke over the bow, lifting Titus into the air—and then he was gone! My friend, my brother—he was gone!*
>
> *The ship was tossed onto the rocks and boulders near the shoreline and was grounded. The tide was out, and by morning there was no way to get under the ship to see if we could retrieve Titus' body if indeed it was there.*
>
> *I write this from the safety of Caesar's camp, regaining my strength. Octavius is healthy again and sends his condolences to you and Titus' parents.*
>
> *I enclose the letter from Titus to Fila as we found it in the strongbox retrieved from the ship. He must have placed it there that evening.*
>
> *Dear sister, I am so sorry to have to relate this sad tale. My heart is broken for you and me.*
>
> *There is more to tell, but it will have to wait until I return home.*
>
> *Love to you all,*
>
> *Cil*

CHAPTER XXI

AFTER THE STORM

Julius Caesar had fought the decisive battle just outside the city of Osuna, on the plains of Munda, while Octavius and his crew were still at sea. Caesar would later say that he usually fought battles for victory; this one he had fought for his life, side by side with his men from the 10th legion.

The night after the battle there was a horrendous thunderstorm with damaging winds. Earlier, Caesar had received a letter from Octavius, who anticipated that his arrival was imminent. When his grand-nephew did not arrive, Caesar sent a scouting party to the harbor where Octavius planned to make landfall on the eastern coast of Hispania. No ship was there.

Meanwhile, Octavius had no idea who they might meet and so was very cautious, traveling close to the shoreline by night and sleeping in the shelter of the forest during the day. One morning as they prepared to sleep, they saw a patrol of Roman soldiers headed inland on the road. When they saw the standard-bearer of Julius Caesar, they let out a whoop. The soldiers were startled because they had found the abandoned ship on the rocks north of their planned landing site. When they saw no one aboard or in the immediate area, they were prepared to give up. But they soon recognized Octavius. The patrol leader relayed the news that the battle was over but that there were still some of Gnaeus Pompeius' men in the area, so Octavius and his men had been very astute to conceal themselves.

They escorted Octavius and his group back to a surprised and relieved Caesar. He was pleased to see Octavius looking so fit, as he had been quite ill when Caesar left for Hispania. That he had survived the violent storm and the wreck of the ship and had brought his men safely to the attention of the search party spoke volumes to Caesar about Octavius' potential.

They spent days talking about the events of the battle and how brave Caesar's men had been. Cil made rounds with the physician in charge, listening to the men's stories and helping tend their wounds. Caesar's men told of their leader's bravery and the tactics he had used to incite his men to battle: going one-on-one beside them against Pompey's son's forces, and at one point jumping into the front lines with his men.

Octavius was delighted to be reunited with his close friend Agrippa. Although he had been taken ill while still in Rome, Octavius insisted that Caesar take Agrippa with him to fight in Hispania.

Caesar had observed Agrippa in battle and was duly impressed by his nephew's friend. He saw that he had a keen mind. During the military maneuvers, Caesar took a personal interest in him, impressed by his brave acts and astute understanding of military tactics. Caesar saw his potential for being a valued ally to his grand-nephew.

One evening, Caesar invited Octavius and his friends to a meeting and dinner. Agrippa was among the guests. As the evening wore on, it became apparent that Caesar had definite plans for Octavius and Agrippa. He had his eyes focused on the Parthians and felt that these two young men would be valuable assets.

Cil sent off the letter about the disappearance of Titus to his family. His grief was palpable to Octavius, and so while Octavius went with his great-uncle to eliminate the remaining pockets of resistance of Gaius Pompeius' men, he assigned his physician, Antonius Musa, to take Cil under his wing and keep him distracted by helping with patients. Cil could put up a strong front during the day when he was assisting the doctor, but when the evenings came, the moments when he and Titus had shared so many good times, especially during those last few weeks, he was inconsolable. The doctor was kindhearted, and when he saw there was no relief to Cil's distress, he felt that the only humane thing he could do was to send him back to Pompeii to be with his and Titus' families and take part in his best friend's funeral.

CHAPTER XXII

RUFILLA'S METAMORPHOSIS

Journal entry—eight days after the funeral.

Because Titus had been commissioned to travel to Hispania in the service of Julius Caesar, he deserved to be honored, so our two families arranged a public funeral for Titus in the forum.

The initial viewing began in the Buccii home. When someone entered the home to pay their respects, Victor, my father, and Cil greeted them at the front door. Then the mourners moved on to the atrium where the empty *lectus*, Titus' couch, was covered with fresh flowers that came from my mother's, Aricia's, and of course, the Buccii's gardens. Cil was given a nightshirt by his shipmates to honor Titus at his funeral. Cil placed it on the lectus. Clodia and her female relatives and friends, including Mater, and I, the betrothed one, sat with our hair hanging down, beating our chests and chanting dirges in time with the somber music played by the flutist. It was very cathartic for the first day, but by the second day, Clodia had lost her voice and had taken to her bed. I was numb by then but wanted to stay with the group of women mourners. My mother was afraid I would start having seizures, so I could only participate for part of the day. Anticipating our problems, Victor had hired professional mourners to help.

On the third day, Clodia was able to rise from her bed to attend the funeral procession in the forum. Even though the distance was short, Victor made Clodia, my mother, and I ride in a carriage. The lectus, replenished with garlands of fresh flowers, was carried aloft by three of Titus' closest friends, including my brother Cil, who wore his military uniform. He seemed taller, thinner, older. Aper had already embarked on his merchant ship duties—sailing port to port—so he couldn't be there. I missed him terribly. Octavius had sent one of Caesar's officers to represent Caesar and Octavius, a meaningful gesture since it showed Octavius' concern for Titus' family and ours. The officer asked to be the fourth lectus carrier. The rest of the men wore their formal togas. Two men walked behind them, wearing the traditional wax mask portraits of his two grandfathers.

The family sat with the lectus on the upper level of the forum. The mourners who stood below consisted of relatives and friends: the extended family of clients, political friends, servants and slaves, and also the towns-people who had been helped in any way by the Buccii or the Istacidii families. There were many people there.

Cil spoke from the rostrum, giving the *laudatio funebris*, an emotional farewell. He started with a quote from Cicero. "The life of the dead is placed in the memory of the living." He then praised Titus' ancestors' military service, then talked of Octavius' fearlessness and determination to find Caesar after the shipwreck, and Caesar's heroism in the battles waged. Finally, Cil remembered Titus' courage to prepare for a campaign under Caesar's command. Cil's words, eloquent and touching, showed that he had learned well his lessons in rhetoric. It also reminded me of the trip we made to Vellitrae several years ago when Octavius' grandmother died. Octavius was only twelve years old, so I was nine. He gave a heartfelt tribute honoring his beloved grandmother. She had raised him for many years, very much like a second mother. Too many funerals.

Clodia was inconsolable. In the carriage, she held onto me as if I was the last vestige of Titus. At that moment, I felt like the torn remnant of the shirt he had worn that night. After the service, the ritual procession exited through the city, out the Salt Gate, and onto the large plot of land that held the burial tomb shared by the Buccii, Melissaei, and the Istacidii families. The property had enough open space to accommodate the burning of the lectus on a funeral pyre. After the group had witnessed the burning, the family held a funerary feast at the tomb site, with extended family and friends included.

As I write this, I can't see through my tears.

Later the same day.

The public display will end with a play, performed in the theater and donated by Victor and my pater. The exact day of the performance will be determined later. Titus and I loved going to the theater. I remember one comedy by Plautus that was witty and sweet, the dialogue facile, and it had a happy ending. Not for us.

The next day.

The private mourning began. Usually, a family would mourn their child for a year, refraining from dinner parties, dressing in white clothing with purple ribbons, and wearing no jewelry or adornments. Since Titus was my betrothed, I felt like family, so I decided to do it in like manner. In the beginning, my parents agreed. For the first few weeks, I rarely saw anyone except my family. I spent most of my time in my room, reading my well-worn book of love poems by Sappho and writing verse. But I did have more than my share of seizures during that time. When I finally left my room, I decided to sketch some flowers in our back garden. That way I was sheltered from my father's patrons who daily filled the front of the house, asking for political or monetary favors.

At first, I wrote love letters to Titus and other letters pleading with Venus to return my beloved. I even wrote a play. In it, Titus had been carried out to sea after the storm and washed ashore on a beach far from the shipwreck. He had survived but had amnesia and couldn't tell the natives who found him who he was. I showed it to my parents. My pater sat me down. "Somewhere long ago," he said, "when I was about your age, I read a poem about Charon, the ferryman. Do you remember he is the one who carries one's soul over the river Styx into the afterlife? He said that the most punished souls are those that are forbidden burial." I burst into tears.

"The reason I tell you this, my child, is that this play you have written gives you hope. I understand. But what I want *you* to understand is that the hope it gives you is only temporary. It picks at the scab that keeps you from grieving for him."

I pulled my tunica over my head, buried my face in my lap and lay screaming. My pater put his hands on my shoulders and drew me to him, rocking me in his arms. "That is it, my child, scream and mourn, scream and mourn, let that pain be purged from your body."

When I calmed down somewhat, I embraced him, and we sat in silence for a long time. Then he told me about Aristotle's description of the concept of catharsis and how the emotions need to be purged when one has experienced a tragedy such as I had experienced.

As the weeks dragged on, I remained angry, cursing and ranting to just about everyone, especially myself. I asked my father to order more ink and papyrus for me, as I refused to write the letters or do my artwork on the reusable wax tablets. It was as if the grief and pain I went through needed to be a tangible record, which I could reflect upon later. All through this ordeal, Hygeia, my cat, never left my side, even during my rants. She would console me by rubbing against my legs until I picked her up and loved her. Somehow she knew she could change my mood. And she usually did.

For a diversion, my mater suggested that I sketch some fresco scenes for the walls of the new rooms they were planning to add to their farmhouse on the outskirts of Pompeii. One night when I couldn't sleep, I took my sketchpad and pen to the porch. The lamp I took with me remained unlit. Some inner force drove me, probably Ariadne. I drew all night by the light of the full moon. It seemed that Dionysus possessed me and his passion became my passion. The story I sketched was of a metamorphosis, based on the Ariadne and Dionysus ritual and brought to Rome eons ago by some long-forgotten Greek.

At daybreak, I reclined on a bench in the peristyle garden and wept as I watched the blue sky fill with clouds reflecting the pinks and blues of the rising sun. My heart was conflicted as I witnessed the start of another day without Titus, but also impassioned by the elation I felt from my inspired drawings. Exhausted, I collapsed on my bed, leaving my night's labors on the table.

CHAPTER XXIII

A SPIRAL BOWL

Aridela and Rufus found Rufilla's sketches as they took their breakfast on the porch.

"She is a talented artist," Rufus said as he perused Rufilla's work. "Why are the drawings of women?"

Aridela picked up the sketches again. "Hmm, I think this is about a women's ritual. It may have something to do with the Orphic ritual of Dionysus," she said. "But how does she know about this? The Senate banned those rituals over 100 years ago."

"What have you been teaching my daughter, woman?"

"Do not worry, I will take care of it," she replied.

Rufilla, when asked about the drawings, told her mother that she had drawn the ritual based on Ariadne's journey to the underworld, where she died, was reborn to a new life, and married the god Dionysus. She compared it with her dark passage to the underworld of sorrow and suffering. "It is what I am feeling right now, Mater," she said. "First I wrote about it, and then these drawings came to me last night. I was possessed. I had to get them all down on paper. And then, listen to this, Mater. I had a wonderful dream this morning. I saw a room where these figures were all painted—life-size. It was beautiful!"

Her mother related the story to her father. "The girl is remarkable," she said. "She has a depth to her that I did not realize."

The euphoria Rufilla felt that day quickly vanished, and she retreated to a bitter, somber mood. More time passed. It was evident that Rufilla's health was suffering. One evening, after her parents retired to their bed, Aridela said, "Rufus, I need to talk with you about Rufilla."

"Yes, I have been thinking about her, too," Rufus replied. "I think some time at the farmhouse might help. You know how she lights up every time we mention going there."

"I agree. She hasn't been out of the house since Titus' memorial service weeks ago," Aridela said. "She won't see her friends, not even Hostia. She has lost weight, too. I have made sure Marcia cooks her favorite foods. She rarely touches the sweet cakes with honey. The cat is her constant companion, and even the dog is depressed. Worst of all, her seizures are coming back. She has had three already this week.

"Oh, spending time in the country house will be like old times." Aridela continued. "I know she misses Hostia. It would be nice to ask her to come as a surprise. We will tell one another of our favorite stories, like the Eleusinian Mysteries story—Persephone and Demeter. She will realize how concerned I am about her if she can see herself as Persephone and me as Demeter. I think it will work. Just as Persephone had to return to the upper realm, so Rufilla must return to the realm of living her new life. She must."

BREAKTHROUGH

The sound of a cooing homing pigeon awoke Rufilla from a deep sleep. She cuddled with her down pillows, wrapped in her blankets and the coverlet she and her mother had made. Her face felt flushed as the morning sun came streaming through the slats of the large shuttered window. She shaded her eyes, recognizing that she was in her favorite place to sleep—the room where she could see anyone coming from town, and the other view was of the sea. She was at the country house. The first thing she saw was a trio of fragrant lilies, in full bloom and fresh from the farm garden, on her nightstand. She thought of the flowers she had thrown on Titus' funeral pyre. The letter, the fateful letter from her brother that was never out of her sight, lay beside the vase. She again ran her fingers over the unique coverlet. It was to have been a wedding gift from her mother, but now she stroked the threads of the elaborate brocade design to comfort the fragile feelings that lingered in her belly.

Her mouth opened, but only a dry, silent sound came forth from deep within her. Tears welled up in her eyes. The familiar pain of the black vortex, churned in the pit of her stomach, returning to fill her day with longing. She noticed that the feeling was not quite as strong this morning, and she missed that intensity. As she lay thinking about it, she realized that this pain was her last connection with Titus. She did not want to let go of it. To feel better seemed like a violation, a betrayal.

She was almost back to sleep when she heard her mother's footsteps coming down the tiled hallway. "Good morning, my sweet," Aridela said as she entered the room.

"Umm," she groaned.

Rufilla turned over in her bed, her back to her mother.

"Time to get up. Marcia has baked some delicious biscuits with honey, and there's fresh fruit to go with it.

"Look here, Rufilla. Melissa brought in some fresh water for you to wash your face."

"I am not dirty, and I am not hungry," Rufilla growled.

"I know, but it is time to be up and out of bed. It is a warm, sunny morning, and I would like you to take breakfast with me on the portico, and then we can go for a walk," Aridela said as she left the room.

She relented, muttering about disturbing a good night's sleep. But the walk sounded inviting, and the vortex in her stomach had turned to hunger pangs. She ate with gusto, hungry for the first time in weeks. "Let us take the path down to the place where the berries grow," Rufilla said. They walked down a familiar path on their property, past the waterfall with the pond below, and found blackberries blooming but no fruit yet. Close by were some rose bushes with buds ready to burst forth.

Aridela walked among the bushes and called to Rufilla. "Come see this spider web, Rufilla." She pointed to a web nestled between two branches. "It looks like a spiral bowl and a deep one at that. Do you remember when you were a little girl, the day we went to the park and saw that unusual spider web, and you said that it reminded you of a bowl? Well, that is how life is many times. We go around and around in circles, trying to find our way out like you are trying to do right now. Even though there seems to be no end, there are points along the way. You are at one of those points. See the two lines of the web as they cross each other? Think of it as a point in time and also a physical crossroad on your journey. It is important at this moment to reflect upon your new life. It will determine where you will go in the future. Do you understand?"

Rufilla nodded. "I think so." After a few minutes, "No, I do not understand."

"You will very soon, dear daughter."

The next morning as they were taking a light breakfast, Rufus joined them.

"Papa, what a surprise," Rufilla said.

"I decided to join you this morning. I have clients to see, but the main reason for my coming is so we could talk about your going to Athens."

"Athens?"

"Do you remember your mother telling you about her journey there when she was around your age? We think that this is the perfect moment for you to make a similar trip."

"I remember that the local priest said that when you were old enough, you should visit the Asclepian Sanctuary at Epidaurus," Aridela said. "It has a building, a sacred space for you to go and sleep, incubating your dreams, and then working with the priests to lessen the frequency of your seizures. You know the god Asclepius can work miracles."

Rufilla could only listen. Her mind was swirling.

"After that, you will go to Athens to visit your Greek aunt, Kallistê, and your uncle, Stephanos." Rufus continued. "I think a trip to Crete will be in order—to see the palace of your beloved Ariadne at Knossos." Rufilla gasped. "And, depending on the weather, there might even be a trip to another sanctuary. Aper will provide one of his ships and personally sail it."

Hearing Aper's name moved her to speak. "I see Bucia from time to time but not Aper. He is always gone."

"That is what Bucia says," Aridela said. "He is home now, but not for long."

"But now? When?" Rufilla said.

"You will have to leave soon," Rufus said. "The spring storms have passed and summer will be quickly upon us. I talked with Aper when he returned recently. He is willing to take you with him as he sails the western shores of Greece and all the way to Corinth."

Around the corner came Cil. "I will be going as far as Brundisium with you. We will have a great adventure traveling the Via Appia together."

"Melissa will be with you for the whole journey," Aridela added, "and Theo will be going for part of the trip."

"Soon, your pater and I will travel to Puteoli with you and Cil so that you can see Aper's ship before he sails," Aridela said. "Isn't this exciting?"

Rufilla's head was spinning. "You all knew?" Her eyes swept around the room and saw nodding heads and smiling faces. "I can't believe this is happening."

"Believe it, and enjoy this turning point in your web," Aridela said.

Rufilla loved and trusted her parents. Everything she thought she had understood suddenly took on a new significance. The trip would not have happened if Titus had lived. Her mind hungered for knowledge as her heart yearned for love and meaning to her life. She felt that answers to her many questions would come as she traveled these new roads of discovery.

"*Adjudicata*. It is settled," Aridela said, gazing lovingly at her daughter as they embraced.

That evening Rufilla noticed a group of women coming up the hill from town, carrying torches and singing and dancing. She recognized the music and the dance steps. They were the girls from her Artemis initiation five years earlier. Hostia was leading the group. "You do not think you could leave without a going-away party with some of your arktoi friends!" Hostia said. "It is almost time for the Festival of Diana, so we all decided to have a small celebration tonight with you so that you could join us before your adventure begins. And look who is here!"

The group parted, and in the middle stood Aricia. "You could not celebrate without me, could you?" She held a diadem of rosebuds to crown Rufilla. "We understand that this has been a difficult time, and we wish you a wonderful and healing adventure."

The girls tossed the diadems they were wearing into the air, shouting, "Safe journey! Many blessings!" One girl said, "Bring back a good-looking foreigner to marry."

"Do not count on that," Rufilla proclaimed. "Look at the 'chaste' moon rising," she said, pointing skyward. "She is in my blood. I will follow her wishes for as long as I can."

She blew a kiss to her mater and Melissa, and then turned to Aricia, who called out to the flute players, "Let us begin with the bear dance."

CHAPTER XXIV

HERCULANEUM AND PUTEOLI

Cil and Rufilla were beginning their ritual journeys. For Cil, it would be an outer journey, learning about ancient and current military medicine and tactics. For his sister, an outer and inner journey into ancient and intuitive wisdom.

In preparation, Rufilla reviewed the story of Demeter and Persephone, of Ariadne, Theseus and Dionysus, and several others, including the Psyche and Eros story. She began dreaming again. She shared them with her mother, writing down the parts that most reflected her outer life. With her mother's encouragement, she also sketched many of the dream figures. Exterior images also came to her quite often during this time, and they, too, were written down and illustrated. It was a growing time for her, giving her new focus and the will to look toward the future. The period of grief moved to one of renewal. She tackled, on a beginner's level, some of the Greek plays of Sophocles, Aristophanes, Euripides, and even an overview of Homer's *Odyssey*. This part she studied with her brother, Theo supervising of course, and thus gained her brother's insights as well as their teacher's. She, in turn, gave her perspectives about the plight and difficulties of Greek women. She felt Penelope was the most intriguing figure of all. Her parents were amazed at her comprehension.

One evening, in preparation for some light, after-dinner entertainment, she asked if she might recite from some of the works she had been studying. Her parents and brother were delighted. She chose Aristophanes.

"For you Mater—'By words the mind is winged' and 'High thoughts must have high language.' Your words to me have always helped me through difficult times."

"For you, Pater—'Under every stone lurks a politician!' We all know your fondness for politicians, if only for a good argument."

"For you, brother—'You are fool enough, it seems, to dare to war with me when for your faithful ally, you might win me easily.' The wars are over, Cil, just a few skirmishes left."

"For me—'Love is merely the name for the desire and pursuit of the whole.' I have a feeling that this is my life's lesson."

Melissa, Theo, and Marcia stood in the doorway of the dining room, listening with rapt attention to the voice of this young girl who had been silenced by Titus' death, and now was breathing her new life forward. Everyone cheered.

At bedtime, she told Melissa, "I feel as if I have come back from the dead. This does not mean that I love Titus any less, but I realize that I must go on with my life. He would want it, I know." A tear slipped down her cheek and onto her pillow as her nursemaid tucked her in. "Thank you for standing by me. I know I have been difficult, and I am sorry if I have hurt you."

"You had to go through this, and now you have come out the other side. It has been a terrible ordeal for one as young as you, and I am very proud and pleased to say that I am in your life for as long as you want me."

They hugged. Melissa put out the oil lamp on the bedside table and gently whispered, "Sweet dreams."

"And to you," Rufilla replied.

The next evening, Rufilla sat in the patio garden, writing in her journal.

> *I am sitting in the garden at our farm outside the walls of Pompeii, wrapped in my blanket and feeling warm as I watch the sunset. As I write, I ponder, what is it that I want from this New Year that starts this summer?*
> *Happiness*
> *Relief from this black hole in my heart*
> *Travel to new horizons—unusual sunrises—uncommon sunsets*

"How long will it be before we can leave?" Rufilla asked her parents, who had joined her.

"Well, there are supplies to gather and also making sure the coaches are ready for such a long trip. We sent and have now received several letters from the people you will be staying with overland. Your father wrote a letter to the priests in the Asclepian Sanctuary at Epidaurus. I sent a letter to Atia telling her of your upcoming adventure. I also wrote to Kallistê in Athens, letting her know that we need to inform the priests that you will be in attendance, starting with the Lesser Mysteries. We want you to be there as soon as possible so that you can settle in before the preparations for the Lesser and Greater Mysteries start. So it should not be too much longer. It is up to Aper. He will let us know when we visit him at Puteoli."

"Tell me again how we will go," Cil said, entering the garden.

"I want you to go the fastest way," Rufus said. "So you and Rufilla will take the road to Nuceria, then head north on the Via Popilia to Nola, connecting with the Via Appia at Beneventum, over the Apennine Mountains, ending on the eastern coast at the harbor of Brundisium." Rufus drew a rough map, as he had traveled the route many times. "There you, Rufilla, will meet Aper and sail to the west coast of Greece—then to Corinth. Your brother Cil—"

Cil joined in. "My trip is short. I will travel by a different ship from Brundisium to Apollonia to meet up with Octavius and our friends. However, I hear that Octavius may be delayed a few months, as Caesar wants him to stay with him for a while longer."

"You, daughter, will be able to experience the port towns and what they have to offer—eating unusual foods, visiting temples and forums, or as the Greeks call them, *agoras*."

"But most of all, it will be the people you meet that will intrigue you," Aridela added. "As you travel east, you will hear many distinctive Greek dialects and be able to practice speaking the language. Theo and Melissa will be an invaluable help to you."

"From Corinth, you will travel by land to Epidaurus, back to the east coast of the isthmus and then on to Athens."

"How long will it take?" Rufilla asked.

"Several weeks," her mother answered.

"It sounds like a long time," Rufilla said.

"Yes, I know you are eager. We are eager for you. It will be the experience of a lifetime."

"You keep saying that—what do you mean? Tell me about your time at Eleusis."

"Well, I was just a little older than you," Aridela said. "Your grandmother took me and participated with me in the beginning ritual. Then I was on my own."

"How long can I stay?"

"At least until the spring," her mother replied. "There are many options. You can study in between rituals and stay for the full year if you want."

"A whole year—without seeing you or the rest of my family! No, no, I cannot do that!"

"As you wish," Aridela replied with a wistful smile.

"What is it? What do you know that I do not? Tell me, Mater."

"It is just that as much as you love to read and learn, you might want to stay longer than you think. As I said, this experience will not come again to you. Think about it."

Aridela and Rufus decided to go with their daughter and son to Herculaneum and Puteoli. It would be a sweet interlude before the long trip that would take their children far from home. Cil would ride a horse most of the time, getting used to the leather-covered wooden saddle. Rufus rode his favorite steed. Rufilla and Aridela followed in a carriage.

The first stop was only a few miles north at a villa by the sea, just outside the town of Herculaneum. Atia had sent a letter of introduction to the owner of the villa, Lucius Calpurnius Piso, who was the father-in-law of her uncle, Julius Caesar. He welcomed them into the atrium and proudly gave the family a tour of his multi-story villa. Each level of the villa was terraced to provide a spectacular view of the sea. Opening out beyond the main floor was an unusually long, porticoed garden that ran parallel to the shore. In the center of the garden was a long rectangular pool lined on either side with plants and trees, interspersed with life-size bronze statues of famous men of Greek and Roman history. At the same time, busts of philosophers decorated the interior of his home. The Istacidii family was overwhelmed by the opulence. Rufus found a moment alone with Piso and spoke to him. "Your *Xenia*, your hospitality, has deeply moved our family." Rufus began. "To take the time to host us is—a man of your stature—why?"

Piso lowered his head and chuckled. "Well, first of all, we both know of Atia's persuasive nature."

It was Rufus' turn to look amused. "Yes, she does have a way of getting what she wants—especially when it comes to her son," Rufus answered.

"Then you understand. Atia heard how upset Octavius was because of the shipwreck and the loss of Rufilla's betrothed. Atia wrote that you have arranged for your son to join Octavius in Apollonia and that you are sending your daughter to Athens to recover from her loss. You are a generous and kind man. I am an old man with a young wife who is caught up in Roman society, and wants no part of living in the 'wilderness,' as she calls this place. She uses the birth of our son to stay in Rome. And so, I enjoy my time alone with my books of philosophy and sharing this—this overindulgence of wealth, as my wife calls it—with someone of *your* stature. You understand."

"I do, thank you," was all Rufus could say.

"I hope you and your family will join me for dinner, and please, call me Lucius," Piso said.

"We would be delighted—Lucius."

A servant showed Rufus to the lavish suite of rooms where he and his family would stay for the next several days. He told them of his conversation with Lucius and emphasized the genuine nature of this very wealthy and influential man. This revelation put everyone, especially Aridela, at ease.

"You will want to hear about our adventures in this enormous house while you and Lucius were walking the gardens," Aridela said. "A man by the name of Philodemus showed us an amazing collection of scrolls—books of philosophy—mostly by Epicurus."

Cil spoke up. "There are several rooms with bookshelves and cabinets that line the walls. Hundreds and hundreds of scrolls!"

"And Philodemus has a very distinctive Greek accent," Rufilla said. "He came from Greece and settled in Napoli. So he learned to speak Latin, but he has a Greek accent. He told me I had a discerning ear for one so young."

Cil rolled his eyes and continued. "He studied in the Epicurean school at Athens and even wrote poetry so he must treasure the written word," he said.

The conversation that evening began with Lucius. "I understand my friend Philodemus showed you the many books I have collected over the years, some that he brought from Athens, some that he has copied while living here. Greek philosophy is a personal interest of mine, but I am enjoying this philosopher's appreciation of the works of Epicurus. He claims he is not so much a philosopher as an interpreter of the Epicurean way of life in today's Roman world. The garden that I have built here is my idea of what the gardens were like where Epicurus and his followers met outside Athens. There they walked and talked as part of what we Romans call *otium*. Leisure time spent walking while discussing Greek and Roman history and philosophy. Are you familiar with that word, Rufilla?"

"Otium. Yes, I am now. Thank you."

After dinner, Lucius brought out some old scrolls. "Cil, you probably know that Octavius is interested in Stoicism. I think that you might be interested in a Stoic philosopher named Chrysippus. Have you ever heard of the theory of the eternal return?"

Cil's eyes darted back and forth between Lucius and Rufilla. "Tell us more!"

"With this theory, time is seen as cyclical rather than linear. At certain times, the world is destroyed and recreated anew." Rufilla and Cil looked puzzled. "Let me put it another way. I must admit, I do not abide by all the concepts of Stoicism, but this theory seems to resonate with me. I believe that it is virtuous to maintain one's will to be in accord with nature. Nature's way. There is a stoic calm that one encounters in a vineyard, an olive grove, or a forest of trees. One might say we take shelter in the arms of the Great Earth Mother. From there, one develops a practice of living in the present moment, reflecting on what might be a problem for that day, maybe seeing that problem as a personal catastrophe, then letting possible solutions evolve in one's mind, thus creating a new way of being in the world. When that puzzle is solved, one often spirals around at a later time, facing a similar problem at a somewhat deeper level—a finite problem occurring over and over again. This is how we learn our lessons in life."

This philosophical theory struck a deep chord within Rufilla's psyche. She knew in her gut that it was right as she had been struggling with coming to terms with Titus' death. It felt as if she had been practicing this idea but hadn't given it a name. "It feels like it is a spiral way of thinking, as in a spider's web," she said, looking at her mother.

"I think you have taught her well," Lucius said, smiling at Aridela.

Cil entered the conversation. "Pater taught us that the four cardinal virtues of the Stoic philosophy are wisdom, courage, justice, and temperance."

"Temperance, or in other words, self-discipline," Rufilla said.

"Were you told of what these virtues consisted?" Aridela asked.

"Not exactly, but—"

"Well, let me tell you about *Roman* stoicism," said Aridela.

Rufus sat back on his cushions, eager to hear his wife's discourse.

"Roman virtues," Aridela said, "include Auctoritas, Comitas, Clementia, Dignitas, Firmitas, Frugalitas, Gravitas, Honestas, Humanitas, Industria, Pietas, Prudentia, Salubritas, Severitas, and Veritas." The words rolled off her tongue as if she had memorized them yesterday. She went into depth explaining several of them. "*Auctoritas*—a spiritual authority but more. It includes *Industria*: hard work and respect concerning devotion to others. For both of you, this includes your vocation and your family. *Firmitas* means tenacity, the ability to stick to one's purpose, once one has found it. *Dignitas*—self-worth—involves knowing not only who you are but also who you are to become. To treat and be treated with respect."

Now her children saw her in a new light. Although they had always enjoyed her quick wit and storytelling, they were beginning to appreciate their mother's depth. She had a sharp mind, and she could help them develop theirs.

"One of the qualities of the Stoics that I appreciate is the clemency toward slaves. This is in accordance with the way we treat our slaves and freedmen in our household. Not every paterfamilias feels that way," she said, nodding to Rufus, "but your pater and I do, and we believe you should be aware and respectful of these men and women who serve you and care for you.

"Know that when you go on your separate journeys, you, Cil, will learn more about the philosophy of balance and moderation when you care for the sick and injured and when you attend the school at Apollonia. You, my dear Rufilla, will learn from the priestesses and priests at Epidaurus, but also at the feet of your Aunt Kallistê. She is a learned woman and will share with you ways of nurturing your soul and giving back to the world. Both of you will learn about social ethics and practice as they relate to your friendships, your marriage, parenting your children, and living in your community."

"Thank you, dear teacher," Cil and Rufilla said in unison. It was a habit they had been taught to thank their teachers at the end of a class.

"We mean dear Mater," Cil corrected, and the two smiled at each other as their mother hugged them both, understanding the compliment they had given her.

Aper arranged to be at the docks when the family arrived at Puteoli, showing them around the ship Rufilla would travel in. "This will be your new home for several weeks, Rufilla. What do you think?" Aper said as they stood beside the vessel.

"It is so tall! And big!" she said.

"Yes, the square mast takes up a lot of room when it is unfurled. You will see that as we get underway."

"The wood is beautiful. How long is the ship?"

"Do you remember the length of the garden you visited in Herculaneum? Well, I have been told that this ship would just fit inside that garden."

"I am certainly impressed. The size alone should keep us safe." As they were helped aboard, Rufilla asked, "Where will I sleep?" Aridela and Aper glanced at each other.

"Come with me and let us get an overall view of the ship," Aper said. Rufilla followed Aper up a ladder. "This is the front of the ship. We call it the bow." He took her into the captain's quarters. "From here, I can see everything I need to see to steer us safely into a harbor and also return us to the sea. And here in the corner is my little cot, rolled up during the day and then unrolled at night—when we are at anchor."

"Not much room," Rufilla noticed.

"No question. Everything and everyone has a place and a space to be. Ships are compact spaces.

Rufilla looked out the window. "What's that carving in the front?" Rufilla asked.

"If you will notice the ships moored next to us, each has a carving on the bow. This ship has a carving of Asclepius. My pater is partial to that particular god. Years ago, he made the trip to Epidaurus, asking for a healing from the god. He was blessed, and from then on, each ship he built has a figurehead of Asclepius carved on the front."

Rufilla was quiet, and when she spoke, her voice had deepened. "Asclepius is one of my favorite gods, too. Seeing this makes me feel very safe." Rufilla left the cabin and leaned forward over the bow so she could feel the smooth texture of the carving and appreciate the artistry.

"Let me show you the rest of the ship." Aper helped Rufilla down the ladder and walked her to the back of the ship, past the large sail rolled up and tethered to the mast amidships. She saw the hole in the middle of the vessel with a ladder going down. "We call that the hold," Aper told her. "The men go below to row when necessary. You will see how that works when we get underway. It is also where we store the amphorae of wine and olive oil that we sell at distant ports. Then at those same ports, we buy exotic items like perfume and spices to bring home for you and your mater. Yesterday, we received a delivery of wine and olive oil from your pater's farm."

Next, they made their way to the stern, climbed another ladder to a platform, and looked forward. "Do you see the linen sailcloth strung just above the deck below us? We will tether it to the front of this platform and attach the other ends to either side of the railings near the stern of the ship. It will form a sort of shelter to give you some privacy, as well as protection from the hot sun or the rain. You and Melissa will sleep under there. And do not worry. You will never be left unguarded."

"I do not see much room for my trunks," Rufilla mused.

"We can store most of your things down in the hold, and maybe you can choose one trunk to keep up here on deck—to hold your necessities."

The mother and daughter looked at each other. "We will be happy to adhere to your rules," Aridela said. "Rufilla, this will be a good exercise in decision making—what are essentials and what are luxuries?" She turned to Aper. "We will resolve it." Aridela changed the subject. "So, when do you sail?"

"We are almost ready. The trip around the southern part of the peninsula and up to Brundisium, where we will meet you, could take up to fourteen days, depending on the weather, wind, and the number of ports where we stop. By the time we get to Brundisium, we will have found any problems with the ship that need repair. At that port, supplies are in abundance for the next part of the voyage, and besides, it is at the end of the Via Appia, where you will meet up with us. I look forward to hearing about your trip over the Queen of the Long Roads and welcoming you to the next part of your journey."

As they prepared to leave the docks to return home, Rufus said, "Thank you for agreeing to do this, Aper. Aridela and I are truly grateful to know that Rufilla will be in such competent hands."

"You are most welcome," Aper said. "It will be a pleasure to see the trip through fresh eyes. I am convinced that she will be a delight. We will ensure her safety and give her the experience of a lifetime."

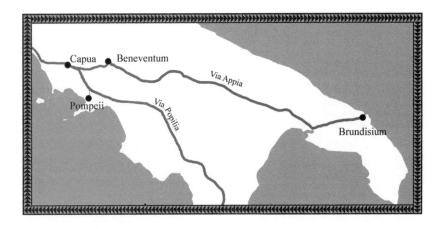

Pompeii to Capua and Brundisium—Appian Way

CHAPTER XXV

CATHARSIS

By the time the family returned from Puteoli, Theo and Melissa had organized everything. Within a few days, Rufilla, Cil, Melissa, and Theo were on the road. The family made their bittersweet goodbyes, and then the foursome, Cil and Theo on horseback, Rufilla and Melissa in the carriage, were off on their adventure, with the Via Appia taking them to the east coast of Italy to the harbor at Brundisium.

Aper had experienced smooth sailing around the boot of Italy and was already in the harbor when they arrived. Friends of Rufus and Aridela hosted the group at their villa nearby.

Soon after their arrival, Cil went to meet the captain and crew of the ship that would ferry him to Apollonia. In contrast, Rufilla went down to the harbor with Melissa and Theo to sit on the pier where the Melissaeus' ship was anchored. Men were busy carrying supplies and cargo on and off the vessels. Rufilla watched them for a long time. Their young, agile bodies made her think of Titus. She still missed him so much. After a while, Melissa decided to walk back to the villa to help prepare for the noon meal. She did not leave Rufilla alone since Theo was there. As they finished their tasks, most of the men went for their midday meal.

One sailor stayed behind as Aper had told him, "Check the hull under the water for any fish that might be trying to take a free ride." He wasn't sure what that meant, but he was loyal to his captain and a good swimmer who was up to the task.

Theo and Rufilla sat on the pier, watching the man dive under the ship, making his way from stern to bow, coming up at intervals for air. His last dive was nearest the bow of the ship. He did not surface for a long time. Theo and Rufilla exchanged glances. All of a sudden, it seemed that two fish jumped from the water, but no, the diver had come up with a fish in each hand.

"Eureka! Look what I found—not one but two suckerfish. My captain was correct. He said that he had felt the boat slowing down and that the rowers had to work harder to get the ship into port."

The fish were long and thin, about the length of the diver's forearm, silver in color, and with strange-looking heads. "What are on the fishes' heads?" Rufilla asked.

"They are a very unusual fish," Theo said. "I have never seen a fish attached to a boat. I was told that these fish can attach themselves to much larger fish in deep waters and survive, but they can also attach themselves to ships as we have seen here."

The diver had climbed onto the pier with the fish. They were flailing about, and Rufilla's first instinct was to tell the sailor to throw them back into the water.

"No, we will not be doing that," Theo said. "We must show them to Aper as his instincts were right in thinking to look for such a fish. I thought that the stories of such a fish were made up, but now I see that it is all true."

Aper reappeared. "What did you catch?"

The diver spoke excitedly about what he had found.

"Let us take a look," Aper said, standing over the curious looking catch. "If I remember correctly, this is called a remora fish, Echeneis remora or suckerfish. Look at the amazing sucker on its head."

"It looks like someone stepped on their heads with their sandals!" Rufilla said.

Indeed, the sucker was scored as if a shoe had flattened the head. That was where it attached itself to the ship.

"Let us take them up to the market and show them to the fish seller," said Aper. "I wonder if he has ever seen a fish like this."

The three men started up the hill, but Theo realized that Rufilla was still sitting on the pier.

"Come, girl!" he shouted.

"I will stay right here, I promise," she shouted back.

Theo paused for a second and then turned and followed the two men up the hill.

One summer, Theo had taught her to swim after Cil and Titus chased her into the water. She had loved the water ever since and had no fear.

Now, she looked down and slipped into the water, swimming to the bow of their ship. She said a short prayer to Asclepius and dove down, her eyes open in the clear waters, her hands following the edge of the keel, where the heavy wooden planks of the ship come together as one. She noticed that the boat below the waterline had a lead hull. She came up for air and dove again, propelling herself as best she could, trying to reach the place where the keel was deepest in the water, where the ship would hit first if it were grounded. She knew this was at the spot where Titus' ship would have rammed into the rocks. She wanted to scream. As she broke the surface of the waters, a guttural sound welled up from a dark place within as hot tears streamed down her cheeks, and her whole body convulsed. She willed herself to be calm as she heard Theo saying, "Rufilla, are you all right?"

"Yes, I just wanted to dive, to feel—" she said, catching her breath.

"I will sit here on the pier until you are ready to come out. Please be careful." He had taught her and her brother to swim years ago, so he trusted that she would be safe.

Minutes passed as she again ranted, at one point submerging even her head—shouting into the sea her muffled roar.

She made another dive, pulling her body along the cold metal plate that covered the bottom of the ship. She kept her eyes closed until she felt again that bittersweet spot where metal would hit rock. She opened her eyes. Before her was an image of a man swimming toward her, and as he came nearer, she saw that he was struggling to get out of his shirt. It was Titus! She opened her mouth to shout, taking in the seawater. And all went black.

Someone was pounding on her chest, and then she was vomiting and coughing. "She is breathing!" Theo shouted. Rufilla opened her eyes to see a worried Theo looking down on her. "Child!" Theo said. "You frightened me. What were you doing under there?" All she could do was cough up more water.

One of the sailors from another ship had heard the commotion. Theo had sent him for help. Soon Aper appeared with four slaves carrying a stretcher, and behind them ran Melissa. They quickly put her on the litter and carried her back to the villa. Melissa never let go of her hand, running beside her all the way.

Rufilla was taken directly to the small bath area in the villa. There, she rested in the tepid waters from the morning baths. The water felt hot to her, and her shivering ceased.

After she dressed, she joined her hosts in the garden for lunch.

Their Greek hosts were concerned and asked, "What happened?"

"I wanted to dive under the ship to see how it might have been for Titus in his last moments," Rufilla replied. "But what happened was beyond my dreams. Or I might say it felt like a continuation of the dream I had before he left."

She proceeded to tell them about the dream she had had of a man struggling under a ship in a white nightshirt—not sure who it was at the time, maybe Titus, maybe her brother.

"This time, there was no question. I saw the man from the dream, but it did not feel like a dream. This time he was closer, and I could see that it *was* Titus! The look on his face filled me with terror. A wave sent the boat and Titus crashing into a huge rock. I saw his body falling to the bottom of the sea. I screamed in horror, and then everything turned black. When I 'awoke,' I was in his arms. He was carrying me to the surface. As he let me free to float to the top, he said, 'You have much to do in your life, Rufilla. I will love you and watch over you forever.' Then he simply disappeared. The blackness enveloped me again, and the next thing I remember was trying to get my breath and looking into Theo's face."

"Remarkable," the Greek host said.

"It was real," Rufilla said. "There is no doubt in my mind that I witnessed how Titus died. You must believe me." Now she was getting upset because she remembered how other men, even Titus, had doubted her past words.

"Yes, my dear, we believe you, but now you must rest. You have had a powerful and disturbing experience, and you must be exhausted," the Greek host said.

Rufilla was softly crying now, and Melissa and Theo took her to her room.

"You do believe me," she said, looking back and forth for approval.

"Of course, we believe you," Theo assured her.

Their hosts lived in a lovely home overlooking the harbor of Brundisium. Rufus and Aper had met the husband years ago while conducting business, and he and his wife always looked forward to hosting Aper and especially to meeting Rufus' children.

Theo and Melissa joined their hosts after seeing Rufilla safely to bed. "We have been very concerned about Rufilla since Titus was drowned,"

Theo said. "She was so depressed. Her parents and we hoped that this would be an experience that would bring her back into life. Could it have been an underwater seizure?"

The Greek man spoke up. "They were to become engaged soon, were they not?

"Yes," Theo replied.

"It has been said," continued the Greek man, "that when someone dies young without using his normal life energy, he can become a ghost."

Melissa gasped. "You may be right, but I would have to say he is a good ghost. If it is the case that she was drawn to him in death, he certainly let it be known that she was to live her life fully."

"A good ghost indeed." Theo smiled.

"What is this about good ghosts," Rufilla asked as she entered the room.

"I was about to say," Theo replied, "that sometimes one has to go into the darkness to realize the pattern of one's destiny. I think that is what happened to you today, Rufilla."

"What a profound thought, Theo," said the Greek host. "I would remember that for your future, young woman. It was a life-changing experience that you should never forget."

"Yes, my pater would say I went through an Aristotelian catharsis," Rufilla said, "purging all my pity and fear." She turned to Melissa. "Please do not worry about me. I am fine. In fact, I am famished!"

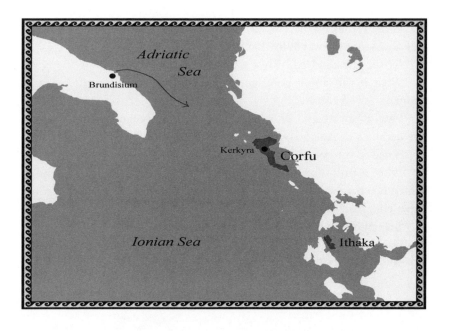

Brundisium to Ithaka

CHAPTER XXVI

CABOTAGE

The next day the winds blew in from the northwest. The captain and crew had made the sacrifice to the gods, and Rufilla, Theo, and Melissa joined in with their prayers. Now that they had loaded the ship, all were eager for the journey to begin. It was mid-morning and the wind was up. The three passengers finished arranging their belongings in their new accommodations. Even the pot had its place. There was one for each woman, in anticipation of the dreaded seasickness. Theo was a seasoned traveler, having worked in the shipyards in Puteoli when he was young and even had a chance to sail to some of the ports on the west coast.

Aper had invited the two women into his cramped captain's quarters in the bow of the ship. Theo stood at the door as there wasn't room for him to enter. "Let us see how quickly you can get your sense of balance," Aper said. He had retrieved his box of first aid items, including seasickness potions, from the lower deck. "I brewed some specially blended spices that will help you get a good start on the voyage." He asked his first mate to pass the tray to him with the brew and two silver cups. "May I pour this for you?" he said.

"Thank you, Aper," Rufilla said.

"I added mint to the brew to make it more palatable." Then Aper spoke in a formal tone. "As captain of this ship, the Asclepius, I, Gnaeus Melissaei Aper, welcome you as my passengers and want you to know that I will do whatever I can to make your trip a pleasant one. This brew will hopefully keep you from experiencing any ill effects from the waves we encounter. When you have finished, I invite you to go down to the main deck and watch as we sail away from the port."

It was a strong brew, but the women managed to drink it down.

"I hope I do not have to drink this every day," Rufilla said.

"I hope we will not need to," Melissa said.

Out in the fresh air, the women ran to the ship's railing. Rufilla watched the movement of the oars as they slipped into and out of the water in unison, the unseen arms and bodies of the crew, creating the motion below. The only sounds were of the oars cutting through the water, a man's voice, and the tap of a drum keeping time for the men in the galley below. Then, when Aper felt the wind was strong enough, the men came topside to set the sail as he shouted orders to the crew master, who in turn, shouted to his men. As the crew unfurled the sail from the mast, it caught the wind, and they quickly sailed out of the harbor. Rufilla turned to face the port.

"Look, Rufilla, you can see the breadth of the harbor now," Aper said.

She had closed her eyes to appreciate the wind on her face. Opening her eyes, she exclaimed, "Oh, what a sight." Like the Asclepius, some ships took advantage of the wind and were well out into the harbor, some were trailing behind them, while the crews from other boats were scurrying on the decks, preparing to leave their moorings.

"Look Rufilla," Aper said. "There is a military ship leaving as well."

"I wonder if Cil is on board," Rufilla said, missing her brother already. It had been an emotional parting with promises of letters between the two. But taking advantage of the wind on this bright, sunny morning was a good omen, Rufilla thought as she tried to raise her spirits. Melissa and Theo stood by her side as they widened their stance on the deck, arms around each other, getting their balance in the morning sun.

As they reached the breakwaters, the waves increased just a little. Still, the women remained topside until they docked for the night. They put into port at the island of Corcyra, Aper, finding a small sheltered inlet to spend the night. The women ate lightly for dinner, at Aper's suggestion, no one mentioning the word *seasickness*. Since it was a beautiful clear evening, crew and passengers slept on the main deck; the women were sequestered in the stern of the ship, separating them from the crew. Rufilla asked that the tarp that served as a roof be left folded up so that they could enjoy the array of stars on this, their first night at sea.

The next morning as they cleared the inlet, the seas picked up, and Rufilla and Melissa stayed in their 'quarters.' Theo tended to the women and coaxed the brew of herbs and spices down them, only to have it come up again and again. He left the tarp rolled up so that Rufilla and Melissa might benefit from the fresh air. However, the pitching of the boat did not cease.

Sailing down the Adriatic Sea, this merchant ship performed its tasks of coastal cabotage—putting into port, unloading the cargo destined for that harbor town, then loading more goods to deliver to the next port. Corcyra was a large island, with many harbors to visit. When they could stay closer to shore, it made for smoother sailing. Aper was careful to be on the lookout for any changes near the coast. Many times, with his critical surveillance, the crew could row to the next anchorage. This slower pace did much to alleviate the motion sickness as the women adjusted to the sea, their morning brew now a ritual.

"And now, the real adventure begins," Aper said. Rufilla and Aper were standing together in the captain's cabin as it sailed out of yet another harbor one morning.

"Does not the beauty of the wind in the sail thrill your soul?" Aper asked.

"You are a poet." Rufilla smiled, looking up at him.

"No, just in love with the sea. There is nothing quite like it. You may come to feel that way about it someday."

Rufilla pondered. Curious what makes a man happy, she thought. Her father loved walking in his vineyards, her brother enjoyed the companionship of military men, and this man loved the travel and adventure of the sea.

"What do I love?" she said, half out loud.

"What?" Aper asked.

"Oh nothing, just musing about the different interests of men—and women."

"It is not about an interest—it is about passion. That is what one feels when one is finding his way in the world. Do not worry, Rufilla. Your father will find a match for you. You will have children and that will fulfill you."

She stared straight ahead, thinking of Titus, the love of her life, lost to a similar sea. She burst into tears and ran to the back of the ship.

Aper started after her, saying, "I am sorry," but Melissa, who had been watching them, stopped him.

"She is still grieving the loss of Titus," she said. "You will just have to get used to her outbursts. It will take time. The whole purpose of the trip is to give her time to experience an initiation back into life."

"I am sorry if I offended her," Aper said. "I would not hurt her for anything—"

"It is not your fault. She will feel better in a while." Melissa patted his shoulder as she left to comfort Rufilla.

As the days progressed, Rufilla was delighted to see many sights and hear different languages or, at the very least, local accents of the same language—Greek. The odors coming from other ships were sometimes foul, but often as they made their way into the port towns, they were replaced with the delightful, heady scent of exotic foods served with spices she had only heard about from her mother and Marcia. In almost every port, there was a basilica used as a court of justice and as an assembly hall. Then there was the agora—a market with booths filled with fruits and vegetables from the surrounding farms, fresh fish, other meats and delicacies, and merchandise for sale. Often there were baths and a temple. She visited as many baths, temples, and markets as possible. A bath after being at sea was always a pleasure. Since she would be returning this way, she was encouraged not to buy remembrances this time around, but only gifts for Aper's friends, with whom they often stayed overnight. Aper guided her purchases as he showed her how to bargain for the best deal. She also bought something appropriate to dedicate at every temple she could, making her offerings to whatever gods or goddesses were honored at each. Poseidon and Asclepius were often the male gods. She particularly liked it when there was a temple to Diana or Venus. No, they are Artemis and Aphrodite, Rufilla corrected herself. These were Greek islands, and so she must refer to the deities by their Greek names.

At every stop, there were chances to have a meal or two on land. That was always a treat, although some ports were not as well suited for young women as others. Because this was a trip he had made many times, Aper steered Rufilla to places appropriate for her station. If none were available, Aper was delighted to have sustenance brought back to the boat, but Rufilla was headstrong about seeing everything and everyone. Sometimes she used another approach. "Please, Aper, I want to see it all, with your kind indulgence," she would say with a slight bow and a coy smile.

Aper would smile in return. He and Theo would roll their eyes at each other, say a few words in Greek, and then Aper would say, "Give me a little time and I will arrange something."

And he always did. She enjoyed not only eating different foods but becoming acquainted with the tavern owners and their families. She especially enjoyed any musical entertainment and was allowed on occasion to join in the dance. She and her mother had practiced some steps that Aridela remembered, but this was different. It was usually Greek men who performed, but now and then women joined them, and that was when, toward the end of their performance, they would often encourage the audience to join them. She found that she loved Greek dancing. Rufilla was even allowed to drink small amounts of wine, always watered down as befit her Roman status.

"Rufilla will want to join the Terpsichore group when she arrives in Athens. You will have to watch her!" Theo said, winking at Melissa.

Many establishments offered not only food but also the services of the women who worked there. Such taverns had backrooms or rooms upstairs to accommodate that lucrative business. This practice was common in Pompeii as well, being a port town, but Rufilla had not been allowed to witness any of this. Many of the women were slaves, forced to accommodate their masters and the sailors who frequented these ports. At one particular island's port of call, Aper and his passengers were preparing to head into town. He noticed that a group of shackled and scantily dressed slaves, women and men, were being unloaded from a ship adjacent to theirs. "Let us go!" he shouted to Theo as they whisked the women down the gangplank and headed quickly toward the town. Aper did not want Rufilla to see what would happen next.

The slaves were paraded from the ship and herded onto a wooden platform near the docks, where slave sellers hawked their wares. Whistles were sounded, which drew a crowd of prospective buyers as well as voyeurs.

One particular woman, strong and willful, had been singled out from the rest.

"Here we have quite a specimen," the slave seller smirked, "strong and voluptuous, ready to serve all your many and varied needs." With that, she spat in his face.

"Has a strong spirit as well," he shouted to the crowd as he lashed at her with his whip. "You see, she even fulfills your basest of needs if whippings are your preference."

The woman had been driven to the ground by the blows from the whip. She lay silent and unmoving.

"Seems like she is easily tamed," the slave seller said. "Who will start the bidding? Stand up, woman. Let them see all your attributes."

When she stood, the men chuckled as blood trickled down her chin and onto her breast. One man came up onto the platform and forced her mouth open with a metal probe. "Seems she is well fed," he said. "She still has most of her teeth. I will start the bidding."

CHAPTER XXVII

ITHAKA'S REVELATIONS

One afternoon while sailing around some islands, Rufilla spotted a secluded beach tucked between two steep hills.

"Oh please, Aper, could we stop for a swim? The water is such a beautiful blue, and it looks so inviting," Rufilla pleaded.

Aper had come this way to give them all a special treat.

"I suppose so," he said, winking at Theo. "It just so happens that the cove you see is one of my favorite beaches." He had already given the order to drop anchor. The crew lowered the small dinghy with Theo, Melissa, Aper, and Rufilla aboard, and they made their way to the beach.

"Oh, this is one of the most beautiful beaches I have ever seen," Rufilla said, strolling the white sandy beach in her bare feet.

"Yes, I think so too. Do you know what island this is?" Aper asked. "I will give you a hint. It is a famous island where a long-suffering woman waited for her husband's return."

"Ithaka!" Rufilla shouted. "Clever Penelope surrounded by all those annoying, obnoxious suitors."

They made their way to the northwest side of the beach. Here there was shade from the cliffs towering above them. They protected them from the strong west winds. She was so happy to feel the tide wash over her as she frolicked in the surf.

"Melissa and I have decided to take a walk," Theo said to Aper.

"There is a beautiful rock formation that looks like a cave a short walk down the beach," Aper said, smiling at the two of them. "I will stay with Rufilla." Seeing the cave would only further remind him of his wife—how he missed being with her. He recalled that they made love in that cave just a few years ago. He had wanted her to join him this time, especially since Rufilla would be on board. But her excuses seemed to close the subject.

"Play with me in the water, Aper," Rufilla said, interrupting his reverie.

They both stripped down to their underclothes and splashed their way through the surf.

"Here, I brought a ball. If we stay in the shallow waters, we will be able to retrieve it," Aper said.

They played for a while in the surf, and when they tired of playing catch, Aper went back to the beach to sit and watch as Rufilla frolicked. Dancing with and against the minimal tide, she sang a lovely tune that she had learned from her flute lessons. She was flirting with him, Aper thought. How much she looked like a young nymph of Venus. When his thoughts strayed to admiring her beautiful young body, he had to rein himself in. "Not to be," he thought to himself. "Not to be."

He looked forward to the time in Patra, thinking maybe a letter from Bucia would catch up with him there. He certainly intended to write to her.

When Rufilla came out of the water, she sat down beside him. "What are you writing?" she asked.

"A note to my friends at our next destination."

"But how will you—"

"You see the other ship anchored close to ours? That belongs to a friend of mine. I will give him the message to take on to Patra. Meanwhile, after the wind dries us, we will get dressed and head into town."

As they strolled down the beach toward the town, Aper and Rufilla talked a little about Xenia.

"Why do not you tell me what you know about Xenia," Aper said.

"Well, I know that it is all about hospitality—how the hosts welcome a guest into their home."

"A guest from a foreign country," Aper said.

"Yes, someone who is far from home is welcomed and offered food, drink, and a bath—whatever the guest wants."

"Then what are the visitor's obligations?"

"The guests must show respect to the hosts and not cause trouble or be a burden. Just as I did when we stayed with my parents' friends or yours on land—I brought a gift to thank them for their hospitality," Rufilla said. "Staying with friends is much safer, too."

"And now that we are in Greece, there is one more step. The hosts will give the guests a parting gift when they leave, showing respect," Aper said. "Now, tell me about Zeus Xenios, Rufilla."

"He is the god of travelers. One never knows when a god will be disguised, just to test a host."

"Can you give me an example of who did not honor Xenia? How about in Homer's *Iliad* and the *Odyssey*?"

"Who could forget Paris? The guest who steals the host's wife and starts the Trojan War! Then there are countless examples in the *Odyssey*. The disregard of Xenia that upsets me the most is those bothersome men who called themselves suitors for Penelope's hand. They took extreme advantage of the situation. Did they have nothing better to do than lie around all day playing dice, eating her food, drinking her wine, and pestering poor Penelope to marry one of them? Suitors, indeed!"

Aper laughed. "I can see you learned your legends well. How about a nasty host?"

"Polyphemus, of course, that one-eyed monster who ate some of Odysseus' men. That certainly would not constitute a gracious host!"

"I give up. You know your history."

Just then, Melissa and Theo emerged from the cove.

As the four entered the tavern in the town, Aper met up with the captain of the ship anchored next to them, a long-standing friend. The captain was just leaving, so Aper had a brief conversation, asking him to deliver his message.

When Aper joined them at the table, Rufilla asked him about the captain.

"He is indeed headed for Patras, and we shall be following soon if the god Zephyr is generous with his wind. The captain and I have a mutual friend that you will be meeting at Patras. That is all I will tell you." Aper winked.

They spent the evening eating, drinking, and telling their favorite stories and versions of the travels of Odysseus. Rufilla was even allowed to have a glass of watered-down wine.

"I thought I saw Circe, the nymph, in the water today," Aper said, teasing Rufilla.

Rufilla countered. "Be careful that you do not take a drink from her. She might turn you into a baby swine and take you to Eleusis to be sacrificed!"

As they made their way back to the ship, Aper suggested that they spend the night on the beach. He had ordered the crew to set up some cushions and bedding.

"Oh yes," Rufilla said, "that would be a wonderful way to end the day."

The moon was rising over the cliffs above them.

Aper stopped in his tracks. "Look up! Do you see beyond the cliffs? It's not often you can see it, but because we are standing in the right place, and the moon is shining on it so brightly—"

"What? What are you looking at?" Rufilla said.

Aper took Rufilla by the shoulders and pointed at what looked like the remains of a structure beyond the cliffs. "The story is told by the people in the town that those are the ruins of the palace—the palace of Odysseus and Penelope!"

Both couples came to a standstill as they took in the scene high above them. No words were uttered at this remarkable sight. Theo and Melissa sat down in the sand, then laid back to watch the moon rise over the palace. Aper and Rufilla stood silent for a long time, his hands on her shoulders, each lost in their thoughts. Rufilla reached into her pocket, removing a dark lava stone she had carried from Pompeii. "Xenia," she said, holding up the rock. "My gift to our ancient hosts. From my homeland to theirs." She placed it at the edge of the water.

He gently took her hand and they strolled barefoot down the beach. As they parted, their fingertips lingered longingly for just a second. Rufilla was confused and a little shaken by the moment of intimacy. Making her way to her temporary bed, she said, "Good night, Aper. Thank you. I will never forget this evening."

"Neither will I."

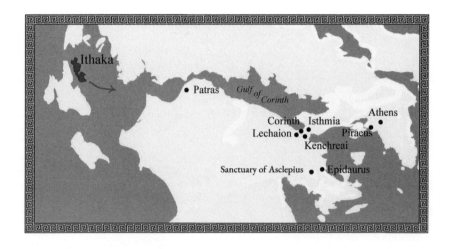

Mainland Greece and the Peloponnese
Visits to Ithaka, Patra, Corinth, Sanctuary
of Asclepius, and Athens

CHAPTER XXVIII

PATRAS

After their picturesque time on the island of Ithaka, one morning they caught an early wind and headed toward the mainland of the Peloponnese. When they were comfortably at sea, Aper took Rufilla aside. "As I said earlier, Patra is our next landfall, and I want to prepare you for what you will see there and beyond," he said. "Let me tell you a few things that Theo and your other teachers, for whatever their reasons, did not convey to you." He looked at Melissa and Theo, who had joined them. "In conquering Greece one hundred years ago, the Roman army, in my opinion, had nothing to prove and everything to accomplish in becoming 'benevolent' conquerors. But instead, a cruel and barbaric general by the name of Lucius Mummius devastated the entire Isthmus. In trying to protect their markets from the Athenians, the Roman sea merchants had urged the Roman Senate to send help, which turned out to be Mummius, who then carried out his ruthless deeds. Corinth resisted the superior Roman forces, which caused untold devastation to the city and the east and west coast ports."

Melissa joined in. "The story has it that he was so ignorant and uncultured that after confiscating all the wonderful art and treasures of Corinth, he told the Roman sea merchants who had contracted to remove it all to Rome that if they lost or broke anything, they would have to replace it. How plebian! Ignorant of the irreplaceable value of the treasure he was stealing from this cultured and wealthy city." Rufilla knew Melissa and Theo were both of Greek descent, but only now, as they drew close to their ancestors' homeland, did she appreciate the depth of their knowledge and love of their heritage and the glory that was Greece.

"I will not go into the brutal details," Aper continued, "but just remember, in killing all the men, which he did, and selling the women and children into slavery, which he did also, he set this country and the Roman and Greek sea merchants back at least 200 years.

"The trading ships like mine could have had the opportunity to expand their trading routes by using the *diolkos* and increasing commerce to everything east of this isthmus, including Athens and all the way to the Bosporus. But those traders were instead shortsighted, protecting their trade routes along the eastern coast of Greece and not appreciating the possibility of expansion of their commerce."

"Said like a true merchant of the sea!" Theo smiled.

"But why did the Corinthians not restore the city and the isthmus?" Rufilla said.

"After killing or running off the inhabitants, Mummius torched the city and the surrounding countryside, making it uninhabitable for anyone. Lechaion, the port town on the west side of the isthmus, suffered because of Corinth, as did Kenchreai on the eastern coast. There was nothing left but ashes."

"Barbaric!" Rufilla said.

Aper continued. "There is some hope recently that if rumors have it right, Caesar will be giving land to a group of Roman veterans and freedman to re-establish the isthmus, restoring Corinth and the port towns to some degree of usefulness. So it will be exciting to see what they have done to secure the harbor."

"Yes, I have heard that as well," chimed in Theo. "I doubt if the diolkos is open for business, but my guess is that preparations are being made to restore the road to at least start the transfer of goods, with the small ships to follow."

"On the road?" Rufilla asked. "Please explain—what is a diolkos?"

"It is a method of portage, a paved road," Theo said, "that allowed boats and sometimes even large military triremes to be towed across the isthmus from west to east from the bay of Corinth to the Saronic Sea. They would unload the cargo and pull it behind the vessel, then reload the supplies when it was safely in the water again. It went both ways, of course."

"That is a lot of work," Rufilla said.

"Yes, but it is far easier and safer than sailing the long route down and around the Peloponnese to get from the Adriatic to the Saronic seas."

Aper continued. "Any progress will require the cooperation of the Greek shippers. We will see how that works out. As far as we are concerned, we will be able to rent drivers, carts, and wagons, and if the Roman soldiers that Caesar sent are there, they will be delighted to take a young Roman girl and deliver her safely to Epidaurus."

Only now did Rufilla fully understand what she had been told before she left. "So, that is why your ship won't be taking us to Athens after we go to Epidaurus?"

"Correct," Aper said. "When I was in the region last year, Roman engineers and soldiers were looking at the area around Corinth, so we will see what has happened in a year. I am sure that the soldiers will have dealt with the pirates, brigands, and squatters."

"I thought Pompey took care of the pirates. That is what pater said."

"Talk and reality are two different things," Aper replied. "I think he wanted to spare you and especially your mater any worry about traveling in the area. The 'Great' Pompey may not have had the success he conveyed to the Roman population. He was commissioned to give the pirates land and help them become farmers, but once a seaman, always a seaman. Anyway, I have kept my eyes out for those dastardly bastards!"

"Watch your language," Melissa interrupted. "Women of culture and refinement are present."

"A thousand pardons," Aper said as he smiled and bowed in front of the two women. "Those men of ill repute. They certainly have been a constant irritation in these waters," he said as he looked out at sea.

"Yes, I thought I saw a suspicious ship in a cove as we sailed out of one of the ports," Theo piped in. "And about your discussion earlier, Aper. The Domina did not want Rufilla to be upset with the talk of pirates, bandits, and mercenaries. But since you are here, Rufilla, I think you are old enough, and besides, you must be aware of what's going on around you. One never knows."

"I thank you all for seeing the need for me to be informed. I will watch as well. And while we're on the subject of Pompey, where was he when Caesar fought his sons in Hispania?"

"Pompey had met his demise in Egypt two years earlier," Aper said. "When his sons wanted retribution, Caesar had to hunt them down—that was what the battle in Hispania was all about."

"Ah," was Rufilla's only reply.

They anchored the ship at the port of Patras, and Aper sent one of the sailors ahead to made arrangements for the four of them to stay at the large and comfortable home of his friends. The Roman party made their way up the broad steps that took them into the town. The hosts were delighted to see their friend Aper again and intrigued by the young Roman girl so eager to speak their language and learn about their customs. Rufilla brought her hosts gifts of wine and also garum, the renowned fish sauce that was produced in the Pompeii area.

Melissa, Rufilla, and their hostess became fast friends. As in the tradition of Xenia, Rufilla was asked what she needed or wanted to do. She requested a bath and then a visit to the local temple of Artemis Triklaria. Aper had told her about this temple and she was eager to pay her respects. Rufilla offered thanks to the goddess for watching over her and asked for continued guidance in the next part of her journey. As she would do whenever she visited a temple, she left a token of appreciation, this time a small terracotta replica of Artemis' Roman counterpart Diana.

"I wish that you could be here for our annual feast of Artemis called the Laphria," said her hostess. "Leading the procession is a virgin priestess. She rides in a chariot drawn by deer!"

"Oh, Diana's—I mean Artemis'—favorite animal!" Rufilla chimed in. "How exciting!"

Their hostess was so taken with Rufilla's interest in the goddess Artemis that the next evening she took it upon herself to introduce Rufilla to her unique version of the local Artemis ritual. Rufilla was led down to the shore by the light of the moon and allowed to bathe at the mouth of the river that flowed into the sea. A mountain range soared in the distance, and there was a strange new freedom that she felt in that moment—at one with Mother Earth. The attentive women, including Melissa, formed a temenos around her, a sacred circle for her to let go of her emotions for ritual cleansing.

She loved once again being the bear-cub of Artemis but also feeling her developing body opening up, ripe and full. She realized that she was no longer the young child of the bear, the arktoi. She felt powerful in her body, which glowed white in the moonlight. She took a quick dip to be sure, loving the sensation of the flowing water on her naked body. Aper and Theo watched from a respectable distance as they did not want to violate her privacy.

On the other hand, she felt no shame, but a freedom here in Greece that she had never felt at home. The experience of the river and the words that the Greek woman spoke, the music they sang, and the dance honoring Dionysus, seemed to purify her in mind and enliven her in body and spirit, preparing her for her next step in life, whatever that might be. Since this god was a part of the local ritual, as she emerged from the waters, a crown of ivy was placed on her head, and Hymns to Dionysus echoed over the rapid waters. Afterward, the hosts and guests enjoyed a wonderful meal of all the local foods with the Greek wine warming Rufilla's body.

Aper made a toast to Rufilla. "You are maturing into such a beautiful young woman that even the gods cannot help but envy you. I am delighted to be part of your journey." Rufilla kissed him on both cheeks and embraced him. She felt alive again.

Again as Aper was falling asleep, he had to hold sway in his thoughts about her. "She will make someone a beautiful bride."

CHAPTER XXIX

THE ISTHMUS OF CORINTH

In the morning, while the crew loaded the cargo ship with military supplies, Aper had the chance to talk with a Roman officer stationed with some of his troops on the wharf. The news from Corinth was that the engineers and the Roman soldiers had made significant progress. Some of the veterans and freedman who had been promised land on the isthmus by Julius Caesar had already arrived. They were in the process of removing the squatters and securing the area from thieves and ruffians. The officer asked whether Aper had any room to take some supplies to the troops. Aper agreed, and in exchange, he secured the word of the officer that he would guarantee safe passage for Rufilla and her group not only to the opposite shore on the isthmus but all the way to Epidaurus and back. The deal was sealed. The officer further promised to give this duty to some of his most trusted soldiers, who would also be delighted to see some fellow Romans and hear the news from the Capitol.

The boat was readied for sailing and pushed from its berth in the harbor. Rufilla noticed an air of excitement as the rowers moved quickly, catching the prevailing current of the sea. Within minutes, the wind came up from behind them, and there was a loud shout from the first mate, and the entire crew came topside to help with the sail. After the sail was unfurled, they all stood, looking forward over the bow of the ship.

"What's going on?" Rufilla inquired.

Aper smiled broadly. "You will see."

He guided Rufilla and Melissa to the bow of the vessel, and the crew stepped aside to give them room. The ship was making good headway now with the wind in her sail.

"The Bay of Corinth is less than a day's sail—with a good wind behind us," Aper said.

Melissa got into the game of things. "Look at that cloud," she said. "It looks like a tiger I once saw in the Coliseum!"

"I did not know that you had seen a tiger," Rufilla said.

"There are many things I have seen that you do not know about," Melissa said with a twinkle in her eye.

Theo appeared on deck and put his arm around Melissa, saying, "There, there girl, do not give away too many secrets!"

"What secrets? Tell me, tell me!" Rufilla exclaimed.

Now Theo enveloped both women in a hug, and they laughed and joked as the wind blew them into a joyful mood.

"Geography lesson," said Theo. "On your left, Rufilla, is mainland Greece, and if you traveled north inland, you would see the Temple of Apollo, where the Oracle of Delphi resides."

"Oh, can we go there?" Rufilla said.

"We will stop there later on our return trip," Aper shouted from his station.

"Now look to your right—what body of land is this?"

Rufilla was puzzled.

"One moment," Theo said. He retrieved two plates and a knife from the galley and laid the knife down horizontally on the deck with a plate on either side. "Let us say that the knife represents the Isthmus of Corinth, and then the plate on the left—"

"Do not tell me—the plate on the left represents Attica or mainland Greece, and the plate on the right represents the Peloponnese to the south!" Rufilla replied.

"Correct, young woman. You win the geography contest for the day! And in front of us, you will soon see, is the isthmus that brings together the two bodies of land that become Greece!"

"Looks like the torso of a woman with the isthmus as her waist!" Aper said.

Melissa shook her head. "Aper, you've been at sea too long."

After several hours passed, Aper shouted, "The port of Corinth—straight ahead in the distance!" Aper looked down from his captain's perch. The crew all cheered. It was an impressive harbor with tall columns lining the width of the harbor and porticoes protecting it. Straight ahead, Rufilla saw hills, rocky ledges at water's edge. As the shoreline came closer and closer, she saw other ships at their moorings and many warehouses on the coastline. It felt like Herculaneum only larger. Aper gave an order to the first mate to turn slightly right to follow a queue of boats and ships as they made their way swiftly toward the land.

"Are we going too fast?" she said, worrying that they might be too close to slow down.

"No, Rufilla, the shore is always much farther away than it looks," Aper said. Rufilla looked up at him. She could tell he was somewhere else, deep in thought. Thinking of his wife again, Rufilla guessed.

Finally, Aper turned back to her, saying, "On the left—do you see what looks like a road?"

"Yes, the road that—I remember—the diolkos! The Isthmus of Corinth—we're here!" she shouted, confirming what Aper had said earlier. All the men returned the cheer.

Rufilla grabbed Melissa, and together they danced around the deck in sync with the heaving of the boat. It was a glorious sight to behold. A few sailors on deck sang and clapped their hands in time with the women's steps, and finally, both women collapsed in a rush of laughter.

Aper saw a large ship moored in the outer harbor, and he could tell by its massive size and structure that it was a Roman military vessel. This confirmed what the soldier at Patra had said. He breathed a sigh of relief that these military men were securing the port and that his friends would have safe passage.

The closer to shore they came, the more clearly they could see the outline of the buildings. The colonnades lining the front of the harbor made an impressive entrance to the isthmus. Behind the columns were makeshift warehouses that had been built to accommodate the new arrivals of men and supplies.

"Not the grand accommodations for the likes of Pegasus," Rufilla remarked. She recalled the bygone story of Pegasus, the winged white horse traveling through the sky during the day and landing in the evening to rest at a stable befitting the stature of a divine horse in what was then, according to legend, the beautiful city of Corinth.

"Can you see the Acropolis of Corinth on top of that tall mountain?" Aper said, pointing inland. "The city at the base of the mountain is Corinth, and this harbor's name is Lechaion. As you can see, after a hundred years of neglect, it will take some time for the new recipients of the land to return it to its earlier order—and beauty." They stood quietly for a moment, and then Aper said, "Harbors, like human relationships, need constant attention." The ship lurched for an instant as the crew started making a right turn. He put his arm around Rufilla to steady her.

"That is a beautiful thought, Aper," she said. "You must miss Bucia very much."

Aper smiled down at her. "Very insightful, young woman, very insightful." He continued. "Now I want you to take in this unusual harbor. Do you see all the waterways to the right?"

"They look like a lot of small coves."

"Exactly right, my dear," Aper said. "As you can see, we are modest in size compared to the military vessel. So we've just passed the outer harbor, and we're heading for the protected inner lagoon. When it is our turn in the line of smaller ships, a tugboat will meet us and tow us down this long canal, leading us to a small quay where we will dock our ship."

"And the lighthouse?" Rufilla asked, looking at the tower in front of them.

"A beacon of light for thousands of boats and ships over the years, seeking safe harbor."

It was so romantic, Rufilla thought, to see the small bodies of water as the ship threaded its way toward a dock contrasted with the tall lighthouse protecting this inner harbor. It felt like another intimate moment. She was falling in love with the Mediterranean Sea, and all its ports.

When it was their turn, they were towed slowly by a tug boat, anchoring in a cove that was deep enough to accommodate the draft of their ship. "We will unload your things here and get you settled in suitable quarters for the overnight stay," Aper said.

"And tomorrow, we will all be off to Epidaurus?" Rufilla said.

"Yes, we will!"

As the group of travelers made their way down the gangplank, the sun shone brightly overhead. Even onshore there was a slight breeze. It felt invigorating to Rufilla and she was giddy with anticipation. Aper had sent someone ahead to secure transportation for them. When a coach appeared, Aper was impressed. "Who would have thought that on this difficult terrain, there would be a coach," he said to the officer in charge.

"We brought it with us on the ship—for dignitaries to use, of course," the officer said, bowing to Aper and his party.

"We are truly grateful for your generous consideration," Rufilla said in her most dignified manner.

As she was about to step onto dry land, she looked down for her footing and saw a string and then something that looked like the top of a pouch. She reached down and dug it out of the dirt. Someone had lost his coin purse.

"I have found a pouch and coin," Rufilla said.

"Come along. Do not hold up the men behind you," Melissa said.

She quickly shook the dirt from the pouch and tucked it in her purse.

At the end of the gangplank, they noticed a group of Roman soldiers, so Aper and Theo went over to talk with them. They came back with a bit of news. These men were part of a scouting expedition sent by Caesar himself. They had landed only weeks earlier and were still in the process of setting up their camp. Because of thieves and highwaymen on the road, civilian travel was tenuous at best, so these soldiers, they said, would be escorting their group across the Isthmus to Kenchreai, the eastern port, and even to Epidaurus if they felt it necessary.

"We are grateful that they are here," Aper said to both women. "I was prepared to escort you, myself, and my crew, that is. Now I know I will be leaving you in good hands. I will travel with you as far as Kenchreai as I want to see what's going on there."

The crew carried the passengers' trunks down the gangway to the pier, just as a row of carts and wagons with Roman soldiers in charge were proceeding toward the ship. They would unload the military supplies that Aper had so generously taken on at Patra.

As they settled into the carriage, Rufilla looked closely at the coins from the purse she had found. Melissa looked too. "These are Greek coins," Melissa said, passing one to Theo that had an image of Athena on one side and Pegasus, the winged horse, on the obverse.

"This one has the head of a woman," Rufilla said. "Oh look, she is carrying a thyrsus—It is a Bacchae!"

"Here, let me look at it." Melissa rubbed it on her skirt and turned it back and forth. She passed the coin to Theo.

"You seem to have found several unusual coins, young lady," Theo said. "This looks like Dionysus with his crown of ivy."

Rufilla grabbed the coin and squealed. "It is. It is!" she said, turning it first to one side showing the maenad, then back to the obverse side with the portrait of Dionysus.

"It is very unusual," Theo said. "I have seen many Greek coins in my time, and it is Greek, mind you, but I have never seen one like this. It looks like it came from another time."

"I agree," Aper concurred. "It is at least a hundred years old!"

"It is a good omen, I know it!" Rufilla said.

"Yes, my dear, it does seem to be a good sign that as you touch the ground of the isthmus, the first thing that happens is that you are given a special gift. Pegasus must have seen you coming from his vantage point in the sky!"

As soon as they had recovered their "land legs," Aper, Rufilla, Theo, and Melissa, along with their entourage, made their way south, on the wide road out of the seaport town of Lechaion. Rufilla insisted she travel by foot, walking through the agora, a market place that was only then starting to redevelop into the international market it was before the ravages of Mummius. Someone remarked how well the restoration of the town was progressing, an optimistic point of view considering the devastation left.

They were going directly on toward Corinth, since the famous Peirene fountain and the surrounding springs were not restored enough to be visited on this trip. Pegasus' favorite watering hole would go unseen. When they arrived at Corinth, they headed straight for the baths as if they were weary sailors eager to wash the seawater away. Rufilla had performed this same ritual on many occasions on the trip, but today it seemed especially invigorating.

"It is a Roman bath with a Greek twist," Rufilla said, delighted with her new surroundings. The baths had been one of the first buildings restored by the military. They were still a bit primitive— that was the "Greek twist"— but were working well enough for these weary Roman travelers to enjoy them.

They had to spend this night out of doors, as there were no accommodations. The soldiers were there to help them get settled. A bank of clouds had come in at sunset. Of course, Rufilla wanted to climb to the top of the acropolis, but she had been told the low lying clouds would obscure the view. When they had all settled in for the night, Rufilla's thoughts went to Mummius, the Barbarian, as she liked to think of him. After a while, she decided to think of something more calming. Her solace in moments like this was to dwell on thoughts of Dionysus. She had heard soldiers talking about the theater of Dionysus near the sacred springs in Corinth. She felt like she was in the land of Dionysus. She remembered how well Aper had played the part of Dionysus in her play so many years ago, and his words from earlier in the day echoed in her ears. "Harbors, like human relationships, need constant care." What if he and she—? Eventually, she had to let go of that thought and settle for the hope that someday there would be a man in her life who felt that way about her.

Quickly, the next day passed as they crossed the isthmus from Corinth to Isthmia. There they visited the Temple of Poseidon, dedicating their offerings at the desecrated building, ignoring its tragic condition, just relieved to be able to enter a space set aside for the god. They thanked him for their safe passage thus far and made a plea for safety on the continuing journey to Epidaurus and beyond. The soldiers were vigilant, paying kind attention to the first women they had seen in months. They told their tales of crossing from Brundisium and how heavy storms had hampered their voyage. It came to Rufilla that these storms had occurred about the same time that another storm had taken Titus' life. She revealed to them what had happened. They were impressed that her brother was a friend of Octavius. Later to Melissa, she lamented the fact that *these* soldiers and *their* ship had come through unscathed, while Octavius' ship had been destroyed, and Titus had perished. Melissa replied, "I do not know what to say, Rufilla, except I am so sorry."

Kenchreai, on the east coast, was as Lechaion had been on the west coast for the last hundred years, an essential port of Corinth reduced to a settlement of squatters at best. As they neared Kenchreai, the soldiers knew where the Baths of Helen had once been. There was little more than a promontory close to the bay to mark the remains of the extensive complex. Bubbling up from a rock was a steady stream of warm water, looking as if it were boiling, as the warm spring water mixed with the cold water from the Saronic Sea.

Rufilla and Melissa were given their privacy, and the warm healing waters soothed their aching muscles. Relaxed, they munched on dried fruits and cheese sent with them by their previous hosts. A shared glass of wine and they were ready to sleep another night, this time under the stars. The clouds rolled by quickly and the moon appeared in the eastern sky. The men, crew, and soldiers had camped at a distance, leaving them time and space to prepare for bed. As sleep overtook them, the towering rock above sheltered the women from the strong winds of the sea beyond.

Later in the evening, Aper and Theo moved closer to where the women were sleeping. Melissa stirred as she saw men coming toward them, then realizing who they were, immediately fell back to sleep, safe in their presence.

CHAPTER XXX

EPIDAURUS

Refreshed by a restful night's sleep, they continued the trip from Kenchreai to Epidaurus. But first, Aper bid them goodbye.

"I cannot thank you enough for all your kindness to me. I learned so much from you," Rufilla said, "but most of all, I learned that you are indeed my friend."

Aper tried to keep it light. "Yes, we had a good time together. I love it that you laugh at my jokes. Many women do not, so when I can make a woman laugh, it makes me happy."

"That is what my pater says about Mater." Rufilla grinned. "You are a pleasure, Aper. I look forward to seeing you when I return to—oh, where will I meet you on the return trip?"

"I will keep in touch with your parents. Knowing you, it may be at the port of Kirra," he said with a twinkle in his eyes.

"Yes, knowing her, Kirra would be the perfect place to meet," Theo said.

Now Rufilla was looking back and forth between the two of them.

"What are you two talking about?"

"Remember the geography lesson on the ship?" Theo said. "Delphi, young woman! Would you not be going to Delphi on your return trip?"

"A chance to see the Oracle, praise Apollo!" Aper said.

"But, of course!" she chimed in. "I wouldn't miss her for all the Roman and Greek world. What a wonderful idea! Then it is settled. Next spring at Kirra," she said. "Oh, that sounds so far away."

"It will go quickly," Aper reassured her. "Your time in Greece will move as quickly as a falling star through the nighttime sky."

"Always the poet," she said. I will miss you, my friend."

"And I will miss you as well. Write to your parents often so that I might keep track of all your adventures."

"That I will. A safe journey to you," Rufilla said as she hugged Aper one last time.

"The same to you, dear Rufilla, the same to you."

The caravan traveled again by carriages and carts down the southeastern coastline of the Peloponnese to Epidaurus. Two soldiers were assigned to see them safely to the Sanctuary. The travel slowed as Rufilla decided to take the advice given to her earlier by the Asclepian priests in Pompeii and begin this sacred journey by walking from Epidaurus to the Asclepian Sanctuary. It was the beginning of her ritual, arriving as a pilgrim, on foot. She was told it would take about three hours, so after staying overnight in Epidaurus, they left early the next morning.

A few wispy clouds made for a beautiful sunrise. There was a crispness in the air as they left the town of Epidaurus behind. The road was wide and paved. The carriages, carts, and soldiers on horseback followed slowly behind Rufilla, Melissa, and Theo. After a long while, they passed between Mount Titthion and Mount Kynortion. Rufilla was at once awestruck by their beauty and calmed by Melissa's gentle thought that she could consider this passage an entrance into her new life.

Rufilla, inspired by the beautiful scenery, reflected upon the walk. "This is also good practice for the trip from Athens to Eleusis."

"That will be a ritual experience with hundreds of people while this is very special, only us." Melissa smiled.

On the way, they talked about Asclepius and his many family members, who were all connected with the Sanctuary. There was Iaso, the goddess of cures and remedies as well as modes of healing. Then there was Panacea, goddess of panaceas—medicines and salves that helped in the cures. She knew something of Salus, or Hygeia as the Greeks called her.

"Oh, let us not talk about Hygeia right now. I miss my cat so much."

"She will be a part of your experience in the Sanctuary," Melissa said. "Her time will come."

The road to the Sanctuary eventually met up with the route from Argos. Looking down that road, in the distance they could see other travelers making their way toward the Sanctuary. Now it began to feel more like what it was—the Sacred Way. A short while later, standing at the edge of a wood was the magnificent Propylaea—the gateway to the Sanctuary. It was breathtaking. With a towering stone archway announcing the way in, it stood on a *crepidoma,* a raised area of ground, with a ramp on each side so that the patients who were infirm could walk the ramps or be supported or carried more easily. It was a massive, open-air structure, dwarfed only by the mountains in the distance. A splendid sight. Six Ionian columns stretched out, side by side, welcoming them as Rufilla, Melissa and Theo walked up the outer ramp. An inner square of fourteen Corinthian columns, taller than any she had ever seen, held up the beautifully decorated marble roof. This design was not meant to accommodate carriages. As Rufilla gazed up at the rooftop, it looked to her like the front of a temple. She stood for a moment, taking in this monumental structure, understanding that it had been built to produce a feeling of reverence in those patients entering to be healed. She understood that she was a pilgrim entering a sacred space, which meant that she must deliver herself, body and soul, to him. She also had every confidence that when she showed true piety, He would come to her, giving her a healing dream for her troubled body and soul.

"Stay calm," Melissa whispered, seeing that the display of grandeur overwhelmed Rufilla. "This is just the beginning. Breathe, child."

Rufilla often did not realize that she was holding her breath until Melissa told her to breathe. Now she took a long deep breath that ended with a sigh.

As the three walked up the outer ramp, a man and a woman appeared on the other side, walking up the inner ramp. They all met in the middle of the arcade.

"Χαιρετισμοί," the two said in unison.

Theo greeted them in Greek and handed them the sealed papyrus, written by Rufilla's father, that Theo had carried from Pompeii.

Rufilla now spoke in Greek: "I am Istacidia Rufilla, grateful and humbled to be here at this sacred Sanctuary, ready to do whatever the god commands." Rufilla had practiced this greeting for weeks before she left. It came out of her without a prompt or a pause, bright as the tinkle of her wind chimes.

The man and woman smiled. The man stepped forward and spoke to Theo. "Please hold onto your letter and follow me. We will begin the process of introductions."

The woman motioned to Rufilla to walk with her through the Propylaea. Substantial marble paving stones covered the floor. Rufilla glanced upward to take in the intricate decorations carved into the ceiling of the inner chamber.

The woman whispered into her ear, words to the effect that "as you enter the sanctuary, your thoughts must be purely based on your devotion to the god." At that moment, she felt humbled in her humanity as they walked down the ramp and into the Sanctuary of Asclepius. It was like walking into a vast meadow, but it was also a Sanctuary with a complex of buildings. They followed, and all were escorted to the closest building, a large stoa—a roofed colonnade with a courtyard within. There, the other new arrivals and their families mingled with each other briefly and then were greeted by a doctor/priest, and a nurse/priestess, who would accompany them through the healing rituals in this unique place. She felt very comfortable as the priests in the Asclepian temple in Pompeii had briefed her as to what would happen upon her arrival.

Since they had traveled a long distance, they were allowed the convenience of giving the priest a pouch containing money instead of an animal to sacrifice. Theo also presented the priest with a scroll, a letter written by Rufus explaining the reason for his daughter's visit. After reading the message, the priest spoke directly to Rufilla. "Please tell me the reason for your visit, Rufilla."

And so the conversation began. Rufilla described her symptoms, her episodes of seizures that she had experienced as long as she could remember. They were often so debilitating that it took several days to recover. Other times they were 'lighter,' and often there was an aura, a warning at the beginning of the episode. The aura, for her, was one of a specific odor, nothing she had ever smelled before. It was accompanied by a hallucination—like a scene from a play. But she could never remember its contents, only the anxiety that went with the aura. If she was lucky, she had a second or two to sit down before she blacked out. Rufilla broke into tears when she spoke of how the seizures had worsened since the death of Titus and how she felt abandoned and alone. As she finished this part of her story, the priest said, "You have given me much to think about. I will be seeing you in the days to come, but you have been on a long journey, and for now you must rest and take care of yourself." He motioned to the couple that had met them at the entrance. The man said he would take Theo and Melissa to the Inn, while the Greek priestess put her arm around Rufilla and gently spoke to Theo and Melissa. "My name is Kharis. If you have any concerns about Rufilla during your stay, please let someone know at the Inn and they will contact me. We want her experience to be a healing one—for everyone concerned."

Theo and Melissa were escorted to the Inn. They were concerned for Rufilla, but almost giddy with anticipation about their time alone together in these beautiful surroundings. They quickly settled in and were accompanied to the baths. They could see the theatre nestled in the foothills right behind the Inn, and were told that they would be able to see a performance there.

After the baths and dinner, they were escorted to the theatre. The play was a light comedy that made them laugh and relax after their long journey.

Except for their afternoon on Ithaka, they had made the long trip with no more than some intimate talk, a hug and a kiss when they had a rare moment of privacy. Now they savored each other's bodies, finding all the familiar, lovely pleasures of being together intensified by the waiting.

Afterward, lying in each other's arms, they spoke of Rufilla and wondered how her first night had been in the Sanctuary.

After Theo and Melissa left that first day, the Greek priestess had taken Rufilla to a building where food and water were brought to them. Her trunks were taken to her room. After a light meal, they walked the grounds of the sanctuary, past buildings, temples, and a round structure that intrigued her. Kharis, as if reading Rufilla's mind, said, "I will give you a full tour of the grounds once you have rested."

She helped Rufilla get settled in her room in the *Abaton*, the building where all the patients slept and where Rufilla hoped to dream a healing dream. Kharis offered to give her time to rest, but Rufilla could not relax, so Kharis escorted her to the baths near the Temple of Asclepius. Soaking in the healing waters, Rufilla realized how tired she was, so she appreciated having the time to absorb and think about what this experience might bring. If she was homesick, she did not let on, even to herself. She thought about the land and sea voyage. So much had happened. She was glad that she had kept a journal of the more important things—really more of a list. She did not want to run out of paper before she reached Athens, although she knew Theo would find her some if needed. She fell asleep in the waters of the bath. Kharis was never far from her side.

By the time Rufilla came from the baths, it was late afternoon, and several people had gathered in the long, columned portico of the Abaton. They smiled and bowed in greeting as she and Kharis walked by, and she returned the greeting. At the end of the colonnade was a spring, more elaborate than those in Pompeii, but she recognized what it was. As they approached, Kharis said, "I will now draw from the sacred waters of this deep-flowing well." She dipped the bowl into the magic waters. "It is known for its compelling powers. We will hope that your reception of the gift will not only quench your thirst but cleanse your soul, making your body and soul receptive to what the god has in store for you."

Rufilla drank deeply as Kharis recited a Greek blessing. Afterward, she continued the litany as she asked Rufilla to turn slowly round and round, using her hand to sprinkle Rufilla's body from head to toe. Then she replaced the bowl, turned Rufilla around to face the colonnade. This time, she saw the people that were coming toward her. "Welcome to the Sanctuary of Asclepius," they said. "May you find healing with the help of the gracious god and all His helpers who dwell here."

Hearing so much Greek all at one time made her head spin. One man introduced himself as a fellow dreamer, open to the god's healing process.

Rufilla asked about the large stone tablets leaning against the wall of the Abaton.

"These tablets are the accounts of others who have been cured before you. They are placed here as encouragement that you, too, can heal yourself," Kharis said.

"Heal me?" Rufilla said. "I, I do not quite understand what goes on here."

"The Sanctuary presents you with this pastoral atmosphere for the healing to occur: the grounds, the setting with the mountains in the distance, the attitude of a holy, healing place. Part of that healing will be to expose your mind to your surroundings. The stone tablets are outside the Abaton not to intimidate you, but to give you inspiration that you, too, will have the experience of healing. Within the Sanctuary, there are exercises one may do—walking is always encouraged. You will be able to have massages, soak in the therapeutic waters as well as attend plays in the theatre, and lectures from the priests. A peaceful mental outlook and a rested body are all part of the healing. Your ultimate aim is to make a connection, bringing your mind and body, soul and spirit together, along with your humility and willingness to accept whatever healing occurs. You have probably noticed that there are many people here. Not all who stay in the Abaton are patients like you. Some have come to honor the god, to take part in the tranquil atmosphere, and to attend the games and the theatre. As you can see, this is not a town, but a place to come and enjoy, a refreshing retreat. Many people return year after year to honor the god and revitalize their souls. These people stay in the town.

"Is that where Theo and Melissa are?"

"No. Do you see the large theatre nestled into the hill? They are staying at the Inn, which is just below the theatre. Do you miss them?"

"A little." She wanted to seem grown-up, but the mention of them gave her heart a little tug.

"You will be able to see them before you know it. Maybe they could come for the next ritual dinner."

"Ritual dinner?"

"Yes, when one has cured oneself—"

Rufilla threw up her hands. "I do not know if I can do that."

"You won't be doing it alone, my child. You cannot will yourself to be healed or you would have done it by now. The healing is facilitated with the help of many people here, and do not forget all the healing partners you have within."

"Healing partners—within?"

"Yes, we do not always know who they are, sometimes ancestors, other times dream images. Then there are all of those negative voices in your head."

"How do you know?" Rufilla said.

"We all have them, voices that help, voices that hinder. We have to learn which voices we want to accept, and the others must either change or be seen for who they are, and you simply choose not to listen to them. Then slowly, over time, they will change. They want to be part of your life."

Rufilla was silent, her mind racing. She had never heard these concepts before.

"This attitude takes time to evolve," Kharis said. "You are very young, but you are ready to start this inner journey. You have experienced more than many young women your age. The seizures caused by epilepsy have set you apart. Uniquely, they have facilitated your growth into woman-hood. From the wound, the god will help you find healing."

That night she awoke several times, hearing strange noises and other people talking in their sleep, but could remember nothing of a dream. The next morning when Kharis arrived, Rufilla expressed her concerns, but

Kharis reassured her. "Do not worry, my child, your dream will come. You have a special calling."

Rufilla looked at her quizzically.

"You must be patient. Come, I want to show you some areas you may be interested in."

They toured the massive complex of buildings. Rufilla was interested in the Temple of Asclepius and all the votive offerings within. But she was more fascinated by the round temple-like building and the areas below, where she was told she wasn't allowed to go. "The round building reminds me a little of the Temple of the Vestal Virgins in Rome. What is it used for?"

"You are a curious one," Kharis smiled.

"But,—"

"In time. All things in their time."

There were gatherings of patients for lectures. They met outside under the shade of the long porch in front of the Abaton. Rufilla attended one that talked about the god and his many family members. She learned that Apollo was Asclepius' father. She also learned more about Hygeia, his daughter. She liked that Hygeia was concerned with problems of the mind.

Kharis had gone with her, and Rufilla questioned her after the lecture. "I know that maybe I am too curious, but I would like to know more about you," Rufilla said. "My sense of you is that you have particular 'talents' too. Would you mind sharing some of your life and how you came to be here?"

"Ah," Kharis sighed. "Well, it started with my family. My mother had epilepsy, and as I was the youngest of her children, I used to come here with her. She was quite infirm by then and so the priests let me stay with her. The priestess who always took care of my mother when we came asked me one day if I would consider following my spiritual path by studying the lineage of the priestesses within this Sanctuary. She told me that over the years, she had observed that I was intuitive and compassionate toward my mother and her plight and that this might be a good direction for me. I was thrilled and she was right!"

"What happened to your mother?" Rufilla said.

"Over the years—you understand, she came to the Sanctuary only later in her life—she improved somewhat, but only to a point. If she had had the opportunity to come earlier, maybe— only the god knows."

"So there is hope for me?"

"Oh yes, my child. When someone with epilepsy comes to the Sanctuary, I am often assigned to care for them. That is why I am here with you. I hold out great hope for you," she said, hugging Rufilla close to her.

This day, her first full day in the Sanctuary, she was to go with others who had arrived recently to observe the sacrifices to Asclepius. The Temple was a beautiful *peripteros*, surrounded by six Doric columns in the front and the rear, and eleven on the long sides. No one could enter, but all stood outside, observing the sacrifices at the altar in front of the Temple. Some brought wine, water, milk, and honey as a ritual sacrifice. Others, one by one, sacrificed animals as supplications to obtain the favor of the god to help cure them of the disease that had brought them here.

Each patient was interviewed again by the same priest they had met at the beginning and given a particular mantra to repeat at times of meditation or times that gave them pause to reflect on their lives. Reflection was a fundamental theme here, Rufilla learned. It was different from the girlish thoughts she had had about herself before she came—about her hair, her makeup, the cloth bought for a new shawl. The affliction had naturally made her more reflective during some of the more extended recovery periods she had experienced. But an odd thing she had always noticed was that she felt more perceptive than her peers. Sometimes she knew what they were going to say before they said it. But she rarely told anyone. Even Titus had not taken her insights seriously. The dream she had before they left for Hispania was a case in point. This was her secret, sometimes a gift, sometimes a curse, just like the epilepsy. She remembered that she had shared her intuitive feelings only with Hostia after the Artemis initiation. Hostia had respected Rufilla's gift from that time on.

Then a thought occurred to her. If I am cured of the epilepsy, will I lose this other gift? She hoped not. She would talk to the priest about it. This was the day for her next interview with him. She was a little apprehensive and wished it were a woman rather than a man, but Kharis escorted her. Until now, she had been restricted from the area where they met. It was in the open air and she liked that. There were seats for the three of them. The priest came and sat across from them. He was very kind and was able to put her at ease almost immediately. He reminded her again of her uncle.

"Let us review what brings you all the way from Pompeii."

She was delighted that he remembered her.

"I came to see if I could receive help from the god to cure my epilepsy," she began. Then she related to him what her mother had told her about her difficult birth and her first mother's death. For the first time in a long time, she felt sadness for the loss of her mother.

"Take your time, child," the priest said. "Your story is all part of the healing."

She told him about her young life in more depth, including her relationship with Titus. Words came pouring from her that she had not spoken to anyone before, spilling forth in a torrent of emotion. The priest was compassionate, at one point, even taking her hands in his as she related her story.

After a short while, the priest said, "This is enough for now. You must be exhausted, but know we will talk again soon."

Over the next two days, Rufilla experienced different and varied therapies. One treatment was a series of baths similar to Roman baths, except the waters were filled with particular substances that made her float as if in the ocean. Others smelled of something strong and irritating to her nose and throat. When she did not react well to this, she was removed and bathed and massaged with fragrant oils that she had never smelled before.

Two more nights of fitful sleep left her longing for her quiet farm. The third night though, there was a fragment of a dream. In the dream, she saw a wood. As she walked into it, she found a rock under a tree.

"Dreams are like life's progression," Kharis told her the next morning. "One dream leads to another. Maybe because you are so impatient, the dream maker teaches you the virtue of patience."

That did not please Rufilla. She wanted one of her full-blown dreams that her mother would help her interpret.

"Can I take a walk today?"

"Yes, being in nature will be a good change for you. There is a wood just beyond that building. Do you see it? You may find Hygeia there," Kharis said with a smile.

"Yes, thank you." Rufilla knew that Kharis had understood that she wanted to find the place from her dream. She was pleased by that but irritated that Kharis had read her thoughts. Rufilla could do it for others, but she did not want it done for her.

The walk was pleasant. It was a chilly morning and she felt as if the birds were singing to her. She responded by trying to imitate them, which made them sing even more with varied tunes. She found several rocks—too big, too small, wrong color, wrong shape. Nothing suited her. She was feeling irritable and realized that she needed to quiet her mind or she might have a seizure. She found herself walking in circles, as in a labyrinth. By mid-morning, it had grown hot. She decided to go to the lecture held under a porch. If there were any breeze, it would be there. The priest spoke of the labyrinth as a way to put the mind in a calm and receptive place. Then he spoke of the labyrinth of King Minos, which pleased her much. Although she still did not understand all the Greek words he spoke, because she knew the story of Minos, the labyrinth, and Ariadne and Theseus, she understood the message. Patience. Receptivity. Relationship. She heard the words but needed to feel them inside. It came to her what she had to do.

CHAPTER XXXI

THE DREAM

That night after everyone in the Abaton had gone to sleep, Rufilla tip-toed out of the dormitory and headed for the curious round building. It was a quiet evening with stars overhead and the moon in its first-quarter—bright enough to light her way. She made her way up the steps and walked cautiously around the circular perimeter. Then she ventured through the first door, walked a little deeper into the building, and became a part of the circular path, each level going deeper and deeper into the center. There was a strong fragrance of honey, and huge frescoes were painted on the outer walls of the inner chamber. One was of Eros playing the lyre instead of holding his bow and arrows. The other painting that fascinated her was of a woman looking through a wine glass. Was it Methe? What were the words to that drinking song she had heard the sailors singing in Ithaka? She hummed the tune and then some of the lyrics came to her: *be merry—drink wine—sing of Bacchus——thanks to him Methe* (Drunkenness) *was brought forth*. Yes! That had to be her in the painting. Then the next words: *Kharis was born*—her priestess!

Her suspicions were correct. She realized she was in a labyrinth. Sitting on the stair, she was afraid but also felt drawn to go deeper. She had to connect with the god. She kept moving through the doors, but when she thought she was about to reach a lower level near the center, she heard from below a sound, a movement of something—snakes, were there snakes? Oh yes, as her eyes adjusted to the dark, she could see the snakes on the lowest level and hear their slithering sounds on the marble floor.

Then a male voice came from above. "Do not go any further. You are not allowed to be here, and now you must retreat before you displease the god."

"Oh, I am so sorry. I do not mean any disrespect," she said, climbing toward the voice floating above her. She kept her head down, eyes focused on the stairs, following the sound of footsteps, guiding herself by touching the circular walls made of bright white stones that somehow radiated their own light. She tried to retrace her steps quickly, her heart now racing. It felt like she was making her way through water—not able to run, but moving none the less. Then she was once again at ground level, outside in the night air. All she could see around her were the white buildings shining in the light of the moon. Nothing stirred except the crickets. There was no man. Had he ever been there? Had she heard a ghost speaking to her? She ran to her room and sat curled up on her bed, shivering and wondering who he was and whether she had displeased him or the god. Tonight, for the first time, she took a sip from the phial of honey that Kharis had put next to her bedside every night. Slowly her breathing became quiet again, and she fell asleep sitting upright, her arms around her legs, her head resting on her knees.

Who knows how long she slept that way, but she awoke with a start and a dream.

In the dream, *she was in her room, but not this room. An old man with caring eyes and a kind smile gently called her name, "Rufilla, come with me." She rose quickly from her bed and followed the man into the night. He walked beside her, talking to her about her life and her journey. When they reached a forest, he told her to sit on the rock he pointed out. "Now, place the gifts you brought on either side of the rock and save one for the altar."*

"But I—" She did not think she had brought the pouch with the gifts, but there it was in her lap. It was so clear exactly where to place the gifts. She sat quietly on the rock, waiting for what would happen next.

She heard the man's voice again. "The time has come," he said.

She awoke upset that she could not continue the dream. The time had come for what? What now? More waiting? She had been there for five days. When would she be able to see the priest again?

The next morning Kharis came to Rufilla's bedside. "You must come with me now. The priest wishes to see you."

At last, Rufilla thought, I will talk with him again. Should she tell him this dream? And what about what occurred the previous night? Had he been told that she had trespassed? Was he calling her to task? Again her heart raced as she dressed quickly in the early morning light.

She was taken to a semicircular stone seat just outside the Abaton. She had passed it many times. Often, people were sitting there in conversation. The seat was able to hold at least six other people, but at the moment, she was the only one there. Kharis left, saying she would return.

Presently, another young woman came hobbling up with a cane for support. She smiled at Rufilla as she seated herself on the cushions that made the stone seats bearable. Her foot was wrapped in bandages.

"Hello," Rufilla said in Greek. Up to now, she had been encouraged to speak only to Kharis, respecting the privacy of the other guests. But she sensed that this girl needed to talk.

The girl looked puzzled and then replied rather timidly in Greek, "Hello."

Rufilla realized she wasn't Greek. "Do you speak Latin?" Rufilla said in Latin.

A smile broke out on the girl's face. "Oh, yes, thank you!" she said. "We must be the only two Latin-speaking people here! It is such a relief. I have been trying so hard to learn Greek. My father insisted I come here while he does business in Athens. He is hoping for a cure, but—" She looked down at her leg and foot. "My mother is here, but they say she must stay at the Inn."

"Yes, my nursemaid and her husband are staying there, too," Rufilla said.

"Oh, I wish my nursemaid were here. I miss her so," the girl said.

"My name is Rufilla. I am from Pompeii."

"My name is Camilla. My father wanted to name me Claudia because of my crippled leg and foot, but my mother said she saw a child with spunk and determination, so she insisted on the name Camilla—it means warrior maiden. Isn't that wonderful!"

So an animated conversation began. They were delighted and relieved to be able to speak their native tongue. But also, each saw in the other a fighting spirit, a spirit of healing with the help of Asclepius. The conversation lasted until Kharis came for Rufilla.

"We will talk later, I promise," Rufilla said as she left.

As she and Kharis walked, she slipped back into the Greek language very quickly. "She is from Praeneste, just outside Rome. It is so good to see someone from home."

Kharis smiled. "Always good to find a kindred spirit."

Rufilla was led past the Abaton, down a set of stairs that had been closed to pedestrian traffic. She wondered about the stairs, but after her encounter at the round building, she dared not ask. They made a hairpin turn to the right and entered an area below the Abaton. Kharis motioned to a chair adjacent to a large wooden door. "Sit here, my child, and center yourself with your mantra. I will return shortly."

Kharis entered the room beyond the door, and a few minutes later returned to usher Rufilla into an underground area under the Abaton. They walked down a long narrow hall that was lit with oil lamps. Entering the first door they came to, Rufilla found herself in a room that was handsomely decorated with frescoes, ornate oil lamps and furniture, a couch and three chairs. There was a man with a beard, white hair, and long robes sitting on one of the chairs. She noticed a second priest, the younger one who had been so kind to her at her initial interview. The older priest motioned to Rufilla to sit on the couch next to the chair where he sat. Kharis sat in the third seat near the door.

"Welcome, my child," the younger priest said, "I understand you have received a dream."

Rufilla was stunned. She had told no one. "Yes, I have, but I am not sure—"

"We will discuss the dream," he gently interrupted her. "Start at the beginning."

She was terrified. "I think I should begin with what happened last night before the dream." She then confessed that she had entered the round building and told them of the man who had called to her.

As she finished, the priests did not comment, but the younger one suggested that she recline on the couch, close her eyes, and relate the dream to them.

"I returned to my bed, and as I was frightened by what I had done, I sat for a long while trying to calm down and finally fell asleep and had a dream." She revealed the dream, saying, "The man had such a kind face, he knew about me and my life, and that I had the gifts for the god." When she was finished, she kept her eyes closed and, after a few minutes, could hear the older priest shift in his chair and breathe a deep sigh.

"Do you remember what the god said?" the younger priest asked.

"The god, was it the god Asclepius? I did not know."

"Yes, we will assume so for now," the younger priest said.

Her heart rate quickened, but with the use of her breathing and her mantra, she soon calmed down again. "I do not remember all that he said, but I do remember that he said that the mind, body, and soul must be in harmony."

"He also said that you had an important and complicated task before you and that the harmony of these three would help you to accomplish what fate had intended," the younger priest said.

"How do you know about my dream?" Rufilla said.

The younger priest nodded to her but did not speak.

The older priest now spoke for the first time. "This sounds like some of the teachings of Chrysippus."

When she heard the older priest's voice, Rufilla's eyes flew open. It was the voice from last night. At the same moment, she saw a wall fresco across the room that she had not seen before. It was a scene of Ariadne and Theseus at the opening of the labyrinth. Then the image of the round building from last night's escapade came to mind—another labyrinth. All of a sudden, she was confused. Her head was spinning.

"Oh, sir, I am so sorry about what happened last night. I did not mean any harm—it looked like a labyrinth. It reminded me of Knossos and the home of Ariadne," she said, pointing toward the fresco.

"You know the story of Ariadne?" the priest said.

"Oh yes, sir, it is my favorite story," she said, gesturing to the fresco. My mother has told me this story many times. I have painted pictures of it. I know it by heart now."

The two priests looked at each other. The older priest spoke. "You seem to be a young woman who benefits from her studies. Do you have any other special gifts you need to tell us about?"

Rufilla spoke tentatively. "I am not sure how to describe it, but it seems that sometimes I know what other people will say before they say it. I never act as if I know, but it sometimes feels like a gift. And then again, sometimes they do not say it for whatever reason, but I trust that I know. It is amazing sometimes when I do not trust myself, and then it happens. So now I try to—oh, the other thing is that I can't make it happen. It is not my will that does it. The gods know I have tried that before." She smiled to herself, thinking that her mother might have said that. "My mother has the gift, too. Not epilepsy, but the inner knowing. Sometimes she says it can be a curse, too." She looked down to the floor shyly, feeling as if she were talking too much. But she needed to ask her question, so she struggled to say the right words in Greek. "If I am cured of my epilepsy, will I lose my other gift—the knowing gift?"

"One gift does not preclude the other," the older priest said. "Rufilla, this is enough for now. We will talk with you soon and try to answer all your questions. Then we will see if the god is ready to release you. We will discuss your gifts at that time."

"Speaking of gifts, what did you bring as a gift to Asclepius?" the younger priest asked.

"I brought two things, a bowl made in Pompeii to offer libations and a piece of black rock that is prevalent in our city. Then when I heard the priests' lectures on the god's family members, I saw an image in my head of Hygeia, and I drew a picture of her to give as a thanksgiving gift to him." With bowed head, she softly said, "I hope he likes it."

The priests could not help themselves. They smiled, and each stood and hugged her.

As Rufilla walked back to the dormitory with Kharis, she remembered something else. "I forgot to tell them that I know a little about Chrysippus. When I heard the priest's voice, it scared me so that I forgot to say something. Years ago, when I was young, a playmate made fun of me; she said that I was not as good as she because my original parents were freedmen instead of aristocrats like hers. It was very hurtful and I ran home to my mother, very upset. My parents sat me down and told me that once a long time ago a wise man named Chrysippus—I remembered his name because I had never heard a name like that before—said that one was not born into nobility, but had to achieve it through living a virtuous life, that virtue was a quality of the soul. That body, soul, and virtue were all intertwined and there had to be harmony between all three," she said, running out of breath. "That is what the priest was talking about, right?"

"Yes, you are right," Kharis said.

"So, to make a long story longer—something my father is famous for saying—anyway, just before I left, we went to visit my uncle, well, he is not my uncle but a good friend of my father's. He lives in Herculaneum and he has a wonderful library, including a copy of a book that Chrysippus wrote a long time ago, and I was going there to study Greek authors, so I asked him if I could read his book. He told me that Chrysippus' Greek was complicated to read, so instead, my uncle read parts of it to me. And I remember what Chrysippus said about being noble. He was a Stoic and thought that *humanitas* was more important than hero-worship. The Stoics preach that—"

"That humans need to develop truthfulness, increase their knowledge of the outer world and be brave and temperate in all things," Kharis said.

"I am sorry. You're such a wise woman, and I am showing my hubris. Of course, you know all of this already. I am so sorry."

"No need to worry, my dear. You are very advanced for your age. It is refreshing. Many of the youth of today do not take advantage of the opportunities given to them. It is so sad."

"Here too? That is what my parents say. I have always felt that if a gift were not developed, it would be taken away. Maybe if my epilepsy is not developed, the gods will take that away."

"You never know, my child, you never know. Epilepsy is very specific and very different from the other gifts you already have. And the ones you will develop."

"What? Other gifts? How—why—when?"

"All in time, my dear one, all at the right time."

"That is what Asclepius talked about in my dream. But he said that 'the time has come.'"

"Yes, I see that this is a time of change for you. Dramatic change. Understand that you will make mistakes, you are human, but that is how one changes and grows. Your trip to Athens will be a wonderful opportunity for you, and I know you will take full advantage of it. I hope you will remain there for the full season of festivals. There is much to learn from the Greek culture."

Rufilla could only think of Titus. "If I were home today and Titus were alive, we would go to the festival of Rosaria. It was always so much fun to go with him and our friends. So many different roses, rose petals, rose water." She paused. "Will I ever find someone to love again? I cannot believe I will. I will probably be married off to some dowdy old man and live the dreary life that he dictates."

Kharis laughed. "Yes, my love, you may be married off to some old man, but you will find love. You are such a beautiful person that I do not doubt that you will. And there is the challenge. Remember *humanitas* from Chrysippus. It is about reasoning and intelligence. It is not about the irrational way that one feels when one falls in love. You will have to listen to the wind."

Rufilla looked puzzled. They walked a while in silence.

Kharis continued. "The Stoics also talk about the Pneuma, the motion of the cosmos. It worries not about the rules of our culture, but about the wholeness of the individual. It is a sort of spirit that lifts you, taking you to places you never believed possible. Then it can let you collapse back to the earth and give you back to this reality."

"That is how I felt with Titus."

"Yes, I am sure you did. It is good that you experienced this so young. When it happens again—and mark my words, it will—you will be able to look back at those wonderful feelings you had with Titus and think, hopefully, with a clearer head." Then Kharis gave her a sly smile. "But then again, maybe not."

They had finished their walk and were sitting in the stoa of one of the buildings where lectures were often given. People were beginning to gather.

"Know that your gifts will guide you. No amount of hubris will ever match the insights you are given. Humility is the virtue that a person with your gifts must develop. Never take it for granted. The muse is with you as long as you remain humble." Kharis stood to leave. "This has been a significant day for you, and it is not even half over!"

"But you have given me a paradox—the rational life versus the irrational life," Rufilla said.

"Ah, good, you have seen the dilemma. Something for you to think about today." As she turned to leave, Kharis said, "Here is a new Greek word for you—*heuristic*. It means discovering something for yourself."

Rufilla thought at that moment that Kharis had the look of the wisdom of Athena in her eyes.

"Remember," Kharis said, "we attend the play tonight. I will come to you and we will go to dinner together before the play. Enjoy the lecture and the rest of your day. Let what we talked about stimulate new ideas. Do not try to figure it out logically. Focus on what the priestess says in her lecture."

The lecture was on Athena. How appropriate Rufilla thought. The priestess talked about Athena's shield with the image of Medusa in the center. Athena had been so taken with Asclepius' exceptional skills as a surgeon that she gave him a bottle of Medusa's blood. The magical properties in the blood allowed him to either kill a mortal or bring him back to life. Asclepius chose to heal people from diseases, relieving their pain.

All Rufilla could think about was writing to Cil and sharing the information she had learned about Asclepius that day. She had received a letter

from him in Patra, describing some of his adventures and passing on what
he had learned about medicine and surgery on the battlefield. She had also
received a letter from her mother saying that her father continued to super-
vise the renovations to the "country house." Rufilla had previously started
a letter to her mother. She had been writing down her experiences thus
far in a journal so that when she returned, she could re-live some of her
memorable experiences. Now she needed to return to her room and write
what had just happened.

CHAPTER XXXII

TRANSFORMATION

After the lecture on Athena, Rufilla hardly ate anything at the midday meal. She was tired, and her stomach was aching, so she decided to take a nap, hoping to walk later. When she awoke, her belly felt a little better, but not well enough to go for a walk. She wanted to make sure she was up for dinner and the play, so she stayed in bed until it was time to prepare. Her mind kept wandering back to the part of the lecture concerning how Asclepius used the Medusa's blood. What exactly did that mean?

When Kharis arrived, she greeted Rufilla with such eagerness about the evening that Rufilla responded in like manner.

But Kharis seemed to pick up on something. "Let me look in your eyes, Rufilla. Are you not feeling well?"

"I am fine! I am so excited about seeing the play tonight. I have never seen 'The Frogs.' I understand it is hilarious," she went on, trying to hide her discomfort.

"If you say so," Kharis said, looking at her sideways. "Yes, it is the amusement that the priest suggested for you. A humorous play to lighten your heart."

Rufilla started talking about what she knew of the play, and Kharis filled her in on some details. "You will be up close, seated with the other patients in the lower seats, but this theatre is so well-conceived that one can hear even at the upper levels, and it is a huge theatre—you will see!"

At dinner, Rufilla still wasn't hungry. Again Kharis asked whether she was all right. "I am fine. I just overate for lunch," she lied. "And anyway, I do not want to get sleepy from eating too much." That seemed to satisfy Kharis.

"I have a surprise for you, Rufilla," Kharis said as they were entering the theatre.

Rufilla was so busy looking at the beautiful, ornate arches that she barely heard what Kharis said. "Those arches look exactly like the arches I saw at the entrance," Rufilla said.

"Yes, you are right!"

Then, there they were—Melissa and Theo. A sweet reunion.

"Hello, young lady!" Theo beamed. They both hugged her.

Many people climbed the stairs to their seats, while the patients with physical disabilities were helped into theirs. Rufilla noticed Camilla a few rows down, waving her cane in the air. She was waving to her. Then Camilla threw her cane down and made her way over to where Rufilla was seated. They greeted one another in Latin. Her mother came with her, and there were introductions all around. "See," said Camilla, "I can walk on my mended foot. I have been healed!" The patients around them started to clap. Camilla raised her arms in triumph, speaking in perfect Greek. "These doctors are wonderful! Asclepius lives in them and through them, and with their help, I am cured." Room was made for them to join Rufilla's group, and there was much to talk about until the announcement of the play settled everyone into silence.

At the end of the play, there was laughter and thunderous applause. Rufilla had laughed so hard, and she whispered to Melissa that she thought she had had an accident. She pointed to between her legs. As she stood, Melissa noticed that the back of Rufilla's *tunica* had a small dark stain.

"Oh, my child! No, I mean, young woman—it has finally happened!" Rufilla looked back at Melissa, who had a grin on her face, and then down at the cushion where she had been sitting. It was stained with blood. Now she recognized that she had started menarche. Her mother and Melissa had talked about it to her many times in the last year. She was well into her fifteenth year and past due for this momentous development. She gave a little squeal and quickly pulled her palla from her shoulders, wrapping it around her waist. The women gathered around her, including Camilla and her mother, hugging her and buzzing with conversation. The men were confused. Melissa quickly whispered to Theo, "She is passing her first blood!"

"Oh, gods above and below, help us to maintain our calm in this moment of transition!" Theo declared. He was delighted that this child whom he had taught and helped raise was crossing into womanhood. "We must celebrate this transformation!"

The next morning Kharis allowed Rufilla to sleep in. Theo, Melissa, and she had arranged to meet with the priests and discuss what kind of ritual they might do to welcome her into womanhood. When they, including

Rufilla, met later that morning, the priests had a surprise. The young priest addressed Rufilla. "Do you remember when you asked me how I knew about your dream?"

Rufilla nodded. "You never gave me an answer."

"Please, be seated," the younger priest said. "You were summoned that morning because I had a similar dream. When such dreams happen coincidentally with one's counselors, it is significant. This phenomenon is called a *symptōma*. Its meaning is two-fold. First, it is a sign of healing. In the instance of epilepsy, I would say maybe a lessening of the occurrences of the seizures."

"The second sign is that your time has come to be consecrated," the older priest said. "We will confer the rites of becoming a priestess upon you. We were not sure it was the right time, since you are so young, but with the coming together of the symptōma and your entrance into menarche, we believe that you are ready."

Rufilla would have collapsed if she hadn't been told to sit. Melissa and Theo sat down beside her to comfort her and also because they were stunned as well.

The older priest continued. "As this will be a combined ritual, your part is to prepare a *paean,* a song of praise and thanksgiving to the god, Asclepius."

"I am honored," Rufilla said.

They decided on a combined Greek-Roman ritual. Melissa and Kharis found it interesting that the Greek and Roman rituals for celebrating menarche were so much alike. A mask would be placed over Rufilla's eyes and she would be led to a sacred space. In this case, there would be an underground cavern that was used just for ritual occasions. A version of the story of Demeter and Persephone was chosen to be performed, with Rufilla playing the role of Persephone. The cave would represent the underworld. The timing was indeed synchronous with her impending departure to participate in the Mysteries in Athens.

As they left the meeting with the priests, Kharis spoke to Melissa and Theo. "I think this ritual is a suitable closure to the work she has done here. The priests have been so taken with her; it seems that they feel she will be an excellent priestess when she returns to Pompeii. Her advanced wisdom at such a young age is rare to see."

"Yes," Melissa replied. "The gifts that she has received from the gods have helped in her development, and her parents made sure that she and her brother were well educated. Aridela wanted a girl child so much." Melissa related the story of Rufilla's birth.

"We must incorporate some of her story into the ritual," Kharis said. "It will be significant to the priests that Rufilla was found in a sacred tree."

With the new information given to them by Kharis, the priests made immediate preparations for the combined ritual. Other priestesses gathered to help with the final plans. The two priests who had helped Rufilla interpret her dream would be the head participants. The younger one would play the part of Hades, the abductor in this world, and the older would perform the role of Hades in the underworld. He would take her through the experience in the cave. Kharis would play Demeter. She would remain just close enough to the cave that Rufilla could hear the signaling of Demeter's plight.

Rufilla was caught up in the excitement even though she couldn't participate in the preparations. She was instructed to indulge her own need for quiet time and reflect on her new stage in life and what that meant to her. She wrote her reflections in her journal and prepared her part of the ceremony. Three days later, the ritual preparations were completed.

The priests met with Rufilla one more time before her ceremony began. "We have created a special ritual for you, Rufilla," the older priest said. "Because you are the honored one in this ritual, you might like to consider your name change within the ritual setting. Just as the innocent Kore changed her name to Persephone when she was released from the underworld—so you will be allowed to have that opportunity as well.

"Oh, thank you, dear priest," Rufilla replied. "As I have mentioned, my mother and I talked about her name change from Lucia to Aridela after she experienced the Eleusinian Mysteries, but I feel that, for me, this occasion fits very well as the start of my new life with a new name. Thank you for performing this ritual for me. I am touched and feel humbled to be chosen for this."

"You have been singled out to participate in this exceptional ritual for several reasons," the priest continued. "You have shown a particular calling, young woman. Your vocation in life will be to marry and have children, but also to attend to the rituals that you will develop with your local priest and priestess. Do you know of whom I am speaking?"

"No," Rufilla said, "but my mother will help me with this task."

"Yes, I am sure she will," the priest said. "Now return to your quiet contemplation and consider your new name."

"Oh, there is no question, kind priest. The name is Arianna," she replied.

"You're sure of this?" he questioned.

"As sure as night follows day," she answered. "My mother and I talked about this before I left Pompeii. The story of Ariadne, Dionysus, and Theseus was uppermost in our minds, especially after the death of my beloved Titus. She explained to me that just as Theseus abandoned Ariadne, Titus, by his death, had abandoned me to enter the next world, leaving me in this world. As she chose a form of Ariadne, namely Aridela, so I have chosen Arianna to honor Ariadne as well."

The priest bowed his head. "It seems that you already understand the responsibility of taking on this new name. I strongly suggest that while you are here in Greece, you visit the island of Crete and go to Ariadne's palace at Knossos. Who knows what you might learn there? Arianna, it is."

CHAPTER XXXIII

ARIANNA'S RITUAL

At the designated hour, Rufilla's *toilette* began. She was given a ritual bath followed by a massage with sweet-smelling unguents. Melissa supervised her dressing. First, the menstrual cloth was placed between her legs and secured with safety pins to a cloth band around her waist. Next, she slipped on a thin linen undergarment, a *tunica interior*. Then Melissa chose the saffron yellow tunica that Rufilla had received last year, altered to accommodate her maturing body. The dress would be an essential part of this ritual. Melissa was delighted that the priests would take such an interest in this young Roman girl. She put the *palla* around Rufilla's shoulders. This outer wrap was worn only out of doors. Next, they sprinkled the outfit with her favorite perfume. Another woman applied makeup to her face. A charcoal pencil was used to accent her eyes. Scented oils were applied to her curly red hair, and then it was swept up off her neck and styled in the Greek hairdo of the day. The crowning glory was a garland of fresh buds of lilies. After the *toilette*, Rufilla was given a mirror. The transformation was complete. She looked and *felt* like a woman. She was near tears but held them back as she looked at Melissa and Kharis. Their eyes, too, were filled with tears, a joyful smile on both their faces.

"You are ready for your ritual into womanhood, young lady," Kharis said. "Come with us."

As Rufilla walked outside, Kharis draped the palla over her head, but leaving the front of her hair and garland visible. She was met by a group of priestesses and a few of the female patients who had befriended her, including Camilla from Praeneste. Rufilla led the procession with Melissa and Kharis on either side, followed by the other women. They walked to a field of wildflowers that she had visited many times—coincidentally, her favorite place to reflect. They stopped and she was told to pick some of the wildflowers.

The young priest approached her in a carriage. "I will now blindfold you so that you will begin to experience your descent into that night voyage into the underworld." He was gentle with her, but the implications of what she would endure were not lost on her. She knew this part of Persephone's story well, but to act it out was beyond anything she had anticipated.

It seemed that she and the priest rode in the carriage for a long time. When they arrived at the mouth of a cave, the carriage stopped.

"Welcome, my child," Theo said solemnly. She recognized his familiar voice and was comforted. As soon as they stepped into the cave, Rufilla heard water falling below. She also listened to the older priest's voice echo off the boulders in the cave. "Come, sweet daughter of the garden, and be with me a while." A sudden chill went through Rufilla, and she clutched her bouquet of wildflowers to her breast. At that point, Theo removed her blindfold so that she could experience the enormity of the cave. It was pitch black except for the flickering torches and candlelight below that reflected onto the shiny, moisture-laden rocks glistening around her. Theo lit an oil lamp, but the light seemed dim in the vast cavern. The sound of women chanting from deep within the cave resonated throughout her whole body, and she was again near tears. As she turned, she witnessed a sight that made her gasp and stumble over the small rocks behind her. On the pillar of stone behind her was painted a pictograph of a horn with blood dripping from it. "Ouch!" she yelled, dropping her bouquet on the cave floor. She grabbed her ankle as she leaned against a boulder and took in this piercing sight, feeling as if she had been pricked by the horn. Theo tended her foot, and then led her carefully down, down, down the slick, moist rocks. At each twist and turn, the "path" seemed more treacherous, and often they scooted on their buttocks as they slowly moved over the slabs of stone to the level below. Again she heard the voice of the older priest, bidding her to join him. This time her body tingled at the sound of his voice. Excitement had replaced fear. She had received advice that helped her prepare for this ritual, but this was beyond what she had imagined.

She held onto Theo as she descended into the belly of the cave. As she approached the bottom, there was a ladder made of hemp anchored deep within the rocks. Theo went first and reached up to guide her as she carefully lowered her body. The rungs were wet from Theo's feet, and as she reached the second to the last rung, her injured foot gave way, and she ended in his arms. Rufilla looked at him with a sigh of relief. They had reached the bottom of the cave. Next, they rounded a corner. Standing in front of them was the high priest in special vestments, and on either side of him were the women who had been behind her in the procession. How were they able to descend so quickly, she wondered?

The older priest spoke to her of many things about life for a woman in the outer and inner world. "Menarche can be seen as an Aristotelian catharsis, a purging of the tragedies that you have endured in your young life, namely your sacred affliction, but also the death of your betrothed."

Her breath caught in her throat as her eyes welled up. With the priest's words, a sudden recollection of what brought her to this moment came rushing back. She started to collapse but felt a wave that seemed to wash over her body, buoying her up, bringing with it an inner stillness. She stood silent and erect, looking directly at the priest, taking in his every word.

"With the release of these tensions from your body, purification has taken place within you. Your dreams of the god Asclepius have assured you of his benevolence and protection. Your accident with your foot is an added expression of who you are to become. Show me your bleeding foot, Rufilla." Theo supported her, and she held her foot high so that the priest could see the wound and the blood that came from it. "It was not enough that you have begun your journey into womanhood with us by passing your first blood in this Sanctuary. This wound is yet another sign from the god Asclepius that you have been selected to endure more." The priest now motioned for her to sit on a stool that had been brought for her. A young boy carried a bowl of water and set it at her feet. He took her injured foot in his hand, placing it in the water and gently washing away the blood with a cloth. "With these sacred waters, your wound will be healed. And now the enigma for you to ponder: the healing is also within the wound," the priest said. "Consider your difficult birth as a wounding which may have caused the epilepsy. But you also have been given the gift of knowing, perceiving things in people before they know them. That is an inner gift, the wound healing from the inside outward and into the world to help others.

When the cleansing of her foot was completed, she stood again.

"Come closer to me," the priest ordered. She moved next to him, and he took her hand and held it to the light of the candelabra. "Can you see the redness in your fingers?"

"Yes, I see it!" she exclaimed, seeing it for the first time.

"That is the life force that will help you heal. Put your ear to my chest." She did as she was told and heard the thumping of the priest's heart. "That is the center of the life force. Now listen closely as you hear me take in a breath and let it out." She listened as he breathed. "That is the spirit moving in and out. It helps the life force. Never forget how these two entities work together, how vital they are to our lives. A balance between these two must be maintained for good health. When you are happy and joyful, know that this life force, this god or goddess, dances within. When you feel bad, the life force needs your attention. This is your first lesson in the healing art of Asclepius."

The priest continued. "By your rescue from the Sacred Tree after your birth, by your upbringing and education, you have been set aside to learn and to grow in wisdom and spiritual understanding. Yours will not be an easy life. You have been chosen to become a Dionysian priestess, and with that task, you will experience periods of profound sadness but also great joy. The gift from the god Asclepius is the virtue of endurance. You have shown considerable strength in your young life, enduring your difficult birth and the resulting sacred affliction. Whether you are cured, only the god knows. But you were guided here with a greater purpose in mind. Take what comes and endure. Your continued countenance in all matters of propriety is paramount. You will be called upon to do great things for your community. Know that not all will accept that you as a woman have different responsibilities. Your marriage will be a natural arrangement. Developing your vocation as a priestess is a different situation, but no less important. Your tendency toward rebellion must be held in check—especially in Athens. Women are treated differently in Greece than in Rome. You will see that very soon. Observe your host's behavior and act accordingly. You are considered a woman now, and will probably be married upon your return home."

Next, a group of women encircled her and unhooked the "pins" on her dress. She stood naked in the women's circle. Then they opened up the circle, leading her to an underground waterfall on the side of one of the rock walls. Kharis motioned for her to step under the waterfall.

The priest read the ritual words as Rufilla turned around and around in the water. "You leave the goddess Artemis' service as a wild and innocent girl, an *arktoi*. Once free to run in nature, you now must realize that the beginning of menarche heralds the time of entering adulthood with all the responsibilities and consequences of your actions."

The women wrapped Rufilla in a towel as she stepped out from under the waterfall. They slipped a white tunica over her body, followed by a Greek chiton, which they belted at the waist. She was led to sit again on the low stool. A long veil was placed over her head, draping her body. Because of Rufilla's connection to Dionysus, Kharis now held a winnowing fan over her head, this mystic *liknon* representing the mystic fan of Iacchos. "The liknon is a symbol of purification," the priest said. Her feet were placed on top of the fleece of a ram's skin as a symbol of the purification of her body.

The priest raised the veil and rubbed her lips with honey. "This is to signify that you will always be truthful in your work as a priestess and that you will be blessed with eloquence and that the prescience, the secret knowing, will serve you well."

He emphasized what the next part of her initiation, in Eleusis, would involve: the paradox that included the necessity for separation from her mother versus her inclusion into the community of women who would nurture and teach her valuable lessons. There would always be those for whom she needed to watch out, he said. Those who would try to deceive her, tell her lies in a voice of sincere intention. So she must learn the process of differentiation and discernment. Not everyone in the outer world would be there to help her. He assured her that her naiveté would wane as she gathered the sound judgment needed to function as the spiritual woman that she was.

As she took in the many points of light in the darkness, the women's smiles were reflected in the light, and the priest, as Hades, looked very benevolent in all his wisdom. Flowers floated down upon all of them as they stood singing a Homeric hymn to the god Asclepius.

I begin to sing of Asclepius, son of Apollo and healer of sicknesses. In the Dotian plain, fair Coronis, daughter of King Phlegyas, bore him, a great joy to men, and a soother of cruel pangs. And so hail to you, lord: in my song, I make my prayer to thee!

Finally, she was brought to stand in front of a table. Before her on the table was a pomegranate that had been broken open. The seeds glistened in the light, the dark red fruit calling to her. She was thirsty for the sweetness of the juice but aware that Persephone was not to partake of that sweetness. With a nod of his head, the priest acknowledged that she sample the fruit. She moved closer to the table where the fruit lay waiting, breaking off a cluster of the rich, ripe seeds. As she ate the fruit, the priest spoke.

"I now acknowledge that you have chosen to change your name. Just as Kore changed her name to Persephone after she ate of the fruit of the pomegranate, you too have decided to change yours. Step forward and tell me your new name."

She stood before the priest, her voice steady, and her words echoing against the stone walls of the sacred cave. "I have chosen the name Arianna, as it is a form of Ariadne," she said. "I have heard her story since before I can remember. She has always been available for me, and so I wish to honor her by choosing a form of her name, and devoting my life to her."

"Now we will all remember that this is her chosen name, Arianna," the priest said.

He walked over to the table and took a few seeds in his hand. "Just as Persephone chose to eat of the fruit of the Underworld, so Arianna chooses to honor the fertile time she will spend in the Underworld, contemplating her new life from time to time, in periods of reflection. When she returns to the Upperworld, she will be able to give herself to her marriage." The priest continued. "The seeds of the pomegranate represent many things, among them the germination and fertilization of your body, Arianna, into a temple that will bring forth a child. It means a separation from being a child cared for by your parents to becoming a woman with responsibilities of husband and home."

When she heard her new name spoken out loud for the first time, her body involuntarily shuddered. Time stopped. This was the moment she had been waiting for. With the sound of her name, time and space dissolved and she was transported into the realm of the gods. Her face flushed, she groaned and sank to her knees. Kharis and Melissa moved to her side to comfort her, helping her gain her composure, once again alert and aware before the priest.

He went on to explain the role that her husband would play in her life and the importance of that bond. Husband on one side. Mother and friends on the other. It was her job to create a space of inclusion yet separation between the two parties. That was the challenge. New responsibilities and old relationships put in a fresh perspective—all-important to her growth.

Kharis now stood beside her and handed her a piece of paper. "Oh, thank you," Arianna said. She had forgotten that she was to sing the poem that she had written to thank the gods. A priestess stood next to her and started playing the double flute. The rest of the priestesses gathered around Arianna, and together they sang the paean of joy and thanksgiving that she had written.

"And now for the 'Whispering'—words for your ears only," Kharis said. She guided Arianna toward the priest, and he whispered into her ear, "Words from a wise Greek named Heraclitus come to my mind, dear Arianna. He said, 'You cannot step twice into the same river; for other waters are ever flowing on to you.' You must keep moving on, dear one."

The priest smiled as Arianna made a low bow to him. He took her hands and raised her, saying, "You are a gifted young woman. May the gods be always with you."

"And with you," she replied.

And with that, she was escorted by Theo into a long tunnel. As she emerged into the bright sunlight, she squinted to see that there were familiar faces gathered to greet her. She was especially glad to see her new friend Camilla from Praeneste.

"You look so beautiful!" Camilla said as they hugged each other.

"Look." Arianna showed the girl the cut on her heel. "I too recover from a wound."

"Come," Kharis said. "We will all gather to share a meal."

Arianna couldn't believe how close they were to the Sanctuary buildings. "You were driven around and around so that you would feel you had gone a great distance to meet your destiny—and you have," Melissa said.

Arianna walked the short distance with her friends back to a building in the center of the Sanctuary, where a ritual meal was to be held. The air was filled with sweet scents, some familiar, some new to her. As she ate, she heard instruments played and songs were sung that she had never heard before. She understood the significance of most of the words and Kharis and Melissa helped her understand the rest. Kharis told her that this was a ritual meal that was celebrated only on special occasions. Arianna understood this acknowledgment and was grateful.

As Melissa watched her, she could see that this short time in the Sanctuary had been crucial to her charge's maturation process. Melissa had worried about how Rufilla would adjust to her new surroundings in Athens. Still, now she felt that *this* experience, becoming Arianna, had been vital in making the next step. It had happened so quickly, as if she had simply opened a door and crossed over a threshold, from childhood to womanhood. The young woman before her was excited, yet Melissa could feel her composed demeanor. The reenactment in the cave had sent her senses reeling back to the times when goddesses were worshipped in caves and on mountaintops, sweet fragrances filling the air and ritual offerings of milk and honey, wine and water made to the goddess who took up residence there and made them sacred places. All this passed through Melissa's mind as she sat thinking first about the sweet baby who had suckled her breast and the young woman sitting before her now.

After dinner, Melissa stood to give a toast. "Here is to this young woman who, as a baby, was taken to the Asclepian Temple on the Tiber River. The priest there foretold of this tiny baby with the holy curse finding her way to her sacred path. Tonight we see how the meaning of his words has come to pass. I am blessed by the gods to be able to see this unfold. Blessed be Asclepius!"

With more toasts, Arianna was welcomed into her new life. Afterward, the older priest took her aside and said to her, "Tell your hostess in Athens that I feel it necessary that you learn about the ritual from Thera. Show the hostess the wounding on your foot. She will understand."

Because of her time constraints—she had to get to Athens for preparations there—they had already arranged to leave the next day. Kharis and her newfound Roman friends made proclamations of keeping in touch. "I will write to you often—in Greek!" Arianna said. Camilla and Arianna made a pact that they would get together upon Arianna's return.

They reached Kenchreai in record time, and the soldiers showed them to their ship. It, too, was a small merchant ship with an affable Greek captain. They would sail the following day.

Arianna spoke to the soldier in charge. "If you would be so kind, sir, could you tell me if the Roman sea captain, Aper, was able to return to his ship without incident?"

"He certainly was. I saw to it myself. He and his men left the port of Corinth within a day of his return."

"Will you be going back to Corinth soon, sir?"

"Tomorrow, as the gods would have it," the soldier said. It dawned on her that Theo would probably be going with him.

The next goodbye became even more painful for Melissa and Arianna. Theo would be returning to Pompeii. Theo and Melissa had said their private goodbyes the previous night in the Sanctuary. This would be the longest time they would be apart since their marriage.

Both women were crying. "Arianna, you know your father cannot get along without me for very long," Theo said, trying to humor them. "I will say no farewells, only 'until we meet again.'"

"Write," Melissa cried and waved as he made his way to the carriage.

"Write often," Theo returned.

"Wait," Arianna said, running alongside his carriage. "Please give these letters to my parents and Aper."

"With pleasure, dear one." And then he was gone.

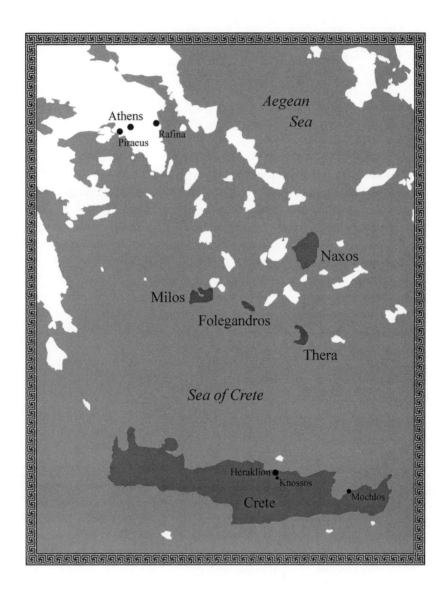

Map of AEGEAN SEA – Athens to Crete

CHAPTER XXXIV

ATHENS

With the wind again at their backs, the sail from Kenchreai to Piraeus was smooth and quick.

"Look, is that the mainland of Greece I see?" Arianna asked.

"Watch," was all the captain said. Now he was focused, navigating the ship through the narrow harbor opening. Slowly they rounded the landmass that was the island of Salamis and there, tucked away was the sheltered but busy harbor of Piraeus, with ships coming out as they were going in to be moored at one of the many docks.

Arianna was interested to see the harbor for the first time and tried to make her questions understood. The captain was enthusiastic with his responses, and she had to keep slowing his speech so that she could understand his replies. Melissa helped.

Again, she saw the devastation that had been enacted at the hands of the Romans. It had been a short forty years since Sulla sacked the harbor at Piraeus. Some re-building had taken place.

The ship's captain said, "After the slaughter by Sulla, who decimated the long wall from Piraeus to Athens, he demolished the harbor and destroyed the city. My grandparents were among the fatalities. The people who escaped, among them my parents and other relatives, traveled to small villages inland that would have been unimportant to Sulla. Little by little, people came back to rebuild their houses and try to start a new life. Most were descendants of the people who were killed during the siege of Sulla."

Arianna remained silent. Although her family wasn't responsible, she felt guilty, just being a Roman.

"Melissa," Arianna said in Latin, "please tell him what Sulla did to Pompeii."

Melissa complied. "Sulla made Pompeii a Roman colony as punishment after it rebelled against the Romans in the Social War. Then he settled hundreds if not thousands of his troops, taking houses away from towns-people who had opposed him. He even changed the name of the town."

Arianna listened carefully, trying to catch all the nuances of the language.

"Do not forget to tell him about how Sulla bombarded the city walls!"

"Just wait. You will see real devastation. We are still recovering," the captain said solemnly. All were silent.

After they docked, Melissa and Arianna were transferred in a less than elegant carriage from the large port to the edge of Athens, which seemed like an eternity to the two women. A porter eventually found them. As it turned out, Stephanos, her host, had told the porter to look for a red-haired foreign girl with a lot of luggage, but she had pared down her luggage at each stop as she gave gifts to her hosts and even more at Epidaurus. Kharis had been the recipient of several gifts along with the priests that were so supportive of her. By the time she reached Athens, the amphora of wine from her father and perfumes from Capua were all that was left.

Arianna settled in with her "uncle" Stephanos and "aunt" Kallistê and their family. Aridela and Kallistê were distant relatives, but because of Aridela's visit to Athens, when they were both in their teens, the families had become close. Kallistê was especially warm and welcoming. She arranged for Arianna to continue the Greek lessons that she had started in Pompeii. This time the teacher spoke no Latin so that it would be challenging, but she would learn a great deal very quickly. Being with so many Greeks along the way and especially in Epidaurus had given her ample opportunity to hear and speak the language. She told her new family the stories of her experiences in Patra and Epidaurus and her name change after the ritual.

Arianna realized very soon that her Greek "uncle" was a no-nonsense disciplinarian as far as young women were concerned, especially foreigners who lived in his house. Arianna, who wanted to see everything Athens had to offer as she had done in previous cities, quickly found herself frustrated by the limitations he imposed on her movements outside their housing compound. One day Kallistê and Melissa decided to go to the vast agora in downtown Athens. Arianna declined to go with them. However, she thought better of it after they left and talked her slave girl into taking her to the agora to try to find the women. Instead of seeing the women, they found a market place full of people: vendors in stalls selling food, others selling exotic gems, cloth, and perfumes. It reminded her of the forum in Rome. It also contained large buildings where court cases were conducted.

One building caught her eye. It was long with columns that held up the roof. The long front side was open, and she could see painted panels of art on the tall back walls.

"Let us go and see what art is on the walls," Arianna said. The slave was reluctant but Arianna persisted. "Just a brief look."

First, they saw an impressive statue of a man. "Zeno," the slave girl said. "This is the Stoa of Zeno."

Not understanding who Zeno was, Arianna passed by the statue and entered the stoa. There was one work of art on the back wall that stood out. A man walked up to them and asked if he could be of help. "Please tell me about this painting," Arianna asked.

"This is a painting of Theseus battling the Amazons," the man said. "Do you know about Theseus, young woman?"

"Oh yes, I am going to visit the island of Crete, where we will see the Palace at Knossos and the labyrinth where he slew the Minotaur. Then he abandoned Ariadne!"

He listened to her accent. "You're not from here, are you?"

"No, I am from Rome," she said.

"Well, young woman, I would suggest that you come accompanied by a male slave the next time you come here. It is not always a safe place." He winked at her.

The wink made her very uncomfortable. "Thank you, sir. Good day," she said. "Let us go," she whispered to the slave girl, who had a worried look on her face.

They made it home quickly, only to be greeted by Kallistê, Melissa, and Stephanos, all of whom were distressed that she had left on her own without a proper chaperone. Stephanos was very angry. He took her into another room to talk. Arianna felt that she had done nothing wrong, because her understanding was that she could go out as long as she had someone with her. He insisted that she should go outside only if a *man* escorted her. He proceeded to beat the slave girl, blaming her.

He then turned back on Arianna. "As long as you are under this roof, you are under my authority, just as you would be if you were back in your father's house in Pompeii."

"But—"

"No excuses in this house," he said as he raised his hand to her.

In that instant, Arianna fainted, and a seizure followed.

"Tend to her," Stephanos yelled to the slave girl as he stormed out of the room.

Kallistê came running into the room as Stephanos was leaving. "What have you done!" she shouted.

"This was your idea. You take care of her," Stephanos snorted.

Kallistê found Arianna on the floor, her limbs still trembling, blood coming from her mouth. "Fetch the doctor," she yelled at the slave.

For days the female household remained subdued. Melissa rarely left her bedside. Arianna remained secluded, not only because she was recovering from a major seizure, but also because she was embarrassed that the seizure had made her seem weak. She did not want to face Stephanos.

"This wouldn't have happened if I had been here. Arianna had been so happy since her time at Epidaurus," Melissa said, talking with Kallistê in the women's quarters.

"Headstrong and spoiled is what I see," Stephanos said as he entered their chamber. "Do you know what might have happened to them—two young girls out for a lark?"

"It was midday," Kallistê said.

"They were not chaperoned," Stephanos said with a cold look at Melissa. "There was no man with them. What kind of rules do you Romans live by that you let young daughters run free? To say nothing of the fact that she is of marriageable age. Can you imagine what could have happened?"

"Calm yourself," Kallistê said.

"Yes, I understand the gravity of your concerns," Melissa said. "This will never happen again."

"Not in my house," he said. Then as if trying to change the subject, he asked, "How is she?"

"She is recovering with Melissa's help," Kallistê said. The tone in her voice reflected her contempt for his feigned concern.

"Much better," Melissa said. "It was a bad seizure, but your doctor is helping her through this. Her tongue is healing and she will be talking again before long. Thank you for your help."

Stephanos nodded and turned to leave the room.

"Your anger was no help," Melissa said under her breath.

Stephanos stopped in the doorway and turned. "What did you say?"

At that moment, Arianna came out of her bedroom. "I am so sorry.

What can I do?" Her words came haltingly as her tongue was still swollen and painful from having been bitten during the seizure.

"Mercy, child." He swooped back in and took hold of Arianna by the shoulders. "I have been worried sick about you." Melissa heard a pompous concern in his voice. "You must understand that I am responsible to your father for anything that might happen. Do you understand?"

"I do, I am so sorry." was all that she could say.

He walked her to a couch and sat down with her. "You must understand that I am the pateras, the head of this household. In Rome, you call it pater familias. Much the same. My wife and children and you are my flock—subject to whatever I deem acceptable." His tone was condescending. "My lineage is of great importance in this city of Athens. We have much responsibility—take, for instance, the Eleusinian mysteries in which you may participate. Each family member has responsibilities. The women must be virtuous above all. I am sure that you learned about virtue and accountability through the ritual in Epidaurus."

"Yes, uncle," she said. Arianna started to say something more, but Stephanos put his finger to her lips. "I will leave you with the words of Aristotle, who said, 'The soul rules the body, and the reasonable mind must rule over passion—it is natural and necessary.'"

CHAPTER XXXV

ARIADNE'S MYTH ON CRETE

Arianna had carried a letter from the Asclepian priest to give to Stephanos. In it, the priest requested that Arianna be sent to Crete to visit Knossos. He did not explain why, nor was Stephanos curious enough to ask. Still, as summer temperatures rose to uncomfortable levels, Stephanos decided that it was time for the women to visit the island of Crete to enjoy the island breezes. He had no idea what Arianna had experienced but only knew that he wanted to comply with the Asclepian priest's wishes. Arianna had shared all the events that had happened to her since she left Pompeii with her aunt, including her dreams, wisdom shared by the priests and priestesses at Epidaurus, and especially the memorable ritual that had been performed for her. Since her initial involvement with Stephanos was so painful, she did not feel that she could trust him. The older priest had also warned her about how her Greek host might treat her. The priest had been right.

Whatever she thought of him, Stephanos had arranged for the group of women and their male chaperone, Timo, to stay at the home of a friend near the ancient Palace of Knossos on the island of Crete. Once there, Kallistê, who was also her teacher, would continue the Greek lessons and introduce Arianna to Greek plays and authors suitable for young girls, along with Zeno, Chrysippus, and the Stoics.

One evening, Melissa, Kallistê, and Arianna had a discussion after dinner.

"Why is it that you like the Stoics so much, Arianna?" Kallistê asked.

"That is a fair question," Arianna replied. "I think it is because when I first learned about philosophy and especially the Stoics, I was taken with what they called 'unruly emotions' and how to control them with peace of mind from living a virtuous life. I related that to my seizures. They often feel like unruly emotions that get out of control and explode in my head."

"Ahhh," Kallistê and Melissa said in unison.

"That explains so much, my dear," Kallistê said. "But your episode of running off to the agora, what was that about?"

"Not a virtuous act—probably just youthful curiosity and stupidity."

The other two women burst out laughing. "We understand all too well. And now, you would not do it again?"

"Next time, I will get my uncle's permission and take a male chaperone with me—maybe Timo!" Arianna said. "But I did find out some important information the day that I was in the agora. Zeno of Citium, whose statue I saw in front of the Stoa Poikile, often lectured, when he was alive, to his followers within that stoa. The philosophical school of Stoicism takes its name from that building! Auntie, do you think your husband might allow me to hear a lecture there from a modern-day Stoic?"

"I think that can be arranged," her aunt replied. "Upon our return!"

Arianna was delighted to be able to visit the island of her namesake, Ariadne. While aboard the ferries that took them south from island to island toward Crete, Kallistê, Arianna, and Melissa often passed the time telling different versions of Ariadne's tale. Arianna shared hers.

ARIADNE, GODDESS OF CRETE

Ariadne was a Minoan princess who lived on the island of Crete. Her father, Minos, for whom the Minoan culture was named, was born the son of Zeus, father of the gods, and the princess Europa. Pasiphaë, her mother, was the daughter of Helios, the old sun god, and Perse, also connected to the sun. As children of gods, Minos and Pasiphaë were divine. As well-known king and queen, they were also considered human.

Minos once boasted that he was so blessed by the gods that they answered his every prayer. So, he dedicated an altar to the sea-god Poseidon and then prayed that a white bull might emerge from the sea, which he intended to offer as a sacrifice to Poseidon. Sure enough, the god sent up the creature, but Minos was enthralled by its beauty and decided to keep it in his herd and sacrificed another inferior animal in its place. Poseidon, offended by this affront, retaliated by causing Minos' wife, Pasiphaë, to fall in love with the bull. Pasiphaë confided her unnatural passion to Daedalus, the master craftsman, and he constructed a wooden cow that Pasiphaë might climb inside and allow the bull to mount her. In due course, Pasiphaë gave birth to a monstrous child, with a human body but a bull's head. It was called the Minotaur. Minos eventually discovered Pasiphaë's terrible secret and commanded Daedalus to build a labyrinth in which to hide their shame.

At this time, the city of Athens was obliged to pay a yearly tribute to Minos as retribution for the death of his son, Androgeus. Henceforth, Minos decreed that the tribute should be seven youths and seven maidens, who were led to the entrance of the labyrinth and never seen again. One year Theseus, son of Aegeus, king of Athens, approached his father that he might be part of the tribute, swearing that he would bring an end to Minos's tyranny. Theseus set sail for Crete and made his way into Minos's palace at Knossos. Luckily for Theseus, he caught the eye of Ariadne, who promised to help him if he would take her away and marry her. Theseus saw his chance and agreed. Daedalus had revealed the secret of the labyrinth to Ariadne. She gave Theseus a magic ball of red thread for him to unravel as he went through the maze so that he might find his way out again. All went according to plan: Theseus killed the Minotaur, rescued the tribute, and he and Ariadne made good their escape.

Some days later, after disembarking on the island later known as Naxos, Theseus left Ariadne asleep on the shore and sailed away. Why he did so will remain a mystery. Some say that while wind-bound on Naxos, he reflected on the scandal that Ariadne's arrival at Athens would cause. Others say that Dionysus, appearing to Theseus in a dream, threateningly demanded Ariadne for himself. Dionysus is thought to have cast a spell that made Theseus forget his promise to Ariadne and even her very existence. Others called him a pompous despot.

Meanwhile, Ariadne became so depressed that she was ready to give up her life, but at her lowest point, Dionysus rescued and revived her. He took her to the Underworld, and placed a crown upon Ariadne's head and made her Queen of the Underworld. After their marriage, Dionysus took the crown and threw it into the nighttime sky to commemorate his love for her so that the entire world might see the crown forever. It is now known as the Corona Borealis.

After a day of settling into a villa near Knossos, the three women and their entourage made the trip up the gradual hill to the ruins of the palace. "Do not be too disappointed at what you see," Kallistê said. "Remember that Stephanos and I told you about a horrific occurrence in the weather, maybe an earthquake that caused extensive damage to the palace more than a millennium ago."

"Stephanos called it Mother Gaia's work," Arianna said.

"Ah yes, blame the woman," Melissa whispered to Arianna.

"The results of the calamity that happened so long ago in this area are still evident in the devastation and debris you will see," Kallistê continued. "The palace will never be restored, but we will still be able to glimpse the enormity of the structure."

After a few more minutes, they came upon a wide road made of enormous flat stones. "Take your time and walk carefully, thinking of all the people over the eons who have preceded you in the journey up this hill," Kallistê said.

"Is this the road that took Theseus and the other tribute to the labyrinth? Is this the Sacred Way my mater told me about?" Arianna asked.

"Yes, the same," Kallistê said, pulling Arianna close to her. "It is tradition to remain silent right after someone gives you the greeting of the goddess. Today that someone will be me." The three stopped and Kallistê whispered into Arianna's and Melissa's ear: "Step slowly with reverence and hold dear the thoughts that come to you from the goddess Ariadne. Know that she is with you now and will remain with you throughout your whole life. Blessed be the Sacred Way."

Kallistê took the lead, then Arianna, and Melissa behind her, walking single file they proceeded onward up the hill. Finally, at the top, they saw the colossal sculpture of the horns of consecration. "Oh, Auntie, it is every bit as impressive as you said it would be. What a wonderful place to conduct rituals."

Next, she saw large pieces of stone, marble columns that had cascaded down the hill when the earth-shattering event occurred. Melissa squeezed her hand.

Making their way through the debris that had lain there for more than a thousand years, Kallistê said, "See, one can easily recognize the top of a column as we pass by. Notice how distinctive the capitols look, resembling a soft, almost cushion-like top, capping the column. Nothing that you've seen in Italy or Greece. The tall trees that were used as columns were turned upside down, supposedly so that they would not sprout."

"How ingenious if it really worked," Melissa said. "Arianna, do you think these columns were as tall as the columns at the Asclepian Sanctuary at Pompeii."

"I think they are. It is hard to tell as the columns of wood have decayed and left no trace. If we could find a base and a capital and measure between the two. Not sure, but that might work."

"Over here." Timo motioned for them to come to where he had found a base and capital that might have accommodated a now-decayed tree column between them. He stepped off the length between the two stone ends.

"Twenty Roman feet," Melissa said. "And each tree the same height," she said.

Kallistê moved on. "Let us take these steps," she shouted from a distance. They ran to see that she was at the entrance to a wide stairwell. She directed the male slaves, "Help the women up. That first step is a tall one."

As they reached the top of the stairs, the Roman women were shocked. Before them was a vast open area. The floor, the only part left of a room, was unbelievably large.

"Many say that artist and craftsman Daedalus designed and built this room for Ariadne," Kallistê said. "She had asked for a dance floor, and here it is!"

"Let us sing the song that Mater taught me before we left." Arianna took Melissa by the hand, and they proceeded to not only sing but dance to their song. The Greek dance came easily to Arianna, and before long, Kallistê and all the women slaves who had been watching were encouraged to join in. They did, and then Timo and the male slaves, who knew the tune as well, stood on the sidelines singing and clapping their hands. One slave pulled a lyre out of his knapsack and started playing. It was as if Arianna was the embodiment of the goddess. They danced the length of the floor and back again—back and forth until they were exhausted.

After they rested, Kallistê had one more surprise. "Come with me, Arianna, and you also, Melissa. We will make this passage together," she said. "Light the lamps." She motioned for the male slaves to bring the lit lamps to them, and the three women made their way through an entrance and down a short flight of steps. They went through a room lined with stone benches, an antechamber. Beyond that room was another room, which had no windows. It felt like a secret room to Arianna, and indeed that is what it was. It was the room closest to *Gaia*, Mother Earth, and the most beautiful place Arianna had ever seen. The floors were finished with intricate mosaics, and covering the brilliant red walls were amazing frescoes of white clouds. One long wall took their focus. The frescoes were of two heraldic griffins, one on each side of the wall, symbolically guarding whoever might once have been seated on the tiny stone seat between the griffins. There were stone benches directly below the griffins, flanking the stone seat.

"This is the secret throne room of Ariadne—I just know it is! This is her throne!"

"This is the *Adyton*, the innermost sanctuary of the Temple of Ariadne," Kallistê said. "No one was allowed here but the priest and priestess. That is why I wanted just the three of us to come. We received a letter from the priest at Epidaurus, and he told me he wanted to make sure that you saw this room. He feels that you will become a priestess when you return to Pompeii. From what your mater has written to me, I think you will be a priestess of Ariadne and Dionysus. That is an extraordinary calling, young woman."

Arianna started to speak but took in a deep breath instead.

"I know you do not understand all the implications of what has happened to you," Kallistê continued. "Only with time will the understanding you gain clarify what needs to be done to carry on your work. For now, you must trust that this will all be revealed to you. Now let us take a few moments to be in this room."

Arianna immediately went to the throne, sat down on the floor beside it and stroked the seat. "This is where she sat. I know it."

After a few moments, Kallistê said, "Beyond this room and down those steps is the lustral basin, the room of purification. But I am sure this room was where the oracle would come."

"Oracle?"

"Yes, the Oracle Iophon of Knossos. Legend has it that he was a favorite of the queen."

"Queen?"

"Queen Ariadne."

"Of course, from princess to queen—Queen of the Underworld."

After a few more moments of silent reflection, Kallistê said, "Remind me to talk later about the Snake goddesses. It is a beautiful tradition. But right now, we had better re-join the group." They could hear the slaves singing a traditional song about Ariadne. As they started up the steps, they heard a flutter of wings. A bird flew around the throne room behind them and then up the stairs, over their heads, and out the doors.

The women looked at each other. "Wasn't that a bluebird?" Arianna asked.

"Yes, it is called a roller bluebird. I have been here many times and have never seen one before. Let us just say it was the spirit of Ariadne blessing us." The women gave each other a knowing smile. Arianna patted her chest as if catching her breath and calming her fluttering heart. They extinguished their lamps and ascended the rest of the stairs, returning to the light of day.

There were more frescoes to see. One that took Arianna's fancy was of young men and women leaping over a bull.

"You know they had to be young and foolish to be doing this at all, much less for sport!" Kallistê said.

"Could it have been a ritual sport? It looks like it must have taken a lot of training. And see, the boy's skin is painted red and the girl's skin is painted white. Girls could do it too!" Arianna said, goading her aunt.

"You are a single-minded young woman," Kallistê said. "Everything and everyone has ritual meaning for you. What a gift to look at the world in this way."

Next they studied the beautiful fresco of a bluebird. It was shown sitting on a rock with wildflowers all around it. Its bright blue body and long black beak made it distinctive and unforgettable.

"Was this the bird we saw?" Melissa asked.

"It is the same," Kallistê responded.

"The fresco was painted so long ago, and the bluebirds are still here," Arianna exclaimed. "Maybe mother nature does not destroy everything."

The massive sculpture of the horns of consecration that had greeted them also served as the stunning conclusion to their visit. "What significance did the bull hold for the people who lived in that time?" Arianna asked.

"You tell me, young woman. What god is often mentioned with the sacred bull?"

"Of course—Dionysus," Arianna responded.

"Remind me to show you one of my most prized possessions when we return home," Kallistê said.

From Knossos, they traveled east to a coastal town, Mochlos, quaint and bustling with people. Kallistê, Arianna, and Melissa settled into their rooms in the local inn high atop the hill overlooking the sea beyond. "What is the island out there?" Arianna asked.

"Look closer," Kallistê said. "See the isthmus that connects the mainland to the—"

"— It is a peninsula, not an island!"

"That is right!"

"Can we visit?"

"Of course, I will arrange a boat to take us over tomorrow morning. Then we will have the day to explore."

"You are wonderful, Auntie. I am so fortunate to be here with you."

Melissa joined Arianna and Kallistê and, accompanied by Timo, they took a walk down to where the isthmus and the ancient structures lay in ruins. "This destruction also happened a very long time ago," Kallistê explained. "Some say there was an eruption on the island of Thera and that the result was the devastation of Creta, especially the northern coast—the rubble you see here, in the water. This could have happened at the same time as the destruction of the palace of Knossos. Who knows?"

Arianna was silent as they walked the shoreline. Finally, she spoke. "It seems that what man doesn't destroy; nature often does."

"But then," Kallistê continued, "see the resilience of man. Here we are in this tiny thriving village."

Melissa added, "And the shops in the agora look very interesting!"

Arianna pointed to a man offshore. "He is walking on water!"

"No, not really," Kallistê said.

The man waved to them.

"What are you walking on?" Arianna asked in a loud voice in her most correct Greek.

The man started speaking very rapidly. Kallistê motioned to Timo who was walking behind them. "Interpret what this man says! He speaks too fast, even for me." To Arianna she said, "His dialect is of this area and almost like a foreign language to me."

Timo asked the man to slow his speech.

"Ask him to explain about the structure he stands on," Kallistê said.

The two men talked for a few minutes, and then the man began jumping up and down, pointing to the concrete under his feet. "Roman, Roman," he said. Timo turned to the women. "He was curious about our guest, and when I told him you were Roman, you saw that he began jumping up and down on the concrete container, did you not?"

"Yes." Arianna was puzzled.

"These are holding tanks for the fisherman's catch. He is standing on one. It keeps the fish alive but contained," Timo continued. "The concrete was made of Roman materials brought from Italy by a Roman official. This officer had been to Mochlos earlier, became enchanted with the area and wished to help the local fishermen. He returned on a ship with workers and with a curious material from Italy."

Now Timo was excited.

"Oh, I know what that is!" Melissa spoke up. "Aper talked about a fine, brownish-red earth like sand from Puteoli. It's mixed with lime, poured into the wooden frames and then it cures in the water! They make moles and jetties and other structures for harbors. That is the magic he is talking about. No one else has used this process but the Roman engineers. And they use only the earthen mixture from Puteoli."

Dinner was at a local restaurant that evening, and all the talk with the local people who were there was about this magic sand from Italy. Melissa was quizzed and told them what she knew, that she and Arianna had even been to Puteoli, the town from which the sand and earth were taken.

"Puteoli?" the innkeeper questioned.

"It means stinky!" was Melissa's response as she held her nose. "The ground bubbles up in places—hot and smelly!" They all laughed. "But people pay large sums of money to soak in the baths nearby."

"We have something similar off the island of Thera," the innkeeper said. "We call it a mud bath!" Again laughter filled the room.

The next morning the group from Athens was transported to the peninsula in a dingy similar to the one on Aper's boat. They explored this projecting mass of land that housed all sorts of remnants from ancient buildings. At one point, they walked down a short set of stairs, making a right-angle turn into a small room.

"This is a special configuration of a room. It may have been a sacred room of ritual purification, like the one we saw in the palace at Knossos," Kallistê said. "There may have been a lustral basin here, a tub for ritual purification." She looked deeply into Arianna's eyes. "Keep this in mind— you may see this again."

Onward they proceeded, ending at the west end of the peninsula that the women had looked at from the inn window the day before. A winding path took them high up to the entrance of a dark cave. Kallistê went in first. "Come, let us follow her," Melissa said. Arianna was reluctant. "You were in that huge cave at Epidaurus. Surely this shouldn't be a major concern for you."

Arianna leaned against the entrance, felt faint, and slowly slid to the ground. Her chest felt as if it were going to burst open. A cool breeze behind her sent a chill up her spine as she felt the sweat beading on her neck. "Whatever spirit lives within does not take kindly to strangers. I will not enter."

Kallistê came out a few minutes later. "See, I am fine. Nothing harmed me! I have been in this cave many times."

"I will not go against my instincts," Arianna said emphatically.

"So be it," Kallistê said.

As they retraced their steps down the path, the fresh air seemed to clear away her feeling of dread and her breathing returned to normal. Arianna looked at Melissa. "I am sure that whatever happened in that cave, the spirit of the dead within does not rest easily."

A few more days were spent enjoying Mochlos and its interesting agora. Arianna bought a lovely weaving for her mother, a stunning red carpet with a diamond design outlined in black. In the center of the rug was a weaving of the bone-colored Horn of Consecration that she had seen at Knossos. Quite a unique weaving, everyone agreed.

Their last evening, they walked the shoreline after dinner. They heard an eerie sound coming from the peninsula. "Listen," she said. "Look, it comes from the cave." They saw the silhouettes of people carrying lanterns and running out of the cave and down the path.

Kallistê and Melissa looked at each other. "Well, maybe Arianna was right," said Melissa.

"Yes, I was right not to go into that darkness."

"Some of the dead do not like to be disturbed," Kallistê said.

With that, the evening was over. As they headed back to the inn, Kallistê pulled Timo aside. "Did you make sure that all is safe for our departure? What about the pirate ship in the harbor?"

"I gave the local pirates the money you gave to me. They will use it to get drunk tonight so they won't rise early," Timo said.

"Then we should leave early. Prepare the boats." He bowed and left.

The next morning they bade their Cretan friends farewell. As the sailors rowed north to catch the wind, Arianna took one last look at the magical island. "There is the palace—see it high on the hill," she said as she glimpsed the palace ruins. She wondered whether she would ever see it again.

"Do you remember the god, Janus?" Melissa asked.

"The god of two faces—endings and beginnings," Arianna said. "When one door closes, turn around and another door opens. But I am not willing to close the door on Ariadne."

"That is not necessary," Kallistê said. "Think of your life as a river. You can sail down the river in your mind and visit her. Then take her with you and sail into the next adventure."

"Whatever that may be," Arianna said.

As the wind filled the sail and they headed north, Kallistê shouted, "Onward to Athens!"

CHAPTER XXXVI

MYSTERY SEASON

INITIATION RITUAL OF MARRIAGE OF
ARIADNE AND DIONYSUS

Returning to the blistering heat of the city, Arianna wished that they were still in the breezy countryside of the island of Crete. But there was welcome mail waiting for her. Her mother's letters were long and newsy. Two sad notes were that their group of friends had had some severe health issues. Aricia's husband, Marcus Arrius Polites, had died quite suddenly while on a trip to the east coast of Italy, shocking everyone. No one knew what had happened. Victor and Clodia were not participating in dinners with the group, as Clodia's health continued to decline. There was also a letter from Cil, telling her of all he was learning in the military medical field. His letter was so enthusiastic that she knew he had chosen the right path. He had made friends with several doctors, one of whom was mentoring him. Everyone was anxious for Octavius to join them. Hostia had written complaining of the hot summer and telling Arianna how much she missed her. Arianna set to answering the letters, filling everyone in on many details, and promising more when she returned home. She said she wouldn't forget anything, as she was keeping a journal.

Seeing the ruins of Knossos and then Mochlos had left a powerful impression upon Arianna. It was compelling not only for her but for Kallistê, who realized her mission in this young girl's life. From the first letter she had received from Aridela, telling her that she wanted to send Rufilla to Athens, Kallistê began to realize now what needed to be done concerning the upcoming rituals. The ritual of Dionysus and Ariadne would be held first. It was a private and personal ceremony that Kallistê had arranged for Arianna. The Lesser and Greater Mysteries of Eleusis were rituals in which Kallistê and Stephanos and their family would have major roles. But the two rituals at Eleusis were meant for the masses, and hundreds of people would participate. Kallistê felt that Arianna might get overwhelmed in the horde of people. Above all, she did not want her so exhausted and overstimulated that it might bring on a series of seizures. It would be three rituals in a very short time. Kallistê spoke with Stephanos, who concurred that it would be better for Arianna to have some time to rest at their countryside villa after the Dionysian ritual while they tended to their duties at Eleusis.

Athens was filled with visitors and bustled with activity. People had arrived in town to attend the Eleusinian games and stay on to take part in the Mysteries—Lesser and Greater. But on an undisturbed street at the edge of the city, preparations were quietly being made for the private Dionysian ritual. The small temple of Dionysus was located at the edge of a forest that had been partially cleared and transformed into a park. The gathering of women involved in the ritual would be intimate: only family and friends, a closed affair.

Arianna was told that this ritual was seldom enacted because an outsider needed to be chosen as the initiate—in this case, a Roman girl. It corresponded to the fact that Dionysus was considered an outsider in the Pantheon of the Olympic gods. Arianna would play the role of Ariadne. The young man who would play the role of Dionysus was one of Kallistê's family members. Kallistê reminded her that she had been introduced to the young man in a social setting shortly before leaving for Crete, so she knew she would recognize him. Arianna remembered the good-looking Greek very well, had even mentioned him in a letter she had written to Hostia, telling her how much they had in common, including Stoicism.

The ritual lasted three days. The first two were for preparation, and on the third day the actual ceremony would begin. On the first day of preparation, Kallistê started by presenting an extensive review of various aspects of the myths of Dionysus. "This particular mystery religion of Dionysus has its beginning hundreds of years ago," Kallistê said. "Orpheus is said to have been the founder. He was a legendary poet and musician of his time. We will hear some of his poetry and music in the course of the initiation. I will begin by defining *cultus* as a religious group," Kallistê said. "It practices rituals that are sacred and secret, otherwise known as Mysteries. The result often produces a state of awe. It is a participation in something that, even though seen and experienced, is not fully understood. For example, let's take the Palace of Knossos. Just being in the presence of the ancient site, knowing from childhood the myth of Ariadne and her father, King Minos, can cause one to be overcome the first time one visits the island. I have visited it many times but still experience that overwhelming feeling of knowing something at a deep level, but knowing nothing as far as being able to explain the experience. If we are fortunate enough to delve into these Mysteries, we might someday have a glimpse of the meaning. But for now, we need to be aware of what we are experiencing and leave the meaning for a later time. Know that cultus is an involvement in something well beyond our understanding. In this instance, it is the story of Dionysus and Ariadne. We must cherish and hold onto the feelings within that conjure up and bring forth the god and goddess within us."

Next, she reviewed the history of the myths of Ariadne. She explained that over the centuries, many and various endings had been created for Ariadne's story, making it complicated and sometimes open-ended. Arianna was told that it was necessary to enact Ariadne's death to show not only the serious nature of this ritual but also to receive the hope gleaned from understanding the rewards of the afterlife. Thus, the goddess Ariadne would be born into immortality, into the world of Dionysus. It was hard for Arianna to hear about the deity's death. Still, she had to look at it symbolically, which meant Ariadne's letting go of her former life on Crete—to be born into her new life as the wife of Dionysus and Queen of the Underworld. Kallistê knew that Ariadne's death and rebirth were painful for Arianna to take in, but going through this part of the ritual would make a profound difference in her understanding of the ceremony for herself and for others whom she would eventually help along the path.

In the afternoon of the first day, the story of Dionysus that would be used in the ritual was told to her. This part entailed the revealing of Dionysus being thrice-born. It was different from the version of his being twice-born because this was the account used in the Orphic tradition—a tradition Arianna would be asked to carry forward. The first birth had to do with Zeus seducing Persephone and thus making Hera, his wife, very unhappy. Zeus had many adulterous affairs with mortal women. This time the child born was Dionysus. He had to be secreted away because Hera wanted him dead. But Hera ultimately found him and incited the Titans to kill him, which they did, tearing him apart and devouring him, save his heart, which was delivered to Zeus by Athena. In the second birth, Zeus gave the heart to a mortal, Semele, in the form of a drink, which impregnated her. But goaded by Hera, Semele asked Zeus to show himself in all his godliness, which was more than a mortal could endure. Seeing Zeus in all his godly power, she burst into flames. Zeus saved the baby by sewing the fetus into his thigh, thus giving birth to Dionysus a third time. Kallistê emphasized his birth, death, and rebirth because this ritual, as well as Ariadne's, had much to say about life after death.

Afterward, they ate a light dinner, and the group of women sang the hymns of Orpheus that would be sung on the third evening. Arianna was unfamiliar with the words and music, so she enjoyed learning some of the stories related to both Orpheus and Dionysus. To her, the melodies were exciting yet haunting.

The second day of preparation was a day of hearing the story of Ariadne and Dionysus that was so familiar to Arianna. Everyone fasted and rested that day with a light meal in the evening.

On the third day, the ritual started with a sacrifice to Dionysus. Again it was a day of fasting. Kallistê and Arianna had a spirited, in-depth discussion about what it might mean to celebrate the ritual back home. She was sure that such rituals were performed in Pompeii, but she had never heard about them. Maybe she had been too young.

That evening, just at twilight, the women were gathered together and clothed in fawn skins, and a man gave them a magic potion, as Arianna thought of it later. The drink was sweet, and she was warned not to consume too much. He also gave each woman a crown of ivy to wear. They were taken to the edge of the woods behind the Temple of Dionysus. Each woman was given a *thyrsus,* a staff made of a tall fennel stalk topped with a pine cone that had been saturated with oil and lit to serve as a torch to carry into the dark woods. By the time Arianna entered, the woods were full of women with torches, dancing and singing to the music of lyres and lutes being played by female musicians around the edge of the woods. Each musician had planted a thyrsus in the ground beside her, forming a semicircle in the woods that served as a *temenos,* a sacred safe place for the women to dance. Pan pipes were played by musicians who strolled along the edge of the woods, keeping the string players in time with the dancers.

Arianna secured her thyrsus into the ground and leaned against a tree. Everything around her seemed exaggerated, including the sensual feeling as she raised her arms behind her and touched the bark with both hands. She circled the tree, and doing her own little dance, felt dizzy and sat down at the base. Looking out into the woods, she could see the torches all around her. They seemed to be moving on their own, disembodied from the women that held them. She closed her eyes but for a moment. As she opened them, she felt someone's presence. She looked up to see an older Greek man standing before her, smiling and holding out his hand. It was the man who had given her the drink and the ivy crown.

"You must be Silenus," she said, having been told earlier that he would be the first of two men to approach her in the darkness.

"Yes, I am the teacher of Dionysus, ancient god of wisdom and the vine."

He led her to the edge of the woods, just behind the temple. There, a gigantic Plane tree stood with long sturdy branches outstretched. Hanging from one of them was a swing held by two strong ropes that secured a seat at the bottom. She sat down on the swing, not feeling anxious as she had thought she would. The drink had calmed her and she knew why she was there. Silenus stood behind her, pushing the swing gently. She felt herself letting go to the experience of dying metaphorically to be received by Dionysus into her new life. All the other women gathered around her, singing a hymn to Silenus. These were the words she best understood:

"Great nurse of Bacchus, to my pray'r incline, Silenus, honor'd by the pow'rs—Head of the Bacchic Nymphs, who ivy bear—Come, rouse to sacred Joy thy pupil kin,—and bless triumphant pow'r the sacred choir."

She heard cymbals clanging in the background and felt a change in the pace of the swinging. Someone new was pushing her, someone stronger. Higher, she soared into the nighttime sky.

The women started to sing again:

"Bacchus I call, loud-sounding and divine,
Fanatic god, a two-fold shape is thine:
Thy various names and attributes I sing,
O, first-born, thrice begotten, Bacchic king."

Coming from behind, the young Greek portraying Dionysus emerged, standing in front of her. He had been the one pushing her. His curly, dark hair encircled his face. His black eyes focused on hers: a spark exchanged, an invitation extended. He was more handsome than she remembered. She hadn't been told his name so that he would forever remain the embodiment of the god, Dionysus.

"Come with me," he said, the Greek words sounded lyric, his voice captivating.

"Jump into my arms." He held out his arms, and she let herself slip from the swing and into his waiting embrace.

In her ear he whispered, "With your leap, you have shown the fearlessness of your spirit. You are ready for this journey to the underworld, which starts your new life."

She felt no trepidation, only an eagerness to comply. She felt lightheaded and a little unsteady on her feet. The next moment, the Greek swept her up into his arms. Her arms embraced his neck, and she smelled the strange, sweet scent of his hair, his neck, and shoulders. She rested her head on his shoulder and fell asleep. When she awoke, she was lying on a couch in a room filled with lanterns and candles. As she looked around, she saw two females pouring hot water into a tub. The man came into the room and sat down upon the couch beside her. He had the same knowing smile on his face and softly kissed both her cheeks. Again, she was overcome by the fragrance of his body and closed her eyes. Her eyes flew open as she felt his hands loosen the belt around her waist. He put his finger to his lips as if to quiet her objection.

"You are safe with me," he said.

Her anxiety left her as he kissed her cheeks again. This was the way of the ritual.

He loosened her gown, removed her clothes, and again took her into his arms, placing her gently into the tub of water. The warm water felt soothing to her skin. A sponge was floating in the water, and the man took it and tenderly started to caress her shoulders with it. She felt no embarrassment about her nude body being exposed to him. On the contrary, the feeling was one of sensual pleasure that she had not felt this powerfully since Titus.

"Lean forward," he said in a whisper.

She complied, and he stroked her back from her shoulders to the bottom of her spine. She was moved to sit up straighter, allowing him to reach the cheeks of her bottom.

Then he said, "If you would like the rest of your body washed, turn over." Without hesitating, she turned her belly to the bottom of the tub, allowing her buttocks to float above the water. In circular motions, he massaged her bottom and her legs.

Without him having to ask, she turned over to expose herself, her breasts and yoni, to him. She closed her eyes as he rounded her breasts with the strokes of the sponge, moving to her belly. As he shifted his focus to her legs, she parted them in anticipation of his touch. He moved to the magic triangle with one motion, then to her inner thighs, calves, and feet.

She raised her arms as if to say, "You missed something." With a single motion of the sponge, he stroked her from her fingertips to the soft hair of her underarm. The movements continued around her breasts and over her nipples, commanding her attention and his.

Next, he stroked her forehead and face with such tenderness that a tear rolled down her cheek. He kissed the tear and then lightly touched his lips to hers. She eagerly returned the kiss and they locked in an embrace.

Again, he lifted her from the tub and placed her onto the lounge, now covered with towels. The two female servants, who had never left the room, were at his side as they dried her body. He reached under the lounge and retrieved a jar filled with a fragrant oil she had never smelled before. He massaged her entire body, ending with her face and another more prolonged embrace. The aromatic oil of Eros filled the room. Dionysus was present.

"You have been chosen by the god," he said. "Stand. You have completed this part of the ritual."

She rose, and again the attendants were there, this time with a tunica and a *himation,* an outer garment of golden color, which they held as she slipped into these new clothes. They tied a ribbon trimmed with gold around her head. A crown of laurel encircled her curly red hair. The man then retrieved the *Kista Mystica,* a sacred basket covered by a veil. A door opened, and in came four slaves carrying a funeral bier. They set it on the floor.

The young Greek explained, "The bier represents the stand that Ariadne would have been carried on to the underworld. Do you understand?"

Arianna had been forewarned. She took a deep breath and said, "I understand."

He offered his arm and helped her lie down on the bier. Sheer curtains were closed around her, but she could still see.

"Close your eyes and lie very still," the Greek said. "I will be with you presently in another place." She was lifted by the slaves and transported down a long hall with women lining either side. Each held a thyrsus and each bowed her head as Arianna passed. They were softly chanting a strange melody. The powerful aroma of incense filled the narrow hallway, almost taking her breath away. Slow, deep breathing enabled her to maintain her calm and take in the intoxicating fragrance.

The bier swayed as it moved in step with the slaves. Moments later she felt a breeze and opened her eyes slightly. She could see that they were back in the night air, heading toward the Temple of Dionysus. The fresh air was welcome.

"You are now entering the realm of the god," the Greek said, catching up with her. "Open your eyes and be aware of your surroundings." Around her, the musicians were playing and the women were chanting as they all walked beside the bier. They paused at the stairs to the temple, which seemed to be rising out of the ground. Unlike Roman temples that were built on top of a pedestal with one set of stairs in the front, this temple consisted of only two broad steps that seemed to surround the entire temple. The four slaves holding the bier ascended a ramp in the center of the front stairs, walking between the columns that held up the roof of the rectangular temple. Thus, they entered the *pronaos*, a narrow, open-air porch. Beyond it was the *naos* or *cella*, the inner room where the statue of the god Dionysus resided. In the pronaos, the bier was lowered onto an elevated rectangle of stone. Tall candelabra stood at all four corners of the bier, elevated so that all might see her with only the sheer curtains to constrain their view. Then the Greek, clad only in a thin chiton, lifted the Kista Mystica over his head and declared, "This is the sacred ritual of the marriage of Dionysus and Ariadne. Know that the penetration is the ritual."

He then opened the curtains and climbed inside with the sacred basket. As he raised his body above Rufilla, he parted her legs, and through the curtain, it seemed apparent that he would be the one to deliver the ritual thrust. As he arched his body above her, she looked down to see that his member was fully erect. "Do not be afraid. I will not hurt you," he whispered. "Breathe."

She had been holding her breath, and as she looked into his eyes, her body opened up to him, mystified by the merging of the sensual, wanting his body, and the spiritual, realizing the sacredness of the moment.

With that, the four slaves who stood next to each candelabra pulled the second set of drapes down over the bier, completely obscuring the view of the participants standing below. After a few minutes, they heard Arianna's cry and saw a red ball of yarn fall from the bier and roll across the floor of the porch and down the stairs. One woman walked to the stairs and slowly raised the ball above her head. One by one, each woman took the ball of thread, unraveling it and forming a circular labyrinth as their bodies swayed with the rhythm of the music, arms stretched skyward, each extending the thread of Ariadne's life back into the world. The sound of Dionysian hand cymbals accentuated the beat of Ariadne's new heart, her new life.

What the participants had not seen or heard the moment before they saw the ball of yarn was this. Hidden within the curtain of the canopy was the winnowing basket the Greek had taken with him into the sacred bed. He had moved the veiled basket next to Arianna, took her hands, and said, "This is the winnowing basket, traditionally thought to be the birth crib of the god. You will find a ritual object contained within. Take into your hands whatever you find, remembering that the fertility of Dionysus is represented by this."

She removed the object and opened her eyes, giving a loud gasp. That was the sound that the participants heard from her. In her hands was a large wooden phallus, fashioned from the branch of a fig tree. Arianna understood at once, having seen large carvings of phalluses in specific festivals that it was the phallus of Dionysus. Voicing her awe, she, in effect, was showing that she understood her entrance into the Dionysian experience in a unique way. "This is not a sexual act for us to consummate but an opening into your innermost soul, receiving the vigor of Dionysus who will fill your life with passion and purpose." The Greek kissed her gently on each cheek. Then he laid down beside her, speaking words of wisdom and counsel to her, words she would write down later so that she might never forget.

The four slaves returned and raised the canopy of curtains, but not before the Greek replaced the phallus within the winnowing basket, covering it from sight. He jumped from the bier and knelt beside it, taking Arianna's hand, kissing it gently.

"You have experienced this ritual for a reason," he said, in a voice only she could hear. "With this honor comes responsibilities to be discussed with you at a later time. Until then, you are sworn to silence—is that understood?"

"I understand." Her voice held a deep resonance.

He helped her from the bier, now considered her birth bed.

Kallistê, Melissa, and the women participants cheered as she stood before them. They understood that this was a ritual marriage conducted by the Greeks and not consummated physically. She was still a virgin in the physical sense, but she intuitively knew that something had penetrated her, uniting body and soul. The women, still holding their labyrinth in place, started chanting, "Ariadne, Ariadne."

The Greek spoke to her. "Go, take the thread of Ariadne. It marks the beginning of the new path of your life that starts with collecting the thread and rolling it into a new ball. It is strengthened through the labyrinth of women as well as your experience within."

She went to the women, and taking hold of the end of the thread, raised her arms and made her way through the human labyrinth, winding the thread into a new ball, her new life. She ran back up to the pronaos, ball of yarn in her hand, and into the arms of the man who had portrayed the greatest god of all, Dionysus! Their embrace brought a roar from the crowd of friends and family who had gathered to wish her well.

"Now, the final tribute," the Greek continued, addressing the group. He uncovered another basket that held a silver crown embedded with jewels from all over the world. He held it over Arianna's head, saying, "This was made to represent the crown that Hephaestus made, and as Dionysus, I give you, Ariadne, this crown as a token of our enduring love on our wedding day. Love and life everlasting to you!" Then, he crowned her and swept her off her feet. Down the stairs, he carried her toward the banquet hall and the waiting celebrants. He stopped at the doorway and lowered her to the ground so that she might cross the threshold on her own two feet. She looked down, stepped into the doorway, felt the cold and refreshing marble of the threshold under her feet, and then paused. She closed her eyes briefly, taking in the sensual pleasure of the moment, without word or thought. She looked back at the Temple of Dionysus, turned to face forward, and then rested her hand on the Greek's arm. Thus they entered with dignity as the beloved couple, Ariadne and Dionysus.

At the dining table, he raised a wedding vessel of wine. He said to the assemblage, "We celebrate this Hieros Gamos, this holy marriage ritual between a god and a goddess, in honor of Ariadne's new life," and in a tone for only Arianna's ears, "And yours."

Now Kallistê and Melissa approached her. "I must share with you the secret that your mother wanted me to tell you at just this moment," Kallistê said, "When she visited me so many years ago, she went through this same ritual!"

Kallistê handed her a box. It contained a ring. "It is a ring just like my mater has!"

The Greek, Dionysius, took the ring from her and put it on her finger. "It is the wedding ring that each initiate receives when she completes her initiation. Your marriage to Dionysus is complete. Wear it only when you perform the initiation rituals of Dionysus for the women of Pompeii."

"What?" Arianna looked from one woman to the other and then to Dionysius. "You mean I will be performing rituals when I return home?" All nodded in agreement.

"Oh, I am so grateful to all of you," Arianna said. "This is indeed the perfect ending to this extraordinary experience." She fell into their arms, sobbing with joy.

CHAPTER XXXVII

AFTER THE MYSTERY SEASON

Stephanos arranged for Arianna to take a well-deserved rest, leaving the hustle of the crowded city and going to their farm in the countryside south of Athens. Although it was different from her family's country home outside Pompeii, it gave Arianna the freedom to roam freely on the acreage located in the foothills, with the Saronic Sea to the west and Mount Hymettus looming to the east. The weather in the countryside was predictable during the summer—hot, dry, and windy, especially by the sea. The rocky terrain was not conducive to farming, as Arianna had experienced in Pompeii. Fortunately, the farm was within a carriage ride of Voúla, a small seaside town. Its market was the primary source of food for the guests and workers at the farm.

Kallistê and Stephanos escorted Arianna and Melissa to the farm and stayed a few days before heading back to Athens to attend to their further duties in Eleusis. The two women's constant companion would be Timo, who had accompanied Kallistê, Arianna, and Melissa on their journey to Crete. Stephanos trusted him because he had saved Stephanos's life when he fell into a fast-moving stream. Kallistê had drawn on that occasion to encourage Stephanos to elevate Timo to the supervisor of all the other servants in the household. She felt he would be a valued addition to her staff, as the servant formerly in that position had often tried to preempt some of her decisions. His duties were similar to Theo's in Pompeii.

Before her host and hostess left, Arianna engaged Stephanos in a conversation concerning riding one of his horses. "Pater taught me to ride several years ago," Arianna said, "and even let me accompany him to one of his favorite outdoor sanctuaries on our land. We have had some wonderful talks there, especially after Titus' death. Because of my experience, I wondered if I might be allowed to ride one of your horses around your property—with Timo, of course," she added.

"Fortunately for you, I was thinking about a ride into our little town of Voúla, to show you and Melissa the market and shopping area," Stephanos said. "Of course, your aunt and Melissa can come along in the carriage to bring back any packages that might be purchased."

"Thank you, thank you," Arianna said, bubbling with enthusiasm. "When can we—?"

"I was thinking about this afternoon, as your aunt and I must be getting back to Athens soon." He beamed at her, enjoying his new role as a benevolent uncle.

The ride into town was brief. Once she felt comfortable on the horse, the young niece challenged her uncle to race, which he accepted. They reached the center of town long before the carriage, and by the time it arrived, Arianna and Stephanos were in a friendly disagreement about who had won.

"Slow down, you two," said Kallistê. "Let us just consider that your uncle allowed you to win, Arianna, genial host that he is."

They all burst out laughing and headed for the market for something to drink.

Melissa and Arianna usually took a daily walk accompanied at a distance by male chaperones. When they returned, they were always hungry, and they often found freshly baked bread in the kitchen. An added treat was the famous Hymettus thyme honey. The local thyme honey had been part of her Crete experience too.

Eating their breakfast one morning, about two weeks into their stay, Melissa said, "I think the drink that you had the night of your initiation in Athens was wine laced with honey. It *is* called the nectar of the gods."

"Melissa, that Greek man is my nectar. I cannot get him out of my mind. I dream about him, and worse, my body is tortured. All it longs for is one more touch, one more kiss."

"I know what you mean, Arianna. I have the same longings for Theo."

"Oh, I am sorry. I cannot even imagine what you have been going through since we left Kenchreai.

"For myself, I focus on the future," Melissa said. "I have to keep in mind that this time we spend in Greece will seem short indeed after we return to our lives in Pompeii."

That afternoon they both received mail, a welcome surprise because they had not expected to receive letters from home while they were in the country. As Melissa finished the letter there were tears in her eyes.

"What is it?" Arianna asked.

"I miss him so much. I wish he could come back and meet us in Delphi in the spring," she said.

"I do not know why he could not," Arianna replied.

"Because it is spring—you know how busy it is at the beginning of the season." She paused. "I must keep in mind that there is a possibility."

Arianna told Melissa the news from her mother. "Mater says that Pater is finishing up the harvest and will concentrate on a project he has in mind for the country house. She says that Victor is helping him design the project." She pondered this. "I wonder why Victor is helping Pater."

"Well, you know Clodia has just died, so it will be a long winter, and I am sure your pater wants to keep Victor's mind from dwelling on the past. Losing Titus and then his wife in such a close period—it is difficult, to say the least. He must look to the future."

"Oh my, yes," Arianna said. "So difficult for everyone." She thought for a moment. "They were an odd couple, Victor and Clodia."

"They say opposites attract," Melissa said. "You know Plato's theory of soulmates. That the gods split humans into two parts and we are forever trying to find our other half."

"But I remember Mater telling me about arranged marriages, that they sometimes worked. I know Titus and I would have made a good couple."

"In the Jewish world, they talk about marriages being made in heaven," Melissa said, "and that arranged marriages—arranged like Victor and Clodia's was—do not always work out."

"Is Victor Jewish? And Clodia? Is that why you mentioned Jewish marriages?"

"Oh yes, Arianna, they are both, I mean Clodia was Jewish too—I thought you knew."

"How did you know?"

"I remember the first time I saw the special garum sauce in the kitchen. I asked what it was and was told it was only to be given to Victor and Clodia, that it was a special fish sauce only used by some religious faiths, including Jews. I think it has to do with a particular kind of fish. I cannot quite remember the details."

"When were my parents going to tell me about this—on my wedding day to Titus?" she said. "I am not opposed to the Jewish religion, but I would have appreciated knowing about this. How would the wedding ceremony have differed? What did I need to know as his future wife?"

"I do not know. You will have to ask your parents," Melissa said quietly.

"I will indeed!"

One evening Arianna wanted to take the horses and ride to town and back, which Timo was willing to do. She had something she wanted to share with him. The first was to watch the sunset from a hill just outside town. As they were enjoying that, Arianna told him that if they hurried to the opposite end of the town, to the beach, they could see the moon rise. A splendid full moon rising at the horizon was her other surprise for him. They were both enthralled by the two natural events occurring so close together.

Starting back so late made Timo uneasy. Earlier that evening, he had seen the man who had previously held his position of supervisor—before his rescue of Stephanos. He had heard that the man was very bitter about being replaced and had asked to be let go, so Stephanos found the man a position in this town, doing work for a friend of his. Their eyes had met, and for the first time, Timo felt the cold glare of an evil eye.

As the two rode side by side at the edge of town, Timo spoke in low tones to Arianna. "If anything happens to me, ride like the wind back to the farm. You will find safety there." Now Arianna was on the alert. All she could see ahead of her was some underbrush in silhouette from the moonshine. As they passed by, she heard a rustling in the dried bushes and saw the glint of what could be a long knife. "Ride, Ari, ride!" Timo shouted.

Abruptly, Timo's horse reared up, and she saw Timo thrown to the ground. Arianna did as he had said. She grabbed hold of the horse's mane with both hands, lowered her body so that she felt at one with the horse, and dug her heels into his ribs, which signaled the horse to take off at a gallop. She focused on getting back to her uncle's property as quickly as possible. Soon she heard the sound of horse hooves behind her. As she saw the barn in the distance, she heard a voice yell, "Wait!" Arianna wasn't entirely convinced that it was Timo's voice. The horse she was riding veered off to the right and started to slow down. She knew that it was heading to the shallow stream that ran beside the barn. The horse and rider had gained on her. She jumped from her horse and a man was on top of her in an instant. He grabbed her by her hair and put his hand over her mouth. Instinctively, she bit his hand, and the man screamed and let go. He grabbed at her cloak, tearing it from her as she scrambled to her feet. "Help me, help!" she screamed, as she started running toward the barn, the man lunging at her. A farmhand ran out of the barn and towards her with his lantern blazing. Melissa followed behind. The farmhand took off after the man, who had run.

"Arianna—what happened?" Melissa said, taking Arianna into the barn.

"Timo, it is Timo," said Arianna. "He needs help."

Other farmhands arrived. "Go!" Melissa screamed at the men.

In short order, the farmhands brought the stranger into the barn. "Where is Timo?" the head farmhand asked. With that, he knocked the man to the ground with his fist. "Tie him up," he said.

"No, no," said the stranger. "I left him just outside town."

"Go and find him," the head man said to two others, and they took off on horseback. They soon returned with Timo, whom they had found staggering and falling as he walked toward them. His head was bleeding and he was delirious. "Find Arianna; I must find Arianna," was all he said before he collapsed.

Arianna ordered the head of the farmhands to take the man who had attacked her and Timo back to his owner and also report him to the authorities in the town.

She also wanted Timo seen by the physician who had taken care of her earlier, when she had her seizures. Arrangements were made to leave the farm as soon as possible. She made sure that Timo rode with her and Melissa in the carriage. A farmhand was sent ahead so that the doctor would be available upon their arrival. Timo had started to regain consciousness but wasn't able to stand much less walk. She sat in the carriage, resting his head in her lap, comforting him with her gentle touch, using cool cloths on his brow.

The doctor was waiting at the house when they reached Athens. After he completed an examination, he took Arianna aside and talked with her. "He is a strong young man, and I think he will recover with time."

Arianna gasped. "How serious is it?"

"I have seen worse, and some have recovered, so let us pray to the gods for their help."

When Kallistê and Stephanos returned from Eleusis, ten days later, they had dinner that first night with Arianna. They were eager to relate some of what had happened in Eleusis during the Mystery rituals. Neither of them had been informed about the incident on the farm.

"The Lesser Mysteries took place first," Stephanos began. "When we arrived, there were several days of preparing for our participation in the Greater Mysteries, which lasted more than ten days, along with a few days thereafter."

"How many people were there?" Arianna asked.

"Thousands. It seemed busier than ever this year," Kallistê said. "Stephanos thought we might not have enough baby pigs for the sacrifice, but we did."

"It sounds overwhelming," Arianna said.

"Completely. In fact, on the way home, we stopped for a few days at a spa to rest and refresh our bodies." Stephanos smiled at his wife. It was the first time Arianna could remember seeing him smile at anyone.

"Well, I am grateful that Melissa and I could rest in your beautiful villa. It made me think of our villa at home. Seeing the stars glowing in the evening sky with only the sounds of the night animals was such a treat. I feel like a new woman."

It was the first time she had referred to herself as such.

They had moved to their veranda, a few lanterns giving just enough light to see one another, but not enough to conceal the starlit sky above.

Arianna moved to sit on the ground between the chairs of Kallistê and Stephanos. Taking one of each of their hands in hers, she said, "Aunt and Uncle, I have something to tell you, but I do not want you to be upset. It is about Timo." Both of them leaned in toward her and held her hand a little tighter. "He is well, or should I say, recovering from an affliction." Stephanos started to rise from his chair. "Dear Uncle," Arianna said, grasping his arm, "please let me finish." He sat on the edge of his chair.

She related the story of what had happened. Melissa, who had been watching from a distance, joined them to add her version of the story. "Your niece took charge of the situation, instructing the farmhands to find Timo and then to return the attacker to his owner—with instructions to inform the authorities of his offenses. They also told his owner that you,"

Melissa said, looking at Stephanos, "would be in touch upon your return from Eleusis."

"I will indeed," Stephanos said. "And you, Arianna, were you injured in all this?"

She shook her head.

"Arianna was upset as you can imagine," Melissa said, "but had the presence of mind to promptly bring Timo back here so that your doctor could care for him."

"You have acted courageously. I would be proud to have you for my daughter," Stephanos said. "Now, take me to him."

Several weeks later, a surprise letter arrived from Victor to Arianna. He wrote that her father had told him that Arianna wanted to know more about him and his Jewish background. "I realize my name is not Jewish sounding, he wrote, but my ancestors from Alexandria were converts, so that is the reason many people, including you, do not realize that I am Jewish. I am not strict in my faith, but I have my own spiritual values. It wasn't that I did not want you to know; it was that it never seemed relevant to our conversations—few as they were." It was a long and interesting letter, laying out his family's history in Rome, then investing in land and starting vineyards south of Rome, and finally settling in Pompeii.

He went on to describe how he was helping her father design and oversee the additions and the remodeling of their country home. "I cannot wait for you to see it, Arianna," he concluded. "I know how much you love the country house and I hope you will be pleased."

He had written to her as an adult, and she liked that. Melissa, on the other hand, wasn't sure why she harbored some anxiety, but she did. Uneasy as she felt, she voiced her concerns to Arianna, who did not take her seriously.

Also, a letter had come from Cil, who was still in Apollonia. This city, since the Romans had conquered it, was where Romans studied at the school of philosophy. There were also facilities for Roman soldiers to prepare for combat. Cil wrote that he was delighted that Octavius had finally arrived along with his teacher, his physician, and Agrippa. Even though Cil was delighted to see Octavius, he was thrilled to hear all about the medical techniques that Octavius' doctor had been able to develop while attending to Caesar's army. He was anxious to work with the physician, and the doctor remembered Cil from their time together in Hispania. Now that Octavius was present, the whole camp was atwitter. Everyone wondered what would happen next. Cil had been told while still in Hispania, that they would be preparing to fight with Julius Caesar in his next round of battles against the Dacians and the Parthians.

Arianna's studies began again in earnest. She thrived on learning something new every day and often shared it with Stephanos, which made for some lively conversations. He started to relax around her and even enjoy her sense of humor.

One evening Arianna was in a buoyant mood. She had learned that the word for a fig tree branch was a play on words for the *phallus*. When Stephanos asked why she was grinning, she decided not to tell him something so sexually blatant, saying only, "I have learned more about the Dionysian ritual today."

"Speaking of rituals, that reminds me," Stephanos said. "Since you have shown some interest in the Stoics, Kallistê and I would like to invite you to attend a lecture on Zeno, the founder of Stoicism, to be held at the Stoa Poikile building in the agora." The name confused Arianna. "I am not familiar with the word Poikile," she said.

"The name of the building means 'painted porch.' It is the long, open-air building in the Athenian Agora where you saw the fresco of Theseus," Kallistê said. "It is a rare day when women are allowed inside, and—she paused—"we have a surprise for you," she said. She ended the conversation there because she did not want to stir up old memories of that upsetting day when Arianna ran off to the agora without a male chaperone and then had to deal with Stephanos' anger and the round of seizures that followed.

The next day they were settling into their seats at the stoa when Stephanos motioned to someone coming into the building. "Over here, we saved a seat for you," Stephanos called.

It was him—Kallistê's nephew. "May I introduce you again to my nephew, Dionysius?" Kallistê said.

Arianna could not believe her ears. She was told that his name wouldn't be revealed, yet here it was. "Of course, your name would have to be that of the god you portrayed."

"Please understand. I am not named after the god Dionysus but Dionysius of Cyrene, a Stoic philosopher." He smiled that smile that made her heart beat faster. His body was so muscular, his dimples as deep as she remembered, and his eyes flashed a knowing smile her way. "I am so glad you are interested in the Stoics. Stoicism is a way of life for me."

At that moment, the lecture started. "I will speak of some of the basic tenets of Zeno and then will take questions," the lecturer said.

The audience assembled were from many different parts of the world. "For those of you who are new to Athens, I will start by giving a little history of this amazing stoa, including the murals on the walls. You probably all know that Zeno of Citium lectured on the porch of this stoa, and because of that, his philosophy came to be known not as Zenoism but as Stoicism."

Dionysius joined them for dinner that evening. After a small amount of watered-down wine, Arianna screwed up her courage. "I feel safe enough with the three of you to discuss some of my thoughts about today's lecture," she said, still feeling some hesitation. "I was drawn to the Stoics initially because of my battle with epilepsy. That part of me seems so out of my control. Then when I heard my pater talk about what Roman Stoics think of as cultivating a kind of serene indifference towards one's plight in life, I grabbed hold of the concept for dear life. And now a differing attitude has taken hold," she said, taking a deep breath. "I am fascinated with the story and ritual of Dionysus, as you all know. It gives me great pleasure when I think about the passion that I felt when performing the ritual, and I cannot be dispassionate about how I feel. Dionysus fills my whole body with excitement when I think of his devotion to women and what I might be able to do to help other women—when I am older, of course." These were words she had never spoken aloud to anyone.

There was a significant pause. Finally, Dionysius spoke.

"We are close enough in age that I might be able to speak to your comment." He looked at his hosts, who both nodded, grateful for him to continue. "I too am enamored with Dionysus, not just for the taste of wine, but also his taste for life. The passion that he brings to my life is significant. But I feel that the two entities, Stoicism and the Dionysian experience, are opposite sides of the same coin. The Stoics call for restraint, while Dionysus is the one who urges us to let go, to be inspired by him. As you know, opposites attract. It may seem contradictory, but in holding the tension between the two, I seek to find a middle way or a balance in my life."

Now it was Dionysius' turn to take a deep breath. "How do you think I managed to get through that evening?" he said, looking at Stephanos and Kallistê hesitantly, clear that he wanted to speak his truth. "You are a lovely, desirable woman." Arianna lowered her head and blushed. "But my responsibility was to seek balance when faced with this pleasurable and sacred task. I wanted to afford a memorable and ecstatic experience for you without violating you."

"You certainly did that." She spoke softly and with emotion. "Then you understand *my* emotions in the situation. And the fact that you did not try to force yourself—"

"The thought occurred to me," he said.

"But you did not. You honored the ritual, as did I."

The four relaxed onto their pillows, exhaling almost in unison.

"Maybe that is enough discussion for one evening," said Stephanos. "The two of you have shown a maturity beyond your years. Wouldn't you agree, Kallistê?"

"I certainly agree," Kallistê replied.

Arianna walked Dionysius to the front door. "Thank you for your spirited and honest answer to my question," Arianna said. "You have given me much to think about. I will never forget what you said that night." She quoted, "'This is not a sexual act for us to consummate but an opening into our innermost souls, receiving the vigor of Dionysus who will fill our lives with passion and purpose.' I thank you for that too. I hope we can see each other again before I leave," she said, feeling emboldened to express the tender emotion she felt for this man.

"I leave tomorrow for an extensive trip with my father, but depending on when *you* leave," he said, smiling, "we may meet again."

"Let me think," Arianna said, counting on her fingers. "I left in Aprilis, Maius, Iunius,—" she said. "Almost nine months ago, and I will be here in

Athens for a few more months and then off to Delphi to meet the Oracle!"

"Ah, so you may be in Delphi in Martius for the Dionysian ritual and the opening of the Oracle's season?"

"Yes, or maybe sooner. Aunt Kallistê wants me to meet with the Pythia before the season starts."

He nodded. "It sounds like an excellent plan."

He reached into his pocket and pulled out a coin cut in half. "Here, take half this coin as a *symbolon* of our friendship. Because of the ritual, we will always share a unique understanding of our relationship with Dionysus," he said, putting the cut piece in her palm, closing her hand within his. "Dionysus will cause problems for us from time to time; trust me. At those times, take this out and think of me and know that what you are experiencing, I will have experienced too."

She looked at their hands clasped together. He lifted her chin and tenderly kissed each cheek and then licked her tears away.

They broke out in laughter. "Remember that Dionysus is eternally playful, so do not let the serious nature of the work he requires depress you. The art of surprise, especially accompanied by laughter, is so welcome to this god, as it will be to you."

"You are—" she stumbled to find the right Greek words— "brimming with profound thoughts, comforting and full of wisdom."

They hugged and kissed each other. As he left, he turned. "Until we meet again."

CHAPTER XXXVIII

SATURNALIA

The season of the winter solstice was upon them. Both Romans and Greeks had their distinct festivals. Arianna's lessons would cease for the month. Melissa and Arianna were longing to celebrate the Roman winter solstice festival of Saturnalia, and Kallistê couldn't resist sharing with them some of the Greek festivals of the winter season.

"There are many festivals at this season of the winter solstice," Kallistê said. "One festival is celebrated only by groups of men who own vineyards. Each man in the group hosts a dinner, which involves opening amphora of the latest pressing, pouring the wine into drinking jars, and judging how well the wine may taste after it has aged. It gives the men an excuse to eat, drink, and celebrate Dionysus, and you can imagine all the wine and food consumed!"

"Well," Arianna said, "Roman men who own vineyards—like my pater—have a similar festival, but they celebrate it in the spring. And their wives participate!"

"Yes, and for better or worse, therein lies the difference between Greeks and Romans," Kallistê said. "It would certainly be more civilized if women were allowed to join. The Greek men left to their own devices can get rather boisterous. You will see—Stephanos will host such a dinner as well as attending several other."

"Well," Melissa said, "I remember being told about the Greek winter solstice celebration for Poseidon. Blazing lights and men drinking is about all I remember. I always wondered why it was celebrated in the winter season when no one sailed."

Arianna thought for a moment. "Maybe it was because, in the winter, Poseidon has time to watch the celebrations, whereas, in the summer, he is too busy with his sea duties such as trying to control all the wind deities!"

"How clever you are." Kallistê beamed, so proud of her Roman niece. "I decided to include the next tradition, the Festival of Lights, or Chanukah after I heard about your letter from your pater's Jewish friend.

Let me begin by telling you a little about the legend of Alexander the Great and his sympathetic treatment of the Jews. Even though he conquered many peoples, he granted the Jews the right to worship their G_d and to live by all the laws of their forefathers. After his death, one of his successors reversed his open-mindedness and violated the Jewish Temple. To be brief, the Jews won back their temple and, in trying to rekindle the tradition of light in their house of worship, experienced a miracle. Supposedly there was only enough oil to keep the candles of the Menorah lit for one day, but inexplicably the oil lasted for eight days, enough time to replenish their supply."

"I love all these accounts of light in the darkness," Arianna said. "It seems that all humans need to focus on the light of day—the longer days returning after so many long nights. We do need the light." Her voice faded away and then returned. "It is about balance. That is what Dionysius talked about at dinner that night. The darkness of Dionysus balanced with the light of Apollo."

"But do not forget, Dionysus is that spark of light in the darkness," Kallistê said.

"Yes, I will have to remember that to get through many nights." Again, her voice trailed off. She sensed a feeling in her body of some future event, strange as it seemed to her.

"You will be going to Delphi as you start your journey home."

"Oh, yes. When will I travel there?"

"It will be your decision," Kallistê continued. "Dionysus is present in the winter months in Delphi, and then Apollo returns to his temple in the spring. You will have to wait at least until the end of Dionysus' time because it will not be safe to travel by sea in the winter."

"Yes, I received a letter from Aper recently. He said that he left his ship at the docks in a small harbor north of Brundisium—Egnazia. That way, he can travel back overland from Pompeii and ready his ship when the winter winds look like they might calm down. Then he'll meet up with us at Kirra."

To ready for the *Saturnalia*, the women spent a day decorating the women's quarters of the house with sweet-smelling boughs of pine and greenery that had been freshly cut from the trees in the nearby forest. "Yo, Saturnalia!" the women repeated each time they passed one another while decorating their rooms and the interior garden that centered on their rooms.

Because gifts were exchanged as part of the festivities, the women visited the agora. Shopping day in the agora afforded many possibilities for gifts. "There are so many terracotta statues. How can I ever decide?" Arianna said.

"Maybe we should try something different," Kallistê said. "We will each take a male servant and go off on our own, then meet up at home."

"Good idea," Arianna said. "I choose Timo to go with me. He can help me decide."

"Of course," Kallistê said, winking at Timo. "As he has fully recovered, I think he can handle you, dear niece."

They parted company and Arianna headed straight back to the vendor with the most intriguing figurines. She looked and looked for something different. There were plenty of animals—pigs, bulls painted black with their horns finished in gold, even elephants replete with ivory tusks. At the edge of his table, she found a grouping of snakes, then looking over to the next vendor's stall, she spied a snake bracelet.

The first vendor tried to keep her interested in his wares. "Here, look here. Do you like snakes? How about a beautiful terracotta image of the Cretan snake goddess?"

Arianna picked up the figurine and turned it around in her hands. She remembered Kallistê's words spoken while they were on Crete. "She had a beautiful, layered flounced skirt with alternating colors of black, red, and white stripes," Kallistê's description had begun. "It was topped with an apron that hung down in front and back, adorned with geometric designs on a crisscrossed pattern. Her bodice fit snug around her tiny waist, upper arms and back, but left her young breasts exposed and alert for the entire world to admire. She wore a bejeweled crown with an animal seated on top. Her silky black hair hung down her back, well past her waist. Her arms were raised, held out on either side of her body, in praise to the goddess, and in each hand, she grasped a small striped snake. She was— what is the Latin word—ahh, yes, magnificent!"

At that moment, Timo whispered in her ear, "Please pardon me, but it is bad luck to buy this for yourself."

"Oh, of course," she said, not understanding but handing the statue back to the vendor. Just as quickly, she took it back. "But I could buy it as a gift for my mother," she said aloud.

"Just wait one moment," the vendor said, and he walked to the back of the store.

He reappeared with a wrapped statuette. As he unfolded the wrap, Arianna could see the figure was not the one she had handed him. It was the body of a woman carved from black stone. "This is a beautiful stone we have in Greece, used because a carver can put so much detail in the work," the man said. "See her tall headdress with a snake coiled on top. Notice the detail of her dress and the snakes around her body, neck, and arms. *This* is the Snake goddess worthy to give to your mother."

She looked at Timo. "Negotiate the price," she said.

Timo did as he was told.

It turned out to be a great day for gift buying. She found a steatite drinking vessel for her father. He could use it in his rituals, she thought. The horns were covered in gold leaf. It too was expensive, but he had, after all, financed this journey—so it was well worth the price. I will present the gifts to them as a token of Xenia, a thank you from a stranger for their hospitality and shelter. That she should see herself as a stranger in her parents' house felt like a revelation.

They arrived home with Timo loaded down with gifts for almost everyone on her list. That evening the servants helped set up all sorts of lights: oil lamps, torches, or, as Arianna now called them, thyrsi. Candelabra completed the illumination of the magical celebration as the women enjoyed a sumptuous meal, drank heated, spiced wine, then sang and danced into the night.

For the days of celebration, Melissa and Kallistê's maid did not have to work. This was, in fact, a role reversal. Arianna and Kallistê treated their servants to a special meal one evening while the servants reclined and let their mistresses serve them.

"Have you noticed how slow the maids are to clear the food from one course to the next?" Melissa joked.

"Yes, I have. And observe how reluctant they are to refill our wine cups," Kallistê's maid Dionne chimed in.

"So sorry, Domina," said Arianna to the maid.

"A thousand pardons." Kallistê bowed before them.

"We will have a meeting when this is over and decide the fate of these two servants." Melissa giggled. "To fire them, or relegate them to chambermaids, or make them cook's helpers."

"Please, please," Kallistê begged. "We will do better. Won't we, Arianna?"

"Of course we will, especially after we have some of the wine that they are drinking!"

With that, the four women broke into laughter and shared the rest of the meal. Afterward, there was a gift exchange. Melissa and Kallistê's servant brought out the *pilleum*, colorful, conical felt hats they had made. They gave these hats to the two "servants" as a mark of freedom.

"Freedwomen one and all," they shouted.

"I want to go next," Arianna said. "To each of my 'mistresses,'" she said, bowing, "I give you something that will always remind you of our time on Crete."

Melissa opened her package to find a beautiful black bracelet, shaped like a coiled snake with the head decorated in gold. "Oh, Arianna, you shouldn't—"

"You deserve it, Melissa. I won't hear another word."

Melissa was close to tears. "No one has ever given me—thank you, Domina, thank you."

"Since we began this trip together, you have become more than my nursemaid and my protector—you are my lifelong friend in whom I can trust and confide!" The two hugged.

"Now, for you, Dionne." Arianna handed Kallistê's maid a drawing she had made. "You inspired me when I watched you pouring wine for us so many times at dinner." Her drawing was of a maid, dressed as for a ritual with laurel leaves in her hair, pouring a liquid into the cup of the priestess she was serving.

"It is lovely, but I am not—"

"Yes, you are that lovely," Arianna finished the maid's sentence.

"And now for you, my Greek mother." Arianna handed Kallistê an elaborate picture that she had drawn on paper she had made by hand back home. "When I made the paper and then decided to bring it with me, I had no idea what I would use it for," Arianna began. "You have inspired me in so many ways, dearest. Even though I did not attend the Eleusinian Mysteries, Mater told me of your responsibilities and the high office you hold in that community. You are so humble, never letting on that you serve as high priestess. You are a role model for me. I give this to you with all the love in my heart."

Kallistê took the paper in her hand. The drawing was a close likeness of Kallistê, dressed in ritual garb and raising a lidded basket. Kallistê's eyes blinked as she took in all the aspects of the drawing.

"This is how I see you in that role," Arianna said.

"How did you know about the basket?" Kallistê asked.

"I did not. But when I closed my eyes, I received this vision, so that is what I drew."

Kallistê turned it around so that the other two women could see it. Dionne gasped. "You have indeed captured the moment!"

"Yes, you have, dear girl. Thank you so very much," Kallistê said, tears welling up in her eyes. "And now, it is my turn." She cleared her throat and dried her eyes.

"For you, my dearest servant, this pair of sandals with a crescent moon decorating the top of each shoe. As you know, the moon represents your namesake, the goddess Diana. May your feet feel the swiftness as your mind holds the focus of the goddess."

"For you, Melissa, whose name represents the sweet honey of the bee, so that you will not forget the time you spent with us on Crete, I give you this honeybee pendant." It was a stunning piece of jewelry—two bees facing each other with a single drop of honey between them.

"Now for the third gift," she said as she reached into her basket. "To you, my Roman daughter, dear and precious as your namesake, the Minoan princess Ariadne, I give this copy of what is thought to be the long lost ceramic original of the Minoan goddess as a young girl."

It was similar to the terracotta figurine Arianna had seen in the Athenian Agora with Timo. "It is so shiny and the colors are so vivid! Oh, thank you, dear Mater. I will treasure it forever."

"This is a ceramic copy made of Egyptian faience," Kallistê said.

Just then, Arianna saw Timo, who had helped her buy the gifts, peeking around the corner.

"Kallistê, I assume you know that your manservant"— she pointed straight at Timo—"told me that I could not buy the statue I saw at the market because to buy it for yourself was bad luck!"

"Good thinking, young man," Kallistê said, smiling at him. "He takes directions well and is also a fast thinker!"

There was a roar of laughter from the men's quarters. Stephanos was hosting yet another dinner party. Two men staggered out of the dining room and headed toward the women's quarters. Timo turned toward the men and stood his ground, prepared to protect the women. Kallistê stood and went into the hallway. "Take your drunken bodies elsewhere," she said. "You are beyond the boundaries of proper conduct. Leave!"

She came back into the women's dining room. "Enough of all this party giving," she said, disgusted. "Tomorrow, we will plan to go to Eleusis, not only to get away from all this but to participate in the winter solstice ritual with some of my women friends.

CHAPTER XXXIX

WINTER SOLSTICE

In Greece and many other countries, the Winter Solstice marks the longest night of the year and the onset of winter. Kallistê and her friends gathered together in a meeting place, exclusively for women, to celebrate when the sun stands still—the true meaning of solstice.

Kallistê opened the meeting. "For these few days, the sun god Apollo holds up the movement of the sun so that we might take time to reflect on what has happened in the past and look forward to the future. It is as if not only the sun but time itself stands still. Tonight we are graced with the presence of a young Roman woman who has her traditions. Arianna, would you like to speak?"

Her aunt had helped her prepare. "Thank you, aunt Kallistê," Arianna said. "I am honored to be included in this group of respected women. Yes, I would like to say a few words about a god who is unique to the Romans. His name is Janus. It is the time of year when we honor him. For us, he is the god of beginnings and endings, entrances and departures. Tonight, I paused as I stepped over the threshold of the door that admitted us to this sacred space. It was only a brief moment, but I wanted to acknowledge Janus and remember that I was leaving the outer world and entering into this world of revered and loving women. As I leave, I will stop again, this time asking for Janus' protection. Thank you for including me."

The ritual continued forward with each woman presenting her symbols of reflection and meaning. Many talked of the light in the darkness, referring to Dionysus. Arianna's symbol for the light was a drawing she made of the nighttime sky, showing the stars of the Corona Borealis, the crown that Dionysus threw into the nighttime sky, displaying their love.

Another symbol, The Spiral Path, was given to the women. This time they could choose how one or more of the four spiral paths had affected them this year. When it was Arianna's turn, she spoke of all four paths. "First, I would like to speak of the Downward Spiral." She spoke of her depression after the death of her beloved spiraling down the path of mourning and heartbreak. Melissa had been by her side the whole time, especially when she experienced an increase in her seizures. Melissa and her mother reasoned with Arianna that the seizures were affecting her in mind, body, soul, and spirit. A turn around had to happen.

"My mater and pater finally realized that the only way to stop this downward spiral was to institute a plan for restoring my health. They conceived of what I will now call the Outward Spiral. It was time to expand my horizons and experiences of the world beyond, learning about other people and their cultures, especially the Greek culture. Through my experiences of meeting new and different people, I also started to add the Inward Spiral, contemplating a new awareness of who I was and who I might become. The Upward Spiral is where I am now as I have reached a new level of being in and relating to the world. And lastly, thanks to my auntie's wisdom, I realize that this is just the first cycle of my life and that the Spiral Path happens over and over again. If I can stay centered within the spiral, maybe I will grow slowly, day by day. In other words, I will make haste slowly."

The last night, they participated in the *Haloea* festival for Demeter and Dionysus, with a procession honoring Poseidon. The women were sequestered for that night so that they could be loud and mischievous without the intrusion of any males. Some women acted as "priestesses," telling lewd jokes. One woman acted the part of Baubo, the old nurse of mythology, who quoted lascivious verses, trying to cheer another woman who acted the part of Demeter.

"Please, Demeter, you must drink some wine and take some food," Baubo begged.

When Demeter declined, Baubo pulled aside her robes and showed her secret parts to Demeter. That brought howls of laughter from all the women. Arianna turned red-faced, feeling embarrassed because she had never seen a woman's private parts that blatantly, but laughing all the while. She felt so grown-up being part of this woman's group.

For dessert, they were served sweet cakes in the shape of sexual organs. Arianna and Baubo got into a shouting match, quoting Sappho poems back and forth until they both collapsed.

Kallistê decided that they should extend their time away from Athens and go again to her country home. It would be the last visit for Arianna, and they would be able to wander the woods and walk the trails together. The weather was less than ideal, but they braved the cloudy skies and winter winds. Arianna surprised her hostess by asking one last favor. "May I ride the horse that I rode that day when uncle and I raced to town?" She did not want to discuss the wild night again when Timo was attacked, but this was the same horse that had swiftly carried her back to the farm.

"Girls riding horses—what is next!" Kallistê laughed, throwing her arms in the air. "Timo, prepare the horse for her and one for you," she said. Timo had traveled with the women, as their male protector, to Crete and now here. The two rode slowly around the barnyard, then moved out into a small field that was within sight, but not earshot, of Kallistê and Melissa.

"How are you feeling?" Arianna asked.

Timo took a deep breath. "It is good to be back. I love this place, I love being in the countryside, and I will not let what happened affect me going forward.

"What a refreshing attitude," Arianna said.

"While we have a few moments to ourselves," Timo said, turning to Arianna, "I wanted to thank you for your kindness during my convalescence. You took care of me, and you saw to it that I was given the care I needed."

"You have protected me on our many journeys together, including when I almost fell in the ruins at Knossos—there have been so many times, so many kindnesses." She reached over and put her hand over his as he let the reins drop.

"I have no right—" he said. Arianna had touched him deeply.

"Given our circumstances, we are—" She too was at a loss for words.

"It is not meant to be, but I am so grateful for your friendship," Timo said. "If I may be so bold to ask, how did you survive after that hostile encounter?"

"When he grabbed me by my hair outside the barn, I was fearful but also fighting mad. I did not know how badly you were hurt, but I knew I had to fight for my life. Fortunately, Melissa and the farmhand were in the barn and heard the horse and then my screaming."

"You were an exact match for that scoundrel. He did not have a chance." Timo cracked a smile.

As they continued talking, the horses, without any direction from their riders, ambled back toward the barn.

Kallistê and Melissa had decided to sit on the porch and watch the riders from there. "Has she always been so adventurous?" asked Kallistê.

"Always," Melissa replied. "Her intuitive nature allows her to explore the world in ways I would never think of—like riding horses and being excited about traveling all this way to see you."

"She is fortunate to have you in her life."

"I feel like I am the fortunate one. I watched this girl, wound tight in the cocoon of her grief over Titus' death, unfold her wings, and open her mind and heart to this wonderful world around her. I hope she will take her next step with as much grace and ease."

"You mean her marriage?"

"Yes."

They were silent for a few moments.

"Aridela writes that Rufus has arranged a marriage for Arianna," Kallistê said.

Melissa took a deep breath. "Yes, Theo more or less intimated as much in his last letter. I can't bear to tell her who it is."

That night, as the three women reclined on the dining couches, the conversation from dinner continued to go deeper into the meaning of their lives as women.

"Frankly, I know you won't hear this from many Greeks, but I feel that the Romans have brought many benefits to us, and by *us*, I mean Greek women," Kallistê said. "Roman women are treated differently by their men. I would never admit to saying this, but I think Greek men are afraid of the power of Greek women."

"Mater says that sometimes Roman men can be dictatorial," Arianna countered. "I overheard Pater and his friends talking about a decree that was passed by the Senate almost two hundred years ago, outlawing all Bacchic or Dionysian societies. Pater said it was because of the terrible things that took place when large numbers of men and women gathered together during the festivals. I wasn't supposed to hear that—but I did. He said that now only five men could gather together at once for any Bacchic festival and no women. How fair is that?"

"It is not about fairness, Arianna," said Kallistê. "It is about the safety of the women who attend the festivals. This is why I think you have been chosen by the god Dionysus to become his priestess, to bring him to the women of the Roman Republic, and especially to Pompeii, in a very different way. By that, I mean that you will only hold the rituals for women—no men involved. Your mother, Melissa, and other wise women will be there for you. I am not the only one who believes this. My nephew Dionysius thinks so too."

Melissa, who had been dozing in the corner by the fire, spoke. "I remember the priests of Asclepius who saw you as you were growing up in Pompeii," Melissa said. "They had the foresight to understand that even in your early years, you had the potential to be a priestess. Your time at Epidaurus, in the Asclepian Sanctuary, and your experience with the priests and priestesses there verified the insights of the priests at Pompeii. Even the friends of Aper that we met at Patra understood that you had a special calling and honored it with their ritual."

"It sounds inconceivable," Arianna said.

"I know," Kallistê said. "You have experienced so much in these last few months, and it feels that you have learned so much, but, my darling girl, this is just a taste of what lies ahead for you."

Arianna shook her head slowly. "I am not sure I am up to the task."

"When the time comes—you will be. I have no doubt. Remember the simple maxim, Know thyself," Kallistê said. "*Know thyself*, that is, who you are, who you are not, and who you are becoming."

Kallistê motioned for Arianna to sit closer to her. " But now it becomes more complicated. There is yet another understanding of this story of Dionysus," she said. "Do you remember that the Titans devoured the body of Dionysus except for his heart?"

"Oh, yes, how could I forget," Arianna said.

"Well, angry Zeus takes revenge on the Titans and strikes them dead. But from the ashes of the Titans, humans arise! So here is the paradox. We are partly derived from Zeus and his thunderbolt and partly derived from the Titans. So we are composed of the opposites, both divine and human. Who we think we are, humans, and who we think we are not, divine, are the same."

"I am confused beyond words," Arianna said. "Indeed, a paradox to ponder."

"Take your time," Kallistê said. "With the help of the wise women around you whom you trust, you will understand it more clearly as the years pass."

Kallistê rose from her chair. "It is time to prepare for bed," she said. "We have a long day's journey back to Athens tomorrow."

"And I have much to think about," Arianna said.

"Please do not think. It will all happen over the next few years. Do not be overwhelmed."

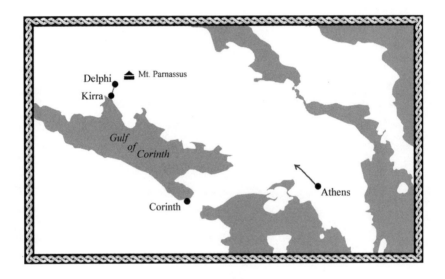

Athens to Delphi

CHAPTER XL

GOODBYE ATHENS

Upon their return to Athens, letters were waiting for Arianna and Melissa. One was from Cil. He was excited because he had just been initiated into the mystery religion, Mithraism. He couldn't reveal much in a letter but promised to share some of the ritual and initiation that he had gone through in person. Arianna had written earlier to him about her Dionysian ritual, with promises to disclose more when they were finally together.

"The weather has been cool enough that the workers do not complain every day," Aridela said in her letter, describing their progress on the country house. At the bottom of the letter, her father added, "Many surprises for you upon your return!"

"What do you think he meant by that, Melissa?" Arianna asked. "Did Theo say anything in his letter about surprises?"

"He said the work on the villa was going well," Melissa said, avoiding her question.

"I miss you so very much," Theo had written. "I cannot believe how quickly the days have gone with the new project, but how long the nights are without you. I hope you are wary of those Greek men. They say their Greek tongues can entice a woman into much trouble."

"No problem there," Melissa wrote back, answering his letter with her own provocative twist. "Stephanos watches out for the two of us. But there was this one time on the road just outside their country home in the mountains. The Greek was very handsome—no, no, no, I am just teasing. I can hardly wait to be in your arms again.

"I will plant this thought—maybe, maybe you could come to Delphi with Aper. I look forward to you planting your seed, my love. Soon." Melissa was ready to go home.

There was also a letter from Aper to Arianna. "It looks like we may have an early spring if you can believe the astrologers," Aper began. "The bulbs are sending up their green shoots, and wildflowers are starting to surprise us when we are out walking the trails—yes, my son Aper walks with me now. You will not believe how much he has grown in the past year. So I would say that I could meet you in Delphi on or before the Ides of Martius. I am trying to talk your pater into letting Theo come with me as you asked. Do not say anything to Melissa yet. I do not want to get her hopes up."

Kallistê had decided to go with Arianna as far as Delphi. "Of course, I am going with you. I do not want to miss the experience of being with you when you see the Oracle."

"Thank you, Auntie. I am sure I will be ready, but it seems a little daunting."

"I have heard about the Sibyl at Cumae in Italy. Have you ever been there?" Kallistê asked.

"No, but Mater told me that that oracle sings the fates and writes on oak leaves."

"Well, the oracle at Delphi does not sing, but she may rave a bit."

Arianna smiled. "Oh, Auntie, are you trying to scare me?"

"Just wait, young one. You will see."

They talked about the journey up into the mountains to Mt. Parnassus, where Delphi was located. "We will make some stops at friends' homes along the way. The higher we get on the mountain, the slower the horses move. We will stop short of Delphi and stay the night at the lovely home of a dear friend. Then the next morning, up we go! That is all I will tell you."

"Will we be able to go to the Acropolis before we leave for Delphi?"

"Of course, let us wait for a warmer, clearer day—maybe in a few weeks."

"That will be my sad good-bye." They both sat silent for a while.

"That is enough for today," Kallistê said. "Let us plan to go to the agora tomorrow. You will want to take some exotic spices back to your cook! Then you will have to show her how to use them."

"Melissa loves to cook," Arianna said to Kallistê. "She will be a great help to me. We need to get together with your cook before we leave."

Arianna's first experience in the Athenian Agora was one that frightened her, because of her misunderstanding with Stephanos that brought on her seizures. She had learned her place in the Greek world—always with a man as a chaperone. There was the time in the Stoa Poikile, where she heard a lecture on Stoicism and met Kallistê's nephew, Dionysius, for the first time. The time of gift buying with Timo for the Saturnalia had been a real treat, and here they were again, buying gifts for the last time.

Athens rituals had been over for a while, and so it was, as Kallistê put it, "A quiet time of year, for which I am truly grateful." The winter days were windy, cold, and often rainy. One day, the women took advantage of a break in the weather and made their way up the steep hill via a wide ramp that led them through the monumental gates of the Propylaea, the enormous entrance with Pentelic marble columns that set the stage for the rest of the buildings on the Acropolis. Its sheer height offered a spectacular view of Athens.

The women headed first to the Parthenon temple to pay homage to the goddess Athena. The chryselephantine statue with her ivory face and arms glowed in the enclosed building. Her massive shield and dress of gold were so dazzling that Arianna wept. She walked around to get a better look at the shield and saw the huge face of the Medusa in the center. It fascinated her as she had heard that Medusa's face with snakes for hair is meant to turn onlookers to stone.

Outside, they moved to the Erechtheum porch, where the caryatids stood, six female figures, their bodies tall as the columns they represented. Kallistê whispered, "You will see two more caryatids at Delphi."

Next, they retraced their steps so that they could enter the Sanctuary of Artemis Brauronia. Kallistê spoke with Timo, who had accompanied them, indicating that he and the other male servants should remain outside the Sanctuary and wait as it was a place for women only. Inside, the women were pleasantly surprised to see young girls sitting in the stoa, helping their teachers make the garments that would adorn the wooden statue of Artemis. They gathered around Arianna and listened to her as she told them of her initiation into the bear clan in Pompeii. Her diction, crystal clear, delighted them because of the strong Roman accent. A foreign woman who spoke their language of love for Artemis!

At the end of the visit, the girls eagerly showed the women what they called a secret stairwell down to the Sanctuary of Asclepius. There, Arianna saw the stoa where patients slept as she had at Epidaurus. They moved on to the small Temple, where she left a token of her appreciation for the god and then drank from the waters of the spring that was so vital to the healing powers of the Sanctuary. After an appropriate time for reflection, they moved on to their final destination, the Theater of Dionysus. Walking toward the theater, they heard music and a chorus singing.

"Look, Arianna, a play is finishing in the theatre," said Kallistê.

By then, large cumulus clouds were moving quickly across the azure blue sky, fueled by gentle but steady winds. The sun beat down on the backs of the women as they watched the audience file past them, exiting the theatre. Arianna hurried past the stragglers to see a flute player and a man playing the *cithara*, working on a sequence of notes. Moving quickly toward the bright marble seats of the theater, she sat down, but as if there were a spring in her seat, bounced back up, pointing toward a sculpture she had missed. "It is the god!" she said, heading back toward the entrance. The women looked up to see a large monument. "Look, he is greeting his audience, welcoming them into his theatre!" The sculpture placed high on a monumental base was of the reclining god Dionysus, holding a cup aloft in one hand, leaning on his other elbow and smiling down as if receiving his guests with a toast. His long hair lay in ringlets on his shoulders, and a crown of ivy encircled his head.

Arianna stood looking up. "How beautiful he is." Lowering her eyes, she focused on the monument's base, where she noticed a line of women sculpted in relief into the stone. They seemed to be moving. "They are maenads! Look how they dance. Oh, oh, look at this one," she said, following the flowing outline of the dress. "How her *chiton* swirls around her body—like mine." She swirled to the music of the two musicians, who had noticed her and set the timing of their music to her steps. She spun the length of the orchestra, the stage that the actors had left only minutes before.

Stephanos wrote a letter of introduction to the Delphic priests who administered the duties and details of the Sanctuary of Apollo at Delphi. A return letter arrived promptly. The priests thanked Stephanos for his generous contribution of gifts and money, reminding him that his Athenian family was held in high esteem. They appreciated that Stephanos' family member wished to visit the Sanctuary and seek the counsel of the god through the Pythia. Stephanos had told the priests that she was a young priestess and so the priests urged the petitioner and the group that would accompany her to start for Delphi before the next new moon.

After Stephanos had read the letter, he interrupted the women in their section of the house. "The letter from Delphi has arrived. Arianna, you are accepted as a member of this family. Thus you will be able to have an audience with the Pythia and submit your question."

Arianna squealed and flew into his arms before he could finish his sentence. "Thank you so much, uncle. I will be forever grateful to you."

He hugged her in return. "My child, you have certainly become part of this family, so I am delighted that you can partake of this inspiring event. Romans are not always well received, as I have said before. You have shown not only your eagerness but your competence and thoughtfulness in embracing the Greek culture." His eyes were full of emotion. She was close to tears.

"Now return to your lessons from my dutiful wife and learn all you can from her. She is a knowledgeable and generous teacher."

"I will. I will." Arianna ran back to where Kallistê was seated and hugged her.

He turned to leave and then asked, "Has she told you the history before the temple was built?"

"No, I have not," said Kallistê. "Please tell the story, Stephanos."

He seemed pleased to be able to impart some knowledge to their eager apprentice. "Before the temple was built," he began, "before the Sanctuary walls were constructed, shepherds tended their goats, which roamed freely on the southern slopes of Mount Parnassus."

He said that the shepherds began noticing some strange behavior, even sounds, from the goats after they ate the edibles from this one particular section of the hill. When they investigated, they found a sweet-smelling vapor coming from a crevice in a rock. The shepherds experienced an overwhelming feeling of euphoria when they smelled the fumes, even talking gibberish to one another. When the shepherds told the holy men of their village about the sweet scent, they investigated to find out for themselves whether this was a sacred place. It was indeed an area where mother earth spoke from the depths of the earth, through the *Pneuma*, the breath rising from the cleft in the rock. It was deemed that this area was sacred to Gaia, and so homage was given to her and Poseidon. A shrine was built around the sacred spring, which became the most important place in all of Greece.

"Apollo enters the story now," said Stephanos, "and I will let your aunt take over from here."

Stephanos left the room. Kallistê waited until he was out of earshot, then leaned closer to Arianna. "Many of the holy people in that era were probably women. Poseidon is the god of waters, as you know, but also the god of earthquakes. He was included here because that crevice in the rock had probably been caused by an earthquake. Also, I want to tell you, dear girl, that I speak to you in confidence, as one woman to another. But when you return home, you must watch how you speak when in the company of men. Most are not receptive to many of the ways that women see the world, especially when it comes to worshiping Gaia, Mother Earth. Your mother has talked of this, I am sure."

"Yes, she has, but I am only now starting to understand what that means. Please go on."

Kallistê continued, reminding Arianna of their time on Crete and all the sacred sites of the Great Mother goddess they had visited and how, when these sites were taken over by the Olympian gods, everything changed. The one exception seemed to be Dionysus. Some said he was a late entry into the Pantheon of gods and goddesses. But stories that came from Crete said he was present *before* the Olympians. Women had always been attracted to him, maybe because he was considered the Great Loosener, the One who freed-up women and allowed them to be their instinctual selves instead of playing a role dictated by male gods and men.

"But mater told me about the followers of Dionysus, the maenads of Greece, and how they became out of control and did wild and vicious things after drinking too much wine."

"Yes, she spoke the truth, which brings me to a significant point," Kallistê said. "On the night of the Dionysian ritual when you were initi-ated—"

"I will never forget it," Arianna interrupted her.

"This is an example of how most of the women followers of Dionysus have changed in Greece, becoming more civilized. You were not allowed to run wild in the woods to perform harmful deeds but were shown instead your intuitive, wild nature within, then allowed to enact an initia-tion process that was full of meaning and that will no doubt stay with you when you return and start your work with *your* Dionysian ritual."

Arianna thought of the drawings she had produced in that Pompeian night of Dionysian possession. "Did Mater tell you of the images I drew after Titus' death? As I look back on that night, in many ways, it was the beginning of my new life."

"She certainly did," Kallistê said. "She shared with me how the images reminded her of her Dionysian initiation when she was here those many years ago, how she has longed for you to be able to explore his mysteries and grow with his insights and wisdom. It was something that she was never able to develop due to family circumstances, and so now she wishes it for you."

"I see my mater in a new light."

"Good. She is a wise woman, and with her guidance, you, too, will grow in wisdom and be able to share your knowledge with other women. I think that is her greatest wish."

Later that evening, Kallistê told Arianna the gruesome story of how Apollo had killed the Python, the serpent that was the protector of Great Mother goddess, Gaia or Ge. The python had its lair next to the Castalian Spring that flowed through the temple built for the goddess in a town called Pytho. As recompense for his lethal action, Apollo was sentenced to serve several years doing menial tasks.

"A slap on the wrist, one might say," Arianna said.

When he returned to Pytho after completing his sentence, Apollo renamed the town Delphi, which means womb. Was this referring to his mother's womb because, after that, he seized Gaia's temple and compelled the Pythia, the priestess who conducted the oracle readings, to serve him? Now, the words of wisdom that the Pythia spoke when she was under the influence of the vapors coming from within the earth were attributed to Apollo, not Gaia. Apollo gave Poseidon an island as recompense.

"What recompense could Apollo give Gaia?" Arianna asked. "Gaia as mother earth is everywhere. How do you give compensation to her?"

"Exactly," Kallistê said. "So when you hear the words of the Pythia, understand that the words come from Gaia, not Apollo. There's much more to tell you, but I would rather show you the rest, in person."

This new adventure meant starting for home, for it was the last leg of her journey. It was a bittersweet moment for everyone. There was a dinner prepared in her honor and a ceremony on the last evening. Having difficulty saying goodbye, Arianna remained very quiet for the first part of the dinner. She was pleasant and smiling, but inside, her heart was breaking. Her aunt was indeed a second mother. She had even won over Stephanos. After speaking briefly to everyone gathered, thanking each of them in very personal ways, she asked to have some alone time, looking at the beautiful city at night for the last time.

The house where she had learned so much sat atop a hill. As she sat on the porch overlooking the city, she started thinking about her time in Greece. Her Greek mother had secured the books she needed to educate her Roman daughter in Greek literature and philosophy appropriate to her station. Kallistê was also versed in the Greek plays, reciting many excerpts from intriguing parts of the plays. Who needed to go to a symposium or attend lectures as the young men did? She had learned not only from books but from the oral traditions of her Greek mother and other women she met along the way. She recalled Kallistê's words: "Just as you will remember the lessons I have taught you, you will also find that each year, you will live your life differently because of all you have learned in this short period. What you think you understand now will change over time, and the life experiences that follow will give deeper meaning to what lies beyond."

From the garden, she could see the Acropolis standing dark and silent in the nighttime sky. As she watched, the waning moon rose over it. Dionysius, who had been a surprise guest at the dinner, approached her. He put a shawl around her and asked to sit beside her.

"It would be my pleasure for you to join me," she answered boldly. "I am so glad your trip was shortened so that you could come tonight."

Moments passed as they sat quietly. Finally, he took her hand in his as they watched the flickering lights from the oil lamps twinkling below in the city streets.

"Look, look at the area just below the Acropolis—there is a light in the theater of Dionysus!"

"Yes, I see it," she shouted, standing to get a better look. "It is a sign, Dio, I know it is a sign!"

He took her shoulders and looked into her dark brown eyes, smiling. "What does it mean to you?"

"He is saying goodbye, I think," she said hesitantly. "What do you think?"

"I think he is winking at you, telling you that he will meet you in Delphi."

They both laughed. It felt familiar—an intimate laugh. They were in each other's arms. Her laughter turned to tears. As he had done months ago, he licked away the tears, and they both laughed once again.

"I had better take you back into the house before I whisk you away on my horse and break all the rules that Stephanos holds dear."

"You tease me, Dio. That is not fair," she said as they walked back to the house, hand in hand.

"Fairness is not always one's fate."

CHAPTER XLI

HELLO DELPHI

Kallistê's entourage stopped for the night at her friend's large, comfortable country house located a short distance from the Sanctuary of Apollo. Tonight was the last night of the journey. Tomorrow they would reach Delphi, and Arianna would visit the Sanctuary of Apollo for the first time: The Oracle of Delphi.

From their vantage point, they could see the tip of a rooftop—the Temple of Apollo as it seemed to rise out of the mountain. A pop-up thunderstorm cleared the air that evening, allowing a dazzling vista of stars. The women rose early and watched the sunrise, casting beautiful shadows that moved through trees and hills in the deep, expansive valley below. "Look off to your left," Kallistê said. "If you could see far enough, down the valley and over the hills below, you would see—"

"Kirra?" Arianna said.

"Yes, my love, Kirra is the port where Aper will dock. I look forward to meeting this young man."

"He is not that young. He is older than I am," Arianna said.

"Whoever is younger than I am is young," Kallistê laughed. "I want to start our tour of the Sanctuary this morning if we arrive in time. It becomes unbearably warm after midday, and unless we are blessed with a wind, the sun can be very intense in the mountains. All that marble will strain your eyes."

"Like the Acropolis?"

"Yes, exactly."

Arianna wanted to walk the road to the Sanctuary as she had done at Epidaurus. She was warned about the steep incline up the mountainside but did it anyway. Kallistê did not argue with her but chose to ride in the carriage and insisted that Dionne and Melissa ride with her. While Arianna started at a fast pace, she slowly lost momentum, and the group moved past her. Kallistê glanced at Timo, and with that, he dismounted his horse, trailing it behind him as he walked with Arianna. Her breath became labored. Timo stopped as she called out that she was going to sit by the road for a few moments. He removed the large flask of water that the horse carried and offered Arianna a sip of water from it. She caught her breath, took hold of the flask, and instead of drinking from it, she let the water flow over her head as she bent over by the side of the road. "My head gets so hot!" Her red face said it all.

"The Castalian Spring is just ahead," Timo said, taking the flask from her. "The freshwater will be much better for you to drink."

He helped her onto his horse and held the reins as he walked beside her. They caught up with the carriage in no time. The animals were struggling with the incline, the altitude, and the loads they carried. Timo was used to the altitude, having made these trips through the mountains with his master and mistress many times.

"The Castalian Spring is very close," Kallistê said. "We are going to stop off at the Temple of Athena Pronaia on the left. If you wish to keep going, you will see the deep ravine on the right with a waterfall above. We will meet you there."

By the time the carriage arrived with the women, Arianna and Timo were both drinking the fresh waters flowing from an early spring melt. Mount Parnassus, crowned with snow, loomed above them, threatening, on the one hand, but with waters quenching their thirst. When he saw that Arianna was safe by the stream, Timo, having quenched his thirst, went back and helped the other travelers, then took his horse for a watering.

The women enjoyed the respite. They noticed another woman, an older woman with short white hair, ambling through the ravine, shouldering a heavy metal object. She seemed friendly, so Kallistê questioned her and found out that this woman was the Pythia-in-training.

"I have been a widow for several years and asked to be considered for instruction." She addressed Arianna. "It used to be that the Pythia was younger, but after one of them was violated by a male visitor, the Pythias and priests decided that going forward, the Pythia should be chosen from the older, less desirable women of the town." She threw a glance and a smile toward Kallistê. "I feel privileged to have been chosen. They are teaching me the ways of the Oracle and how to be open to the skills, which includes knowing how to protect myself."

Arianna tilted her head. "Protection?"

"Yes, the fumes can be overwhelming if one does not pay attention.

Also, some of the pilgrims can be insistent because they do not understand the danger we face with the fumes." The Pythia seemed embarrassed. "It is time for me to leave. I probably should not be talking with you."

Kallistê thanked her, and they watched her walk away toward the Sanctuary.

"Well, Arianna, what do you think of this, your first experience meeting a Pythia?"

"It certainly was unlike anything I had expected. Why was she so reluctant to talk with us?"

"Her duties require that she remove herself from the world and live the life of solitude and reflection, sharing her life with very few people. Sometimes not feeling a part of the outside world is what gains one the insights necessary to live the inner journey. Your journey may indeed call you to withdraw from the world at times for the same reasons. Like Dionysus, you will be asked to live a two-fold life—the inner world and the outer world. Light and darkness."

Kallistê paused to let her words sink in and then continued. "I was not going to tell you until later, but it seems that later has arrived," she said. "The reason I wanted to come to Delphi with you is that there is an experience you need to start to understand. You must see Dionysus in his dual life. You have gone through the marvelous ritual of Dionysus in Athens. Now, some of the women you met through that ritual will be here as well. This time you will experience the dark side of Dionysus. These women are very skilled in what will seem to you like chaos. It is anything but that. You will not be participating in the Dionysian ritual but will be witness to it. I will have to make sure our hosts understand this. For now, do not say a word."

Arianna was holding her breath.

"Enough, dear girl," Kallistê said. "Take in the clear breath of the day so that you may let the cool air of the night fill you with wonder." They walked together, Arianna deep in her thoughts. The women settled back into their carriage, and the conversation continued. "What was the Pythia carrying over her shoulder?" Arianna asked.

"I think it was the key to the temple of Apollo. I would imagine that carrying the key with all its heft and meaning gives her much to ponder. It will be part of her responsibilities to help decide when to open the temple. The day when they receive the supplicants is usually the seventh day after the new moon, and since this is the month that opens the new year, there will be numerous pilgrims lined up to gain entrance."

"Who gets to ask their questions first—I mean, what order—how will I—?"

"The priests manage those affairs," Kallistê said. "Since Stephanos sent our letter to them, we might be some of the first ones to be admitted. I will ask our host."

"Our host?" Arianna said.

"Patience, my dear," Kallistê said.

Delphi was a small community but had many beautiful homes, and they would be staying in one of them. Their host, Nikolaos, was a friend of Stephanos and Kallistê. He graciously welcomed them, and because it was a hot afternoon, they decided to get a fresh start in the morning.

Arianna learned more of the legends that evening. Delphi was considered the center of the world and, therefore, the most important sacred site in the Greek world. "It was said that to find the center of the world," Nikolaos explained, speaking low as if revealing a secret, "Zeus released two eagles, one from the far east, another from the far west. They flew towards each other and landed in Delphi. With that event, it was forever after considered the center of civilization.

"From ancient times, the grounds of the Sanctuary were already felt to be numinous. Heads of state, local and foreign dignitaries, all recognized the importance and power of the Pythia, whose role it was to reveal to these important men answers to their questions. Before battles were fought, territories were settled, or towns were built, the Oracle of Apollo was always consulted. The god Apollo gave the answers to their questions through this woman, the Pythia, whom they would see, sitting on a tripod in the *Adyton*, the sacred inner sanctum of the temple of Apollo."

"On the way here, we saw a Pythia carrying the key to the temple," Arianna said.

"That is indeed an auspicious beginning, young woman," Nikolaos said. "You need to know how fortunate you are, to be sure, an exception to the rule. Usually, only men are allowed to go into the temple and ask a question. But because of your uncle's status in Athens, you have been granted a dispensation." Arianna smiled at him and also at Kallistê, giving a little bow of her head in recognition and gratitude. Even though Arianna had heard some of this from her Greek parents, she acted like it was new information for which she was grateful.

The next morning Arianna asked that Melissa be able to join them on the tour of the Sanctuary. Nikolaos agreed and led them back up the winding path they had taken the day before, crisscrossing past the terraces of houses built up the side of the hill of Mount Parnassus that together made up the town of Delphi just below the Sanctuary.

"This part of the mountain is shaped like a giant amphitheater," Arianna commented as they ascended toward the Sacred Way.

"Earth Mother's handiwork," Melissa whispered to her.

Nikolaos continued. "Look up at the columns of the Temple of Apollo." The temple, built on a plateau, dominated the skyline halfway up the mountain. "Now turn around and take in the spectacle of the Pleistos valley below."

It was breathtaking. The valley was so deep and wide that Arianna became lightheaded as she whirled around.

"Living here is like living near the gods," Nikolaos said. "We settle for two—Apollo and Dionysus." He smiled. "Speaking of that, you have come just at the change of seasons—from the Dionysian winter rituals to the return of Apollo from where he spends his winters in the land of Hyperborea."

"Where is that?"

"The Hyperborean means the place beyond the North Wind, where it is forever springtime."

Kallistê added, "The last of the winter Dionysian rituals will take place within three days. Women who have come from Athens will climb the mountain, and, with the Pythia in charge, reenact an ancient ritual."

Arianna started to speak.

"No, Arianna," Kallistê cut in, "you may not participate. Remember, we talked about some of the rituals being intemperate in their origins and therefore, the women are carefully chosen as they must be fully aware of what they will be expected to do. It is not a ritual for everyone."

"Well said." Nikolaos was duly impressed with Kallistê's answer.

"I have spoken to Nikolaos," Kallistê continued, nodding to him, "and it has been determined that you will ascend the mountain as the women from Athens ascend, to witness but not to participate in the Dionysian ritual."

Arianna grinned from ear to ear.

"We will see how much you are grinning when you return," Nikolaos said. "This is serious business, and if your aunt had not convinced me that this is part of envisioning the whole experience of the Dionysian ritual, I would not have allowed it. There seems to be a path for you as a priestess of Dionysus upon your return to your homeland. I see it as a blessing and a curse—but that *you* will see only in time."

Sanctuary   **DELPHI**

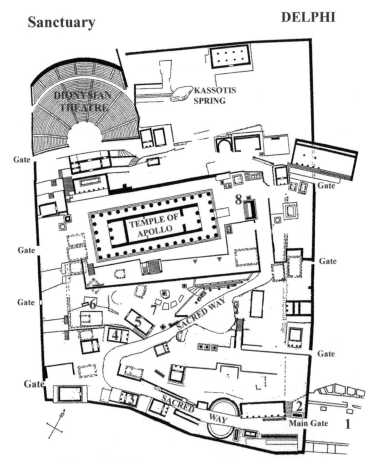

1 Roman Market   4 Treasury of Athenians
2 Bronze Bull -   5 Bouleuterion - council house
   votive monument   6 Asklepieion
   of Korkyra   7 Rock of Sibyl
3 Treasury of Siphnos -   8 Altar of the Temple of Apollo
   two Caryatids

CHAPTER XLII

APOLLO'S SANCTUARY

DIONYSIAN AMPHITHEATRE

"I will share the current history of the Sanctuary," Nikolaos said as they stood at the entrance gates of the Sanctuary. Since your father is a Roman citizen, you may be aware of a Roman general by the name of Sulla. When he decided to ravage Athens, he chose to fill his coffers by raiding several treasuries in our beloved Sanctuary. That you will see as we pass by."

Arianna couldn't resist. "You should see some of the holes left from his catapults in *our* walls around the city! He saw to it that the Pompeiians would surrender to his rule by occupying the city and setting the Roman troops in place. My pater says Sulla plundered our coffers because we did not immediately surrender—"

Nikolaos interrupted. "So, I am pleased you know of this Roman officer's tactics. Let me tell you now about the buildings in the Sanctuary along the Sacred Way," he said, changing the subject.

Through the open gate, they went. "On your right and left, you will begin to see the offerings by the people of Greece and territories abroad," he began. "This bull, for instance, is a gift from the island of Corcyra." He had told her the story the night before. "Do you remember?"

"Yes, yes," Arianna was quick to say. "The people were very appreciative that the Pythia had solved their problem and sent the bull as a token of their gratitude. I did not realize it would be so huge!"

"Excellent, young woman."

As they walked on, Kallistê asked to stop at the Siphnian Treasury. "Look up, Arianna. See the carved characters enacting the Battle of Troy."

"Beautiful," Nikolaos continued, "and full of votive offerings of gold and silver that were mined on the island of Siphnos. These buildings are not temples"—he swept his arms to include all the temple-like structures within view—"but are called treasuries in that they secure the safety of the votive offerings. You will see the whole known world represented on this one street."

When he finished speaking, Kallistê walked Arianna to the front of the treasury. "Now, what I wanted you to see are the two maidens, the caryatids I talked about when we saw their sisters at the Erechtheion on the Athenian Acropolis."

"I remember," Arianna said.

They paused there for several minutes, looking at the caryatids up close, even closer than she had been able to see their sisters on the Acropolis. The two sculptures were shaped in the form of young women and used as columns to help support the entablatures of the treasury. "It shows the strength of women to carry heavy loads, both figuratively and literally," Kallistê said.

"This is one of the most beautiful buildings in the Sanctuary," the host continued. "Notice the flawless, pure white Parian marble of the porch and columns."

By then, it was midday, and the marble reflected the brightness of the sun so that Arianna was almost blinded by it. She raised her arm to deflect the light. Melissa opened the parasol she carried and shielded her.

"Let's move on. We have so much more to see," Nikolaos said.

At this juncture, the Sacred Way made an abrupt right angle and turned up the hill, past more treasuries than Arianna could have imagined. The buildings stood almost side by side, on both sides of the Sacred Way.

"Is each treasury from a different city?"

"City, or polis, as we Greeks call it," Nikolaos said. "Let's keep walking. The Athenian Treasury is up ahead on the left. Your auntie will want you to see this."

When they reached it, they stopped to admire its splendor. The metopes were sculpted into thirty different images in the Doric frieze.

"See the images of the Amazon women fighting," Kallistê began. "Also, do not miss the nine labors of Theseus," she said as they walked farther around the building. "And you must not miss the Labors of Heracles. I know he is near and dear to your heart."

"He is important to me, but I have yet to understand why, except that he is essential to my pater's religious beliefs."

Next, tucked behind the Athenian treasury, which was full of votive offerings, was the Asklepieion with its temple and a little fountain at the Sacred Spring. "I did not want you to miss the god who was so important to you in Epidaurus," said Kallistê.

Seeing it made her homesick for Cil. "I wish my brother could be here to see the Temple of the god of Medicine, so dear to him. We will have much to talk about."

"Next of note is the building where Delphi's fifteen councilors meet," Nikolaos said.

Melissa spoke up. "It is similar to the buildings at the end of the forum in Pompeii, where the city magistrates meet and make speeches to the populace."

"Look above you at the Rock of Leto, where it is said that Leto held her young son, Apollo, so that he might kill the Python," Kallistê said.

Arianna shook her head, not wanting to see it.

They walked on. "The next part of the Sacred Way gives you a sense of entering the Holy of Holies," Kallistê said. "Look on your left and see the Rock where it is thought the first Sibyl sat and prophesied."

"It is enormous!" Arianna said. She and her aunt stayed there for quite a while. They also took in the place where the Kassotis Spring emerged from within the temple—flowing through the *Adyton*, the Holy of Holies, where the Pythia sat on the tripod and received her insights from the Oracle.

"The Mother goddess," Arianna whispered, taking it all in. She was utterly dazzled with the natural wonders before her. But more than that, she wanted to live out of a place inside her, where the myth was alive, a place to breathe and grow into her own womanhood.

Meantime, Nikolaos had arranged lunch for them just outside a nearby gate. Several shade trees took the edge off of the blazing sun, and they were able to continue their conversation.

"Maybe, we should separate this into two days," Kallistê said after they had eaten. "We have another day before we need to prepare for the Dionysian journey."

"Please, Auntie, I am rested now. I want to see the origin of the Sacred Springs above the Temple of Apollo. I know I cannot go into the temple, but I at least want to see the spring where the water emerges from the mountain and then flows underground, under the temple. Is the emerging water the place where the Pythia and her patrons purify themselves before entering the temple?"

"The same," said Nikolaos, realizing that there was no possibility of saying no to this determined young woman. He shrugged his shoulders and smiled at Kallistê. "To the Kassotis Spring we go." They re-entered the Sanctuary. "I will make sure that you can drink some of the waters." As he glanced up the mountain, he stopped in his tracks. "Look up for a moment at the Phaedriades, the shining ones above you," he said.

They all turned and looked upward toward the mountain. There was a cleft in the mountain where a pair of colossal cliffs emerged, a natural rocky barrier enveloping them as the group stood in the Sanctuary. The cliffs, set in a semicircle, protected the Sanctuary on three sides with the fourth or southern side open to the valley below. This was the place where the Sacred Kassotis Springs first emerged from the mountain—between the cliffs that glistened in the noonday sun. "Thank Apollo for this sunny day to enjoy their sparkle."

Next, they came face to face with the Temple of Apollo. And there, high above the entrance to the Temple, were the Greek words, *Know Thyself*.

It had been a maxim that her aunt had discussed with her. But here were the words, taller than she, etched in marble above the entrance to the temple above her.

They stood in silence, but the words rang in her head until she put her hands over her ears, trying to silence the persistent voice within her. Kallistê gently placed her hand between Arianna's shoulder blades. Her touch seemed to ground Arianna and she relaxed a little. "Take these words into your heart, your soul and your body as fertile seeds which will hibernate, incubate and grow within you over time," Kallistê whispered. "We will talk about it tomorrow. For now, just take it in."

"Follow me up the hill, and I will give you a closer look at where the Sacred Waters emerge from the ground at the Kassotis Spring," Nikolaos said, leading them out of the Sanctuary.

After a brief respite at the springs, tasting the sweet-smelling waters, they continued to the Theater of Dionysus. The view from the theater was panoramic, even more breathtaking than when they started their climb that morning. Apollo's Temple stood below them, and below that was the Sacred Way, winding its way amid all the treasuries gleaming with gold and marble. In the distance, one could see the glistening Corinthian Sea. "I can hear Aper now, whistling one of his favorite songs," Arianna said.

"You do have a vivid imagination, child," Nikolaos said.

As Arianna had done at Epidaurus and Athens, she climbed the steps of the theater that was cradled into the hillside, leaving the others behind. Melissa stood in the center of the orchestra and quietly talked to the group around her. "We'd better watch that girl. She'll climb into those shining cliffs behind her and we will never see her again."

Because of the acoustics of the theater, Arianna heard every word. "If I had food, you would be right," she shouted to those standing below. "As it is, I will be right down." She clamored down the stairs as fast as her legs could carry her.

Arianna had finished climbing for the day, and as she retraced her steps down the hill, Kallistê called her attention to a tall column that Arianna hadn't noticed before. "See the three dancing girls at the top of the column?" Kallistê said. "They are celebrating the rituals of Dionysus like the one we will witness tomorrow."

"How graceful they look. Are they standing on Acanthus leaves?" Arianna said.

Kallistê nodded. "Representing life, death, and rebirth—just like Dionysus."

Arianna imitated them, twirling with her raised hand as she danced down the path toward the Sacred Way. Kallistê and Melissa looked at each other, smiling. "To have all that energy!"

As they reached the Temple of Apollo, they heard men's voices coming from the temple.

"Listen." Nikolaos paused. "Do you hear the rhythmic sound of the music? That is the cadence of Apollo—order and reason in his music. Tomorrow the music will sound quite different—Dionysus."

That evening as they finished dinner, Arianna gathered her courage. "I have had a question," Arianna said, "You spoke of Apollo killing the Sacred Python who was the protector of Ge or Gaia. Then today, Auntie showed me a place where Apollo's mother, Leto, held up her young son so he could shot the arrow and kill the Python."

"Yes, that is part of the story."

"Why did Apollo kill the Python?" she asked. "It was the animal protector for the Mother goddess."

Kallistê started to answer, but Nikolaos interrupted. "I will answer this," he said. "The Python he killed was the same Python that Hera had sent to chase Leto when she was looking for a place to give birth to her twins, Apollo and Artemis. Hera was determined not to let her give birth anywhere on earth, but Delos, the island where she gave birth, was a "floating" island, not connected to the earth. Remember, her husband Zeus was the father, and Hera was very jealous."

"Jealous that her husband had seduced yet another mortal woman!" Kallistê chimed in, shaking her head.

"So killing the Python was retribution for the wrongdoing of Hera?" Arianna said. "It had nothing to do with Gaia?"

"We could say it was both," Nikolaos said. "The Olympians, especially Apollo, are sometimes very complicated. In taking over the Sanctuary of Delphi, Apollo had to destroy the animal that is symbolic of the wildness of Gaia. Do not forget, Apollo represents order, and Dionysus represents the wildness of the mountains of Gaia."

"But even today, those who have access to the Holy of Holies room within the temple say that often one sees small snakes twining around the tripod of the Pythia," Kallistê said. "Again, the dichotomy of Apollo and Dionysus sharing the same temple."

"I see," Arianna said. "Thank you for your explanation.

Arianna with Thyrsus on Mount Parnassus

CHAPTER XLIII

DIONYSIAN RITUAL ON MOUNT PARNASSUS

The next morning Arianna came down from the women's bedroom area and strolled in the walled garden of the house. It had rained overnight and the stones on the walkway were still wet. She noticed the raindrops poised on the leaves and flower petals, ready to release the nutrients that would let the young plants grow. She heard music and voices coming from the Sanctuary.

Kallistê shouted over the railing and into the courtyard garden. "Come back upstairs. We have to start the preparations." Arianna ran up the stairs to the balcony. "Do you recognize the music?" Kallistê said.

The male voices and the instruments were growing louder.

"Dionysus—is it his music?" Arianna asked.

"It is. Notice the difference?"

"Yes, not Apollo's solemn cadence of yesterday. This music makes me want to dance."

"Did you hear the roar of the bull last night, calling the Athenian matrons to begin the Dionysian ritual? The aulist was playing and the women were singing," Kallistê said.

"I heard the bull, but I thought I was dreaming. Did they go up the mountain last night—without us?" Arianna looked up the mountain past the Sanctuary.

Kallistê chuckled. "They did. But we will join them today."

"Later, I thought I was awakened by women howling and shouting."

"Yes, the first night of the ritual is particularly animated," Kallistê said. "One might consider it controlled chaos."

"I am sorry we missed it," Arianna said.

"Well, there are events of the first night that are secret even from us."

"Mysterious mysteries," Arianna said.

"Yes, indeed! Now we must prepare for the trip. It is quite the climb and essential that we dress accordingly."

They went into the suite of bedrooms that the women shared. Arianna watched as Dionne helped Kallistê, binding her dress with long strips of woolen fabric that wound around her waist, then in between her legs, wrapping the dress material around each leg, to create a pant leg of sorts out of the long dress. When the adjustments were made, Kallistê leaped into the air, coming down with both legs and arms outstretched, and shouted, "Ready!"

They burst out laughing. Next, it was Arianna's turn, and then Melissa's, and finally Dionne's.

"If Cil could see me, he would laugh and make fun of me!"

"We're not finished," Kallistê said.

Dionne brought in several pairs of sandals.

"These look like men's shoes!"

"And so they are, but smaller—made for a woman's foot," Kallistê said. "They will have more traction going up the slippery slopes of the mountain. You will see. It is quite the trek. Now put on as many layers of clothing as you can. It will be chilly tonight."

"We're staying overnight!" Arianna whispered to Melissa in Latin.

Later that morning, the host bid the women good-bye. "Timo, take good care of these women. As you know, it is not an easy trip!"

Timo and his horse, carrying the overnight supplies on the horse's back, had to take an alternate route, as only sacrificial animals were allowed to go through the Sanctuary. Usually, no horses were able to negotiate the steep incline, but Timo and his dependable horse had made the trip several times over the years.

"Meet us at the theater," Kallistê said to Timo. She, Arianna, Dionne, and Melissa walked slowly up the hill through the hairpin turns of the Sanctuary and paused at Apollo's Temple.

Arianna noticed that there were three maxims carved at the entrance. "*Know thyself. Nothing in excess.*" Arianna said, reading the inscriptions. "But what is that third saying?"

"It is difficult to interpret even from the Greek," Kallistê said. "The three work together, but each individual has his own unique understanding. Some say that the third maxim means that one should be careful what promises one makes when asking for wisdom from the Oracle.

Others say that one should be careful what one asks for, and yet another interpretation says that it is the third maxim because you must first take time for introspection. Remember the story Nikolaos told us of King Croesus and how he misinterpreted the message from the Oracle and lost his empire!"

"These Greeks are deep thinkers," Arianna whispered to Melissa.

"All of us are impulsive at one time or another, so we must strive for reflection in thought and deed," Kallistê offered her young protégé. "Spontaneity would be an aspect of Dionysus, while restraint would be a characteristic of Apollo."

"I think I am beginning to understand," Arianna responded.

"It will take many years to understand fully," Kallistê continued. "Think of the two gods as sons of father-god Zeus. Now think of their images on opposite sides of a coin. They have contrasting qualities. Apollo is the bringer of the light of the sun, while Dionysus is the light in the darkness. Music and poetry, even though expressed differently, are something they have in common. Most importantly, they share this Sanctuary."

"Enough for now," Kallistê said. "There will be more discussion tomorrow. There are some surprises in store for you." Her eyes twinkled as she hugged her Roman daughter. "Let us move on!"

They met Timo and trekked slowly up the mountain on a steep, narrow path that snaked back and forth. At one point, they could see the origin of the Kassotis spring burrowed deep in the fissure between the Phaedriades, the shining cliffs.

"Think of this as the holy mountain of Parnassus and these cliffs as the twins, Apollo and Dionysus. We are right between them!" The path took them staggeringly close to the edge of the abyss so that they had a breath-taking view of the falls. After a light lunch and a rest, they continued and made the mountain clearing by late afternoon. Exhausted, the woman collapsed at the edge of the field, where Timo had set up camp near a small cave. Toward evening Arianna saw a white-haired woman making her way toward them.

"You arrived safely!" the older woman said. "What did you think of the falls?"

Kallistê spoke first. "Hello, dear friend. The falls are spectacular as always!" She turned. "Let me introduce you to my Roman daughter,

Arianna."

Arianna did not know what to do, so she bowed her head. She assumed that this was the head Pythia that Kallistê had mentioned.

"I understand you met our Pythia-in-training recently," the woman continued. "She is a bit shy and unsure of what to say."

"We were delighted she talked with us at all," Kallistê said.

"We will have more time to talk later," the Pythia said, turning to Arianna. "I hope you enjoy this part of the ritual. It is more intense than the one you participated in Athens."

Arianna found that hard to believe as her head was still reeling from the experience.

Then turning to Kallistê, the Pythia said, "Look out for your young friend. She may be surprised at some of the happenings." She turned and left, saying, "I must return to prepare for the evening's ritual and prepare the women for their roles."

Dusk came later at the higher elevation. Finally, the sun set behind the top of Mount Parnassus, which, even though they had climbed a long distance, still loomed above them. Soon, stars could be seen in the clear, calm evening sky. That was a good omen. It was a signal for some of the preparations to start. The boundary markers of the ritual were defined by small stacks of wood placed at intervals. In between were thyrsi, staffs with pinecones on top like those that Arianna had used at the Dionysian ritual in Athens. These were decorated with ribbons and had been pounded into the ground. Slowly, the musicians took their places to complete the rectangle that was formed to delineate the boundary of the ritual dance. The musicians tuned up, speaking back and forth to one another, finishing one another's tunes. It was a playful time and reminded Arianna of the ritual in Athens.

The small bonfires and thyrsi were lit. The music, sung by a chorus of an elite group of local women, the Thyiades, became more identifiable as the dithyramb of Dionysus. It was full of modulating rhythms, wandering in and out of tempo and heightened by the interwoven shouts of female voices. It sharpened the ears of everyone within listening distance. In contrast to the deep voices of the men heard the previous day coming from the Temple of Apollo, they could now hear the women's voices, gentle at first, then gaining strength, contrasting yet complementing the instruments of Dionysus. There was the *aulos,* a double-piped instrument; the *cithara*, a stringed instrument, larger than a lyre; and the *tympanum*, a type of tambourine. It was as if the women recognized their voices as instruments of longing and desire. Their bodies seemed content to be singing in the minor mode. The rigorous behavior of the night before had left them in a mellow mood, voices muted, as if still exhausted from the riotous clamoring of the first night of ritual.

The group of women who had come from Athens, emerged, one by one, from an underground, wide-mouthed cave and joined the Thyiades in the ritual space. Musicians intuitively followed the lead of the women as they swayed to the music. Slowly the tempo escalated, and each solitary dancer felt the ebb and flow of her own body's tempo. A musical seduction. Were the musicians imitating the motion of the dancing Thyiades, the Dionysian maenads, or were the women mimicking the frenzied music? It was hard to tell. A synchronized connection between dancer and musician was certainly in play.

By now, Arianna had surrendered to the music and was dancing at the outer fringes of the ritual space. She saw a graceful, elegant woman enter the sacred arena, her white gown caressing her body, showing each sensuous curve, flowing as she twirled. She danced and sang with a flaming thyrsus in her hand. Soon, the musicians were affected by the woman, their bodies swaying to the music. Her radiance seemed otherworldly.

"It is the Pythia!" Arianna tried to whisper a shout.

Kallistê nodded, putting her finger to her lips.

As if on cue, a group of men entered the space, carrying flaming thyrsi. They gave one to each of the maenads. Almost in a state of frenzy, Arianna put her hand over her mouth so as not to scream, but pointed excitedly to the men. Before her, she saw men sporting long hair and full beards, imitating satyrs, naked except for goat-like horns coming from their heads, pointy goat ears, and a thong connected to a goat tail.

Slowly the satyrs set a staccato beat with their legs, dancing in and around the maenads. One after another, each man grabbed a maenad, twirled her round and round, then danced with her, lifting her into all sorts of beautiful positions that Arianna had never seen. The women's gowns were rippling in the breeze. At times their legs flew high above their heads. One of the women floated close by, her feet and legs tripping to the staccato. She was barefoot, and by the light of her thyrsus, Arianna could see her nude body under her thin white gown. Yet she did not seem embarrassed as the frenzied music emboldened the sensual movements of her erotic dance.

"The god possesses her," Arianna murmured. She wanted so much to be a part of the dance, but refrained, moving close to but not crossing the boundaries. She mimicked the dancer's movements, twirling her body, humming the music, and extended her arm as if holding one of the flaming torches.

Slowly, maenads formed a circle around the Pythia, dancing and singing to the Dionysian dithyrambic music with all its rhythms. Satyrs again circled the maenads and, one by one, took the thyrsus from each woman. Some of the women ran to retrieve the tympanums from the musicians, rhythmically beating them on their hips or with the palms of their hands, making their way back to the circle. A tall, broad-shouldered man emerged from the cave. Encircling his long, curly hair was a crown of ivy leaves atop a glistening, golden mask that covered his face. Draped over his shoulder was the skin of a panther, and wrapped around his waist was a sheer piece of cloth that revealed his muscular legs and his boots. He held a *kantharos*, or double-handled wine cup, in his hands and took sips of the wine-water mix as he strode to the circle of dancers. The music and singing ceased when he appeared, and Arianna recognized that the man was dressed to represent Dionysus. Both groups of maenads, Athenian and Thyiades, let out a squeal, their heads thrown back. They started running in every direction within the ritual space.

The music began again. Throwing down his kantharos, Dionysus grabbed the maenad closest to him, twirled her around, and picked her up. She screamed as she looked at him, and a nearby satyr took her from him as he danced away to capture another maenad. He circled the perimeter, repeating his actions, each time a woman swooning in his arms. Then he strode past the lighted thyrsus closest to Arianna.

I know that swagger, she thought to herself. Without another thought, she shouted, "Carpe Noctem!" and crossed the boundary.

Timo started to run after her. "Wait," Kallistê said, clutching his arm.

"Dio, is that you?" Arianna asked.

The man looked down and then threw his arms up to the heavens. He had heard the Latin words—*seize the night*! "A Roman maenad—

Arianna!" he shouted. Without looking at her, he moved quickly, twirled her into his arms, and ran off with her into the darkest area of the ritual space—the center.

"Follow them, and when she screams, be there to retrieve her," Kallistê told Timo.

As Dio reached the center, he stopped as the satyrs circled the couple with their lighted thyrsi.

Then Arianna looked up at him and, seeing his animal eyes staring at her through the mask, screamed. Dio handed her off to Timo.

Arianna was still clinging to Timo when they reached Kallistê and the group.

"His eyes, his eyes," she kept saying. "They were glowing like the eyes of an animal!"

"A serpent?" Kallistê said. She had seen this before at previous rituals.

"Yes, yes, yes, that is it—a green-eyed serpent!" Arianna blurted out. "What—how?"

The group of women and Timo carried Arianna to sit under a tree. Kallistê gave her some watered wine. Timo left to retrieve the only lighted thyrsus remaining in the ritual space. He saw the man representing Dionysus and the Pythia leading the retinue in a procession toward the cave as everyone—the musicians, singers, maenads, and satyrs—followed.

"I think this was left for you," Timo said, returning with the flaming thyrsus.

Arianna looked up at the light. Melissa sat behind her and cradled her in her arms.

"This is the part of the ritual that we couldn't do in Athens," Kallistê said. "It is better understood after experiencing Delphi with all the stories of Ge and the Python.

"Isn't the snake one of the symbols of Dionysus?" Arianna offered.

"Yes," Kallistê continued. "Therefore, he is the perfect god to reenact the return of Dionysus as Python. That is what you saw in his eyes."

"How did he—?"

"We do not understand everything that happens with these rituals. We do know that the Pythia is in charge of what goes on here. It is a sacred space, controlled yet meant to re-enact the wildness of the reveries."

"What a paradox," Melissa said.

"That is the mystery," Kallistê said. "As I have said before, controlled chaos."

"Try to explain that to a Roman senator," Melissa said to Arianna.

"We will talk more about this when the Pythia visits us. For now, let's get back to our camp and try to calm down and get some sleep. I am drained from the evening's events."

Walking in a single line, the women headed back. Kallistê chose Arianna to lead the way with her thyrsus. Timo had gone ahead to tend the large bonfire he had built earlier just outside their cave. The women bedded down in the small rock shelter. They were chilly now and lay next to each other, spooning to warm one another's bodies.

The final secret part of the ritual would be conducted without them, in the massive cave on the opposite side of the ritual space. From a distance, Arianna could see in the moonless night the fiery stars above. Below, the mammoth cave looked like it was aflame, the light in the darkness filling the night. The god was present.

CHAPTER XLIV

THE PYTHIA

The sun shone into their cave, awaking Kallistê first. As she lay there, she heard women's voices. She woke the others, and they went out to watch the women participants as they made their way back down the mountain. Last in the line was the Pythia. She headed toward Kallistê's group.

"Good morning!" the Pythia said. "Come and look at what has emerged." They walked with her into a field that yesterday had been filled with greenery, but with the morning sun, several mullein plants, tall and green, were beginning to open their spray of vertical yellow blooms and interspersed were tiny plants that had started to give up their little buds. "Narcissus!" she shouted. "Can the vernal equinox be far behind?"

Arianna spied something. "Look, one lone purple iris in this field of yellow."

"You know, Arianna," said the Pythia, "that Iris is a messenger of the gods; I wonder what message she might have for you."

"What message, indeed," Kallistê said.

"Let us return to the town," said the Pythia, "where we can bathe, rest and nourish ourselves."

And so they followed the Pythia down the mountain. The trail switched back and forth as they made their way down the steep hillside and were soon behind the theatre of Dionysus.

"I will show you a way to get back to town so that no one will stare at you, especially those on the Sacred Way," said the Pythia. Only then did they look at one other, laughing at their tousled hair, their gowns in disarray, shoes caked with mud. "It is not unusual to see women coming down from the mountain after a ritual night looking a little bedraggled, but I will save you any embarrassment."

"Why is it you always look so neat when *you* come from the mountain?" Kallistê said, having witnessed this phenomenon before.

"I take a change of clothes with me," the Pythia whispered as if telling her a secret. "You might also notice that the shortness of my hair eliminates much care. The shoes—will take some work!"

The side street they took skirted the walled Sanctuary. "Here we are, back on the street that will take you to your house. I will leave you here to find your way home." She smiled and pointed to Arianna. "I will see *you* tomorrow morning."

The next day, Kallistê had business with the women who had come from Athens and participated in the Dionysian ritual, so she took Arianna to the Pythias' home and left the two alone. "Understand that this is a distinct honor to be in the presence of the Pythias, and especially in their home," said Kallistê.

The Pythia had welcomed Arianna at the front door, talking briefly, and then the two moved to a private place in the Pythias' garden connected to the house. She was frank and to the point. "I see something in your young face, your eyes—intense—eager to learn. And there is more. Your aunt and I have discussed where your life's journey might take you. You must understand that I speak to you in closest confidence," the Pythia said, drawing nearer. "I understand that you have abilities far beyond what you comprehend at this moment. This is why I will share some of the wisdom that has been passed on to me."

She paused, closing her eyes. When she spoke next, she seemed other-worldly, choosing her words carefully. "You may not have noticed, but I am different today. I am beginning preparations to move from the Dionysian ritual, which started on the night of the new moon, to seven days hence, when we Pythias have to be ready to undergo the first day of the New Year—communing with the Oracle. Isolation and fasting are just part of the discipline. We must create a perspective that will meet the god's demands—a heavy responsibility. As this week progresses, we move into a period called Kairos, a moment in time in which the impossible becomes possible. Every day that I am called to the Temple of Apollo and down into the *adyton*, the holy of holies, I sit on the tripod and inhale the sweet-smelling aromas flowing through the waters, the fumes moving upward from the cleft in the rock where I sit. Going within, I embrace this Kairos moment in time, and if I am present and aware, I will hear the questions of the pilgrims put to me by the priests, will breathe in, and surrender to the words of the god that speaks through me. Each moment is different from the next, so in between, I try to cross into the Kairos moments, receiving the gift—the gift of speech—from my lips to the questioner's ear. It is not always clear. Sometimes it comes to me like a riddle for the questioner to figure out. Other times the *Pneuma*, the sweet-smelling vapors that escape from the fissures in the rock, is too strong for me, and what I utter comes out as babble, and I do not remember what I said. When that starts to happen, the Priest and I know it is time for me to remove myself from the chair. That is when another Pythia comes in to take my place so that I can recover from the fumes. The energy expended is enormous. Someone compared it to running a marathon. The third Pythia, the one that you met at the sacred spring when you first arrived, will also be called upon to do her part. From a distance, she observes us only briefly so as not to be overcome by the fumes. When it is time, she will take her turn in the holy of holies. Working as a unit is the only way that we can make it through the day. So you see that we perform dangerous work. It can often make one ill, and over the centuries, some of us have died."

She paused again. "I tell you this for a reason. You will be leading rituals to honor Dionysus, and you must be aware of the code of behavior for you and his followers. You need to know that Gaia understands what Dionysus represents, that he flourished in other places long before the Olympian gods. He was accepted as one of them only later, so in the Olympian pantheon, he is the oldest of the gods, but also the youngest of the Olympian gods. One of his secrets is that he is a god for women. He understands us. But we must be careful. Because he understands us, he may take advantage of us, so we must be ever on our guard when we are within his powers."

"The power of the vine?" Arianna asked.

"Yes, that, and what occurs after that also—the power of Eros. He is called the Loosener for a good reason. Dionysus is Eros incarnate. The hardest part for a woman is to maintain control, yet to be able to let go when the god calls."

"It feels like a contradiction—holding on and letting go." Arianna's eyes lowered and she fell silent. Her aunt had uttered similar thoughts about Dionysus and how he affected women, but the concept of him as Eros incarnate took her understanding of him to a deeper level.

"Some women find it a curse. Others see it as an opportunity to flourish. And there are those, like you, who will have the struggle of both curse and kindness. Each woman will experience him differently. He will ask much of you, but will also give you the courage to do what needs to be done in his name. In time, you will grow in wisdom. You will understand so much more."

"I have so many questions—I do not know where to start."

The Pythia continued. "Think of the paradox of the brothers, Apollo and Dionysus, sharing this temple. See them as two opposites coming together in the arms of Mother Nature on this mountain sanctuary. These are the two parts within you that you need to hold in tension." She extended her hands, gripping a string stretched tight between her fingers. "Slowly, the balance of the third way will evolve." Her hands came together as in a prayer.

"I find it hard to accept Apollo after what he did to the Python and Gaia."

"He was only defending his mother. Think instead of the Stoic ideas that you have embraced. That is part of Apollo's order."

"Then Dionysus balances that out?"

"More or less." The Pythia smiled at her perplexed student.

"I wish I could stay longer," Arianna said. "You and my auntie have been so helpful to me. I am not ready to leave."

"Because you mentioned the Python, I will share this last revelation with you." The Pythia took Arianna to the back of the garden. In the corner was a tall, cylindrical piece of pottery. "This is a secret you must never reveal—do you understand?"

"I do." Arianna grew anxious and started to breathe faster but caught herself and deliberately took some deep breaths.

The top of the cylinder ended in a teardrop-shaped handle. The Pythia slowly removed the lid to reveal—

"A python!" Arianna said.

"Yes, but look, it is a most unusual snake."

Arianna leaned in for a closer look. The huge snake was coiled and sleeping. "It is iridescent—blue and silver and purple. I have never seen a snake like this."

"And you never will," the Pythia said. "She is our namesake, and as her ancestor protected Gaia, she now protects us. We rarely allow anyone to see her."

"Not even the priests?"

"Especially the priests. They suspect, I am sure, but have never challenged us. Our confines are sacrosanct. They understand the volatile position we put ourselves in, and there is respect for us, and therefore, a line they will not cross. They understand the power of the god who speaks through the unpredictable rock beneath us. The older priests show us reverence, while the younger priests learn this in time, but initially are impressed by how wealthy this town, this region, has become because of what we Pythias do."

"I cannot tell you how honored I am to have been entrusted with such knowledge."

The Pythia and Arianna walked slowly back to the house. "You are entering a new stage of life," the Pythia continued. "As a young woman, you will commit yourself to marriage, bear children, and learn from the women around you, especially your mother and Melissa. You are indeed a woman blessed by the god Dionysus. Remember that even though he is a god, he too has matured from teaching men how to grow the grape and dipping low into the revelry of drink to finally creating his theater for all to learn our stories and from them, life's lessons. I understand that when you were much younger, you composed a play of your own about Ariadne. You are definitely on your way to creating your rituals."

As the Pythia prepared to dismiss Arianna, she turned to the subject of the Oracle. "Dear one, when it is your time to come to me in the *Adyton*, observe everything I do and say." They were holding hands now. "Carefully listen when I deliver the Oracle's words and make sure that the priests do not distort them. You have the gift of listening and observation. Use it with wisdom and patience. Bless you."

Arianna returned to her host's home. "Melissa, I need my stylus and ink," she said. The Pythia had given her blank scrolls so that Arianna could transcribe as much of their conversation as she could remember. She wrote the sacrosanct words in a code only she could understand.

CHAPTER XLV

THE ORACLE'S PRONOUNCEMENT

Apollo's Day occurred the seventh day after the new moon, resulting in one day a month from March through November—nine days total—that the Pythias would allow themselves to be touched by the god. These women were indeed the high priestesses of the land. In stark contrast to the misogynist society they lived in, the Pythias flourished in an illustrious world of privilege. They lived an independent life that most Greek women could not even fathom. Because of the Oracle's predictions over the centuries, the Pythias had achieved respect and admiration around the world and were showered with expensive gifts and money. It was said that Homer referred to the wealth of the "rocky Pytho." The drawbacks were that if a woman, always from the town of Delphi, applied and was chosen to be a Pythia, she had to give up any relationships with her family and remain celibate until death. While these rules were a sacrifice, those chosen were older women, often those whose husbands had died. It was a way to be taken care of for the rest of their lives. Their celibacy remained the holiest offering the women could make to the gods.

Because it was the first consultation of the New Year, occurring after winter's three-month hiatus, the Pythias would be swamped with many pilgrims flooding into the Sanctuary. Those who gave the most gifts and money were often the ones who had their questions taken to the Pythia first. If one was in a hurry or happened to miss the day, some priests could advise for a lesser price. It was a business. For the most part, priests acted as prognostic mediators between the human and the divine. By contrast, the Pythias, who had given up their human families, entered into a *Hieros Gamos*, a holy marriage with Apollo. They breathed in the Pneuma, or vapors, rising from the rock below them, giving human breath and voice to the god's words.

The night before, the Pythias of Apollo had begun their fast and performed the last of their ritual preparations in the solitude of their secluded home. The priests kept their distance but were always there to provide security. Long before sunrise, the women left their protected home and made the trip to the Kassotis Springs located above the temple, accompanied by the oldest priest and another that he had chosen for this task. They provided privacy so that the Pythias might be purified. After bathing in and drinking of the chilly, sacred waters, they changed into simple dresses, white chitons, and himations, bridal garments that were pleasing to the gods. They put on their warm cloaks as it was still nippy in the mornings. Tucked in their knapsacks were special shoes, to be worn only in the temple. When they reached the place where the sacred waters flowed into a well, they paused again, drinking the sweet-smelling waters. Priestesses and priests all walked down to the altar in front of the Temple of Apollo. One of the young priests was finishing up preparing the temple—sweeping the steps leading to the temple and sprinkling sacred waters on them.

The Pythias offered prayers to all the Delphic divinities and burned laurel leaves and barley meal on the altar located outside the temple. "We offer these prayers, honoring you, Apollo, Dionysus, Poseidon, and Mother Earth Gaia. We are your humble servants. Please protect us."

The newest Pythia opened the locked door with the massive key to the temple. As they entered, the Pythias put on their temple shoes and walked the length of the building to a room at the back of the temple. Here they could prepare for their strenuous day and take periods of rest.

Tradition held that the priests also bathed in the Kastalian waters. When finished, they would move to the altar outside the temple. They sacrificed only one animal at the beginning of the day, which represented the whole group's sacrifice. It was a ritual offering involving the correct way the animal shivered when sprinkled with the sacred waters. If those signs proved to be favorable, the sacrifice of the animal was carried out on the altar. They also checked the animal's organs for a portent of good omens.

In addition to the extravagant gifts, goats and sheep were brought to Delphi by the pilgrims and offered to the priests. They, in turn, offered the animals to the gods at different festivals during the year, providing food for them, the Pythias, and the townspeople.

Getting ready for the long line of pilgrims was an enormous task. All the priests had been commandeered into service to help on the opening day. The oldest of the group had relegated many of his duties, but the most precious duty—watching over the Pythias—was his alone. He made his way to the Pythia's room at the far end of the temple and escorted the Pythia, who had spoken with Arianna earlier to the central area of the temple where the eternal fire was burning. They paused, chanting words that only they could know. She was barefoot, and a crown of bay leaves topped the white veil that covered her white hair as a gesture of purity as the bride of the gods.

Before dawn, Nikolaos, Kallistê, and Arianna had made their way from the house to the side road that took them up the hill outside the walled Sanctuary. "This is the road we took when we walked down the hill from our night at the Dionysian ritual," Arianna remarked. They had passed by the road that went up to the entry gate of the Sanctuary, and even though it was not yet dawn, there was already a line of men standing before the gate. "Why are we not standing at the gate, waiting to enter the Sanctuary?"

"Because we're going to the Kastalian springs for your purification ceremony," Kallistê said.

"Do they not have to purify themselves too?" Arianna asked, referring to the men.

Kallistê and Nikolaos exchanged glances. He avoided the question.

"Since we are the first participants of the day, we will make our way to the springs and then into the Sanctuary," the host said. He was not going to go into all the arrangements that he had to make to allow her to go first. "Now, I suggest that we maintain silence in preparation for this wondrous occasion."

The biting cold waters of the Kastalian spring gave Arianna a start, so she made quick work of her "shower" in the waterfalls. Nikolaos removed himself to give her privacy, and Kallistê helped her quickly change into the dress made just for this occasion, covered by her cloak. Walking down the terraced path from the Kastalian Spring, the threesome made their way to Apollo's temple. Nikolaos knocked as he had been instructed.

"Good timing. Come in, come in," said the old priest as he opened one of the tall double doors. Arianna started forward with Kallistê and her host behind her. The old priest shut the heavy door behind them. "Wait here until I come back for you. In the meantime, behold the temple." He raised his arms as if opening up the sights of the temple to them.

Arianna stood riveted as she watched the priest and Pythia. He stood once again next to the Pythia, both meditating on the eternal flame. She took his arm, and they slowly moved down the staircase. For one brief moment, she turned and looked at the three petitioners. Later, Arianna would swear that she had offered a secret smile meant only for her. And so it was. She watched until they were out of sight, and then gazed at the spectacle before her, focusing on the eternal flame coming up from the floor. "The fire reminds me of the fiery sun as it rises to illuminate the front of the temple," she said.

"Remember the fiery sight that came from the cave the night of the Dionysian ritual?" Kallistê spoke in whispered tones. "Keep in mind that on the back wall of this temple, there is an inscription honoring Dionysus. That means, the west and the fiery sunsets are his. So, this is his temple too."

At that moment, the little priest appeared and motioned for them to come to him. She noticed how his white hair and stooped shoulders belied the fact that his energy was certainly not diminished. Observe and listen, she told herself, remembering what the Pythia had told her.

Nikolaos went first, followed by the two women, past the eternal flame and down the same short flight of stairs. Nikolaos gave the priest the piece of paper with Arianna's question written on it and then moved into a small waiting area cordoned off with curtains so that the Pythia could not be seen by the visitors. As Arianna walked down the steps with Kallistê, she took in as much of the scene as possible. She was fascinated with this room called the *Adyton,* the holy of holies. First, she noted the venerated stone, the sacred Omphalus, a beehive-shaped stone that represented Delphi as the navel or center of the earth.

"Look," said Kallistê. "The stone is decorated with the worker bees that protect the Mother goddess. Remember seeing an omphalos like this at Knossos?"

The omphalos was flanked on either side by two eagle statues made of gold. It reminded Arianna of the story of Zeus and the two eagles.

Immediately adjacent was a golden statue of Apollo, and next to that was what Arianna had been told was the grave of Dionysus. A laurel tree stood beside the Pythia. Arianna peeked around the curtain and was startled by the sight of the Pythia sitting on her tall tripod, legs dangling above the ground as she straddled two fissures that crisscrossed in the middle of a large rock. She grabbed hold of the curtain and smelled the sweet fragrance, first in the curtain, and then from the Sacred Pneuma coming from the fractures in the rock.

The Pythia was barefoot and slightly slumped. She held a sprig of laurel in one hand and was intently focused on a dish filled with what Arianna assumed was the sacred water from the Kassotis spring that ran under the temple. The Pythia was in a trance, gleaning some divine pronouncement from the liquid in the plate.

The old priest kept a close eye on the Pythia, and when he saw that she was in the altered state necessary for an oracular reading, he made his way over to stand in front of her, a pillar separating them. He read the words of Arianna's question so that they were almost inaudible to those in the waiting area. Arianna had worked very hard to ask the "right" question, and now she could barely hear it.

As he finished reading it, the Pythia closed her eyes and slumped even more. She chanted a prayer as she poured the clear liquid from the *Philae*, the ritual dish, onto the rock below.

A few more minutes passed, and then she threw her head back and straightened her spine as Arianna had seen the maenads do in the Dionysian dance performed for them earlier. She mumbled a few words, but then her voice changed—becoming stronger, lower in tone than Arianna had ever heard it. Through the Pythia, the Oracle spoke these words: *"Is your Fate in my hands, or is my Fate in yours?"*

Arianna gasped and fainted. Nikolaos caught her and lowered her to the floor. He saw her body became rigid and the violent contractions followed.

"Priest! Priest! We need some help in here!" Nikolaos shouted.

The priest in the Adyton could not leave his charge, the Pythia, while she was in this liminal state, but two other priests who were stationed in the temple heard the screams and ran to help.

Kallistê had witnessed one of Arianna's seizures in her home, so she knew what to do. After the convulsions stopped, the priests moved Arianna to the Pythia's place of rest at the back of the temple. Nikolaos followed until a woman stopped him. "We will take care of her from here," the woman said emphatically.

"Do I know you?" Nikolaos inquired.

"Yes, you were on the council when I was granted retirement from my duties as Pythia after the unfortunate incident with the Oracle," the woman replied.

"Now I remember who you are. I did not know—"

"Yes, I am still living. I serve by helping the Pythias on their oracular days. Even though I cannot serve in that capacity, I can be very helpful in times like these. If you will excuse me." She bowed and moved back into the Pythias' chamber before he could say another word.

He grabbed one of the priests who was leaving the Pythias' chamber. "I did not know she was still alive," Nikolaos said, motioning to the woman no longer in sight.

The priest understood who he meant. "Her oracular encounter with death has earned her a reputation well deserved in the Pythian community. She wants no attention and prefers to keep her whereabouts private."

Arianna awoke to see Kallistê and a stranger peering down at her. Immediately she knew what had happened. "Oh no, not today of all days," she said.

Just then, the senior Pythia came in and sat next to her.

"I am so sorry," Arianna said.

"I am glad you are recovering," the Pythia replied. "I understand from the priest that the words were not from Apollo but from Dionysus! That must have been quite a shock—I am sorry the words were too much for you."

"It had nothing to do with my question," Arianna said.

"But everything to do with the answer," the Pythia said. "A wise philosopher by the name of Heraclitus once said, 'The gift of words spoken by the gods does not reveal or conceal one's life path, but implies the direction that one's path might take. Only Dionysus would have asked that question."

Still in a state of confusion, Arianna shook her head and closed her eyes.

"Here, give this to her when she has regained her strength," the Pythia said to Kallistê. "I must return to my duties." It was the piece of paper that Arianna had written her question on, and under it was the barely legible writing of the priest, transcribing the words as they came from the Oracle. His trembling hand reflected Arianna's emotional and physical state of mind. He too had been touched.

Melissa was called to the temple. She brought with her the familiar unguent that comforted her charge, her familiar touch soothing Arianna's body and soul.

"I should have insisted that I be there with you," said Melissa.

Arianna handed the paper to Melissa. Melissa's mouth dropped open. The only thing she could think to say was, "I will always be here for you. We will solve this mystery together."

When Arianna was stable again, she was escorted out the Pythias' secret entrance, the door that she would forever call the Dionysian door of eternal sunsets.

CHAPTER XLVI

PARTING

The next few days of Arianna's stay were spent in the house. Nikolaos was little seen as he was tending to his duties as a diplomat to the visiting dignitaries there to consult the Oracle: hobnobbing, making deals, establishing new contacts for future visits.

One evening, Kallistê stayed up until he came home. "How are you?" she said.

"Tired of eating, drinking, and carousing with all these men. This was the final night, and everyone should be gone by tomorrow night—I hope," he said, collapsing into his chair.

"Well, I waited up to talk with you," Kallistê began. "I received a note from Stephanos today. He sends you his greetings and thanks for taking care of my entourage for all this time. He also said he had heard from Arianna's friend, who will be escorting her back to Italy. He has not been able to sail due to bad weather. I wonder if we could prevail upon your kind hospitality for a little longer," she said.

"My friend, the house is yours. I usually take some time off after this first cycle of consultations. I will be heading to Kirra in a few days to take in some sea breezes and visit friends of ours who live in the area. My wife used to love these visits," he said.

"I am so sorry, but I have had little time to talk with you. You miss her, I am sure, but are you planning to remarry anytime soon? It has been— what?"

"Three years this month. Always a sad time of year for me. Going to see our friends helps me over this rough period. And having you here this year, along with your charming niece, has meant a lot to me," he said. "No, I am not going to remarry anytime soon, unless," he said, teasing, "you are available!"

Kallistê blushed. "Now, now, I am sure there are matchmakers out there looking for prospects at this very moment."

"Frankly, I have been so busy with the council and all the activities going on in Delphi. We do have several events—from the athletic and music competitions coming up to the theater presentations and festivals to the gods and goddesses of Parnassus. We are a small but very vital community. I enjoy my involvement. And then there is the Oracle—the attraction from which the rest has developed, thanks be to the gods!"

"Yes, the Pythia is quite lovely. I cannot thank you enough," Kallistê said.

"It was your doing, you and she have been friends for—"

"Since her husband died many years ago. I think she was meant to be a Pythia. She is a very spiritual woman and devoted to her calling." They both sat in silence. "So be it. I will say goodnight." With that she hugged him.

"Ah, but I miss the warmth of a sweet woman," he whispered in her ear.

"Take yourself to Kirra," she laughed, breaking from his embrace. "I hear there are many women there to give you solace—and the 'warmth' you desire."

REUNION

Another week went by, and one day Arianna asked that they go up to the theatre of Dionysus. She wanted time to "just sit and be with the god," as she now preferred to say. It was late afternoon by the time they returned, and dark thunder clouds were rolling in from the west.

"No beautiful Dionysian sunset tonight," Arianna complained.

While Kallistê and Melissa busied themselves with the cook, Arianna lingered in the enclosed garden of the house, watching the fast-moving clouds.

The rainstorm started with soft claps of thunder that seemed muffled by the mountain top above them. Arianna ran outside and thought she caught a glimpse of someone carrying a torch near the stairs leading to the temple.

Was it her? Was it the Pythia?

A louder clap of thunder brought Melissa out into the garden. "Come in, Arianna, the storm is upon us," Melissa said.

Large raindrops started falling as Arianna scampered under the shelter of the peristyle roof that bordered the garden, drops of water suspended in the ringlets of her curly red hair. A sudden chill shook her body as Melissa covered her with her woolen shawl.

They moved into the kitchen and warmed each other before a roaring fire in the large fireplace, turning and shaking their bodies as if in some ancient warming ritual. A round, iron pot suspended on a tripod stood above a pile of slowly burning embers. The unmistakable fragrance of stew meat in the pot turned their thoughts from the storm to their stomachs.

Night was upon them. A flash of lightning followed closely by a loud crash of thunder startled the women. In the next instant, there came a pounding at the door.

"Open up, women," a familiar voice shouted through the wooden front door.

The two women ran to the door, only to be met there by one of the male servants. Arianna heard another voice, also familiar, coming from outside the door.

"Open then the door!" Arianna shouted. "I would know that voice anywhere."

The door flew open, and another flash of lightning lit the faces of the men on the porch.

Nikolaos entered first. "Look what the storm blew in!"

"Aper," Arianna shouted as she flew into his arms.

Then another surprise. "Theo is that you," Melissa said, jumping on him as a small child would, Theo twirling her round and round.

Another man stood in the shadows, waiting outside the door. Arianna squinted. "Cil, is that you?"

"Yes, it is your favorite brother waiting to be acknowledged." The women grabbed his arms and pulled him inside. "Surprise!" he said as Arianna embraced her brother, tears streaming down her cheeks.

"What are you doing here? I thought you were with Octavius in Apollonia."

"I was until we received the incredible news that on the *Idus Martii*, Julius Caesar was assassinated by members of the Senate. He considered them his friends. Unbelievable!"

Cil said that Octavius learned of the news when a freedman of his mother, Atia, delivered her letter. "After the first letter, Octavius was unsure of what to do. All of us stayed up all night talking about different options. A second letter arrived from his mother and his stepfather in short order. She wanted him to come back quickly, but without drawing attention. After that, he was very decisive about returning to Rome, seeming to have a plan in mind," Cil said. "Among other things, he insisted that his cousin Quintus take me by land to Delphi to retrieve my sister. But before we could leave Apollonia, Aper and Theo arrived."

"I was preparing to leave Brundisium when the soldiers got the news," Aper said. "We were all horrified. Bad weather had kept us in port, but it was just starting to clear. I immediately readied the sailors I had hired, and we set sail that day for Apollonia. I assumed that Cil would want to retrieve his sister and take her home."

"Your father was most generous in allowing me to travel with Aper to bring you home," Theo said, smiling at Arianna as he squeezed Melissa's hand. "And here we are. The winds were with us and we've made good time getting here. All we need now is a good omen from a sacrificial goat and we're back on the water. We're more than willing to do whatever it takes to get you two women safely back home."

Nikolaos spoke up. "My reason for going to Kirra was not only to take a rest by the sea, but also to keep my eyes out for these young men. And find them, I did."

It felt as if there was no time for long goodbyes. That night they all sat down to their last meal in Delphi, talking about the days to come.

"Octavius was not sure how he would be received by Caesar's troops, so he is sailing to a small harbor south of Brundisium," Cil said.

Aper chimed in, "I have another port in mind—Egnatia, just north of Brundisium. I know the people in the little town, and it is a safe Roman harbor—I wintered my ship there. They will have the latest news from Rome. We think the assassins have fled Rome and could be heading our way, so we must be ever vigilant as we travel toward the Via Appia."

Aper spoke specifically to Arianna. "It will not be as fast sailing back as it was coming, Arianna. The winds blow out of the north and west. They will be in our face, so the rowers will have their work cut out for them. I hired each man, specifically for his strength, endurance, and loyalty. No need for you to worry."

At the end of the evening, Arianna gave her parting gifts to Nikolaos and Kallistê, and they returned the favor. Kallistê had decided to stay on for a few more days. She wanted to spend some time with the Pythias.

"I am jealous of your time with them," Arianna said. "Promise you will write and tell me all the happenings."

"I promise," Kallistê smiled.

Theo and Melissa excused themselves early as Nikolaos had found them a room in one of the town's hotels so that they might have time for each other before the long journey home. A generous gesture. Besides, he was a romantic.

A dense fog had enveloped the top of Mount Parnassus overnight. From the village of Delphi, one could barely see the Sanctuary of Apollo jutting out of the mountain above them. The theatre of Dionysus sat even higher into the mountainside and was completely concealed.

Arianna had been awakened that morning by the sound of horses snorting and stomping their feet, their earthy scents strong just below her window. Pulling the comforter up around her shoulders, she lay in bed for another minute. Her sparkling dark eyes fluttered and closed. She imagined the draft animals at the barn, waiting to be tethered to the carriage that she and Melissa would travel in, down the mountain. Following behind them would be small wagons pulled by oxen, full of precious cargo that she had collected on her extended sojourn. She was worried about going too fast, and the animals swerving out of control. Coming up the mountain from Athens had been a gradual climb, but the procession down the steep incline to the seaport of Kirra was a more serious situation in her mind.

"No need to worry, my dear," her host had told her the night before. "These animals have traversed this mountain many times. That is their job. They will not put you in danger, I promise you. The serpentine road down the mountain slows their descent and will give you expansive views of the green valley below with its orderly olive groves and sweet-smelling lavender fields. That will make you forget all about going down a mountain."

She wondered where Melissa was this morning, and then she remembered that she and Theo had spent the night together—their first and last night alone until all were safely back home in Pompeii. Over these many months of travel, she could not have asked for a better companion than Melissa. She had become more a confidant than a nursemaid. But, after all, Arianna had grown in wisdom and competence, from teenager to young woman.

She used the chamber pot, then dressed hurriedly in the brisk morning air, her nightgown dropping to the floor as she wrapped a cloth around her breasts, as much for warmth as support. The underpants came next, followed by her tunicas. The first one stopped at her knees; the second had sleeves with a skirt that touched her ankles. Looking for the next layer of clothing and not finding it, she hopped back into bed, rubbing away the goosebumps from her arms. She had left her bedroom shutters open to catch the mountain breezes one last night.

Arianna caught a whiff of honey cakes, and Melissa peeked around the door holding a plate of the freshly baked pastry. "Morning," Melissa sang. "Anyone hungry?"

"Ravenous—come!" Arianna said. She devoured the two cakes with gusto. "Ravenous, too, for the next part of this adventure." Their knowing smiles said it all—they were both ready to go home.

"Your smile shows me that it was a good night for you and Theo," Arianna said, cupping her hands around Melissa's beaming face.

Melissa blushed. "It felt like our first night together," she whispered, "only better!" The two women hugged and giggled as Melissa helped Arianna finish dressing.

Arianna squealed as she glanced out the window, starting from the room but pausing at the door. "Can you finish up? Timo is here with his horse. I must go down."

"Go, go." Melissa shooed her away. "Wait, take your shawl." Arianna grabbed it. "And your shoulder bag."

Arianna eyed the bag for a second. "Yes, thank you—you are right—the gift! Such a dear. What would I do without you?"

"Very poorly," Arianna heard Melissa call after her as she ran down the stairs.

The mountain that morning reminded Arianna of Mt. Vesuvius, which she had seen blanketed in cloud cover many times, but she was always at a distance from the mountaintop back home in Pompeii. Here the mountain enveloped them, which only heightened her feelings of longing to stay yet wanting to go home at the same time.

"Timotheus," Arianna called to him as she reached the outer threshold of the entrance to the house.

Two other riders stood beside him, waiting to make the journey down to Kirra. They motioned for him to heed her call. He stood before her, angular as the jagged mountains towering above them. "We have been on so many journeys together—to Crete. Remember, you played the lyre at Knossos, sang your traditional songs. At the countryside villa, you taught me to ride the horse in the mountains, protecting me when we were attacked, so many other times—" Her voice trailed off. "Here," she said. "This is to remind you of me." She handed him something wrapped in a piece of cloth.

"But the memory of *you* is my gift."

"Open it," she said. He unrolled the material to find a small clay statue, whitewashed and in the shape of Pegasus, wings and all.

"They say that Pegasus is the Muse's favorite horse," she began. "I say that with his ability to travel long distances, he will bridge the distance between us, for now, and for always. Remember the bridge that we crossed on horseback as we rode into the countryside? Each time you cross it, you will remember our time together."

Now it was his turn to tear up. "You are my muse. I, I—" He could not speak the words of love that were in his heart. He realized that his love could never be returned. The image of Pegasus would have to bring together the two opposites, her aristocratic stature and his humble station in life.

She looked around to make sure no one was watching, and then touching his shoulder to indicate that he should bend down, she kissed his cheek. "Leave now, but return to give me safe passage down the mountain. Go, Go!" she said, shooing him away. "You may have yet to save me if I tumble out of the carriage and roll down the mountain," she shouted after him as he mounted his horse and rode toward the barns.

The exodus commenced, Timo leading the procession of mules pulling carts behind them. The Roman men mounted their horses, and the carriage was brought to the door of the villa. This chilly morning, Arianna would not argue about wanting to ride a horse. Kallistê kissed Arianna and spoke her parting words to her loving, Roman daughter in her Latin tongue:

Vocatus atque non-vocatus, Deus aderit—Bidden or not bidden, the god is present.

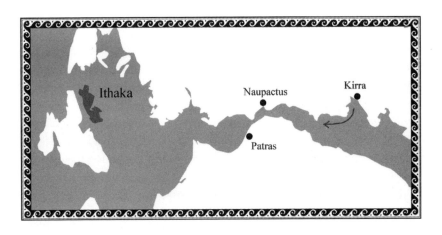

Returning Home

CHAPTER XLVII

THE JOURNEY HOME

Aper's second-in-command had been told to keep a watch out for his captain and esteemed passengers. That morning, he had raised the specific flag that told the sailors to head toward the ship. He had given them the previous evening off as he wasn't sure when that would happen again. Aper had chosen a ship that would hold more sailors for rowing. It was long and lean and carried only the supplies necessary to give comfort to the Roman voyagers. The "cargo" this trip was travelers only. The ports entered would be few as they made their way west on the Corinthian sea, turning north into the Ionian and back up the Adriatic. The rowers knew that their only job was to get these Romans safely back on Italian soil as quickly as possible even though no one knew how the Roman military would act toward civilians once they arrived. Octavius had promised to send a letter to Cil via a military transport ship that would dock at Corcyra, the last island before making their way to Italy's mainland. The written communication would also act as an introduction of the ship's ranking officer to Cil and Aper, securing safe passage for Aper's civilian vessel.

Kirra's port buzzed with activity. The spring sailing season had started. Many merchant ships had begun their daily docking: unloading then loading merchandise to take to the next port. So, too, the pirate ships were out to ransack and take booty at every opportunity. Looting in port wasn't prudent, for there were usually guards assigned round the clock, but on the open sea—that was a different story. Aper planned to stay close to other ships as much as possible. The more ships around them the safer they were. Still, the journey was in the lap of the gods. If the wind was coming from just the right direction, they could use the sail to get through the Corinthian Sea heading west. But as they turned north, northwest, there would be no need for their square sail rig as they would be heading into the wind. Instead, the crew would use all of their energy to pull the oars for more extended periods, stopping only for brief intervals to rest.

Aper had taken particular notice of the currents and tides coming down the Adriatic and into the Corinthian sea, but now the reverse, rowing against them in the open sea, would be especially tricky. It was not winter, but not yet summer, and the winds often collided with each other at this time of year. Sacks of sand had been added to the ship to provide just enough ballast to maintain the weight necessary to give the ship its heft. When they docked in Kirra, Aper had directed the first mate to hire a few extra able-bodied seamen to assist in general duties, and more importantly, act as rowing relief. This decision was, in the end, to the ship and its passengers, a detriment as well as a saving grace.

All the necessary gear had been checked and double-checked early on—mast, yard, sail, ropes, steering oars with tiller bars and brackets, oars, companionway ladder, landing plank, ladder, winch, mooring lines, tow rope. The list went on and on. Of course, there were the mandatory amphorae of wine, only for the passengers, not the crew. When they reached Italia, and if any wine was left, a toast would be given to thank the gods for their safe journey. Olive oil was stored for use by all, but two distinctive amphorae would be saved to take back to Pompeii as a gift to Arianna's parents. The oil in these containers had been harvested from the olive groves on Stephanos and Kallistê's land, near their country estate. Next, six jars of dried figs, three crocks of Chian cheese, ample containers of wild boar and goat's meat along with other dried meat and fish were loaded on board to feed the crew.

When the group arrived from Delphi, a wagon load of gifts for the return trip, earmarked for Arianna's parents and friends, would have to be loaded at the last minute. Arianna had saved two small amphorae of her favorite honey from Crete. On a trip to a fabric shop in the agora at Athens, Arianna had purchased gorgeous textiles, including everything from fine local wools to exotic fabrics such as silk. Lastly, there were spices imported from the east, cosmetics unseen in Rome, and unusual ornate pieces of jewelry for Arianna, her friends, her mother, and her friends.

The group arrived at the ship in the early evening, and everything was transferred aboard. Arianna watched as Timo led the teams back up the hill, only joining her group when she could no longer see him. He had been a dear and faithful friend.

A light supper was prepared on board for the group so that their stomachs would not be too full when they started their sea journey early the next morning. Arianna had her herbs to soothe her digestion, and she prayed that night for a smooth journey.

FIRST DAY AT SEA

It was not quite dawn when the crew stirred. One could hear the activities on the other ships as well. Soon, the faint aroma of incense came floating across the waters. The crews from other ships had assembled on their decks to offer prayers for a safe journey. So, too, on this ship: the altar had been set up on the stern deck in front of the captain's cabin, and the distinctive fragrance of the glowing embers of frankincense and myrrh filled the air from aft to bow. The sailors gathered around the incense burner in a semi-circle, and Aper encouraged his Roman friends to join them, forming a full circle. He started with a prayer.

"I pray to you, Asclepius, the patron god of this humble vessel. We offer our bodies, minds, and souls to you that we may receive from you safe passage to the shore of our homeland. We promise to give thanks to you upon our arrival and pray to you for good weather, light winds, and protection from harm afforded by your noble spirit."

The first mate started a sailor's song that was one of Aper's favorites. Music in the minor mode kept the hymn somber, but in the middle, a triple time helped enliven the singer's moods as the circle swayed arm and arm, from side to side, smoke and firelight bellowing up from within the center of the altar. The haunting melody caught on, and, by the end, the entire group had given up their harmony to the gods of Delphi—Apollo and Dionysus, as well as Apollo's son Asclepius.

Arianna had taken part in this travel ritual on numerous occasions, but this was a singular moment in time. As the men moved away, she stepped in front of the altar. The smoking incense was still flowing upward; she opened her cloak and closed it around the smoke, enveloping it so that it permeated her clothes with the delicious aroma. Melissa joined her. "I love the smell of frankincense and myrrh together. They should make a perfume of it," Arianna said.

"They probably do," Melissa said. "We will have to look for it the next time we go to Rome."

"Oh, yes, we are *going home*!" She hugged Melissa and whispered words in her ear that only another woman who had gone through this incredible journey could appreciate. "Let us give thanks to the Great Mother goddess of us all, and seek Her blessing as well."

"And so, with your words, this part of our voyage is complete," Melissa spoke in a low and appreciative manner. "Thank you for allowing me to be present for your metamorphosis. I feel so blessed."

Arianna whispered once more in her ear, "And thanks, or no thanks, to you—I am still a virgin!" They both burst out laughing.

Slowly, each ship in port readied its sail, just in case of a fortuitous wind. The mooring ropes that tethered the ships to the quay were detached and thrown on board. One by one, the ships inched out into the waters beyond the docks. One could hear the voice of the first mate, directing the rowers with his rhythmic song, and the rowers answering him with their voices and the swish of their oars. When the singing stopped, constant, rhythmic drumming punctuated the action of the sailors dipping oars into the sea. The harbor of Kirra was tucked away in a northern arm of the Corinthian sea, so once they were out of the congestion within the harbor, the sailors unfurled the sail and continued south. A good omen in the guise of a morning breeze flew down the mountain, across the valley, and into the bay. The land fanned out, the bay expanded, and ships chose which way they would go, east to Corinth or west to Patra and beyond.

The latter was Aper's plan, sailing west close to the northern shoreline of the Peloponnese; he would take advantage of the winds coming off the sheer cliffs to make some good sailing time before heading into the Ionian Sea. Aper had hired a pilot to help with the navigation along the shoreline areas, where knowing the depth of the waters and the headlands were crucial.

After they were underway, Aper asked the pilot to join him as he assembled Cil and Arianna, Theo and Melissa, to explain to them how the trip might take place. Nothing was set in stone. "As I said earlier, sailing back to our homeland is much slower as we will be going against the winds most of the time. I chose this ship because it has a captain's quarters where you two women can be safe and secured if necessary."

"Secured?" said Arianna. "Not secure, but secured. It sounds like we are cargo, Aper."

"Hopefully, you will not have to experience the rough sea that would make that necessary," Aper said. "Let us leave it at that for now."

The pilot now spoke. "I will give you the history of the area as we progress. While we are still in the Corinthian Sea, it will not be complicated." He spoke in Latin with a heavy Greek accent. "I have traveled these waters many times and know the landscape well. Each day your captain and I will plot the course for the day, and then I will explain where we are as we pass certain landmarks—headlands and bays."

Arianna perked up. "Would you explain those last two terms?"

"That is easy," said the pilot smiling at her. "Simply speaking, headlands are often promontories, tall boulders surrounded on three sides by water, and bays are water surrounded on three sides by land."

"Enough for now," Aper said. "We plan to arrive at Naupactus in time to make our oblations at the Asclepian temple this evening, and then leave early in the morning to pass through the narrows before the winds pick up."

The steep and rocky coastline they had witnessed all day opened into a long bay, where the harbor town of Naupactus lay sheltered from the surrounding winds, a welcome relief as the crew's strenuous first day came to a close. Captain and crew knew that this was also the last protected stopping point from winds and from pirates for some time.

The next morning they woke to a thunderstorm. Theo and Cil scurried to collect their bedding, abandoning the tent-like shelter set up the night before and made their way quickly down into the hold of the ship. Aper, the pilot, and the crew had already left the deck and were crowded below. They made their male passengers as comfortable as possible, lighting some of the oil lamps. The sailors were used to bad weather and enjoyed the free time to play some of their favorite dice games.

In the captain's quarters above the main deck, Arianna and Melissa had awakened when Cil and Theo left their sleeping post just below the captain's quarters. The women had tried to go back to sleep but soon heard the men laughing and became curious about what fun they were having—without them. When a short break in the weather allowed, the women dashed to join them. Cil challenged Arianna to one of the games the men were playing.

As the storm blew on and on, they all tired of the games. Cil started to recall the terrible storm he had encountered on the ill-fated ship with Titus and Octavius. The sailors' ears perked up as they had heard about the storm and shipwreck off the coast of Hispania. Arianna had never before heard Cil relate the complete account of what had happened.

Cil realized he had brought up a delicate subject. "Rufie," Cil said, "I am sorry. I know you probably, maybe I shouldn't—"

Arianna did not even correct his use of her childhood name. "No, Cil, I wasn't able to hear the whole story at the time, but now I am ready—I want to hear what happened to all of you."

"Well," he started slowly, addressing the sailors. "My friend Titus, my sister's betrothed, and I are friends of Octavius—the grandnephew of Julius Caesar." Heads nodded. They all knew Octavius.

"We were to meet up with Caesar and his troops in Hispania to do battle with Pompey's sons, Sextus and Gnaeus Pompeius," Cil continued. "Unfortunately, our ship was delayed several days by foul weather and rough seas. When we finally got underway, we sailed straight toward the east coast of Hispania. We were anchored just off the mainland and would have disembarked the next day."

Arianna fidgeted in her seat. Cil looked at her. "Please continue," she said.

With that, Cil told the men about the terrible storm, the rogue wave, and the grounding of the ship. He spoke of someone last seeing Titus in a white nightshirt. Arianna gasped as Melissa pulled her close.

Cil continued. "One morning, we heard soldiers on the road as we prepared for sleep after a night of making our way through enemy lines. As we peered through the trees, we realized, after seeing the standard-bearer of Julius Caesar, that they were Roman troops."

"What a relief," Aper's first mate offered.

"A relief to us and a surprise to the soldiers," Cil continued. "They had found our ship abandoned and feared the worst. They then informed us that the battle was over, but there were still enemy troops in the area, so Octavius' plan was a good one. The rescue commander told of the desperate circumstances of the battle. He told Octavius that his uncle was the bravest of all of the men. 'We were losing the battle,' the commander said, 'and Julius Caesar stepped forward to the front of the line shouting his defiance and showing his courage, turning the tide, and leading us back into battle. His strength and resilience outmatched any man half his age. It was a sight I will never forget.'"

The crew sat in stunned silence. Several had been soldiers in other circumstances and rarely if ever, had they heard of such bravery from a leader. Arianna leaned back into Melissa's arms as she gave her comfort.

"And now," Cil continued, "as fate would have it, we are looking to another leader, Caesar's grand-nephew, to carry on his tradition. I have been working with Octavius and his troops in Apollonia this past six months, helping and learning all about military medicine from Octavius' private physician and military doctors. Octavius and his physicians have many new ideas about how to help the troops in battle. One idea is to retrieve those injured in battle, giving them medical care as quickly as possible. Those of you who have been soldiers I am sure can understand how that might make all the difference in regaining one's strength."

The men nodded. "Do you want to hear one more story about Octavius?" Cil asked.

Everyone agreed. "Tell on!"

"There is the time in Apollonia when Octavius and Agrippa went to see an astrologer by the name of Theogenes. Agrippa went first and was told that he had an incredible future in store. Octavius was reluctant, but when he finally gave his birth date, Theogenes fell at his feet in awe."

Another stunned silence from the crew.

"So," Cil concluded, "when Octavius recently received news that his great uncle Caesar had been assassinated, he was determined to return to home. He instructed me to come and retrieve my sister, but before I could leave, Aper and Theo showed up. And here I am!"

Arianna extended her arms to receive a hug from her brother.

"Listen," Aper said.

The group listened and heard nothing except the boat creaking in the water.

"The storm is over," a man replied.

Aper climbed the ladder and opened the trap door that kept the rainwater out and the hold dry. Back on deck, they all felt enlivened by the fresh air after the storm. But the wind was still blowing hard. "No sailing today," Aper said. "Let's go into town and get any supplies we might need, have a meal, and then turn in after sunset for an early start tomorrow."

The Romans went to an eating place considered respectable enough for women. The crew went to another place where they could be rowdy and burn off some of their energy. They seemed anxious, anticipating the trip into open waters. The first mate and pilot went with them.

As they all returned to the ship, the passengers, Aper and his crew all gathered on deck to watch the sunset and moonrise. The pilot was still full of stories. "Seeing the moon reminds me of a story I have heard, about a mysterious mechanism made in the recent past by some very learned Greeks," the pilot said, "maybe even some Stoics." He had heard Arianna espousing the qualities of stoicism.

He told of a mechanism with gears and dials that predicted astronomical positions of the sun and moon, zodiac and solar calendars. "It would make my job much easier if I could set my position with that machine, and it would help guide the way. But it would seem that if the device existed once, it might have been lost at sea. No one knows for sure where it is or if there is another one as unique."

"Tell us more about this curious machine," Aper said.

"Well, you understand I have never seen it but have been told that it could coordinate the annual solar calendar with the lunar religious calendar at Athens. Some say that it could even be used to predict eclipses and the four-year cycle of the Olympic Games."

The pilot and Aper talked on and on, as the rest of the ship's populace, including the women, prepared for sleep. When all were asleep except for the two men, the pilot lowered his voice to a whisper. "I wanted you to know that when we were in the tavern this afternoon, one of the new crew members went on at some length about Cil's earlier story, bragging that we had some important passengers on board," the pilot said. "I mention it only because some suspicious-looking sailors were sitting close to us that started asking questions. I immediately attempted to downplay the blustering crew member's comments, and the first mate chose to cut off the drinks and make for the ship immediately. I wanted you to know this."

"We must keep a close lookout tomorrow for any ships that leave the harbor when we leave," Aper said. "Pirates are often hard to identify."

"Until they show their true colors."

THROUGH THE NARROWS

Arianna woke to the sound of the first mate rousting the crew from sleep. She and Melissa quickly dressed in layers and cloaks to keep warm. They stepped out on deck to find that everyone was up, and shortly after they were underway. Aper had taken his post, standing on the highest point in the aft of the ship—the deck on top of the captains' cabin. From there, he could take in the sweeping view of his ship and the waters below. He could appraise the situation and bark his orders to the two helmsmen who manned the rudders and stood just below and on either side of him. The steerage was tricky and challenging at times because of the cross-currents, eddies, and shifting winds. The rowers below deck remained steady as the first mate kept the cadence going with drum and song. He sang about a sailor courting a young maiden. The oarsman answered in return, keeping them focused on the speed they needed to maintain in the choppy waters. The currents grew stronger as they changed direction.

The pilot motioned for the two women to climb, with Cil and Theo's help, to the highest point on the bow of the ship. He started his morning's lecture to the four of them. "If you will notice, the land is starting to narrow. On the left is Antirhion's point, and on the right is Rhion's point. This, my fellow passengers, is the entrance of the Gulf of Corinth," he said with a dramatic flair. "It is of strategic importance because it controls the sea route from Corinth to the Ionian Sea."

Arianna felt that the ship was out of control, at the mercy of wind and currents shifting the vessel to and fro. Standing between the pilot and Cil, she was caught by them several times as she swayed with the ship. "Do you want to go down below?" the pilot said.

"No, no, no, I feel better with the wind in my hair, and when I'm able to see the horizon and movement of the water." She had wisely not eaten that morning. Finally, the pilot tied a rope around her waist and tied it to a rung on the railing.

"You're a pilot in the making," he shouted over the increasing wind. "As you will notice, if you dare to look down that the currents change from east to west and back again. In other words, this is where the Corinthian Sea meets the Ionian Sea, which causes this tug of war of the waters."

The passing through the strait seemed to take forever, as Arianna would tell it afterward. "I think the pilot tried to divert my attention from my queasy belly by relating the story of one of the wars that took place 'in these very waters,' but war stories do not settle my stomach."

In the end, the two currents came together as one, pushing the ship forward out of the strait and into the Ionian Sea. Aper and his family of Romans gathered on the deck to celebrate the safe passing. They were ravenous after the adventure, and Melissa and Theo brought up food from the hold.

"Coming up, Arianna, you will notice to your left, in the distance is Patra, where you first encountered the southern part of the Peloponnese," Aper called to Arianna.

She ran to join Aper at the railing on the port side. They stared into the distance, seeing only the stretch of a vast landmass and the shore.

"Unforgettable memories, Arianna," Aper said as he looked down at her. "The Fates are certainly watching over you."

"Yes, *Clotho*, spinning the thread of my life, took care of me when my first mother died, and my second mother appeared."

"She did indeed. I think *Lachesis* has measured enough thread for you to accomplish your life's tasks."

"And *Atropos*?" Arianna asked.

"Let us ask that she will honor you and her sisters by giving you a long life."

IONIAN SEA

Aper avoided sailing in the open sea due to the unpredictable winds, choosing instead to use the expertise of the pilot to guide the ship between landmasses—islands and the mainland—which helped give shelter from the winds.

The oarsman took turns rowing. Half the group rested while the other half rowed. They switched back and forth, day and night, so as not to lose momentum or get thrown off course. That was part of the pilot's job—to keep them on the course that he and Aper had mapped out at the beginning. It was a relief to Aper to share those duties.

"We will next touch land on Ithaka," the pilot declared one night during the evening meal.

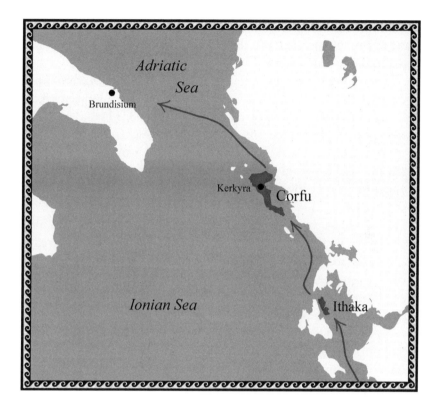

Ionian to Adriatic Seas

"How soon?" was, of course, Arianna's first question.

"If the winds and currents do not wreak havoc with us, I would say within a day or two."

The concern of pirate ships was still on Aper's and the pilot's minds. Aper did not want to worry passengers or crew, but there were times when one man or both would gain sight of a ship trailing behind them—far enough away not to be identified.

They were on a northwesterly course, and because the winds were coming out of the southeast, the crew was able to set the sail and Aper, and his friends could have a relaxing evening meal. "We have indeed been blessed by the gods," he said. He went on to explain the difficulties of this region. "Not long ago, our beloved statesman, Cicero, was sailing from Patra to Brundisium. This trip took him three times as long as it will take us—due to the winter winds."

Cil perked up. "Octavius wants to have a meeting with Cicero before Octavius returns to Rome. I think he is concerned about his safety. Since the murderers killed his uncle, they might want to kill him as well." Cil stood up and walked to the railing, deep in his thoughts about his friend.

"I think I can see a ship behind us, Aper. Did you know that?"

Aper walked over to where Cil was standing. "Yes, the pilot and I noticed it several days ago. We will forge on and be in sight of land anytime now."

That evening, the lighthouse located on the southern tip of the large island of Kefalonia was a welcome sight in the darkness. They steered to the right of the island, heading toward Ithaka. The ship behind them seemed to come closer but then veered off to the left. "There are ports along the coast," the pilot said, relieved that the ship no longer appeared to be following them.

Aper showed Cil the navigation maps that the pilot had brought on board. "You see that there is a narrow passage between the large island of Kefalonia and the smaller island of Ithaka to the east."

"I remember hearing of pirate ships slipping next to other ships, taking cargo and passengers and making off in the night," the pilot said. "We will spend our first night on the east side of Ithaka, taking shelter behind a tiny island in a bay. From there, our sailors standing watch will be able to see if any ships are coming our way."

On the deck, Arianna heard Theo whispering. "Who will tell her—when?" Theo was asking.

"This should come from our parents," Cil said.

Melissa said nothing.

"What should come from our parents?" Arianna asked, joining them on the deck. "Are you talking about the man that I will have to marry? Silence fell upon the trio like the silence of the split second between the fall of a wounded gladiator and the roar of the crowd.

MORE SURPRISES

The tranquil waters in the bay where they had spent the night were stirred as the ship lurched to the port side. Waves created by an incoming vessel were causing their ship to roll.

Aper saw the distinctive trim on the other ship's sail as it turned into the bay. He shouted to the crew, "Heave the anchors," followed by "man the oars," and in his next breath, "secure the women—now!"

Melissa had staggered and fallen on the deck with the rolling of the ship. Theo picked her up and carried her to the captain's quarters, and together, Cil and Theo, following the orders given to them earlier by Aper, unwound the ropes that had been coiled in the corners of the room. They tied the rope around the women's waists and secured the other end of the rope to metal rings mounted on either side of the cramped room.

"These ropes are for your protection. Stay within this quarter," Cil shouted to the women as he and Theo ran back on deck.

The menacing ship continued into the bay, sailing straight toward them, as Aper's vessel attempted to evade it on its way out. As the ships passed side by side, they saw the other crew's faces for the first time. A scruffy lot of pirates to be sure! The pirates threw their grappling hooks at Aper's ship. Only two of the hooks found their mark, and Aper's sailors quickly cut the ropes and freed them.

The pilot instructed the first mate to hug the shore, while the pirate ship's captain made a strategic error. Instead of sailing close to the shore to follow Aper's ship, he sailed into the open sea lane, realizing too late that there was an oncoming warship bearing down upon him.

"Behold a Greek warship, a trireme with three rows of oarsmen, one hundred and seventy rowers strong!" the pilot on Aper's ship said. "Long, lean, and low to the water, there is no faster ship in the fleet."

Aper caught sight of the warship and shouted to the helmsman, "Right rudder—pull! They headed even closer to shore to give the warship a wide berth. The trireme swiftly moved past them, heading directly toward the pirate ship that had nowhere to run. Aper could hear the panic in the voices of the pirates.

There was a loud thud as the ram of the warship hit the underbelly of the pirate ship. Pirates dove over the side as the trireme pushed the wounded ship down the waterway.

"Look!" the pilot shouted. "The cadre of archers on the deck of the warship is unleashing a flight of arrows, annihilating the pirates still on deck as well as the ones in the water!"

The oarsmen on all three levels of the trireme moved quickly to their stations and, with their verbal cadence set, backed away from the pirate ship to watch it sink.

The women had loosened themselves from their tether and joined the men on Aper's deck.

"Listen to the cadence call and the rowers' response," Arianna shouted. "These are the same words I heard in the play *The Frogs*. Charon was setting the cadence for Dionysus to row across the River Styx. The same words!"

"O-opop, O-opop," the pilot repeated the words. "Also, listen at this moment to the pirate ship crack and groan as it takes on water. What a sight you are witnessing—you can't imagine how rare it is to see this action!"

"What is the eye that is painted on the bow of the warship?" Arianna asked.

"It is the eye of a god, protecting the course of the ship as well as keeping away bad spirits," Aper said. "With this wind, they should be in the taverns of Patra before nightfall. Heroes one and all!"

Aper turned back to the bay where they had spent the night. Arianna looked around. "This is the bay we anchored in on our first sail. I didn't recognize it before!"

"*Legitimus*!" Aper said. "News of the sinking of a pirate ship will travel rapidly, so I think we are out of imminent danger and safe to stay another night. Let us give everyone a day of rest and continue tomorrow."

The crew dispatched their passengers onto the beach and then headed to their favorite taverna for a hearty meal and drink.

"I know I am on solid ground," Arianna said as she stood barefoot in the sand at the edge of the crystal clear aquamarine waters. "But in my head, I am still swaying back and forth."

"I am famished," Aper said, as they headed to his favorite tavern.

Cil and Arianna walked up the beach together, deep in discussion. "Octavius' teacher taught me about the sun motif in the Mithraic Liturgy," Cil said. "He says that the sun motif appears in many places and times and that the meaning is always the same—that a new awareness has been born. It is the light of illumination, which is seen in the skies above. And so dear sister, I have seen many signs that a new awareness is being born within you. You radiate the light seen in the skies, but it is also within you."

Melissa and Theo followed behind, giving them their privacy. When they saw Arianna tuck her arm within Cil's, they knew that her brother had told her.

NORTHBOUND

They ended up back on board before nightfall. "I will sleep soundly tonight," the pilot said to his Roman friends. In the next part of the trip, he would be guiding the ship by night as well as by day. He knew the coastal landmarks well and had plotted his course, watching for the sequence of headlands and promontories on the islands. "When you line up these Ionian Islands on a map," the pilot said to Arianna, "they progress in a straight line. That is the secret. Then one cannot get lost. All I can hope for are clear skies with lots of moon shining down on us."

"Believe me, I pray for that every night," Arianna said. "And also that the god Notus blesses us with his winds."

Early the next morning, under clear skies and favorable winds, the crew rowed out of the harbor far enough to catch the morning breeze, which had changed once again. They were able to set the sail. Northward!

That night, Arianna made her way to the captain's quarters slowly, unsure whether Theo and Melissa might still be enjoying the last few moments of marital bliss. She stopped short when she heard the men's chorus starting on the deck below. The rowers performed their yeoman's duties by day and by night whenever the winds calmed. It was hard to keep rowing but even harder to keep awake at night, so they often would hum a tune with the accompaniment of the piper. Tonight, however, they were singing a capella, and it was stunningly beautiful.

It was a clear night with so many stars above that Arianna had to quit looking. She sat down on the deck, closed her eyes, felt the steady pull of the oars, listened, and fell asleep.

CHAPTER XLVIII

CORCYRA

BRUNDISIUM

Further north, they sailed into the lane between the island of Corcyra to the west and the coast of mainland Greece to the east. "I have a special surprise for you," Aper said as they prepared to land at the major city on the island. "Remind me, what was the first temple we visited in the Peloponnese?"

"Not that you would ever forget the first and only time you saw me naked. Artemis at Patras, of course." Arianna said, watching color come into his cheeks. "I made you blush."

"No-no-no, just the wind on my cheeks," Aper stuttered.

"I would not have said that to you a year ago."

"Is that a sign of maturity, my sweet young woman?"

"No, just a sign of my bold feminine nature coming through," she said, laughing. "Why could I not have married you?"

Aper did not miss a beat. "What would I do with all those vineyards? I know—you want to tie me down to the land and take me away from my mistress—the sea. You just want me to stay home and make—oops, I had better stop, I have made *you* blush!"

"Make love, make babies—which was it?" Arianna asked.

"Both, do not you know?" he said, pulling her to him. They stood motionless, looking at each other, both wondering—if things had been different. Arianna leaned her head against his chest.

"Break it up, you two," Cil interrupted. "I will have to tell your wife about your philandering ways."

"See, my brother will not let us have any fun—what can I do with him?"

"We could throw him overboard." Aper grabbed Cil by the back of his shirt.

"Not worth it," Arianna said. "Then you'd have to fish him out—the sea doesn't want him."

"Oh, but the water nymphs might!" Cil said. "No, I will wait for the baths, a good rubdown, and then a hearty meal and a cup of wine—or two."

"You had better at least take the baths before you go to the temple with me at Corcyra!" Arianna said.

"That is the order of things—the baths for purification, then the votive offerings, then the visit to the Temple of Artemis," Aper said. "It is one of the oldest Greek temples. Very unusual. I will be anxious to hear your reactions to the image on the pediment—quite different from anything you've seen, Arianna."

"She *will* have an opinion—she is now the expert on temples, you know," Cil said.

"Yes, and do not forget it," Arianna replied.

In fact, after landing, they took the afternoon to relax in the baths, women separate from men, and then a leisurely meal. The next morning, they all went to the temple with their votive offerings. Arianna was struck at a distance by the massive pediment that capped the stark white stone temple. "I thought you told me it was a temple to Artemis. That looks like Medusa!"

"It *is* Medusa," the pilot said, interrupting her conversation with Aper. He had offered to come with them to the temple as he considered himself an expert on this building. "I think if you understand the history of this island, it may make sense to you. It was earlier affiliated with Corinth, then Athens, conquered by Spartans, Illyrians, and now you, the Romans," the pilot said. "I could go on and on, but the point I want to make is that here is one of the first temples that was decorated with mythical figures. Here the Medusa head is reunited with her body. She protects the temple of Artemis from evil. She protects this virgin goddess from harm, the harm that was done to Medusa by the god, Poseidon." he stopped mid-sentence and looked at Arianna. "Do you know what happened to Medusa?"

"Yes," Arianna, uncomfortable with the question, but even more distressed by the answer. "Poseidon raped her in the temple of Athena," she said.

"And who was blamed for this violation of Athena's temple? Poseidon? No. Athena blames not her fellow god, but the mortal woman. There is much to think about here, young woman. Understand it as you will."

The pilot then walked on, taking the group with him to explain the other images on the pediment, the architecture of the building and Sanctuary. Arianna stayed behind, where she was left alone with her thoughts—usually, Medusa had no body, only the ugly mask. Here her body was poised to spring into action or flight. Was she protecting her goddess from the evil outside? Or was she about to take revenge on Perseus, who cut off her head at the behest of Athena? And what did all this have to do with her?

Melissa returned to Arianna's side.

"I am not sure what this is all about, but I feel that it has to do with the mask," Arianna said, trying to understand. "The image—I need to sort this out. Let us sit down." The two women found a shaded area beneath a big oak tree where they could still see the images on the pediment sculpted in high relief. "The mask is the result of her being violated. To me it shows her pain. It shows how she now protects herself—and others—like Artemis. Why has this jolted me? Is it the meaning of the mask that I need to understand? What meaning does the mask have for me?"

"Let us think about the body for a minute," Melissa said. "As you mentioned, one usually sees the head, but not the body. Showing the body in this position says to me that she is ready to defend herself or Artemis. What if you see the mask as a way to force the enemy, whoever that may be, to flee, just by looking at her face?"

"But I remember in the story it talks about anyone that looked at her decapitated head was turned to stone," Arianna said.

"Remember when you talked with the Pythia and Kallistê?"

"Yes, they talked about the mask. We were talking about creating a mask of Dionysus in a fresco, and maybe a real mask," Arianna said. "It would show a frightening face, a powerful mask to let a woman know that she had two options, either stand behind the mask, protected if she followed the god's commands, or if she betrayed Dionysus and did not listen to his message, she would have to live with his wrath, forced to gaze at the mask and the dreaded consequences."

They sat in silence for a long while. The mask of Dionysus would take on more meaning in the coming years. Arianna was only beginning to reach deep within her heart and soul.

The men came back from the pilot's tour of the building, discussing what a rare opportunity it was to see this archaic-style architecture that was built hundreds of years before this group's arrival.

On this last night on Greek soil, Aper arranged for a private dinner at a taverna for his Roman friends and the pilot who would not be traveling across to the mainland of Italy. The room was open-air and afforded a spectacular view of the bay.

As they entered the taverna, Aper was approached by a friend, an Italian shipowner who had recently traveled from Brundisium to Corcyra. He pulled Aper away from his group, giving him a letter. At the bottom of the letter was one word—SECRET! Aper folded the letter and tucked it away.

A bittersweet smile crossed his lips.

"What are you up to, Aper?" Arianna asked when he rejoined the group. She did not miss a thing.

"Did you see me talking with that captain?"

"Of course I did!"

"He just came from Brundisium and said that maybe we should land there instead of going up the coast."

She paused. "I think he is right. I am ready to be back—on terra firma. Now, let us dance."

The musicians were in full swing, and her reluctant partner ventured into the line of dancers, if only for a few minutes, but soon Aper broke off from the line, begging, "Please, I would rather watch *you* dance!"

And so he would. Arianna was a sight to behold: dressed in the latest Athenian garb, her gown translucent, showing every curve of her young body, her curly hair pulled up, topped with a tiara, a necklace falling around her neck, the jewel almost hiding the cleavage that she now so proudly revealed. Dazzling in her youth and zest for life. Who knew what the landing in Brundisium would bring. Only this starlit night of music and wine remained as a treasured moment in her life—and his.

At dinner, Aper thanked the pilot for his excellent "pilotage at the bow of the ship and also for the education afforded to our Roman passengers—they are now ready to fill those empty moments at meals, with loved ones, and not so loved ones with the knowledge imparted to them by your infinite wisdom and rhetoric." Aper paused, refilled his wine cup, and then continued. "At last, I raise a cup to my friends, for taking this opportunity to travel abroad. My congratulations for taking this extended trip full of endless adventures with great experiences that will live with you forever. A special toast to the two fearless young people whom we have all watched grow and evolve. One, a man who wishes to spend his military years healing rather than hurting people. The young woman, this lovely vision before us tonight, who has prepared to fulfill her destiny by taking this journey. A toast to your health and continued good fortune."

Aper sat down beside Arianna. "I found something in Corcyra's market today that made me think of you." He gave her a small wooden box, hand-carved with inlays of different colored woods.

"Thank you," Arianna said. "It is beautiful."

"You're not finished. Open it!" Aper said.

"Be careful, Rufie, remember Pandora's Box," Cil said.

Arianna shushed him and opened the box to find a beautiful gold necklace with a pearl pendant. "Oh, Aper." She touched her hand to her chest.

Aper rose to fasten the necklace around her neck. "The pearl is known for its calming effect and also for strengthening friendships. We will always be friends."

Then he took the pearl in his hand. "You see this mark on the pearl? It is a sign that Zeus has blessed it with his lightning bolt. His protection is with you."

As they made their way out of the restaurant, an old woman called Arianna over to her table.

She pulled on her arm and whispered in Arianna's ear. "You have the good fortune to be blessed with a man who loves you. I hope you and your husband have a beautiful life together."

"Oh I wish, but—"

"Be careful what you wish for." The old lady laughed and dismissed her.

BRUNDISIUM

Two days later, the spacious harbors of Brundisium welcomed the weary but grateful crew and passengers. They gathered around the temporary altar for a short ritual. Aper opened an amphora of wine, and they celebrated a successful landing, this time on Italian soil. Home at last.

As she stood on the pier, Arianna looked up the long flight of stairs that led to the landing above. Two columns quietly announced the beginning of the Appian Way. She looked closer. A couple was standing at the top of the stairs between the columns, the very spot where she had stood several months ago, ready for her trip.

"Melissa, please retrieve the mask I was given at the Dionysian ritual in Athens," Arianna said. "I want to wear it so that my parents can see who I have become."

The mask was of a priestess of Dionysus, with hair that looked conceived in a rush of wind and a small snake curving down her forehead and onto her cheek. Arianna held it to her face.

Cil and Aper offered their arms. Together the trio walked slowly up the stairs.

Arianna thought of the virtues that her mother had taught her: *Firmitas*, the ability to stick to one's purpose, and *Dignitas*, knowing not only who you are but also who you are to become.

Arianna wore no jewelry. Instead, she had tied a red thread, representing Ariadne, around her neck. It would say more than any words. Aloud she repeated her mantra with every step: *Firmitas, Dignitas, Firmitas, Dignitas.*

Almost at the top, she could see the smiles on her parents' faces. Behind them stood a man. She recognized the shock of white hair, a wig she knew well since childhood. Even though she had known for days now, upon seeing him, the breath went out of her. She heard a voice within whisper, "Breathe." With that breath, she gained her composure. She greeted her parents warmly and then addressed the man who now stood in front of her.

"Victor," she said as he extended his hand to her. She hesitated, looked down at his hand through her mask, knowing that putting her hand in his sealed her fate. She gave the mask to her mother to hold. She looked at Victor, clear-eyed, and then placed her hand in his. He replied to her gesture, merely saying. "My only wish is to bring you happiness."

Consummatum est. Novum Iter Incipit.
It is Finished. A New Journey Begins.

324

EPILOGUE

A Dream

She watches.
A red thread swirls and moves like a musical note that soars
high and free with joy. Her hands reach out to grasp it,
but it darts away, plunging into unknown depths.
Please come again. Don't abandon me.
A mirror is held up to her face. But it's not her face she sees.
An old man's face, and the kind countenance she knows starts
to contort, his eyes blacken as they gaze into hers. His mouth
opens. He is speaking words, but she cannot hear them. It goes
on and on. He seems ready to strike her. Her body shivers with
frozen despair and she cannot look away, cannot move.
It finally stops and as the image dissolves, hands appear, very fine mascu-
line hands. Elegant. He is holding a brush, full of crimson paint.
There is nothing but silence as she watches the hands
and she wills the mirror to show her his face.
She longs to reach out for the red brush, to touch those hands.
Is it you, Dionysius? Is it you, Titus? Free me.
She has become the brush. His hand holds on to her like a lover's
embrace and she is immersed in the viscous liquid, becomes one with
it. She feels herself propelled toward a wall. Faces, wings, weeping
women. She can see where she has been. She sees what is coming.
Is my fate in your hands or yours in mine?
From the edge of the dream, she strains to keep
listening. Her eyes open as the voice dies away.
Is there freedom in duty?
It's her wedding day.
She knows now what she will do.

APPENDIX

GODDESSES AND GODS

APOLLO—**The prophetic deity of the Oracle of Delphi.**
He represents reason, restraint, and order—the twin brother of Artemis.

ARTEMIS—**The virgin goddess of the hunt, the wilderness, the Moon, chastity, and childbirth.**
Nurturer and protector of young children. The twin sister of Apollo. The Romans called her Diana.

ASCLEPIUS—**The god of medicine.**
His sanctuary, the Asklepieion, near Epidaurus, was a sacred site to spend time in reflection, incubating, and working with dreams of healing given by the god. The son of Apollo.

ARIADNE—**A Cretan princess and wife of Dionysus.**
Her myth concerns the Minoan Labyrinth, where Ariadne helps Theseus kill the Minotaur, then is abandoned on the island of Naxos. The god, Dionysus, rescues her, and they marry.

DIONYSUS—The god of wine, fertility, death, and rebirth as reincarnation.
He was also the god of theatre, encouraging the development of the culture through poetry and plays of comedy and drama to express the human condition. The Romans called him Bacchus and Liber. The Greeks called him Iacchus and Zagreus.

FORTUNA—A farming deity.
She is often pictured with a cornucopia to represent the land and fertility for women. Or with a ship's rudder resting on a globe, as she steered the lives and fates of those who sought her blessings.

HYGEIA—The goddess of good health and hygiene.
Daughter of the god of medicine, Asclepius.

RITUALS

During Classical times, rituals were a religious way of honoring and paying homage to the gods and goddesses. In return, humans hoped that the deities would think kindly of them, easing their pain and suffering, and granting them wishes.

Other times these rituals were to honor the transitions of human development. All of the rituals in this book are based on actual ancient rituals of the time, and sometimes incorporating several versions of the ritual.

Rufilla goes through two Artemis rituals.
Both of these rituals represent a transition of Rufilla's development through the goddess.
Artemis Arktoi Ritual: For young girls, an instruction on respecting their independent thoughts and feelings while living in the outer world. Rufilla was 10.
Artemis Ritual at Patra: This was a unique ritual created for Rufilla by her hostess because she saw the depth of this young woman and the importance of honoring her spiritual journey.

This *Transition Ritual* for Rufilla takes place in the **Asclepian Sanctuary** after the beginning of her menarche. It is about her new life with a relationship to **Persephone**: Going to the underworld, dying to her old life and being born again to her new life. As Persephone did, Rufilla also takes a new name—Arianna. It is about recognizing the importance and necessity of a contemplative spiritual life as well as giving back to the world in creating a Dionysian ritual for other women.

The *Ritual* of the *Marriage of Ariadne and Dionysus* takes place in Athens, with Arianna playing the role of **Ariadne**. She accepts the responsibility of taking on the spiritual tasks of **Dionysus**, the holding of the tension of the opposites between divine and human, and finally, the coming together of the opposites to show a middle road, a third way toward living in the world but also developing spiritually.

Dionysian Ritual: The Dionysian ritual on Mt. Parnassus at Delphi is celebrated at the end of winter months to announce his rebirth. It is a ritual of religious ecstasy, music, dance, fire, and frenzy. He was known as the Loosener, the Liberator, the one who brought counterpoise to Apollo's rule of order.

Saturnalia: It is a light-hearted Roman ritual honoring the agricultural god Saturn. Arianna and Melissa introduce this ritual to the women of Athens's experience with songs, decorating their homes and giving gifts. It was common for role reversals between the upper class and their servants.

Winter Solstice: It is a time of reflection, looking back and looking forward, endings and beginnings.

330

ILLUSTRATIONS

MAPS
Plan of Pompeii

FIGURES

ACKNOWLEDGMENTS

In 1991, my now long-time friend, Susan Bettis, introduced me to the meaningful world of ancient women's rituals, ones that we as westerners have all but forgotten. The slide presentation Susan presented in 1991 changed my life. When I saw the frescoes from the Villa of the Mysteries, I was transported out of space and time, never to be the same. What I have learned about the lives of these women who lived in the classical period has transformed my understanding of mythology and the wisdom of the ancients. Thank you, Susan.

My curiosity was whetted by a Jungian analyst, Gary Sparks, who introduced me to the writings of Jungian analysts Linda Fierz-David and Katherine Bradway on the Villa of the Mysteries. Also, analysts Marion Woodman and Edward Edinger's writings have been pivotal in my understanding of the Greek and Roman psyches. Gary's guidance over the years, conducting classes in the study of C. G. Jung, has given me a depth of experience and meaning I would not have received anywhere else. The members of this Jung group have given me enormous support over the years. Cathleen Guthrie has traveled with me on many of my trips to Greece and Italy—a gracious and generous companion. Carol Spicuzza has been an integral part of the illustrations in the book as well as collaborating with me on an awe-inspiring painting that I chose to use for the cover of the book. The wisdom and insights of these women have been invaluable to me as we reach decades of friendship—my enduring gratitude to all.

Trips to Greece and Italy with Jungian Analyst, Nancy Qualls-Corbett, to the sacred sites of mother/goddess worship gave me a deeper understanding of the early religions of Western civilizations.

The Archaeological Institute of America introduced me to the work of classical archaeologists, art historians, and anthropologists. Professors Robert Hohlfelder, Nicholas Rauh, John Hale, and Steven Tuck were among my earliest teachers. I worked with the Pompeii Food and Drink Project under the guidance of Professors Betty Jo Mayeske, Robert Curtis, and Mary Meier in 2011. Thank you.

At Indiana University, Bloomington, I studied under Professors Nancy Klein, James Franklin, and Eleanor Leach. These generous teachers gave me the will to persevere.

An American archaeologist, Wilhelmina Jashemski, started the field of garden archaeology in the 1950s in Pompeii. One of my research papers was written about her professional life. It opened a window into how essential the gardens were to the Pompeiians. Thanks to the Indianapolis Woman's Club, also, for listening to my papers and encouraging me over these many years.

Along the way, I have received reassurance from Professors Rebecca Schindler and Pedar Foss. Dr. Foss and Dr. John Dobbins permitted me to use the map of Pompeii from the book they wrote and edited, *The World of Pompeii,* for which I am grateful. I met Dr. Bettina Bergmann and Dr. Eric Poehler while attending lectures at the Chicago Field Museum exhibit, *POMPEII, STORIES FROM AN ERUPTION.* Their encouragement for my writing project has inspired me. Drs. Sandy MacGillivray and Alastair Small were especially helpful with their insights into ancient Greece and Crete, and the Campanian area.

Charles Hill, with his B.A. in the Classics from Wabash College, and his M.A. in Art History and Archaeology, was the perfect person to read my manuscript with his eye on the Classical information that I have written into the book. His comments and corrections were very constructive. Thank you, Charles.

My first writing mentor was Laura Gaus, who taught me the value of the written word. I'm sorry that she is no longer with us to see the completion of this book. I have been fortunate enough to have had two excellent editors, Nancy Zafris, and Lori Ostlund. Without their help, this book would never have been written. Currently, my friend and coach, Carol Faenzi, has helped me move from finishing the manuscript to finding a publisher and so much more. Her tour of Tuscany was an eye-opener into the ancient Etruscan world and modern-day Italians.

The Indiana Writers Center has been an integral part of my writing life spanning decades. I am grateful to many of those teachers, among them Jim Powell, Barbara Shoup, David Hassler, and Candace Denning.

Terry Kirts, a teacher at the Writers Center and a senior lecturer in creative writing at Indiana University-Purdue University Indianapolis, helped me form my earliest concepts of character development, as well as giving me the fundamental skills in how to write a work of fiction.

I want to thank all the authors whose works I have collected over the years for helping me in my research and providing me with a priceless research library. The Herman B. Wells Library at Indiana University, Bloomington, and Indiana University—Purdue University Library in Indianapolis has been a constant and valuable resource.

A significant acknowledgment goes to Nancy and Art Baxter at Hawthorne Publishing, who have taken on this book project to help me reach publication. Thanks for sharing your wit, guidance, and expertise.

Erika Espinoza has been an extraordinary formatter these past months. So patient. Gracias.

Many thanks to Drs. Shelagh Fraser, Paul Phipps, Divya Narayanan, and Lauren Paladin for helping me stay strong physically so that I could be at my computer all these years. No small task.

Special thanks to Maria Luisa Gagliardi for making it possible for me to do extensive research in Pompeii and the surrounding area. A dear Italian friend.

A dear American friend, Deborah Gindhart, has been at my side for the last twenty years, making the bad times bearable and the good times joyous. Thank you, Debbie, for putting up with me.

To all my friends and family who would say, "How's the book coming?" Thank you so much.

My husband, Stan Hurt, deserves heartfelt accolades for his patience, and always supporting me as my research travels took me to many places in the U.S., plus trips to Europe, and countless years alone at my computer. Our cat Tigger could always tell when I needed his calming presence, curling up close but not too close to me in his kitty chair.

If you are not mentioned here and know you should be, consider it yet another senior moment on my part. *Mea Culpa!*

For better or worse, I take full responsibility for all errors in this book.

Gratitude goes to the superintendency of Pompeii, now known as the Archaeological Park of Pompeii, for all their help, granting me *permisso* to visit many of the houses in Pompeii. Gaining access to these sites has been invaluable in my research efforts over the years. *Mille Grazie!*